THE
MESSENGER

MEGAN DAVIS

Megan Davis was born in Australia and grew up in mining towns across the world. She has worked in the film industry and her credits include *Atonement, In Bruges, Pride and Prejudice* and the Bourne films. Megan is also a lawyer and is currently an associate at Spotlight on Corruption. She has an MA in Creative Writing from the University of East Anglia. Her debut *The Messenger* won the Bridport Prize for a First Novel in 2018, judged by Kamila Shamsie, as well as the Lucy Cavendish Prize for unpublished writers in 2021. She has lived in many places, including France for a number of years, but now lives in London.

THE MESSENGER

MEGAN DAVIS

ZAFFRE

First published in the UK in 2023 by
ZAFFRE
An imprint of Bonnier Books UK
4th Floor, Victoria House, Bloomsbury Square, London WC1B 4DA
Owned by Bonnier Books
Sveavägen 56, Stockholm, Sweden

This is a work of fiction. Names, places, events and
incidents are either the products of the author's
imagination or used fictitiously. Any resemblance to
actual persons, living or dead, or actual
events is purely coincidental.

A CIP catalogue record for this book is
available from the British Library.

HB ISBN: 978-1-83877-857-6
TPB ISBN: 978-1-83877-858-3

Also available as an ebook and an audiobook

1 3 5 7 9 10 8 6 4 2

Typeset by IDSUK (Data Connection) Ltd
Printed and bound in Great Britain by Clays Ltd, Elcograf S.p.A.

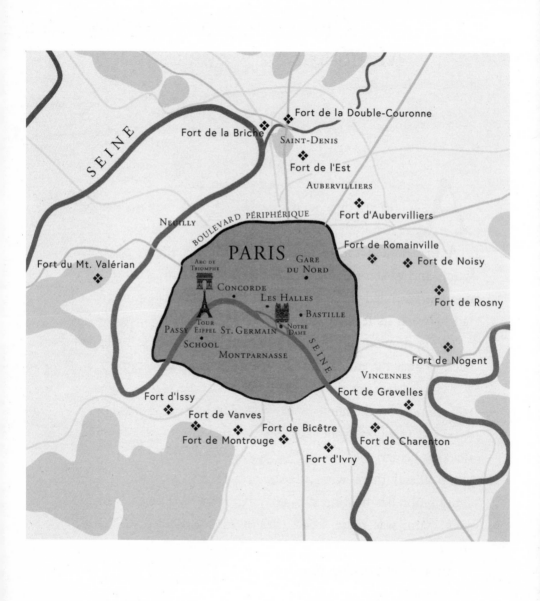

Prologue

Christmas Eve
Montparnasse Cemetery

A SHOUT FROM THE DARKNESS UP ahead.

Then a dog – some kind of muscled mongrel – nosed at my ankles, a low growl rolling in its throat.

A man jerked the leash bound double round his fist, flesh white and glistening, puckered by the links. He smacked the dog with a rolled-up newspaper, then laughed as it scuttled on, tail between its legs.

'Gotta show 'em who's boss,' the man said to me, as I stepped back against the railing that wrapped around the cemetery.

I glanced towards the corner – Sami was fifteen minutes late – enough time for the rain to soak through my clothes bringing with it second thoughts while dark, earthy smells crept over from the shadows behind me.

Up ahead there were yellow headlights and slanting rain, shiny umbrellas floating through the night. And when I turned back, Sami was there, hood up, his face shadowed under the street lamp.

'Start by just asking him for money,' I said. 'Tell him I owe you money.'

It was cold, and my breath hung in the air.

Sami smoked as we walked along the tall black rails with their gilded spikes, back towards the Boulevard Raspail.

'Tell him I'm in trouble. Get him to hand over his wallet. He always keeps a lot of cash. Cards and cash.' I was jabbering now, teeth chattering with the cold.

'Uh-huh. Cards and cash,' Sami repeated.

'In his wallet.'

'OK,' said Sami, checking the road before we ran across.

'I know the PIN codes – always the same ones. I told you.'

'Yeah.'

'If he thinks it's a one-off payment, he'll go along with it,' I said, grabbing Sami's arm. 'Make it clear it's a one-off thing.'

'It *is* a one-off thing,' Sami said quietly, drawing half a step ahead.

'He puts his wallet on a tray by the door,' I said, as a wave of nausea engulfed me, thinking of the warm apartment and Sami's cold intrusion.

Sami checked his phone and then scanned the street as though there was somewhere else he needed to be. He looked at me as if he'd only just heard.

'Yeah, yeah, you already told me.'

I tried to breathe, the air catching in my throat. 'There are gold cufflinks and stuff in his bedroom. On the chest of drawers in a little silver bowl.'

Sami grinned, and I felt like throwing up. He quickened his pace, and I ran to keep up, my stomach lurching like the sea. We hadn't talked things through, not properly, not beyond getting into the apartment and a few things Sami should take. As for what we'd do afterwards – we hadn't even thought about that.

We came to the church, crossed over and turned right into

my street, the rain needling our faces, sharp and silvery under the street lamps. Our footsteps echoed along the narrow footpath between the buildings, dark and shuttered save for a faint glow on one of the upper floors.

'Just let me in and leave me here,' he said at the entrance to my building.

'It's raining. I'll wait in the lobby.'

'That's not what we agreed.'

'So what?' I said, suddenly not trusting him at all. 'It's better if I'm here. In case there's a change of plan.'

I pressed the numbers on the keypad, but the door didn't budge. A surge of relief coursed through me – they must have changed the code.

'Try again,' he said, his breath warm and rank on my cheek.

This time the door clicked open and we went inside, shaking off the rain. The radiators were cranked up and it was stifling. A Christmas tree stood in the corner, its red fairy lights dancing round the small, mirror-panelled lobby as if to some upbeat Christmas tune.

There was a note taped to the *gardienne*'s door, her perfect cursive saying she was away for Christmas and New Year, and wishing everyone *Joyeuses fêtes*. Outside in the street, there was a shriek of laughter – someone singing a drunken song – but inside was quiet as a tomb.

I pressed the interphone and stood back. My father took a while to answer. I almost heard the squeak of the chair as he pushed back from his desk. In my mind I saw him take off his reading glasses, rub his eyes and smooth the thin grey hair from his forehead, his hand pausing for that last irritable scratch of the nape. I imagined the swig from the crystal glass before he stood,

3

replacing it on the well-worn coaster with the faded sailing ship, lone ice cube swirling in the coppery liquid as he walked towards the door. I could smell the apartment – that sour, old man's reek, and the soft, leather-bound mustiness of the bookshelves.

Sami eased back his hood, checking his reflection in the mirrors all around. He cocked his face to either side, cheeks sucked in, and raked a hand through his hair. He puffed his chest and drew a finger across his lip, wiping clear a light sweat.

'Hello.' My father's voice crackled through the interphone. 'Yes? Who's there?'

A pause, as the interphone scratched.

'Speak.'

Finally, Sami stepped forward. 'It's Sami, Alex's friend.'

'Is Alex there? Alex, are you there?'

Sami glanced at me. 'He's on his way. He said I should wait for him upstairs.'

More static through the interphone, then the lock released. A rush of cold air blasted in from the back stairwell as Sami pushed the door open and then entered the lift at the foot of the stairs, his body strange and unfamiliar in the wrought-iron cage. He turned, and a halo of light cast shadows on his face as the lift jerked upwards. I had the urge to run upstairs, warn my father he was coming, to call the whole thing off. But I didn't move, and the door to the apartments closed softly in my face.

I stood there listening, counting off the floors as he glided upwards. I imagined the lift juddering to a halt with that familiar last jerk, Sami stepping out to the darkened landing, pressing the doorbell. I swear I almost heard the soft tread of my father's loafers on the parquet as he stepped forward and opened the door.

I turned and saw my image in the cold mercury glass of the

mirrors that surrounded me. My face was damp with rain, flushed red, and the lights from the Christmas tree flashed crazily in time with my heartbeat. As I looked around, my reflections receded into the corners. The images mocked my movements, and in each of my eyes there was a tiny, flashing red blob of light.

A chill ran through the lobby and I wiped my hands on my jeans.

Minutes passed like hours and still Sami hadn't appeared. I walked to the door that led to the apartments, pressing my ear against the crack, against its cool brass edge. My tongue rasped on the roof of my mouth, humid breath over dry lips, blood throbbing in my ears.

Where was he? What if he'd screwed it up? What if the police were on their way?

I rattled the handle, pushed against the foggy glass. No sound from beyond the door, nothing. Then I pressed the buzzer to my home – three quick blasts – hurry up! I waited and pressed again, then again, longer now. Still no sound.

Then I heard it – someone coming down the stairs fast, taking them two, maybe three at a time, the pounding getting closer, louder. I stood back as Sami burst through the door, fear and adrenaline rising from him like steam. He held a white plastic bag, the handles twisted round his fist. There were dark shadows on the inside, the weight of the hammer warping the bag, pulling it sideways.

He fumbled with my father's wallet, shaking as he held it out.

'Take this,' he said, forcing the wallet into my hand.

I stared in horror at the blood on his hands, on the wallet, the dark smudges on his jeans.

'He was drunk. He went for me!' Sami said, wiping his face,

my father's blood blooming across his cheek.

My head burned, the muscles in my neck like twisted ropes, skin flaming across my chest. I turned towards the door, catching it with my foot before it closed.

He grabbed my sweatshirt. 'Do not go up there! It's OK. He'll be all right. He was still speaking.'

'*Still speaking?* Jesus, Sami, what have you done?' I said, tears streaming down my face.

Sami's eyes were crazed, red and flashing, and they locked on mine. 'We've done this now. Come on.'

'Done *what?*'

He pulled at me. 'Come on. Don't be so gutless. We need to get out of here. Let's go.'

They say the human body replaces itself every seven years, but that some cells, like those in the lens of the eye, can last a lifetime. That's why, more than seven years on, images from the night my father died still haunt me. Most of the cells in my body have died and regenerated, yet these images recur. Each night the dream's different, but the feeling is the same, and it's like I'm seeing it again for the first time.

And in the back of my eyes there's always that tiny red flash of light.

NOW

Seven and a half years later

One

Aubervilliers

'ARE YOU GOING TO ANSWER me?' my parole officer asks, her head on one side, brow heavy.

I glance around the room – plates in the sink, unmade bed. From behind the bathroom door, the loamy stench of bad plumbing.

'No comment.'

She rolls her eyes. 'Don't give me that. You're not under arrest.'

My throat contracts and I look outside. Wet clothes strung out along the balconies of the tower block opposite, and satellite dishes tilt towards us like cupped ears. The wind lashes rain against the window, forcing it into diagonal streaks. Drops race like needles, wet tracks along the glass.

She glances at her notes. 'Let's go through it again. Lisa Dallet says she saw you near her apartment in the sixteenth arrondissement.'

'Wasn't me.'

'You know you can't contact her,' she says, her brown eyes straining against mine. 'Or stalk her.'

'I wasn't *stalking* her,' I say. 'I was here all night.'

She leans back, arms folded. 'I didn't say it was night-time.' Then a smile. 'You're a bad liar, Alex. But you know that already.'

I start to object, then stop. I need to learn to shut up. It's always safer to say nothing, do nothing, and for a while we just sit there listening to the drone of rush-hour traffic on the autoroute below.

She goes over, pours a glass of water from the tap. 'You'll be on CCTV, you know. There are cameras at the stations and all the main roads, probably right outside her house. Dashcams, buses. They're everywhere now.' She puts the water in front of me and leans in close, placing her hand on my mobile. 'I can also track your phone.'

She gives the screen two hollow raps with her fingernail. I reach over, and she grabs my wrist.

'You need to be straight with me, Alex. I can't help you otherwise,' she says, releasing my hand. 'Lisa hasn't made a formal complaint, but this is a warning. If you do anything stupid, I'll have to tag you or put you on curfew. Things are tighter now with the new laws. I have fewer options.'

She bags my urine sample then holds out several sheets of paper. 'You asked for these.'

'The new laws apply to terrorists. I'm not a terrorist.'

She slides her coat off the chair, and for a second, her eyes say, *No, you're worse than that.*

My hand shakes as I smooth the papers on the table. 'I didn't kill my father.'

'So you keep saying,' she says, shrugging the coat on, her face tight with distrust.

9

'But you're free now, Alex, so just stick to your parole conditions. If you breach those, you'll be back at Fleury-Mérogis where no one cares what you are.'

Images of the place rise with the name – that dull concrete sprawl packed with the worst kind of men who dealt violence as easy as breathing. The sick reek of fear that shot through days of relentless boredom. No, they didn't care who I was, they weren't picky like that. And free? I'm only free now in the way unwanted things are free – unwelcome and with no real place.

At the door, she turns. 'Do you have any reason to be in Zone One? Is it essential travel?'

I want to say, *Yes, it is essential,* and make her see that my only option is to go back and prove I didn't do it, but I just shake my head.

'Then just stay out of there,' she says.

I watch the door until her footsteps recede then look at the article on the pages she's given me. They've used an old photo of my father and me. It's the same one the papers used after the trial, one my aunt had taken the previous summer. The top of my face is a pixelated blur because I was a minor then, but you can still tell it's me. In the picture, my father's tanned face beams into the sun, his expression relaxed and self-assured, like he's just said something he thought was clever. He has an arm slung over my shoulders and has drawn himself up to his full height, so he has maybe half an inch on me. It's a country club kind of pose – both of us looking as though we'd just stepped off a tennis court, as if we'd just played a match that he'd won. It's the sort of picture that, under different circumstances, you might use as a Christmas card.

I fold the pages carefully into my jacket pocket and leave the flat.

The quickest way into Zone One is on the high-speed commuter train. The tracks feed into tunnels at Saint-Denis then fan out at the Gare du Nord like frayed wire. The train lurches forward, the platform stretching to a sliver of grey concrete then it's gone. I never used to like travelling backwards, but I do now. These days I'm more focused on where I've been than where I'm headed. The train gathers pace in the tunnel and I feel a rush of vertigo, receding fast towards something unknown.

The journey takes nine minutes, passing under Boulevard Périphérique – the ring road that slashes around Paris like a blade, severing the city from the suburbs. The Péri lies along the shadow of the old city wall that once defended Paris from invading hordes. Today it does the same thing for a different age, as eight lanes of gridlocked traffic keep the suburbs from tarnishing the glittering centre better than any barricade.

A man sits next to me, his thigh pressed against mine. He stinks of fast food and wears dark, wraparound shades even though it's raining outside. He nods as if he knows me and places his forearm on the rest. I steal glances at him, wondering where I've seen him before. *Was it prison? School? Is he one of my father's friends?* His closeness makes my skin bristle and I move so we don't touch, the muscles in my neck tightening.

I change seats and his shaded gaze follows me across the aisle, then he leans over holding a roll-up, wanting a light. I shake my head and quickly turn away, the rain-streaked window a two-way mirror. Yellow bulkhead lights flash by, illuminating blurred graffiti on the concrete walls and I close my eyes, feeling the vibrations in the pit of my stomach.

The train emerges from the tunnel, and I glance towards the man, but he's gone. The tug of brakes as the train slows, screeching over sidings at the Gare du Nord. Checking first for guards, I leap over the ticket barriers and take the metro to the other side of town.

Elena Landis was an old friend of my father's and she lives in a tall apartment building that flanks the Champ de Mars. I stand outside, scrolling through my phone. A few people leave the building, and then an old lady comes out, her dog pulling at the lead while she checks the sky for rain. A courier picks out the code on the keypad and when they've gone, I tap in the same numbers and enter the large, wood-panelled lobby.

At the entry phone I press the button for Landis.

'It's Alex,' I say when she answers.

There's crackling over the receiver then silence. I press the buzzer again, and the lock releases on the heavy iron door. The pungent smell of wood wax as I walk slowly up four carpeted flights to a landing and three polished doors. The middle door is ajar, chain on. She checks I'm alone before closing the door and opening it again.

When she steps out, I don't recognise her – she's so thin, her skin papery, almost transparent. She must be nearly seventy, the same age my father would be now, and she's aged so much.

'I told you I couldn't help,' she says, her hand on the door. 'I'm sorry, Alex, I really have nothing to say.'

I step forward. 'Just a few minutes. Please.'

She sighs and ushers me inside, standing back stiffly to let me pass instead of kissing me on the cheek as she's done all my life. She hangs my backpack on a coat hook and leads me down an unlit corridor to a large, triple-room salon. There are imposing bookshelves all around stacked with old volumes and darkly framed photographs. Gesturing towards a sofa, she takes two cups and saucers from a shelf. The brown dye in her hair has stained her scalp, and damp wisps cling to her nape.

'You said you were going away,' I say.

'I leave tomorrow.'

'You're still travelling for work?'

She pours coffee and hands me one before taking a seat. 'No, I stopped all that years ago. I'm visiting Nathan.'

I'm glad for the opportunity to talk about her son, once a friend of mine. She answers quietly, giving few details – *final year of medical school in Lyon. Yes, I visit him often.* Then our conversation falters. It's her turn to ask about me, but she lets those questions hang in the air as she takes her coffee to the window. Her apartment is so close to the Eiffel Tower it feels as if we're perched on one of its pedestals, and the massive brown carcase dominates the window like a cage, its thick ironwork keeping light from the room.

She checks her watch. 'You're not here to talk about Nathan though, are you?'

I shake my head, taken aback by her abrupt tone.

'You said you had some questions about your father,' she says.

'Yes, I do in fact. Do you know ...?' I start, but then pause, wondering how to frame it since she'd been so dismissive on the phone. 'Do you happen to know what he was working on when he died?'

Her expression shuts down, and she looks tight-faced and stern. Dusty afternoon light filters through the high windows, emphasising the shadows under her eyes.

'Your father and I weren't that close when he died.'

I ask about their relationship as she sips her coffee, but my voice catches and the questions backfire. I imagined approaching this slowly, teasing out details like a cop – firm-voiced and steady-eyed, but my enquiries slip, lacking traction, and then slide back into a void.

'We were very close once, but that was many years ago. Long before he died,' she says, replacing her cup abruptly on its saucer, the noise echoing around the room like an exclamation. 'You know all this, Alex. Why do you want to rake over it now?'

'What about Patrick? Did he know—'

'My relationship with your father was over long before I married Patrick. And yes, of course he knew about us. We had no reason to hide!'

'No, I don't mean that. Did Patrick know what my father was working on?'

She shakes her head slowly. 'No. Why would he?'

We've reached difficult ground, and I'm not sure how to navigate. When we talked on the phone, she told me her husband had died. I already knew, having seen the reports two months ago, when I was still locked up. They'd dredged his body out of the river near Issy, and everyone blamed his job as a war correspondent – Afghanistan, Iraq, Libya, with no real break in between. After twenty years on the frontline, it had become too much. He was working out of bunkers next to airfields, his informants blown up or beheaded. Patrick could handle all of that, she'd told me, but he couldn't deal with the desk job back in Paris.

'Do you know if Patrick spoke to anyone about him? Is there anyone I could ask about it?' I say.

'Ask about what, Alex? What's this all about?'

I look towards the glass cabinet. It's packed with small wooden figures arranged in rural scenes. Miniature farmers lean against tiny bales of hay, playing flutes to their sheep and goats. Families spill out of caravans and cook over fires, while others weave baskets and chop wood. The vibrant displays are a distracting contrast to the gloominess of the apartment.

'I'm trying to piece together what my father was doing before he died – who he was seeing, what he was working on.'

'Who he was seeing?'

'I need to know who killed him. I have to prove it wasn't me or Sami.'

She stares at me. 'You always said it was Sami. Why this sudden change?'

Her words lunge at me, piercing the shame I'd carefully buried. I take the papers from my pocket and smooth them on the veined marble coffee table, feeling the chill beneath my fingers as I push them towards her.

'My father was alive when we left that night. Injured but *alive*,' I say quietly. 'Someone came after we left. I heard them on the stairs.'

She looks at me in disbelief. 'On the stairs?'

'He told me he was expecting someone. Perhaps a woman?'

She comes over, resting her hand on my shoulder to steady herself as she scans the article about Patrick's death then turns away. Although it's from an obscure website, it's clear she's seen it. Comments on the site say that at the time of his death, Patrick had been looking into my father's murder seven years earlier. There's speculation that my father wasn't killed by Sami and me, but by someone else, and that his death had something to do with an investigation he was working on.

'I've found other articles that say the same thing.'

She walks to the windows and lights a cigarette. 'You can find a conspiracy theory on the Internet for just about anything, especially where journalists are involved,' Elena says, opening the tall windows a crack. They move on their hinges in the breeze, reflections rippling over watery glass as she stands with her back to me smoking, her silhouette very straight and still.

I tap the article. 'This implies Eddy was working on something dangerous, and that his and Patrick's deaths are somehow linked.'

She shakes her head. 'You said at your trial that Sami attacked your father, and you both left him for dead. How many times do you need to relive this?' She turns to face me, her voice catching. 'And now you're just making things up. It was clear Patrick killed himself. I can understand the attraction of other theories, but if Patrick—'

Her voices wavers, then she clears her throat. 'If Patrick suspected anything, I'd have known.'

She pauses a while, collecting herself. 'Patrick wanted to see you before he died,' she says quietly. 'In prison, I mean. He'd want you to know that.'

The mention of my trial, of Sami, brings it all back and I see Patrick's face as I emerge from the Juvenile Assizes Court all those years ago, his worry turning to shock as my aunt told him the sentence they'd handed down. The feeling is overwhelming, like the jury, the judge and all the lawyers are in the room with us now, crowding around and threatening to send me all the way back there.

'He always liked you, you know,' she adds, as if it were a weakness.

'You think I killed Eddy, don't you?' I say, pushing back against the weight of her judgement.

She shakes her head, exhaling slowly. 'No, I don't. Do you think you'd be in my apartment if I did? But that doesn't mean you can play the innocent with me, Alex. My God, you were sixteen!' Her face has a ravaged look as if the idea has only just occurred to her.

I stare at my hands, clasped together between my knees.

I want to tell her Patrick actually had visited me in jail not long before he died, asking about my father's work, and that it was Patrick who'd given me these ideas.

'If he wanted to see me he could have,' I say.

'No, he couldn't. I forbade him,' she says coldly.

'*Forbade* him?' The idea of forbidding Patrick to do something is ridiculous, and I nearly laugh aloud. Then I feel a surge of anger. I want to puncture her self-righteousness and let her know he'd disobeyed her, that he'd visited me in prison, but something in her tone stops me.

'I banned both Patrick and Nathan from seeing you.'

There's silence as she stares out of the window. 'Patrick always saw the best in people, including you. He was like that with Eddy too. Loyal until the end.'

She shakes her head as if to erase a thought and then blows smoke through the crack in the window.

Finally she grinds the cigarette into an ashtray and turns to me. 'As for your question, I have no idea who'd know what Eddy was working on back then. I don't know who you could ask.'

At the door she hands me my backpack. I see the fine silver roots at her temples and smell her stale smoker's breath as she kisses me drily on each cheek and says goodbye.

THEN

The September before the murder

Two

Saint-Germain

ALTHOUGH I REMEMBER EVERY DETAIL of the night my father died, I can't remember what it was about him that used to piss me off so much. I think that's because I can't nail it down to just one thing. Sometimes it was his arrogant manner and the pompous way he spoke – as if there were someone nearby taking notes, ready to quote him. Other times it was the way he looked at me – the way his hair hung over his glasses as he gawped at me through thick, foggy lenses like I was some kind of philosophical question, or puzzle to be solved.

In fact, his looks bothered me. I was grateful I hadn't inherited his worst features, but these things are never guaranteed. His eyes were a vague sludgy green, normally murky and impenetrable, but occasionally they'd clear and then drill right through me. As for the rest, I only looked at him closely when he was asleep – slumped in his armchair, or passed out on the couch in front of the TV. Then I'd scan his face, staking out the worst of it while tracing my own for similarities. I hoped my jaw wouldn't take on that stubborn, square set, and I'd have to watch out for those blubbery chins. Later in the mirror, I'd check my nostrils for the same wiry hairs that sprouted from his own puffy and bloodshot nose. He had a beak that reared up on his face like a battle-hardened soldier, virile and ripe to bursting while everything around it lay sagged and defeated.

My father had a habit of walking around the apartment naked, often barging into our only bathroom while I was in the bath. At such moments, my eyes would be at the height of his groin, so I had to make an effort not to look there. If I looked away while he was speaking, he'd know I was embarrassed, so I just stared straight ahead over my feet towards the wall. I knew this annoyed him because he'd move into my line of sight and carry on talking. Stepping out of the shower, he'd pause to lecture me before he'd even reached for a towel, the water streaming down his naked body and pooling at his feet. Or, if he were brushing his teeth, he'd nag me through a mouth rimmed with toothpaste, spitting white foam into the air like some kind of fanatical preacher. To acknowledge him was to give in, so most of the time, I just sat there staring ahead as he droned on. The topic? It was always my shortcomings.

And so it was one Friday morning, six months after we'd moved back to Paris after ten years in the US. It was mid-September and my new school had just gone back after the long summer holidays. We were both getting ready at the same time that morning, and while I was in the bath, soaking the eczema that had flared up during the first week back, he'd just stepped out of the shower, all freshly scrubbed and in the mood for a back-to-school pep talk.

'You need to work much harder this year,' he said, running a towel between his legs like a length of rope. 'You need to start thinking about university.'

He'd usually start this way, adopting a tone that sounded fatherly enough but you could tell he was just gearing up to blow. It was like listening to the slow hiss of a valve somewhere.

'For once, your mother agrees with me.' He arranged the towel on the rail and sauntered over to the sink. 'Don't forget she's collecting you after school today,' he said, pointing at me as he walked past.

I waited until he squared up to the basin.

'*You* didn't,' I said.

'What?'

'You didn't do any of that crap when you were my age. The Bac, university.'

He squeezed a line of toothpaste onto his brush and carried on in a chatty, upbeat tone like he was being interviewed. 'You're right. I didn't. That's because I never had the chance, unlike you. You'll regret it, you know, if you don't go to a good university.' He punctuated the air with his toothbrush, and then looked back at me in the mirror.

Even though he hadn't gone to university until he was much older, my father refused to admit that it made no difference. He gave the impression he'd scaled massive odds to get where he was, but as far as I could tell it was an advantage for him to have been an outsider, not wasting time at university when he was young. It meant he hadn't run with the pack, or been part of the elite, and this gave him something to prove, someone to expose, or some point to make. But he didn't see it that way. He just saw me pissing away the chances he never had.

'There aren't any jobs, Dad. University's no guarantee. Not anymore.'

The water had cooled, so I leaned forward to the hot tap. He gargled, spat in the sink then walked over to the side of the bath, wiping his mouth as he looked down.

'It's not about a guarantee, Alex. It's about minimising the fucking risks.' He put a foot on the bath as he towelled between his toes. 'Christ, your eczema's bad,' he said, peering into the oily bath.

A wave of irritation burned across my face, and I leaned back, partly to distance myself from his crotch, but mostly to give the impression I didn't care.

'All right, say I go to a good university, whatever that is.' I turned my head slowly, my eyes following a shaft of light from the high window that lit up half his face. His mouth twitched, and one sunlit eye glinted like a beacon. 'What then? Do I become an academic like you?' I said, looking out over my feet. 'Help kids rack up qualifications for jobs that no longer exist? Or maybe I could try journalism and report on the job shortage?'

Academia seemed pointless enough, but *journalism* – what a fucking waste of time. He did both these things.

He started towelling hard around the back of his head. It made his lips vibrate.

'You don't have to follow me. I simply want you to have an interest in *something* other than your computer. It's not as though you—'

I drew my knees up and slid back, submerging my ears. Water from the tap pummelled the bath, drowning his voice. I lay there watching his mouth form words I couldn't hear. Releasing the air from my lungs, I sank slowly beneath the waterline and watched his hazy outline shimmy over the end of the bath.

A hand gripped my shoulder, and I came up spluttering.

'Don't ignore me when I'm speaking to you!' he yelled, his steaming pink face inches from mine. He released me and stepped back, glaring. 'We'll discuss this when you return on Monday.'

I didn't answer, just slid back again beneath the water. The colours blurred and faded, and then disappeared like a cloud on the horizon.

Three

Boulevard Périphérique

MY MOTHER DIDN'T MAKE IT that weekend, after all. She was coming in from New York and missed her flight. Since their divorce ten years earlier, arrangements between my parents had been haphazard, often made or broken at short notice, so it was no real surprise when my father messaged to say I'd be spending the weekend with him again.

'Jesus, you gave me a fright,' he said, as I opened the passenger door of his old blue Citroën after school. The close heat of the day still hugged the pavement, and low clouds gathered in the east, giving the afternoon a heavy, static feel.

'Relax, Dad. There's not much carjacking in the fifteenth arrondissement,' I said. 'Unless you count *Grand Theft Auto*.'

He started the car. 'Those games of yours have infected my brain too – seeping through the walls like this heat.'

I glanced at the satnav. 'Where are we going again?' Perhaps the plans had changed.

'The Chambières'.'

He checked the rear-view mirror then pulled into the street, cutting left at the Boulevard de Grenelle. Crossing the bridge at Bir-Hakeim I looked down. Canal boats flanked the river all the way to the Trocadéro and phlegmy water stretched out below, laced with the sun's glitter.

We drove along the Right Bank in silence, the Eiffel Tower looming on the other side, its latticed ironwork spiking skywards.

'You said old Chambière was a prick,' I said eventually.

Paul Chambière and my father had worked together decades ago when they were journalists. They'd been good friends once, but there had been a falling-out.

'No – wait. You actually said he was an arsehole.'

My father was silent for a while then glanced over. 'You might want to speak to him. He runs the Journalism School at Sciences Po now.'

I groaned, sensing a set-up. Sciences Po was exactly the kind of university my father hoped I'd attend after the Bac. I felt the weekend slipping from my grasp as we drove along the river towards the Péri and a weight of doom settled in, not so much because the weekend was ruined, but because there was a chance Paul Chambière's son, Tomas, might be there. Tomas was in my year at school and trumped his father by being both a prick and an arse. He'd taken a sudden dislike to me, and made my life hell at every opportunity.

Approaching Notre Dame, I looked across to the left bank. If he released me here, it would take ten minutes to walk home.

'Before you ask, yes, you do have to come. I'm not leaving you home alone.'

It was coming. I could hear it in his voice. *Last time I left—*

'Last time I left you home alone, you used your bedroom as a crack den.'

And left trails of coke—

'And left trails of cocaine in the bathroom.' My father winced at the memory of the only gathering – one friend and a pizza – I'd ever had at our apartment. He brought it up regularly, amplifying the details each time. According to him, the cigarette butt he found on the balcony contained crack, and the dusting of eczema powder on the toilet seat was coke. My father loved to dramatise the horrors of living with a teenager.

'Come on, Dad. It's too late for me to have anyone around, even if I wanted to.'

He had no idea it wasn't just a matter of inviting people to a gathering, you had to be in with the right crowd before anyone would even consider attending, and I was light years from that. I was the new kid at school who didn't speak French – not properly like them, and in six months I hadn't made a single real friend. Even the person who came around for the pizza had given up on me.

'You're coming, and that's it.'

'I don't understand why you want me to spend the weekend with a prick?'

'An arsehole, remember?'

I laughed, despite myself.

'It's not as though I had a choice. Your mother only called—'

'It's my weekend too.'

'Look, the evening was arranged at my request. I need Paul's help with some work I'm doing and I can't back out now. Besides, they were good to invite you at short notice.'

My father had always socialised with his colleagues, and we spent many weekends with these people when I was younger, when they all worked for the same newspaper. He hadn't seen them for years, but since we'd returned to Paris, they were back in his life again. He told me we had left the US because there were more opportunities for him in France, but I didn't really see any evidence of that. I knew things had changed because he'd gone freelance as a journalist and had a temporary teaching job at a university, and I got the sense that he didn't enjoy being back at all. There was much more urgency about work all of a sudden, which I guessed was anxiety about money.

I sighed. 'Oh, great. A work weekend and *they* don't want me either.'

'That's not what I'm saying. They were kind to invite you, that's all. Elena and Patrick will be there. And an old colleague, Jean-Marc Garnier, and his wife Anne.' He glanced over with a strange expression, almost embarrassed, as if he knew how bad it sounded. 'Look, I know it's not your idea of a wild Friday night, but just be polite.'

'Polite?'

'Yes, you remember the old routines – shake hands, say please and thank you. Smile if you still can.'

I forced a smile.

'That's it. Bravo! Think of the weekend as a challenge.'

'An endurance test.'

'Yes, treat it as one of your *games*. Teenage hero beats back an army of cruel adults hell-bent on ruining his weekend.' He lit a cigarette, its red glow flaring in the corner of his mouth. 'At least you won't have to speak much French. There'll be some ex-pats there,' he said in French.

My father usually spoke to me in English because he thought it would be better for my education so even though I understood French, my conversation was patchy. We'd moved from France to the States when I was five, and so the only French I retained from then was the kind a child would speak, and I hated it when he talked this way – alternating from French to English, his words patronising but disguised as humour. He knew I loathed ex-pats with their smug worldliness and constant references to '*home*', and though I'd always been an ex-pat myself, I didn't know where I belonged. It was impossible to have a discussion with my father when he was in this mood. If I took him on, I'd always lose the argument, so I settled back and kept quiet.

We made it to the Péri, the car slowing to a halt in the rush-hour traffic. Up near the intersection, a few ragged people made their way towards us, begging and cleaning windscreens.

As we crawled forward, he started up with the school stuff again. In those days he only talked to me when I was trapped – places like the car, or the bath. The car was a real favourite for this kind of chat. His grip on the wheel gave him a sense of power, and the absence of eye contact meant he could almost pretend I wasn't there, and deal with it all like a badly planned experiment.

'I spoke to Béa today.'

My heart sank. It was always a bad sign when he mentioned his sister. She was a teacher at my school and had pulled strings to get me in.

'I'm worried you're not settling in.'

I almost laughed. I knew he wasn't worried about whether I was 'settling in'. This was about my grades. We had stopped in the traffic, and I squinted into the glare of a white lorry as a woman in a flowery headscarf approached my father's side. Brushes and rags hung from a belt around her waist, and she drew a soapy heart on the windscreen with the rubber blade of her wiper.

He blasted the horn, waving her away. '*Non! Vas-y!*'

The woman laughed, deep wrinkles spreading like a sunburst over her cheeks as she smeared the glass with foamy slop, stretching her body across the windscreen as she wiped. Large perspiration stains darkened the fabric under her arms.

A boy about my age stuck his forearm in on my side. '*Réfugié syrien,*' he said. He had a puckered scar on his forehead and crooked teeth behind a sad smile. I fished in the side pocket for change, and the woman blew a kiss as they hustled off to the next car.

My father turned on the car's wipers. 'Damn them! They're no more refugees than I am. What a mess she's made.'

'She might have done a better job if you'd let her finish.'

'Bullshit. And next time give them *your* money, not mine.'

As we inched forward, he turned in his seat, aiming his whole body at me. 'Béa mentioned your *exams*, Alex. Eight for Chinese. Five for history! History used to be your best subject.' He shook his head.

I pretended to be interested in the traffic. A car had broken down and four lanes pinched into two. The sun beat through the window, and as I leaned forwards, the seatbelt strained against me and I felt stuck, like an insect under glass.

He was still facing me, harping on about exams, when the car drifted sideways into the path of oncoming traffic.

I screamed as he pulled on the steering wheel, just missing a lorry that roared past, its horn blaring.

'Jesus, Dad. Pay attention!'

'It's you who should pay attention,' he bellowed, as he wound down his window and reached for a cigarette. He worked a plastic lighter to get a flame, and then jabbed his cigarette at me as he spoke, his eyes now fixed on the traffic ahead. 'It's all about *competition*, and that's why you need to work harder.' He released a cloud of smoke. 'Your generation has to compete with the whole world now, so work hard at Chinese. They'll be running the place soon.' His tone relaxed with the influx of nicotine and the mention of Chinese, as though soothed by the thought of a Chinese-speaking son.

I kicked off my shoes. The sour reek of my feet enhanced the foul atmosphere, making it my own. A sea of characters drifted through my brain as I reached for my headphones. 'Chinese is a waste of time, Dad. They all speak English.'

He rambled on about the intellectual benefits of learning Chinese, his voice muffled now through the headphones as I scrolled through my playlists.

'It's all about hard work and application. The problem is you've had it too easy,' he said, working himself up as he trotted out the tired old monologue.

I could barely hear, just caught the gist of what he said: '—handed to you on a plate – *Chinois* – slave my guts – *ta mère* – school fees – *racaille*.'

I shouldered away towards the window, trying to decipher the graffiti on the tangled mess of overpasses and high-rise blocks of the banlieue. A mixture of Arabic and French, some Neo-Nazi slogans over posters for the far right and the Communist Party. He carried on talking, stuck in his groove, busy replaying the same old soundtrack.

Chinese? What planet was he on?

Four

Épernay

IT TOOK OVER TWO HOURS to reach the Chambières'
hamlet – a cluster of damp farmhouses slung low in the battle-
weary flatlands east of Paris. I wore my headphones for the
rest of the trip, feeling my father's resentment metastasising as the
miles ticked by. He jabbed the radio buttons for a while, and then
focused his irritation on the road ahead. He drove fast, drawing up
behind slower cars, tailing them at close range, and then leaning
on his horn as we passed, muttering obscenities. The motorway cut
through a landscape of bleached-out fields buffered by low grey
clouds, the horizon a faint line in the disappearing flatness. As
we drove east towards the wine region, the sky darkened, and the
pale fields gave way to a rolling patchwork of vines whose gnarled
limbs bore deep green leaves and bright yellow clusters of fruit.

By the time we drove through the tall stone pillars of the
Chambières' driveway, there was a light drizzle and barely enough
air to breathe. As soon as the car stopped, I pushed my feet back
into my shoes and leaped out. My father sat for a while, unrolling
his shirtsleeves and staring ahead as if gathering strength for
the visit.

He took a wheelie bag from the boot, and together we crunched down the gravel path towards the farmhouses. His trousers were creased, his shirt stretched tight across his gut, the damp fabric clinging to his armpits like remnants of the irritation he couldn't shake.

It was not yet dark, but lanterns illuminated a path flanked by stone boulders engraved with a family crest and *fleurs-de-lis*. My father told me years before that Paul Chambière had bought the hamlet from a debt-ridden seller in the eighties, so I already knew this display of a noble pedigree was a complete hoax. My father had laughed as he explained that even though the Chambières no longer spoke to the relatives who owned the neighbouring chateau, they were proud the estate was held by the same family and boasted about their 'line' as though they descended from the aristocracy.

A tall woman stood smoking under the awning of a small farmhouse. Mme. Chambière wore a loose white shirt, tight skirt, and a thin beige cardigan. Her legs were tanned and smooth above shiny heels. The drizzle had made no impact on her hair and it hung in stiff caramel waves. Apparently, she'd been a model once, and she still held herself as if she expected everyone to be watching, but the years and the fags had had their effect. Like many of my father's female friends, she'd tried to rectify the damage with some kind of facelift, but it hadn't worked, and her skin was stretched tight over her face like the canvas of a faded painting.

I hung back a bit and stared at my trainers. This approach usually got me ignored, but I sensed her looking at me. I thought perhaps my fly was gaping open, so I checked my crotch then met her gaze. My father greeted her with lingering kisses to each cheek, said something stupid about how lovely she smelled, and then stepped aside for me to do the same. I just stood there, not heeding his cue.

Just be polite.

'*Bonsoir*, Alex,' she said, smiling, then rattled on in French. *Almost as tall as Tomas. He's fifteen too. You're in the same year, no?*

She took a drag, peering at me down the length of her powdery nose. Her son, Tomas, had skipped a year on account of his genius and was top of the class and captain of the ice hockey team. He was on his way to a good university, no doubt about it. Maybe even Harvard on account of the ice hockey.

'Alex is sixteen, Céline.' My father glanced over as if willing me a few inches taller.

'Oh, yes, of course. Your mother was also *petite*,' she said, her smile tightening. Most people have a way of speaking about divorced couples as though one of them were dead. It's usually accidental, but Céline's remark was perfectly aimed. Her cigarette lingered near her mouth, pinched between beige nails and when she spoke her thin, down-turned lips gaped open and closed like a fish.

I looked around. Their place was in the middle of nowhere. I doubted they even had Wi-Fi.

'Is Tomas here?' my father asked.

'No, the boys stayed in Paris this weekend. They wanted to have a *soirée*, so we thought, why not let them have fun since they did so well in their exams.' Then she turned to me and winked. 'Mind you, I'm a bit worried about it. Do *you* know anything about this party, Alex?'

I shrugged, relieved to have it confirmed that at least Tomas wasn't there. I'd heard rumours about the party, but Tomas and his brother would never invite me, and she knew it.

33

And the wink. It was OK to wink at young children but after a certain age winking across the generations was too familiar, almost obscene.

Céline exhaled theatrically as if releasing the anxiety of leaving her teenage sons home alone. She dropped the cigarette and ground it into the gravel with the toe of her shoe.

'Let's not stand in the rain, come inside.'

She led us into the farmhouse, its deep-set windows edged by dull green shutters, heavy curtains framing the fading daylight. We walked through the small entrance hall, passing a room off to the left where a highly polished table was set for dinner under a low-beamed ceiling, a fire looming in the grate at the far end. The house was full of ornate furniture and lavish upholstery – a showy contrast to the humble exterior. We filed through a side door into a dismal courtyard, ducking our heads as we went. Outside, there was a crumbling pool filled with murky water and next to it, three chairs and an iron table with a large, flooded ashtray. A group of shabby outbuildings hunkered just beyond the courtyard.

Céline looked towards the dilapidated buildings as if surveying a vast estate.

'Our main guest cottage has a leak in the roof, so I've put you in one of the barns.'

She walked quickly over the wet gravel towards a small stone cowshed. We followed, my father trailing the wheelie bag, which refused to roll. Instead, it operated like a plough, pulling gravel into a mound. He dragged it for a while, and then gave in and picked it up.

She spoke over her shoulder as she walked. 'We don't use the barn much these days as it has no heating, but it's not too cold yet, so you should be fine. There's a bathroom next door. Paul keeps his cars in the other buildings.'

She opened the door and a damp gust wafted up from the darkness, bringing with it the reek of mildew and engine oil.

'Thanks, Céline. I'm sure it will be perfect.' My father stooped to peer into the gloom.

She turned to me as I got out my phone. 'No Wi-Fi out here, I'm afraid.'

I knew it. What kind of people don't have Wi-Fi?

She followed my father into the shed and I listened by the doorway as she spoke quickly in French, saying something about the spoilt plans for the evening, firing questions at him, and then they started whispering. I walked to the pool, the crunch of my footsteps echoing around the courtyard.

When they emerged from the building, my father looked uneasy. Céline kept her eyes fixed forward, ignoring me as she strutted past.

Inside the barn was like a fridge. Limewash coated the thick walls, and there was just enough space to walk around two narrow beds. Cobwebs hung in the corners, and a dusty bulb on a rickety wooden table cast a dim, cold light, making the shadows move.

My father sat on a bed and bounced softly, checking the springs. 'At least it's stopped raining.'

Old beams crossed the low ceilings, leaving dirty yellow stains at either end. I reached up to touch one.

'Careful,' he said.

I withdrew my hand. A patina of tiny black specks covered each beam.

'Fly shit,' he said, as we stared at the ceiling. 'This was where they kept the animals. And that's the petrified excrement of the flies that buzzed over them.'

He turned his gaze on me, taking in my T-shirt and faded jeans.

'Why don't you change into . . .?' he started up in his usual, bossy tone and then stopped, his voice trailing off as if even he'd become tired of the role. I sat on the bed next to him, exhausted by the trip and everything he expected of me.

He looked at me as though he had something else to say, then sighed, squeezed my shoulder and smiled. 'It's just one night. Come on, let's go and find a drink.'

Five

Épernay

THE FOUR OTHER GUESTS WERE already in the dining room. Elena and Patrick stood talking to an older couple – an American woman with a foghorn voice, and a bald man. Céline passed around champagne to everyone but me, and I stood there, empty-handed, listening to their chatter. I learned that most of them had worked together at some point, and that the older couple were the Chambières' neighbours in the country as well as important friends from Paris. The man, Jean-Marc, had been editor of *La Globe*, my father's boss at one time, and was now a successful businessman who owned the paper. He had a rough, reddish face and sharp blue eyes beneath a bushy monobrow.

'It's good to see you again, Eddy,' he said to my father who stood by the window, smoking. Then Jean-Marc turned to me. 'You must be Alex.'

Jean-Marc shook my hand and told me how much he'd heard about me already. He saw I didn't have a drink, so he reached over to the tray and passed me a glass of champagne while Foghorn's eyes scanned me vacantly then drifted over my shoulder. She was the victim of another bad facelift, and her short blonde bob curled in around her face like parentheses. Everyone gripped their drinks, steeling themselves for the small talk. Jean-Marc waded in first. He was loud and enthusiastic, the way adults are when they know they have an evening ahead of eating and drinking themselves senseless.

'You've moved back to Paris, I hear,' he said to my father.

'About six months ago. It's good to be back,' my father lied. 'Congratulations on the acquisition of *La Globe*. It must be like coming home,' he added.

'Yes, indeed, it is. The building hasn't changed at all since you were there. Except for the smoke! Back then you couldn't see across the newsroom.'

'I bet some of the old guard are still there with their microfiche and pagers,' said my father, stubbing his cigarette. 'Saving *La Globe* is a worthy cause, but it can't have been popular with your backers, given the paper's performance.'

'It was a tough sell, but they're used to me by now,' Jean-Marc said, taking a sip and rolling back on his heels. 'And I'll show them that news can still make money!'

I stood staring at my father as he laughed at Jean-Marc's boasts and bad jokes. I'd never seen him suck up so hard. I thought for a second he was about to drop to his knees and polish his shoes.

'Yes, well, your business acumen has certainly paid dividends. The shareholders must be delighted. Your other businesses are booming,' my father said.

'Everyone wants security – economic, political and social. It's a sign of the times, unfortunately, and my companies are proud to be able to fulfil that need. We've pitched well, and have other projects in the pipeline too.'

'Speaking of pitches, I'd like your thoughts on a story. I think it might interest you,' said my father.

'Anything from you interests me, Eddy,' said Jean-Marc.

We took our seats for dinner. Céline ushered me in between Patrick and my father, who was chatting with Elena on his left. Foghorn looked dissatisfied with her assigned position at the table and came over behind me, putting her hands on my shoulders as she leaned in, whispering for me to take her place opposite. I felt her rings against my collarbone, and her heavy perfume almost knocked me out.

We swapped places, my father looking anxious as I took the seat between Jean-Marc and Elena. Perhaps he was worried I'd sabotage his efforts with Jean-Marc, or maybe he was afraid of Jean-Marc's wife Anne, but by then Anne had turned her attention to Patrick. I checked the data settings on my phone, thinking of Tomas's party and my classmates in Paris, and I saw a Wi-Fi network nearby. Céline had been lying.

The table fell quiet as Paul spoke and Céline brought food to the table.

'We were talking earlier about the increase in migrants on the street, since it's been in the news lately,' Paul said, addressing the table. 'They're kept outside the system, and have to beg and steal to survive.' He took the plate of veal from Céline, served himself generously, and passed it on.

Migrants and other street people were always in the news back then, the papers full of stories about the scams they worked to separate tourists from their cash. Their camps were tolerated in the suburbs but when they moved inside the Péri, it was another story. The mayor said he wanted to *purge* them from the city, and I'd seen police in riot gear rounding them up into vans across our neighbourhood. My father said it was a waste of time, and they'd return to the same places a few days later. I'd looked, but hadn't seen them since.

Jean-Marc took the plate from Paul and served me a portion before serving himself. 'Some of them deliberately make their children sick to get on the system. They have no moral compass whatsoever,' he said.

There was silence. Everyone was looking at him.

'They're coming in from all over. The borders are wide open, unpoliced,' Jean-Marc added, scanning the table, his eyes widening to illustrate the breadth and emptiness of the borders. 'It's dangerous. Today we give them hospitality, tomorrow we will question it.'

'But many are allowed to come here and work, and if they fall ill, they're entitled to healthcare. It's terrible to see them on the streets with their children,' Elena said, coaxing a few buttery carrots onto her plate.

I kept an eye on my father, wondering how long he would put up with the discussion. I knew he hated this kind of talk, but he kept his mouth shut and played the helpful guest, keeping everyone's glasses filled.

Anne slammed down her fork. '*Work?* They work the streets in gangs, stealing thousands of euros. They set up filthy camps in the city and fill the hospitals to the brim.'

'Yes, they have no conscience. And the people who wear burqas on the streets. It's aggressive. We must resist all forms of hostility – at our borders, in our suburbs, for our safety, and the security of the nation,' Jean-Marc said, moistening his lips.

'And as someone with an interest in the security of our nation, how should we manage that?' asked my father. The question sounded unfriendly and was a surprising change of tack given his performance earlier, but he was smiling.

'Oh, it's already happening. They're putting in more security for communities in the problem areas. A system of controlled access to the estates, and better law enforcement. All of this on a much more ambitious scale than we have now.' Jean-Marc glanced around the table. He loosened his collar, stretching his neck. 'It's not just about policing or private security, of course. There are also our charities, the ones Elena runs in the suburbs for young people. They do excellent work stopping tension escalating in the first place.'

'We all need to take responsibility for the disruption in the suburbs,' Elena said quietly, while Jean-Marc drew breath.

My father laughed. 'Take responsibility? Sounds like you're just shifting blame.'

I focused on eating as they carried on like this. The religious topic had stirred Jean-Marc, and he turned to me after a while, asking about school. *Did the canteen serve halal food? The girls, did they wear headscarves?* My father cast nervous looks in our direction and so I hammed it up, replying that the canteen was completely halal, that we were taught in Arabic, and that my girlfriend wore a burqa.

'But they've banned that,' Jean-Marc said.

I shrugged. 'Not everyone complies.'

He moved closer, lowering his voice. 'So here's something I've always wondered. How do you know what she looks like?'

'She sends me photos when she's at home.'

I started scrolling through my photos.

'Really?' he said, looking at my phone with interest.

His focus was shattered by a ringing crash on the other side of the table. Anne had knocked over the champagne bucket and ice cubes skidded across the floor, followed by the bottle, rolling and foaming at the mouth. She shrieked and apologised for her clumsiness as my father leaped up to help. I looked at Jean-Marc, expecting him to follow suit, but his face was beet-red. A rush of irritation surged from him that was almost physical, like the sudden blast from a furnace.

I took the opportunity to excuse myself and went outside.

Outside I got a faint Wi-Fi network signal by the pool, so I took a seat at the table there. The drizzle had stopped, and the sky was clear. Sunken lights illuminated the murky depths of the pool, and tiny bats flew over from the barns, skimming and rippling the surface of the water.

I could hear the party through the still night air – the waterfall of cutlery, plates and drunken laughter, opening verses of *La Marseillaise*. My father was part of the generation I'd grown up hearing about constantly, and even studied at school. Les soixante-huitards who, in their radical youth, tore up paving stones and flung them at the authorities. He'd told me stories about those times and later, when he, Patrick and Paul had been journalists together at *La Globe*, speaking truth to power, fighting the good fight. It was hard to believe all that now as I watched them belly up to an antique table, whining about immigration and border security through flutes of champagne, fixated now by their jobs, pensions and taxes.

'So here you are,' said Patrick, his silhouette at the door, hands cupped around a lighter. 'Not smoking, I hope,' he said, walking over and offering me a cigarette.

I shook my head as he sat down.

'Don't start. It's a slippery slope,' he said, and then laughed. 'Don't listen to Jean-Marc either. He wants everyone signed up to the far right.'

We chatted for a while. He asked me how I was finding life back in Paris and then we spoke about school. He mentioned that his son, Nathan, had started there that term.

Patrick surveyed the barren courtyard. The outdoor lights emphasised the shadows on his face, and his crooked nose and sunken cheekbones gave him the look of a Cold War spy. The ruggedness of his face had always fascinated me when I was younger. He'd been injured by shrapnel years ago when he was a war reporter, and a slight paralysis meant he could wear different expressions at the same time, which I thought must be useful in his line of work.

Paul emerged from the house leading Jean-Marc, Anne and Elena towards the outbuildings.

'Come and see Paul's cars,' Anne hollered. She had taken off her shoes and was leaning on Paul for support.

Patrick waved at her.

'Save me a cigarette,' she called, picking her way over the gravel.

'You're still in Baghdad?' I asked.

He nodded. 'I head back on Monday, but it's coming to an end soon. Once the troops withdraw, that'll be it for me. Time for a quiet office and my feet under the desk.' He smiled. 'But the good thing is I'll see more of Nathan. I'm looking forward to that.'

'Is it still dangerous there?'

'Not for me. I sit in a concrete bunker in the Green Zone and wait for bad news. But for others, yes. Everywhere is more dangerous for journalists now.'

'Even Paris?'

He nodded, an uneasy look on his face. 'There's a new world taking shape and the city is the new conflict zone. You can feel it closing in.' He put his hands together as if wringing the air. 'A stranglehold of wealth and corruption.'

I pointed to the dilapidated barns, to the sound of old horns and spluttering engines. 'No new world in there though.'

'Not yet,' he said, smiling now.

'At least you're doing something, not just collecting vintage cars,' I said and Patrick laughed.

'Paul and Céline haven't always been like this. I think your father's in shock at the change in them.'

'He's too busy sucking up to Jean-Marc. He wants a job or something.'

'It's not a job he wants – your father could have had Jean-Marc's job, or any of ours, for that matter. But that would have been too easy. Look at him now, here, coming back to all this,' Patrick said darkly.

A worried expression crossed his face and he paused as if considering whether to carry on. Like most adults, he spoke in riddles, especially when he was drunk.

'The two of you seem to be getting on better,' he said after a while.

I shrugged. 'I just wish he'd get off my back.'

He smiled. 'That's his job, Alex, he's your father. He wants the best for you.'

44

I didn't reply and we chatted about other things for a while as Patrick smoked. Then he emptied the rainwater from the ashtray, stubbed out his cigarette, and walked back to the house.

Patrick had left his cigarettes and lighter on the table. I didn't smoke, but I thought it was something I should practice, so I lit one and resumed my search for the Wi-Fi network. It had disappeared by the pool, so I headed off down the side of the house towards a softly lit window. Underneath, there was a signal, so I got a chair and peered into a small room. A rack of clothes took up one side, and a desk with a lamp and a computer stood against the other wall. An Orange Livebox winked up at me from beneath a mass of cables under the desk.

There was no password so I got straight into the network. I downloaded my emails then checked out the party snaps Tomas had uploaded to Facebook. There were a lot of selfies with his arm around Lisa, a girl in my class.

I heard voices nearby and looked around, throwing the cigarette into a bush. The courtyard was empty, so I glanced back through the window just as the door opened, and my father and Céline burst into the room. He pressed her against the desk while she undid his belt, the two of them so close to me that I could almost feel the heat coming off them. He unzipped her skirt and eased her knickers down her legs, reaching to pick them off the floor, nuzzling his face into her crotch. Then he lifted her onto the desk, his hands gripping her hips as he started a slow grind against her, his belt hanging from the trousers that puckered around his thighs.

My phone beeped with an incoming message, and they both froze. I ducked away from the window and jumped off the chair, treading carefully across the gravel. Behind me, hushed voices, a door closing, and then silence. I went over to the barn, my heart pounding in my head.

I switched on the lamp, clamped my headphones over my ears and lay on the bed. The room was draughty, so I pulled over the covers, watching the ceiling and the shadows that wouldn't settle, like the spidery darkness between Céline's thighs.

It took a while to get those images out of my head, but I must have fallen asleep eventually because I woke to the sound of crunching gravel. Then talking – the same rhythm of questions and the rapid-fire French, both of them making no effort to whisper this time. After a few minutes, the sounds receded.

I woke again when my father came in after dawn. Light splintered the shutters and birds squawked outside as he crept into the room. He fumbled and groped around, then lost his footing and fell on the bed, sending the lamp crashing to the floor.

'Alex, are you awake?' he whispered.

'I am now,' I said, rolling away from the alcohol fumes.

He kicked off his shoes and lay back heavily. 'Don't shay anything 'bout what you shaw.

'And don't shmoke,' he added before his slurs turned to snores.

I lay awake, staring up at the darkness and a hundred years of fly shit.

NOW

Six

Aubervilliers

I T'S LATE AFTERNOON WHEN I leave Elena's. Back at the Gare du Nord, rush-hour commuters weave around knots of tourists pointing at maps and hauling luggage. Then it's standing room only to Saint-Denis where beyond the oily ballast, bleached litter clings to trackside weeds, and razor wire separates the station from a junkyard of rusted equipment.

I push through the turnstiles to a busy marketplace, cobblestones slick with grease and food scraps. Dark clouds mottle the sky, the air heavy with smoke and the smell of charred meat. On the edge of the market, hawkers call to passers-by as they thread raw meat onto kebab sticks, grilling them in shopping trolleys rigged as barbecues. Broken umbrellas shield the kebabs from the rain, their spokes jutting into the air like the ribs of spinning ballerinas.

Shoppers hurry now through the drizzle to a tram stop on a bridge that spans the canal. The wind has picked up, and there's a rank smell coming off the water where cigarette butts swirl in oily eddies towards the banks.

On the tram, I sit opposite a man and a boy dressed in matching brown djellabas, the baggy hoods slung behind their heads. The man has his arm around the boy's shoulders and watches him play with a snow globe. Inside, Paris is submerged under a plastic cover speckled with the night sky. The boy gives it a shake and smiles up at his father. Flecks of glitter blast a landscape of tiny silver monuments and the snow settles, falling quickly against the dome's starry night.

I get off at La Courneuve and walk towards my block. Up ahead, a car throbs with music, the windows fogged. As I cross the road, I notice someone behind me. Short, dark glasses. It looks like the guy from the train this morning, but a raincoat covers his head and flaps around him so I can't tell.

He follows me over, his shoulders hunched against the rain. If I take a shortcut through the park I'll get home sooner but it's safer here on the main road, so I carry on, quickening my pace.

Now he's closer, gaining on me. My palms are prickling, sweaty, and I glance back again. He's not the man I saw on the train. He's younger, one of Sami's mates for sure, I think, panicking as I scan the street for a refuge – a shop, a café, but there's nothing. There are quick footsteps behind me then he tugs at my shoulder, grabbing my backpack. Close up, he's smaller than I thought, so I throw myself at him and we both go down, the bag squashed between us. Pushing hard, I dig an elbow into his chest and jump up, kicking out as he gropes for my legs.

The adrenaline's in me now as I pull my backpack from him. He lunges at me, and almost has an ankle before I turn and sprint to my building, wet fingers slipping as I punch in the code. The door clicks open to the sharp reek of disinfectant and

I rush inside, pushing heavily against the door, cursing the gasping hydraulics as it shuts slowly, my heart pounding against the cold steel frame.

I run to the first floor and peer down to the street. There's no one there – just a grey pavement pitted with rain. I wait for the shadows to reveal him, but he's gone.

The main lift only goes to the eighth floor, and I'm on the twelfth. That lift is broken because some kids melted the buttons with their lighters, so I take the stairs four storeys up, stopping on each floor to check the street.

I lean on the wall outside my room, light-headed, lungs raw, and my mind spins back to that night – more than seven years ago now, but it feels like another life. I'm standing outside a different apartment, an older, wooden door. I close my eyes, but that's where the memories are, as stark and real as ever.

The door is open, and in the gap, my father's legs sprawl across the prayer rug we used as an entrance mat. His socks are the same shade of red as the rug, and one of his loafers has slipped off. He slides his knees up, the rug buckling as he twists and groans. The sounds are muffled and weak, just a kind of hoarse mumbling, and the look he wears as I back away is the one that still haunts me – his face wide with terror and disbelief. There are blood smears on the doorframe – two short streaks and one longer, like a child's finger painting.

I wait until my breathing slows and the vision recedes.

In front of me now is my own door – a cold sheet of metal in a buckled frame. Last night there was rattling on this door and now the frame's all warped with deep scratches round the keyhole. I try to recall if it was damaged before but I can't remember – there have been so many doors like this. I slam it hard behind me, pushing across the bolt, and then fall down on my bed, staring out at the charcoal sky.

I live in a hostel for juvenile offenders now out on parole. It's a halfway house, a kind of refuge, and mine for three months while I find a job. My room faces west over the Autoroute du Nord, which cuts through the suburbs from Saint-Denis to Drancy. Outside, wet tower blocks stretch out like a sprawling citadel and the whole terrain is illuminated, its dull throb extending to a dark horizon. Tonight there are no stars, just a low cloud haze that reflects yellow light back on the city. Rain pricks the windows, and I'm on that train again, barrelling backwards through the night.

My room's not much bigger than the bed when it's pulled out, and if I stand with my arms spread, I can lean sideways and touch one wall, take a step and touch the other. There's a small kitchen at the back with a broken door that leads to a mouldy bathroom, and the whole place stinks of cigarettes and backed-up plumbing. On nights like these the wind shrieks along the open passages outside, merging with the roar of traffic into a wild scream that shreds the building like a freight train.

I stay inside most days, staring at this view, or waiting for visits from my parole officer. Just getting downstairs is an ordeal. The building is a warren of fire doors, stairs, corridors and lifts, and each jangle of keys sends my heart racing. Signs everywhere yell from the walls: NO ENTRY! GO BACK! QUIET! DON'T SLAM! NO VISITORS! NO DOGS! NO SMOKING! 24HR CCTV!

I'm trapped here because of the broken lift, but also because outside feels strange. On the street there are too many people and as they walk past, they stare. One day they'll figure it out, point at me and shout, *There he is, that boy who killed his father!*

Out there I feel naked, exposed, and my legs don't move like they used to. They have this weak, bloodless feeling. I can run, of course, like I did tonight, but my muscles are limp, just waiting to cramp and smack me down, forcing me to stumble. This is the kind of freedom that makes you nervous. It makes your head spin.

The way Elena spoke to me today made me nervous too. It wasn't just her cold manner or what she said; it was the way she looked at me as she smoked at the window. It was as though I'd frightened her, like a ghost or shadow from the past. It was as if I reminded her of how close she was to something desperate, something she couldn't control.

That same sense closes in on me now. It's the guy on the street, the presence of Sami, I can tell. I've felt him nearby ever since my release – watching and waiting, and wanting revenge. *You always said it was Sami,* she said.

It was a shock, that blatant reminder of what I'd done, how I'd blamed him. I was in too much trouble back then to think about anyone but myself and I feel the shame of it now, potent and sharpened by fear.

But would it have made any difference if I'd told the truth? Maybe not, but I didn't need to lie. I could tell from the way the jury looked at him that he was doomed, that he was already convicted. The cards were stacked against him but I ratted him anyway, just to be sure. The same way you hit the hammer one last time even when the nail's in as far as it will go.

The balcony door slides open, the gale lifting papers off the table, sucking under the front door. I stare through the wet haze to the street below. I know he's still in jail – I even checked and made sure – but that doesn't stop me thinking he's always right behind me. And one night he will be – slouched in that doorway or against that wall, smoking and waiting and wanting me to see him. But tonight there's no one. The rain claws my face as I yell his name to the wind, 'Sami, Sami, Saaaammmiii.'

The building sways and the clothes on the balconies flap wildly, wrapping around the lines.

Later, at the fridge, I hear my father's voice.

'A drink will calm your nerves after a fright like that,' he says softly, like a medicine man with an ancient remedy. I check the window, half expecting him to be there, a shadow beside my own.

My reflection is startled, guilty.

'Go on, take one,' he whispers, waggling a bottle and egging me on so he doesn't have to drink alone. 'Your friend wasn't the one who killed me, you know that. You need to deal with that guilt, or else drown it.'

I turn from his memory, pulling a bottle from the box and flipping the lid with the opener I've tied to the drawer handle. That's a trick I learned from him too: a drinker can't trust his memory, let alone what he sees. I've taken on many of his habits, even the ones I used to hate. I guess those are tougher, more deeply ingrained. Resentment hardens things, it makes good mortar, and he's stuck in my head, whether I like it or not.

Back at the window, a line of red lights traces the perimeter of the building site below and inside, cranes and diggers flash like ships at sea. Further out beyond the scar of cleared earth, apartment blocks recede like blunt teeth, glinting and shining in the darkness. I think of all of the people who have a home there, and those who don't – the outcasts, criminals and vagrants. The exiles and refugees. Vast stretches of the unwanted, forgotten and the uninvited.

I hold the bottle out to them.

I'm one of them now.

Seven

Aubervilliers

MY FATHER WRITHES ON THE threshold, his knees up as he twists and groans. I strain towards him, but a rope jerks me back. There are sirens and blinding red lights flashing to a manic Christmas tune.

Interrogation.

Confinement.

It's the same dream of mirrors, of the night he died. Twisting and turning, sweat pooling on my chest, slickening my armpits.

Sami's eyes are crazed, red and flashing, as they lock on mine. He thrusts something at me then grabs my arm.

We need to get out of here. Let's go.

I wake to light searing across the mattress from a gap in the blind and then roll from the glare, pulling the sheets from my throat.

Stumbling out of bed into empty bottles. They roll like skittles, leaving a pissy trail on the carpet. I crack open a window and the drone of traffic rides in on a blast of polluted air. On the building site below, a jackhammer tears up concrete and tremors wrack the building, juddering my jaw like a dentist's drill.

On my desk is the article about Patrick, the one I showed Elena. There's a picture of him squinting into the sun against a shimmering desert backdrop that fades to a bleached horizon. He's dressed in beige camouflage under a blue flak jacket, PRESS stamped across his chest in big white letters. I read the final paragraph again:

> Patrick Landis was a friend and colleague of Edouard Giraud, who was killed in his home in Paris on Christmas Eve, more than seven years ago.
>
> The case received extensive press attention as Giraud's son, Alex, and his friend, Sami Lantou, were convicted of his murder in a closed trial. No details of the proceedings were released to the public due to the ages of the accused. Alex Giraud received a reduced sentence of seven years on account of his youth, whilst Lantou, just two years older, received a sentence of twenty-five years.
>
> Recent speculation has drawn a link between the deaths of the two journalists and their investigation into corruption allegations.

Beneath the article is the same photo of my father and me. He's grinning, with his hand on my shoulder like a soft white paw. It's from a website, Society to Protect Journalists, and this page is headed UNSOLVED JOURNALISTS' KILLINGS & DISAPPEARANCES.

On the next page, there's a map of the world. Any suspicious death of a journalist is depicted by a red bullet hole. It's only May, and already a spray of red artillery extends from Afghanistan, through Turkey, Iraq, Syria and the Middle East. In France, there's a single puncture mark for Patrick, followed by an obituary and details of his work.

I emailed the link to my parole officer before her visit and asked her to print it out. I said I was a friend of Patrick's and had only just learned of his death.

I'm not your secretary, she emailed back. Then minutes later, *You're meant to be focusing on your job search.*

She doesn't look like a secretary. With long, dark hair and tattoos on her fingers, she doesn't look like a parole officer either. She actually looks like someone who might, in other circumstances, be all right. That was what I was counting on, and she brought it to me the next day.

When I showed it to Elena, she turned away. If Patrick killed himself, then why is he on this site? By 'unsolved' did they mean his death wasn't suicide? Elena seemed so sure about it that I couldn't ask – it would have been picking at a fresh scab. It didn't make sense that Patrick had killed himself, let alone thrown himself into the canal, where he'd be someone else's problem. The Patrick I knew would have done it at sea, where he'd be nobody's business but his own.

And why did the article mention my father? Why did it mention *me*?

You can find a conspiracy theory on the Internet for just about anything, especially where journalists are involved.

It's just after midday and the sun radiates along the walkway outside my room, sending up a wall of heat. Doors are open and the smell of fried food mingles with the stench of rubbish and dope. Everyone uses the passage as an extension of their flats, a kind of storage area for useless and unwanted things even though there are signs everywhere telling them not to. Broken bikes, shoes, anything they don't mind losing, all scattered among the sagging pyramids of rubbish. A man leans against his door frame in a string vest, damp towel around his waist. He smokes a joint and yells into his phone, competing with the drills on the construction site. I haven't left the room for two days and I'm just waiting for someone to yell at me like I'm an animal, as they did in prison, or warn me against doing the wrong thing, like those signs everywhere.

The cleaner scowls as I squeeze past her on the stairs, poking my ankle with a mop. Disinfectant seeps through my sock and muttered abuse follows me down the stairs. A few floors below, I work up the courage to yell back, and my voice sounds pathetic, her laugh a further insult.

The library is two bus stops down the Avenue Jean Jaurès, but I take the road that runs through the estate, past the shops and the playground where kids throw a basketball through a broken hoop. Men in a cherry picker pollard trees, their pruned branches reaching up to the sky like drowning hands.

It's hard to say where one estate ends and another starts. Clusters of tall buildings spreading like an epidemic between the pharmacies and betting shops, all of it hemmed in by six-lane roads. Everyone ignores the signs to keep off the grass, and cars nose up against sickly trees, their tyres thick with dried mud as if they've been there forever.

The hostel building is a garish pink, and other high-rises radiate out from this central core like prison blocks. The whole place is like an open jail – hurricane fencing, barbed wire, gang fights, drugs, and the unwritten curfew at night. In fact, the only difference between here and prison, the thing that makes it even more hopeless, is that there's no parole from this place. Poverty is a better jailer than locks and bars can ever be.

I pass the main car park where dealers sell dope from cars, ready to drive away if the cops arrive. But the cops don't come, or at least they don't come *looking* for crimes. If they respond to a call, they arrive late, in groups of four, hoping things will have blown over. They stay in their armoured vans, knowing they are targets too.

A drunk staggers towards me, asking for change. He's bleeding from a gash to his head, his eyes wild and bloodshot, like a pair of cracked saucers. He grabs my arm, pulls me towards the road. There's a guy on the median strip in his underwear, palms outstretched, wailing and singing at the top of his voice. The first man hops from one foot to the other, calling to his friend over the din of song and traffic. I help him cross, and he turns to thank me with tears streaming down his face.

The library is set back from the road, wedged in between a kebab shop and a discount supermarket. The librarian takes my card and nods towards the computer.

I key Patrick's name and scroll through his feed from last year to get a sense of where he was before he died. My father always said the best journalists couldn't help putting themselves into their work so that when you finished their piece, you knew what they thought. It went against everything they learned about being objective, but what good reporter is ever neutral?

At the beginning of the year, he wrote about problems in the regions – unemployment in the North, gangs, oligarchs and gambling on the Riviera, the unstoppable rise of the far right. I skim through looking for a pattern, a gap or a change in tone. Midway through the year, he followed a group of kids in Toulouse who'd swapped schoolbooks for a jihad training camp. The story is compelling, and I read the whole thing. In a city where youth unemployment is the highest in France, where violence happens on a daily basis, a jihad camp is a no-brainer. There's a series on terrorist financing through people smuggling and drug trafficking, and a piece about money laundering through property deals before a pause in February this year.

His work tackles gloomy topics, but nothing suggests he was depressed or suicidal. It's reporting from a person who was interested in the world, not someone who wanted to escape it. He'd seen terrible things, but he was used to it. It was his work.

I'm near the end of my hour when I come across an obituary with the same picture from the blog – Patrick in a barren landscape, the sun on his face, eyes squinting under a green army helmet.

Patrick Landis, a former freelance war correspondent, died in Paris on 25 March of apparent suicide.

In a career spanning 30 years, Patrick covered conflicts on the frontline, across Africa and the Middle East. He was renowned for his writing on the realities of war and the need to 'give people the facts of war so they understood the truth'. He often said 'the hunger for truth exceeds the craving for lies'.

While covering the US war in Afghanistan, Patrick received a shrapnel injury that left his face partially paralysed. In circumstances where most soldiers would seek a medical discharge, Patrick carried on dispatching frontline news for another ten years.

At the time of his death, Patrick was working in Paris and had shifted his focus to organised crime and corruption within Europe.

I scroll down the list of comments – more stories and links to Twitter feeds, all adding to the unanimous chorus of praise for his bravery and investigative courage. Then there are comments on his death, throwing doubt on the suicide verdict:

Jo Paul
Patrick was looking into Eddy Giraud's murder. This is where the focus should be.

Abu
Terrible and sad news about Patrick. Let's not forget the other journalist who was looking into the same thing. RIPx2 and how many more?

I scroll down, past more comments and then there's the same photo of my father and me, but this time my face is clear, unpixelated. The roundness of my young face shocks me – full cheeks and pouchy lips, my head bent in towards my father's. The date stamp says it was posted by an anonymous user just over a week ago.

The librarian calls over, tapping a pen on her computer to say my time's up.

I scroll up to a new comment and a blurred photo file with a timer indicating something's being uploaded. It comes into focus. It's a picture of me at the door of my apartment building. I'm wearing the same clothes I have on now. Beneath the photo the words:

PATRICIDAL MANIAC ON THE LOOSE –
ALEX GIRAUD LEAVING HIS APARTMENT NEAR
AUBERVILLIERS TODAY!

A chill spreads across my shoulders. Then the screen goes black.

Eight

Aubervilliers

L EAVING THE LIBRARY, I WALK quickly along the canal before getting spooked and doubling back to the road. Was this how they got Patrick? Ambushed as he walked down a side street a bit too close to the water? Did he survive the worst war zones only to be murdered in the suburbs?

The last time I saw Patrick was a fortnight before his death, and about two months before my parole. He'd visited me a few times when I was first convicted and wrote to me in prison from time to time, but then the contact petered out and I didn't hear from him for several years. I'd always been interested in him – he'd seen some shit, and unlike most of my father's friends, he didn't just boast about his achievements, or those of his son, though he sometimes did that too. Like most adults, his favourite topic was himself, but he never tried to ram his ideas down my neck, or corner me in a debate about politics. I've always been wary of people who tell you what they think. They usually have an agenda, and sooner or later, they want something in return.

When Patrick walked into the visiting room that day, I didn't recognise him at first. He'd lost weight, and his clothes sagged around his body. His hair was cut short, the bones of his face visible beneath his sun-worn skin and one side of his face was completely immobile.

He scanned the room and its wall of cameras, and then turned back towards the guard as if he'd changed his mind about the visit. He hadn't recognised me either, and when he did, his mouth froze into a lop-sided smile, his wrinkles like carvings beneath the strip lights.

He leaned forward, embracing me as best he could over the desk and the Perspex barrier, and then squeezed my shoulders, his eyes shining. His grin was strange against the tears, and I looked away, embarrassed.

He poured some water into a plastic cup and started telling me about the past few years – his job in Paris, Nathan. I tried to look interested, but couldn't muster any real enthusiasm, so I just let my eyes wander over his face. I saw the war hero I'd admired as a kid but the original had faded, together with his stories, so I tried to imagine him as a gangster who'd been in one too many fights, but really, he just looked old and tired, white dog hairs clinging to his raggedy blue sweater.

'You know, Alex, we want to help you when you get out. I know you have your aunt Béatrice, but Elena and I are here too.'

I stared at him, wondering whether he was for real. It made me want to laugh – his earnest look and words of vague help after all this time, but I just smiled, putting on what I hoped was an expression of gratitude.

He looked embarrassed, perhaps sensing the fraud. Then he shifted position and plunged in.

'That's not the main reason I'm here. I'll get to the point, as we don't have much time. I need your help, actually.'

The first thing I thought was that he wanted me to grass someone up. He was a journalist after all and reporters were always visiting their contacts inside. There were messages stamped on the walls in the showers:

ANONYMOUS INFORMATION ABOUT A CRIME COULD EARN YOU A CASH REWARD

I used to focus on the Wild West type and the words 'Cash Reward', wondering how much they'd pay, how much each betrayal was worth. There were plenty that made a career from it, grassing up friends and competitors, and God knows, I'd done it to Sami. I'd given him up to save my own skin, and just look where that had got me.

I sat back. 'What kind of help?'

'It's about Eddy.'

He saw me flinch and waited a moment. 'I'm trying to find out what he was working on when he died,' he said quietly. There was a hopeful look in his eye that was a bit apologetic too. The plastic cup buckled noisily in his hand. 'Do you recall him talking about work at all before he – before he died?'

I thought back to that time, remembering a few chats about work, but no real details. In the old days, my father spoke about work all the time – the people he'd met, where he'd been, the stories he was working on, but once we moved back to Paris, it all died down. He didn't talk about it too much then, and I certainly didn't want to think about it now. His death still loomed so large it obscured everything else. It was like the glare of a lighthouse that warns of rocks beneath the surface, and I preferred to keep well clear in case I went crashing into something unexpected. I moved further back from the table, annoyed that Patrick assumed I'd be able to remember any kind of detail, given what I'd been through.

'Do you tell Nathan about your work?' I asked. Nathan had never seemed to know where Patrick was, let alone what he was working on.

Patrick smiled. 'Sometimes. In vague terms – concepts and ideas. But I usually keep the details to myself.'

'Well, Eddy never discussed any *concepts or ideas* with me, if that's what you're wondering.'

The smile fell from his face, and he looked at me sadly. 'I'm sorry to ask, Alex, but let me know if anything comes to mind,' he said. A slight sweat gleamed on his forehead.

I was ready to let it go, but his cautious approach disturbed me. 'What's this about?'

He hesitated, and I felt a cold stab of dread. 'A friend of Eddy's told me about something she was mixed up in. She said she'd sent him some documents before he died, and that it might have had something to do with his death.'

'Something to do with his *death*?' I repeated.

'Yes, but she didn't say. In fact, she wasn't at all clear. She kept asking about Eddy and whether I knew what he'd been working on. She said she'd call back, but she hasn't, and now I can't contact her. She was worried, very anxious.'

My heart beat faster, a sudden gallop of hope and fear. 'What was it?' I asked. 'Do you know what she meant?'

He shook his head. 'Whatever it was had her spooked and I want to know why. I'm following up some leads, but it seems your father died in the middle of a puzzle, Alex.' Patrick sat forward in his chair like a hunting dog, watching for my reaction, his voice suddenly urgent. 'Let me know if you remember anything he said about work, or if he started seeing different people. That kind of thing,' he said, his eyes not leaving mine.

I was stunned by this sudden flow of confusing information. 'Different people? He always saw different people.'

'I mean people who weren't his usual friends. Other people, especially in the months before he died.'

'When you say *seeing*, do you mean women? This woman you're talking about? I mean, he saw anyone who'd drink with him, you know that. He wasn't choosy. Especially with women.'

My words sounded bitter, but I didn't mean it like that. I was speaking quickly, thinking faster, trying to understand what Patrick was saying. There were nights with Paul, and my father's affair with Céline. There had been other women, too, that winter.

'Yes. Women were always your father's motivation. They were his weakness. It was never money,' Patrick said with an odd laugh.

Women? Money? I never had the sense my father had been motivated by either, at least no more than anyone else.

'You think he died because he got mixed up with a woman?'

'I'm not sure. Perhaps.'

'Well, I guess, why not? He could be a bastard when he put his mind to it,' I said, sitting back. 'A real bastard.' Again, I didn't mean to sound harsh, but I'd seen what he was capable of – blatantly carrying on with Céline right under Paul's nose, for example, and why wouldn't that kind of thing get him in trouble?

But would it cause his *death*? I was confused, struggling to remember anything specific, and again, my comment fell flat.

I was about to ask Patrick if he knew about my father and Céline, but he was already on his feet. 'Right, then,' he said.

When we said goodbye, there was that same sad look in his eye.

'You're quite a lot like Eddy, you know. Especially when he was younger. I think that's why it's so hard to understand why you disliked him so much.'

I didn't know what to say, so I just looked at my hands and waited until the door slammed behind him.

What Patrick said that day stuck with me, and I thought about his words a lot in the weeks that followed.

At first, I didn't want to think back too far. I was supposed to be making a fresh start, after all, and I'd already had a lot of thinking time in prison. As Elena said, I couldn't play the innocent, but I wasn't guilty either. For seven years I'd whittled away the sharp edges of culpability and created around me a fuzzy no man's land where blame and fault, truth and lies, were just labels depending on your perspective. Or to put it more plainly, I convinced myself I was more sinned against than sinning. I didn't kill my father, yet here I was in prison. Who said anything about degrees, and the many shadows the shifting facets of guilt can cast once lodged in the heart? I was guilty of setting Sami up, of bringing him to the apartment, then lying about it afterwards. And although I'd laid the blame for my father's murder on Sami, I knew it wasn't him. It was awful to think I'd let that lie fester for so long, and so I didn't like to dwell on it too much. The shame of betraying Sami came and went during my time in prison, and it sat particularly heavily on me then, in those few months before my release, enhanced, of course, by a growing fear of the kind of vengeance that might be waiting for me in the dark recesses of those shadows.

As for my father, I know there were many things he didn't tell me about his work in Paris. Perhaps he wanted it to appear ordinary, and maybe the stress of the pretence explained his short temper with me, fuelled by the fact that I didn't share his anxiety.

Although there didn't seem anything unusual about his habits back then, the loaded way Patrick referred to women as my father's 'weakness' now cast an erotic glow over his activities, and I scoured my memory for details. I tried to recall the smell of the perfume in the corridor, and the low, night-time murmurings that drifted out on the thin band of soft light from under his bedroom door. There were frequent trips to the suburbs, late nights out, and staggering in with the dawn. All these things, exhausting perhaps for someone in their late fifties, were ordinary enough for a single man in Paris, but they now took on a much more fatal significance. My own limited experience with girls had taught me something of their power, and although I'd had no further practical experience in prison, I knew enough to be aware that as far as women were concerned, the level of the indulgence, and the danger, was limited only by imagination.

I didn't speak to Patrick again, and then two weeks after visiting me, he was dead. I made a few enquiries, got in touch with the lawyer who defended me and asked for all the transcripts and records of my case. I didn't receive anything until I got out of prison but then I devoted myself to the task. I stayed up late, endlessly researching and reading through the court documents, visited the library to surf the net, got lost in Twitter and obscure news websites.

My parole officer made it clear I was on my own with these investigations, but if a woman had spoken to Patrick about my father's death, then I had to find her. I started tracking down my father's old friends and colleagues – the people he saw in the months before he died, and the first person I met was Elena.

When I arrive home, I stand at the entrance to my block. In the photo I saw at the library, you could see straight through the open door to the mailboxes in the lobby. I turn and scan the car park, then beyond to the road. The shot could have been taken from the car park, the road, or a window on the estate opposite.

Are they there now, somewhere nearby, watching me? Is it someone I know, or a lunatic stranger? A vigilante with a crazed sense of justice. You hear of some prisoners, often those convicted as children, who are forever hounded by the public, never able to lead normal lives.

'What are you looking for, boy?' comes a voice from behind me. An old woman I sometimes see around the place leans heavily on her stick as she rolls her shopping trolley towards me. I forget her name – something unlikely, like Brigitte or Colette.

'If you've lost something here you'll never get it back,' she lisps, the words whistling through the gaps in her teeth. 'You put something down and when you turn back, it's gone.'

There aren't many white people living on the estate. This woman and her husband are the only ones I see regularly. When I first arrived, they greeted me as though we'd known each other for years. Now they always nod, their eyes seizing mine like navigational points in an unfamiliar landscape.

'Are you Muslim?' she whispers, cupping her ear. Flecks of dandruff gather in greasy ridges at her scalp, and moisture pools in reddish hollows beneath her eyes.

'Yes,' I say, knowing this is the best response. If I say no, she starts up against the Muslims, her hand trembling on her stick. She says they're all thieves, that they've overrun the place, that there are no real Christians left. It won't be long before there are none in France either, she's heard all about it on the news. When she first cornered me, she stood there like this, blocking my path with her stick and shopping trolley. A freezing wind blew into her face, making her eyes stream, but it didn't stop her.

'It's no good out here,' she says, gesturing around with her stick. 'Too many gangsters. And the young kids with drugs and knives.' She shuffles closer, bringing a hot blast of halitosis, her throat a vase of rotting flowers. Her tongue is obscenely pink and plump in her shrivelled mouth as she immobilises me with foul breath and walking aids, and I think how strange it is that bodies age not all at once, but in stages.

'I must have left my bag upstairs, *Inshallah*,' I say, pushing her stick aside.

'None of us is safe. He was here again, asking after you,' she says, pointing behind her. 'I saw him over there taking photos this morning.'

'What? Who did you see?'

'Like all the young people today, they are so rude. So rude! On the trams, no one gets up, always on their phones. The drugs, the loud music—'

'What did he look like?'

'What?'

'The man you saw. What did he look like?'

She leans in close as I hold my breath. 'Osama Bin Laden.'

*

71

There's a red trail on the stairs. The drops get bigger, forming streaks on the landing where something's been dragged along. I peer over the rail to see the same pattern spiralling down the stairs. It disappears for a couple of flights and then starts up again – a dark wet smudge. It stops at my floor and I follow the trail along the passage to my gaping front door.

The first thing that hits me is the smell, then the blinding glare of sunlight burning across the floor. In the kitchen, a pile of fish heads simmer on the tiles, bleary-eyed, their mouths wide. Next to them is a mound of bones and guts – pink and grey tubes crawling with flies. Blood pools between the grout lines, marking out the slaughter in expanding squares. Plates and cups smashed near the wall. Packets of sugar, salt, coffee, rice, scattered across the worktop.

Beyond the kitchen, there's rubbish everywhere – scraps of food, takeaway boxes, bottles, cans. Plastic bags ripped open and strewn across the carpet. Cupboards and drawers turned out. In the middle of the room, yellow foam bulges from the slashed mattress like fat from a corpse. Even the electric sockets are ripped from the walls. I stand frozen at the door, straining to piece it together. I check the number – is it even my apartment? Back down the corridor the air is quiet, full of menace, as if whoever did this is still here.

I pick my way to the bathroom. Cupboards open, tubes and jars smashed, bed sheets stuffed down the toilet.

A door slams along the corridor and I rush outside, but no one's there. The sun has moved and the walkway is in shadow, but free of litter, clear of anything. I knock next door, but there's no answer. Then I notice my door. It's scratched like before, but there's nothing wrong with the lock, no sign of forced entry.

I don't own anything worth stealing apart from the TV, and they've left that. And whoever did this took their time – hauling the fish upstairs, gathering rubbish from the corridor. Surely someone will have seen them. This whole set-up, this style, it must be Sami's people, but what do they want? Are they watching me now, through their cameras and those dead fish eyes?

THEN

October

Nine

Montparnasse

MY FATHER GENERALLY AVOIDED PEOPLE who were more successful than him, but he made an exception for Paul Chambière and they saw each other again a week after our visit to the farmhouse. I wasn't sure what to make of it after what I'd seen him doing with Paul's wife, but if anything the episode seemed to have strengthened their friendship. I guess they now shared something, even though one of them didn't know it.

They also shared a thirst for alcohol. Paul had that saturated look – bloodhound eyes, a low-slung paunch, and a permanent beading of sweat that made his bald patch shine. My father didn't need any encouragement to drink, and could match anyone, bottle for bottle, in the cafés around our neighbourhood.

There was nothing else happening that Friday night, so I tagged along with them to a restaurant in Montparnasse. After we'd eaten, we moved outside so they could smoke. The evening was mild but a steady rain slid down the plastic canopy, projecting the light of passing traffic around the terrace.

'The weekend wasn't a complete waste of time, I hope,' said Paul.

'Not at all,' said my father, studying the wine list.

'You got something out of it, then?'

My father flinched, disguising the move in a gesture to the waiter who stood nearby in a bow tie and a long black apron.

'It was good to see Jean-Marc again. His acceleration's been astounding,' he said, ordering two more cognacs.

Paul smiled. 'I thought you'd like that. He's done well for a provincial lad.'

'Done well? He's spent thirty years churning out propaganda, now he owns the paper. That, on top of his other interests. It's incredible.' My father's voice bristled with irritation.

Paul shrugged. 'Shit floats,' he said, raising his glass to study the contents. 'Have you offered him your piece?'

'He won't have it. Says their focus is online now. They want short, choppy pieces for the attention-deficit generation.'

Paul muttered his assent. '*Génération déficit.*'

'Generation Deaf, more like it,' my father said, reaching over to ruffle my hair. 'Single message, nothing complicated. Boost the likes between the clicks.'

Paul swirled his cognac. 'Listen, don't hold the past against him. Judge him by his behaviour.'

'His behaviour *then*?'

'His behaviour now.'

'You think he's changed?'

'He's an important man.'

My father laughed. 'That wasn't the question.'

'People change.'

'Not that much.'

Paul wiped the perspiration from his brow. 'It depends who's pulling the strings.'

'Now it's the money men and the politicians. It looks like journalism, but it's window dressing. Built from the Internet up.'

'You sound like a Luddite. A *Boomer*. Times change, Eddy, and people change. It's what we always said – get behind it, or get left behind.'

'It's what *you* always said.'

'And I was right about that too.'

They shifted in their seats, squaring up for the next bout.

My father got in first. 'Speaking of which, last weekend had me thinking back over those times. The Messenger, the Matrix Club. You know that old place is just around the corner? We passed it on the way here. It'd make a good story.'

The skin on Paul's scalp lifted with his eyebrows. 'Jesus, Eddy. You're not serious, surely?'

'Why not? Sex, lies, betrayal. People love that.'

'Now who's talking click-bait?'

My father leaned back. 'I never worked out who was really behind it all, and it's about time I did.'

There was a pause and Paul lowered his voice. 'Listen, it's not a story. All the stuff that happened back then – none of that had influence, it didn't change things in any way. You know that.'

It was my father's turn to smile. 'I've never heard you speak so honestly about your own persuasive skills. Or the power of journalism.'

'Come on,' said Paul, putting down his glass. 'This is one of the worst ideas you've had.'

My father sat forward. He looked like a shark that had just sensed blood in the water. 'You seem very agitated. You always said you weren't involved.'

'And I wasn't. But it's a bad idea.'

'Aren't they the ones worth writing about? You always said that too: *Things are never what they seem on the surface. Dig deeper!* Was that a lie as well?'

'Times have changed.'

'So you mentioned,' said my father. 'But the story's more relevant now than ever.'

Paul raised his hands. 'Don't start digging all that up, Eddy. And if you do, count me out.'

I took my laptop to an empty table and loaded up *Rome: Total War*. They kept drinking and smoking, shirtsleeves rolled up to the elbows, laughing and stirring each other up as they went hard at the booze. The rain-filled light mottled their faces, and they looked like the stone gargoyles that crouched in the eaves at the church I went to as a kid. I'd watch from the pew as the stained glass threw garish light across their faces, distorting their bodies with lengthening shadows.

I increased the volume, filling my head with the roar of the battlefield. I was winning now, and with each thumb click, I thrust the might of the world's first superpower against forts and cities, redrawing the borders of the Ancient World.

An hour passed and we were the last in the restaurant. Paul was doing most of the talking, my father most of the drinking, and I could tell by the lazy roll of his eyes and his slow grinding jaw, that he was now fully loaded. I went back to the game, concentrating on bringing victory to the Republic and when I looked back, Paul was leaving. Their faces were stony; there'd been an argument. Paul tied his trench coat angrily and left without saying goodbye.

I returned to the screen, forced my army ahead and trapped the enemy in a pincer. Then I mowed them down and installed myself as Emperor. My centurions cheered, and I felt the exhilarating buzz of victory as I gathered my things and walked over to my father who was slumped in his chair.

His phone buzzed in front of him, and the word 'SALOPE' blazed across an unflattering photo of my mother.

'Hi, Mum.'

'Alex, where *are* you? Why aren't you answering your phone?'

'I'm at a bar with Dad—'

'A *bar*?'

'A restaurant.'

'It's after midnight there.'

'We're just leaving. Dad's phone's running out of juice.'

'Can you put him on?'

My father gazed at me, unfocused. 'He's in the bathroom. I'll call you later,' I said, then hung up.

'Whossat?' he said.

'It's Mum.'

He straightened up, his eyes darting around the empty terrace as if she might be there.

I passed him the phone. 'She's gone now. Come on, let's go.'

He leaned heavily on me as together we weaved past iron tables and stacked-up chairs. Nearing the exit, the waiter appeared, squinting through the smoke of his roll-up, and thrust a silver tray towards us.

'Bastard's left me with the bill,' said my father, swaying. 'He's always on about the money. He never lets it go.'

I reached into his jacket, flipped open his wallet, and withdrew his Mastercard. The waiter passed the handset to my father who tried unsuccessfully to peck out the PIN, and then handed it to me. I punched in the numbers.

'Bravo,' the waiter said, stuffing the receipt in my father's pocket.

Outside, it had stopped raining, but there were no taxis and it took me a while to navigate us home, my father staggering beside me. Finally, we reached our apartment building and I put my arm around his shoulders and led him inside. Mirrors clad the lobby walls and our reflection, like limping conjoined twins, or some hideous Quasimodo, receded into infinity in the corner panels.

He steadied himself in the doorway leading to the lift as a blast of air blew in from the back entrance. 'You should be in bed. I bet that's what she said.

'You should be in bed, Alex,' he repeated in the lift, swaying with the rhythm and mimicking my mother's accent.

When he saw our front door he made a U-turn for the stairs. 'I'm not ready for bed yet,' he said.

An overwhelming sense of exhaustion came over me, which soured quickly into rage. I had the sudden urge to send his bombed-out carcase and inane chatter plummeting into the dark, silent mouth of the stairwell.

Instead, I led him inside where he tripped and lost his balance. He lay sprawled on the floor, slack-mouthed and grunting. I thought of leaving him there – the air from outside might bring him round, sober him up a bit – but eventually I coaxed him onto all fours and got him to crawl to his bedroom. Once he saw his bed, he climbed up like an obedient toddler and lay across it, feet dangling off the end. I stripped him down to his underwear and rearranged the sheets, moving the debris. There were piles of newspapers, pens, spiral-bound notebooks on the bed, even a full ashtray. I put a pillow under his head and settled the covers. He tried to lift his head to speak, but it fell back, his mouth moving, trying to form words.

I walked into the gloom of the empty hallway, closed the front door and went to bed.

I woke early the next morning to the sound of his groans. There was retching and the muffled rustle of papers as I rolled away from the wall that separated us. In the bathroom, he coughed and flushed the toilet then I heard him in the kitchen filling the coffee machine. The clang of glass and stainless steel as he rifled through the drawers, preparing a drink.

'A beer often settles the stomach,' he'd say, as if it were a doctor's prescription whenever he opened one before midday.

I waited until he returned to bed then got dressed. I could feel the shape of the day ahead and I didn't want to be around. He'd probably sleep for a few more hours then eventually he'd rise, prowling around the apartment in his dressing gown, a vacant expression on his face. He wouldn't say much, but occasionally he'd grunt or swear as hazy details pierced the fog. Then later, when the morning had soaked through to the afternoon, his hangover would really take hold, and he'd bitch about everything I did. It was best to get out of his way on days like this and not return until nightfall when he'd probably be drunk again. Like most people, he was better drunk than hungover.

I found his wallet and took fifty euros, tucking the note into my own wallet. He never missed cash after a night like that.

I heard him moving around so I went into the kitchen, grabbed the remains of a pizza from the fridge and left the apartment.

Outside, I heard him calling from the balcony. He was in his bathrobe, holding something that caught the light and glinted down at me. I stopped, struggling to make it out, but I couldn't. I waved at him, clamped my headphones in place and walked away.

Ten

Montparnasse

I HEADED SOUTH ALONG THE BOULEVARD Raspail, past the cafés of Montparnasse with their chairs lined up like theatre stalls. Outside the restaurant from last night the same waiter sluiced the pavement, filling the air with the sick smell of disinfectant. I edged around the tables and cloudy green puddles, past several early drinkers clutching goblets of yellow beer. They drank slowly, making each sip count as they stared into the distance like the baffled audience at an avant-garde play.

I turned into a narrow street that led to the cemetery. Some joker had named it Passage D'Enfer, passage to hell, and it was lined with nightclubs, bars and cabarets, their neon signs dulled, windows shuttered with boards and metal grilles. Above me, the trees were almost bare and the leaves that once threw shards of light across the summer pavements now filled the gutters in spiky drifts.

Halfway down the street, a faded blue tarpaulin sagged between some low scaffolding and a line of traffic barriers. Through a gap in the sheeting, I glimpsed a girl with a baby on a stained mattress surrounded by plastic bags. A black plait wound around the girl's head, and the baby was bundled with scarves. The girl emerged from the tent and walked to a small iron fountain where a guy was filling a bottle with water. He wore a pair of loose jeans but no shirt and he spoke to her as she bent to wash her face. I guessed from his young appearance and lightly stubbled chin that he was probably only a few years older than me.

I stopped, feeling like an intruder, not sure whether to cross the street or turn back. Then the guy called out in English with an American accent asking for a cigarette. I smiled, pleased he could tell I wasn't French, but I didn't smoke, so I shook my head and crossed the road. He muttered something I didn't catch, and they both laughed as I rounded the corner.

Outside the cemetery, long trestle tables bowed under buckets of carnations and funeral flowers. Water trickled from the tables to the gutter, and I bought a small bunch of violets from an old woman selling wreaths.

With the flowers as a prop, I entered the cemetery. It was a place I often went to be alone – it was always quiet, and no one bothered me there, especially at this hour. Near the gates, the plots were laid out like a mini suburb, all neat borders and picket fences, everything held within tight boundaries. Further inside as the ground rose, the place became more chaotic, the tombs bigger. Older graves buckled up from the earth leaving jagged cracks, and soil clung to the hairy roots that reached across the cool darkness like stitches.

Cresting the hill, I sat on a bench and took out my headphones. Trees flanked the distant walls, and yellow leaves fell and caught the light, flickering like lanterns past dark, wrinkled trunks.

After a while, I noticed someone on the path heading towards me. I could tell from the loose way he walked that it was the guy from earlier. I didn't want company, so I stared at him, hoping to push him back with the force of my glare, but he waved, his pace quickening.

'Serge Gainsbourg. You are a fan?' he said when he reached me gesturing to a grave behind the bench. It was piled so high with tributes that you couldn't see the slab beneath. Washed-out photos pitted with rain lay propped against flowers wilting under cellophane. At the head of the grave was an old record sleeve featuring a topless girl cuddling a rag doll and next to it, the same kind of doll, now sad and waterlogged, its head slumped to one side.

My mother loved Serge Gainsbourg. I could hear his gravelly voice against sparse, twanging instruments, the lyrics rutted with sex and innuendo, slaked over with a thousand Gauloises.

'Do you speak English? Are you American?' he said.

'No,' I said, and looked away, hoping he'd get the message and piss off.

Instead, he placed his palms together like he was praying. He said his name was Sami and pointed towards the gates of the cemetery. 'You saw us outside. Please, some money.' He brought his fingers to his mouth, rubbing his belly, his face full of suffering.

I ignored him, so he smiled and made as if to walk away. But then he stopped and lit a cigarette, flicked his collar up and launched into a Gainsbourg song. He had a beautiful voice and adopted a brooding swagger – one hand on his hip, the other with the cigarette. It was one of my mother's favourite songs. I'd heard it thousands of times, but never this way.

When he finished, he leaped up among the flowers and the photos and sang another song. I couldn't help laughing – it was absurd to see him thrashing around on the old man's grave, singing his songs like that.

Finally, he jumped down, slung his shirt over the bench and edged in close. Our hips touched, and I felt a shudder along the outside of my thigh. He gave off a strong, sour smell like an animal, and I felt suddenly panicked.

'What are you doing here, my friend? You need to be careful, a rich boy like you in here alone.' His eyes were light brown – bright and clear, like a pair of polished beads. They locked onto mine, drawing me in.

'There are strange visitors here. Not only at night, *tu vois*,' he whispered, gesturing around at the tombs. 'In here we have daytime ghosts too.' He offered me his roll-up. Behind his gleaming eyes was a mocking flicker.

I shook my head. 'Get lost.'

The sun went behind a cloud, and he put his shirt back on, gesturing towards Gainsbourg's cluttered grave. 'Great French man. The voice of France.'

'Piss off. Leave me alone,' I said, looking around for one of the attendants.

He followed my eyes and saw the place was deserted. 'Why do you ignore me, brother? It's just you and me here this morning.' He spread his arms wide. I could see the stained ridges of his teeth and the dirt under his fingernails.

'I hate Serge Gainsbourg,' I said, louder than I intended. He sensed my fear and moved in closer, his face almost touching mine.

'Ah, yes. He is terrible. You should listen to me. I play good music. I do this for money, on the metro and elsewhere. I can also do other things—' He laughed, a strange, deep cackle.

He relit his cigarette stub, took a drag and put his arm around me. His smell was suffocating – stale breath, unwashed clothes.

I pushed him away and stood up. Grabbing a stick, I scraped it loudly along the railings as I walked. I hated anyone being so close to me, touching me like that. I could hear him whistling and singing, calling out to me from the bench. I glanced behind, and he waved back.

'OK, bye-bye, brother,' he called in a mocking tone. I walked faster, past a section of higher crypts and vaults. I could hear him behind me, on his feet now scuffing and kicking the gravel, tailing me and calling out in his sing-song voice.

'Fuck off!' I yelled.

His deep laugh followed me as I walked back, quickly now, past all the tombs, statues and stony idols of France.

I left through the main gates, crossing the street and heading towards home. I felt shaken, my heart racing with fear and a strange kind of exhilaration as if I'd just escaped something. Despite his American accent, his total otherness unsettled me, and I looked back a few times to check he wasn't there.

I was thirsty, so I went into a store to get a drink but my wallet was missing. Adrenaline rushed to my head. Then anger.

I raced back down the Boulevard Raspail, towards the tent.

I looked under the tarp and down the laneway, but there was no sign of them. A couple of bars along the street had opened so I checked inside – no sign there either.

I found the girl a little further up on the pavement near a busy intersection, the baby sleeping beside her. There was a pink baby's bowl in front of them which served as a sad little begging dish.

'*Monsieur, s'il vous plaît.*'

'Where's your boyfriend? Where is he?'

She shrugged helplessly, her teeth all stained and crooked.

87

I lunged for the bag beside her, thinking the wallet might be there, but she snatched it up, her plait whipping against my arm. In the scuffle, something shiny fell out of her hand, and I grabbed it. It was cylinder-shaped like a large bullet, wrapped tightly in foil.

She sprang at me, her plait slithering over her shoulder as she dug her fingernails into my wrist.

I twisted out of her grasp and pushed her away, knocking over the bowl and sending coins scattering onto the road.

She scratched my face, and I leaped back, fists up, ready to defend myself if she came for me again. But she just collected the bowl and the coins and stood next to the baby, glaring at me, her hands on her hips, eyes like slits.

I went back to the cemetery, wandered the streets for a while, checking the bins, this time *wanting* to see him again, but of course, he wasn't there. Tearing the foil from the silver bullet, I saw compacted leaf. It had the dense fruity smell of weed, so I tucked it away and carried on south, past the catacombs to a small park somewhere off the Boulevard Saint-Jacques.

As I ate the pizza from my backpack, I wondered how to smoke the weed. I'd never tried it, so I'd have to find someone at school who knew how to do it. I took a pinch and chewed it, spat it out, then went over and drank from a fountain on the edge of the grass. There was a sign with a long spiel about the park, saying it used to be part of an island in the middle of a river that flowed to the Seine. The tanneries on its banks had polluted the water, so they buried the river in the sewer networks of Paris.

I lay on the grass, smelling the weed and thinking about the old river powering mills and bringing life to the city. Then its end, as it became thick with skins from the tanneries that sent poison and quicklime eddying to its banks. I imagined the water all clogged up and sluggish, trailing muck through the town – oily and stinking and full of disease. The river now ran beneath me, shoved deep below, out of sight, condemned to the borders beyond the periphery. I wondered what it would take to dredge it up, to untangle it from the sewers and gutters.

I held the silver bullet up to the sun and listened for the sounds of the old river, gurgling through valves and whistling in the drains all around me. I heard its hiss and rasp, and I smelled its stale, swampy breath.

My father was rustling around in the kitchen when I arrived home. He'd cleaned the place, and several rubbish bags sat by the door.

He stepped into the hall. 'So, where have you been all day?'

I shrugged. 'Around.'

He opened his mouth to continue and then saw the scratches on my face.

'Right, well, I didn't think you'd get far without this,' he said, holding out my wallet.

It seemed to pulse in his hand.

'Where did you get that?' I said, certain he'd tricked me somehow.

'I was waving it from the balcony. What did you think I was doing?'

'I couldn't see.'

'You need your eyes tested,' he said, looking at me over his glasses. 'Oh, and by the way, I repatriated that fifty euros.'

Eleven

Saint-Germain

MY FATHER DIDN'T MENTION THE fifty euros again and in return, I didn't mention how drunk he'd been. Things often passed like that between us: I ignored his bad behaviour and mostly, he ignored mine, but the incident hung between us like bad air for several days until one morning at breakfast he started talking about my allowance, saying he would have to reduce it by fifty euros unless my grades improved.

I was about to get up and walk out of the kitchen when I felt my phone vibrate. I glanced down at the screen – sunglasses and white teeth against a bright blue sky.

It was my mother, but I didn't answer. Then it buzzed with a message as if she knew I was there, watching the phone:

Let's have lunch today! I'll send Philippe to collect you.
Don't tell your father.

I flicked it to silent in case she continued. Anything she wanted kept from my father often meant trouble for me, and I couldn't engage with her now with him right there. I was often dragged into my parents' battles in this way, each of them demanding my secrecy so that it was impossible to weave a path through the maze of traps and lies they laid for each other. I usually messed it up by saying too much or too little, and I could already sense the danger ahead.

The last time we spoke, my mother apologised for missing her plane the weekend of the Chambières' party. She said it was because of the traffic at JFK, but I could tell she was lying because her voice went down to a whisper – as if even she couldn't bear to listen to the stuff she made up. She usually fooled people with her deceit, including my father and her new husband, Olivier. They were smart men, and not the kind who were easily duped – or at least that's what I thought.

Although I resented it, my mother always impressed me with her ability to lie convincingly. I thought it proved she was smarter than us, but now I know deception is much more complicated, more instinctive than clever, and that most successful liars are just actors on a good run.

At least there wouldn't be a lecture about school, I thought, relaxing a bit. She was never interested in that kind of thing. My mother didn't stress about grades, and she didn't buy into the fuss my father made about universities either, so at least we saw eye to eye there. She'd got by on her looks and her wits, each victory making her more fearless and irresistible, like a wave that gets stronger on the incoming tide.

My parents were so different it amazed me they were ever together. I didn't understand how they'd managed four years of marriage when now they couldn't even share a phone call. They'd met in the early Nineties when my mother was twenty-one, an intern at *La Globe*, and my father was exactly twice her age. This was before he started drinking, back when he had a full head of hair and was the paper's star columnist.

'I was a catch back then. Women love journalists, and they loved me,' he would boast. But it was only when he was drunk that he could say her name, recounting hazy stories from the past, and letting his eyes film over as the memories drifted back. He told me she had burst into the office one summer, dazzling everyone in her orbit, and burning those who got close. Sometimes he'd present their story as a tragic romance – doomed yet profound, whilst other times he'd raise a finger as if it were a cautionary tale.

According to him, my mother arrived from Croatia with barely a word of French but acquired it within months thanks to a string of men who were more than happy to oblige. She blazed through the office like a gambler on a losing streak until she got to my father whom she sized up as, if not quite the alpha male she was hoping for, then at least a soft touch and the crucial first springboard into a life of no turning back. Her talent lay in making it seem as if it were all his idea, as if he were the one that needed her. In the end, she had him eating out of her hand.

She became pregnant almost immediately, he'd say, with a helpless look that I found insulting. The facts blurred at this point, but in one account, I was conceived in a nightclub to the muffled throb of 'Gangsta's Paradise' by Coolio. There was always a lot of wild invention to my father's drunken tales, and none of it seemed like my mother at all, but the story about the nightclub might be true because they were married by Christmas and I was born the following June. Within a year, she had what she needed, and school grades had nothing to do with it.

Heat shimmered over the bonnet of my stepfather's black Mercedes as Philippe, his driver, craned around to chat. I saw my reflection in his gold aviators as he brought me up to speed with his family and his recent holiday to see them. He had a soothing voice, so I let him talk as we drove to the swanky restaurant to meet my mother.

I waited behind a velvet rope while the concierge checked my name and then let me into a place decked out like a strip club. Dark, mirrored dining tables filled the room, while heavily fringed lamps muted the light. My mother sat in the middle of it all, scrolling through her phone.

She kissed me on each cheek, her eyes darting from mine as we took our seats.

'I was worried about you the other night. In a bar at midnight?' she said, tut-tutting as though it had been my idea.

There was an awkward silence as I refused to get drawn in.

'I heard he's drinking again,' she said, looking at the menu.

'Not so much,' I said, choosing my words carefully. 'He's pretty busy with work.'

She snapped the menu shut. 'What's he working on now? Wait, let me guess – a conspiracy theory about people he envies?'

Here we go again, I thought. I hated the way she laid straight into my father whenever we met. I knew she still had a score to settle, but she didn't seem to realise I was the one who actually had to live with him. In a strange way, it made me feel defensive of him and that was the last thing I wanted.

93

After a while, she changed the subject, and I zoned out. I watched the waitresses as they weaved around the tables balancing trays of food while she chatted about her life and the places she'd been recently. One of the girls had long hair, and a tiny golden padlock pierced the flesh of her navel. She reminded me of Lisa from my history class at school.

About half an hour into the meal, my mother cleared her throat and looked around. I thought for a horrible moment she was about to rise and address the crowded restaurant, perhaps even propose a toast. Instead, her focus returned to me.

'Listen, darling, there's something we need to discuss.' She looked sideways at our neighbours as she leaned forward. 'It's not very good news.'

Her lowered voice chilled me, and I braced for what was to come. I stirred the edges of my steak tartare, forking in spoonfuls of diced onion then capers, sprinkling Tabasco on the glistening yolk that wobbled on top of its meat cushion.

'There's some tax nonsense on one of Olivier's projects, and we need to leave until things are sorted out.'

I worked in a streak of mustard and watched the yellow flare swirl through the meat.

'It's these new laws the government's imposed,' she said, whispering now, her eyes mournful. 'We're moving to Monaco.'

It was my cue to feel sorry for her, but how could I when she was basically telling me she was leaving me here with my father full-time? I didn't spend many weekends with her, but they were a relief when they came, and she usually spoiled me by taking me to restaurants like this. I knew we were only there because she liked the place, but so what.

I reached for the pepper grinder. My mother must have thought I was extending my hand in sympathy, and she grasped my fingers. We sat there, holding hands awkwardly in mid-air for a moment or two.

'It's not until the New Year, at least,' she said with a sigh.

I focused on my food, adding mustard, ketchup, more Tabasco until it turned a lurid shade of terracotta.

'I knew you'd be disappointed,' she said. 'Imagine me as an *exile*. We're being treated like criminals!'

I looked at her. What on earth was she saying?

Then I had a crazy idea. She'd always promised I could live with her one day. I knew it was difficult because she had another child – a half-brother I barely knew, and they travelled so much, but I was older now and less trouble. They could leave me alone while they jetted around.

'I could come and live there too,' I said.

My mother stiffened, and I regretted the words immediately.

'Oh, Alex. We'll hardly ever be there, and ...' she said slowly. 'And what about school?'

It was like she'd slapped me in the face.

'Oh, that's right, I forgot. They don't have schools in Monaco,' I said.

She gave a smile like a squeezed lemon. 'Of course they do, darling, but the one you're at now sounds *wonderful*. Everyone says it's the best in the country, how difficult it is to get in.' She pushed salad around her plate then forced a laugh, her face still sour. 'You have your father's sense of humour.'

I stared at my food. Piercing the egg, I watched the yolk ooze over the meat and pool in the bloody crevices. I dug in my fork, bringing the meat to my mouth.

As I bit down, a fireball of mustard shot up my nose, setting off a coughing fit. I dropped the fork, which fell off the table and rang on the stone floor drawing everyone's attention to me as bloody lumps of meat rained across the table.

My mother stared at me, aghast.

'Why don't you just fuck off, then? Fuck off to Monaco,' I said, through threads of saliva.

'Alex!' she said, backing away in horror.

I tried to breathe, staring at my reflection in the mirrored table as the waitresses fussed around.

My mother gathered herself, dropped some notes on the table, and led me from the restaurant, her head high.

Outside, she drew me to her. 'You have to understand, Alex, it's not like that. Things are much more complicated than you know.'

'What *things*?'

She shook her head, and for the first time ever, she looked worried, suddenly much older, and her eyes glistened slightly. 'One day I'll explain, but for now, it's out of my hands.'

Then, before I had a chance to find out what she meant, she smiled and put on her sunglasses. 'Tartare's never a good choice in warm weather. It's very hard to keep the meat fresh.'

She stepped forward to kiss me, but I'd already turned towards Philippe, who was waiting across the road.

I left school with Nathan that afternoon, feeling sick and empty after the lunch. I didn't want company, but it was too late to change the plans we'd made to experiment with the weed while my father was out.

'I've asked them along too,' Nathan said, pointing to Lisa and Jeanne up ahead, dressed identically in ankle boots, leggings, and designer puffa jackets. 'Lisa's an expert. She's probably already smelled it on you.'

I held the door of our apartment building as the others filed in. We all squeezed into the tiny lift, and I felt Lisa's breath on my neck as we climbed to the fifth floor.

Our housekeeper, May, was ironing in the hall and looked up, surprised since it was the first time I'd ever brought friends home after school. I knew both of the girls lived in vast apartments in the sixteenth arrondissement and I watched their reactions to our ordinary flat. They wandered through, opening doors until they found my bedroom.

Lisa took a small metal pipe from her bag, opened the window and sat on the ledge.

I passed the foil bullet. 'You do it,' I said, having no idea how the thing worked.

Peeling back the foil, she stuffed a pinch of weed into the pipe, tapped it then held it out to me. She put her lighter over and I sucked it in, the heat of the flame searing my throat. I held my breath for a few seconds before it hit me with a massive head rush.

The pipe was passed around, and soon it was my turn again. I couldn't work the lighter and pipe at the same time because my hand was shaking, so Lisa helped me.

'Alex, this is really strong. Where did you get it?' she said.

I could barely form words, my head spinning. 'A girl in Montparnasse,' I squeaked eventually. 'I don't know who she was.'

Lisa raised her eyebrows. 'Little Alex scoring drugs on the street.'

After that, the room started pitching, slowly at first then gathering momentum. I lay down, and my head felt pinned to the bed with my body whirling fast around it. Someone said my name, and it felt like hours before I could reply. Nathan was laughing and holding the pipe, but I waved it away.

'Come on, Alex,' Lisa said, millennia later. Her hand shook, and flakes of grass spilled onto the bed. When I finished, she lay next to me, holding my hand as the room pulsed and swayed around us. I tried to sit up, but my head was anchored to the pillow. Someone dropped the pipe and crashing cymbals filled the room. Finally, I rolled onto my side, my body leaden.

'You look bad,' Nathan said, his voice reaching me as if through an echo chamber. My ears burned, the blood throbbing in my head, my throat on fire. Smoke hung heavy in the room, thick and reeking.

Then panic whipped up through the haze.

What if this feeling was permanent?

What if my father found us like this?

You used your bedroom as a crack den.

I leaned over the bed, feeling like I was going to puke while Lisa pressed her hand to my forehead. 'Just lie back. Breathe. The spinning will stop.'

She brought my head to the pillow and stroked my forehead. Her hand felt cool on my burning skin, like a cloud passing over the sun. I tried to control the panic by breathing slowly, keeping my eyes fixed on tiny cracks in the ceiling, and then finally, everything calmed and the room just pulsed with shadows and light, the bed covers rippling in the breeze, wafting over my face like soft ribbons. Lisa was fanning me and loose threads tickled my cheeks. Someone played some music, and the edges of the world softened and blurred. My arm drifted off the side of the bed, and I felt I was on a gently rocking boat, numb and peaceful, floating.

Lisa continued to stroke my arm as sunlight shone in, bouncing off her hair in a Technicolor halo, blonde strands drifting across her face.

Finally, Nathan loomed above me, asking if I was OK. He looked serious, but the things he said were absurd. Laughter welled up inside me and rolled out like bubbles bursting, each one setting off the next. The look on his face was the funniest thing I'd ever seen and I was doubled up, laughing uncontrollably, carried now on the waves of light and sound. We all clutched each other on the bed, laughing into each other's faces.

Lisa kissed me. She tasted of smoke, her lips hot and dry. Then she lay beside me, her hand tracing patterns on my chest. I flinched, worried about my eczema, but amazed that for once it didn't itch or hurt. We lay there kissing, and awkwardly rearranging our limbs until we were in each other's arms beneath the sheets. Then she smiled, and I thought she was going to laugh at me, but her hand moved down as she watched me, registering each move she made, and its effect on me. I'd never had such close attention. She was looking right inside me, her gaze so intense it was as if she was taking something from me. I was only half-aware of the other two – they had slipped out of sight.

Later, there was a soft knocking at the door.

'I'm going now, Alex,' May called gently. 'Papa will be home soon.'

Lisa went to the window and lit a cigarette. The sky was indigo and someone was singing in the street below. It had rained, and tyres lapped the road while distant car horns beeped in the rush-hour traffic. Lisa finished her cigarette and turned to face me with that same intense look she'd given me earlier. Then she ran her fingers through her hair and tied it up in a knot. She put on her boots, kissed me goodbye and walked to the door, glancing back as she left the room.

Twelve

Paris 15ème

BEFORE THAT AFTERNOON WITH LISA, I was nobody – just some new kid at school. But now I meant something to Tomas who, as well as being the Chambières' son and an ice hockey playing genius, was also Lisa's sometime boyfriend. She hadn't made this clear to me, of course, and although I doubt it would have made any difference to my feelings for her, what *was* clear was that Tomas already hated me for some reason and had just been waiting for an excuse to express it.

Somehow, he'd heard about us being together at my place, and it all came to a head the next week after a history class. We'd been studying Napoleon and the dates of his battles. I'd memorised them all for the exams the previous term, but then promptly forgot them, apart from those that fell on my birthday.

Napoleon liked a summer battle, but only Waterloo and Trebbia took place on 18 June, and since they're battles France lost, they were never discussed in class. It was a shame. I liked the fact that my birthday fell on the anniversary of Waterloo, and that each year I'd celebrate France's greatest defeat. It gave me a secret thrill, like I was somehow responsible for the disaster.

As the morning limped towards the afternoon, a sense of inertia slid into the classroom, settling over us like a low-pressure system. Detecting our lethargy, the teacher marched down the aisle, her boots pounding the boards.

'Battle of Austerlitz!' Mme. Joubert barked, smacking a steel ruler on my desk. She twisted it slowly as the silence expanded then pointed it at me like a bayonet.

'Alex! Do you recall a single date from last term?'

There was a long pause. I had no clue about the Battle of Austerlitz, but I did know one date.

'Waterloo, 18 June 1815,' I said, then burned with embarrassment as everyone turned to stare at me.

It was a stupid thing to say and the atmosphere electrified, bringing everyone together as a unit. Backs straightened, eyes flicked away from hidden phones, all bodies still and upright in their rows. Lisa looked at me, amused, but shook her head, scraping a red fingernail slowly across her bottom lip.

'Alex, you're an imbecile! Give me your *carnet*,' Mme. Joubert said, her face like a fist.

There was a sour blast of caffeine and smoker's breath as she bent over me and scrawled a detention in my book.

The bell rang and I rushed out of class, wondering what had possessed me. I was still muttering to myself in the quad when Tomas drew up alongside. We fell into step, and I thought he was going to commiserate, but when he didn't, I slowed to let him go on ahead. When he slowed, too, I knew I was in trouble. As we approached the toilet block, he turned and stood in front of me, a sneer blooming across his face.

'*Imbécile*,' he hissed, jabbing my ribs.

I swore back in French, but pronounced it badly. My lips stumbled on the consonants and blubbered through the vowels.

Tomas grinned. 'You speak like a peasant.' Then he switched to English, the same fake, trans-Atlantic drawl they all had. 'No, your French is worse than any peasant's.'

'Who cares? It's a stupid fucking language.'

We were alone now in the damp concrete bunker and my armpits started to pool. I smelled the sharp stench of adrenaline on him as he bit down on his lip.

'Maybe you understand this language better,' he said, grabbing my shoulders and kicking me in the shin. Pain blasted through me like an electric shock as he released his grip and spat in my face, laughing like a maniac. There was sweat above his lip and he ground his jaw for a split-second as if he could barely contain himself, then swung around and punched me deep in the guts, the breath hissing through his teeth.

I fell to the ground and lay on my side gasping for air, the floor cold and rough against my cheek.

Another gob of spit landed in my hair, its warmth seeping through to my scalp. His boot smelled like damp earth and shit as he ground it on the concrete near my face. 'Next time I'll break your fucking teeth.'

I lay there winded, gulping like a fish. Tomas's footsteps receded, and I heard nervous laughter as someone passed close by. My shin throbbed as I worked on breathing through waves of pain, voices and footsteps swirling around me. The bell rang again and, finally, my breath came back, spooling through slobber and bile as I dragged myself to a bench and sat there with my head between my knees.

At the sink I mopped his spit from my hair and looked at myself in the mirror.

Imbécile. What was I thinking?

'Alex, what happened?' my aunt Béa said, stepping from her office after school. She traced the scratches on my cheek. 'How did you get those?'

I said something about basketball as we headed to the metro, past the café on the corner where everyone gathered after school. I waved to Lisa, who pretended not to see me.

But my aunt saw. 'How are you finding it here with everyone knowing you're my nephew?'

'It's fine. Everyone likes you.'

She laughed and squeezed my arm as we took the stairs. 'I don't believe that, but it's nice of you to say. I'm sure it's a lot different from your old school. The Americans tell me it's nothing like school in the States.'

I looked down the platform. 'Americans say that about everything. They think everything's better in the States.'

She kept on about school as we stood in the carriage, asking about my teachers, my subjects and whether I liked the school in general. I couldn't see the point in telling her the truth – that I hated it, that I could barely communicate with anyone, and that not only did I have no real friends, I already had enemies. It would only make things worse if she started to meddle, and I didn't need any more problems. When we came out of the metro, I let her go up to the apartment by herself while I went to the shop for a snack.

When I got home, I closed the door quietly, thinking I could sneak past and go straight to my room.

I heard my aunt's voice. 'And these women, Eddy. Can't you for once find someone appropriate? She's the mother of a boy in his class, not to mention the wife of a good friend of yours. My God!'

'He's hardly a good friend. I've told you what he's like.'

'That's not the point! Where on earth do you think this is going?'

My father scoffed. 'Come on, Béa. We're adults, not teenagers – it doesn't need to *go* anywhere. And besides, I don't need to justify myself to you. It's none of your business.'

'It *is* my business. Her kids are at my school, so is your son. If I've heard these rumours, others will have too.'

'That's the real problem, isn't it? *Your school.* You should be the one having an affair. You need something in your life apart from that school. You'll be having a fling with a student if you're not careful.'

'Don't be disgusting.'

'Well, you wouldn't be the first. Plenty of female teachers find themselves attracted to their—'

'Eddy, stop it! Please just think where all this has got you in the past.'

'All this? What are you saying?'

'You know exactly what I mean.'

There was a shuffling and creaking of floorboards as they moved to the sitting room. The doors along the corridor gaped open, and I couldn't pass without them seeing me, so I opened the front door again and slammed it loudly.

'Alex?' called my father. 'Come in. We were just talking about you.'

When I reached the sitting room, he gestured towards a chair, and I sat facing them, interview style. They were both flushed and wore the same anxious look.

My aunt started to speak, but my father cut in, looking at me over his glasses. 'Béa was just telling me about your grades. You'll have to repeat most of last year. It's worse than we thought.'

My aunt turned to him. 'It's not entirely his fault—'

My father raised his hand to silence her then shook a bunch of papers at me. 'These reports,' he said, looming over me like a thundercloud.

They went back and forth, cutting each other off, my father wrestling with my grades, my aunt trying to defend me. Finally, she suggested we look at different schools, ones that weren't so *fast track*. A French school. The local lycée where I'd be immersed in the language and pick it up much quicker.

What was she *saying*? The French schools were the worst, especially if you barely spoke French. I didn't understand how a French school would make things better. They must know that.

In that moment I hated them both – my father's fixation with grades, my aunt's useless sympathy and the way they both got off on it. I wished they'd just leave me alone and focus on their own pathetic lives.

My father spoke to me as if I was five years old, telling me he needed to see me trying much harder, that he didn't want any more bad reports, that he didn't have the *bandwidth* to worry about it anymore. His jowls shook, his green eyes peering down at me, bulbous and magnified through his glasses, and I hated him then more than ever.

I kept clear of Tomas and Lisa for the rest of the week until Friday when the class went on a field trip to Versailles. Tomas was off school with hockey training, but word had spread about us, and people kept their distance as though I was contagious.

The guide led us to the art gallery – a hall of paintings celebrating fifteen centuries of French military conquest. Mme. Joubert clasped her hands in rapture as she identified the various battles. I'd never seen her so happy. There was Napoleon at Austerlitz, luminous in white breeches and military regalia, his horse trampling over the bodies of dead Russians. The guide lowered her voice in deference to the military glory all around, while the blank-eyed busts of generals watched from their marble perches.

We spent over two hours trawling through the main rooms where dusty air hung in mirrored corners, and light shone from every gilded surface until finally, the guide led us up a narrow staircase to the rooms of the kings' mistresses.

Lisa stood near me at the back of the group. I caught a whiff of smoke as she turned and smiled, swinging her hair so it grazed my face. We hadn't spoken since the afternoon in my bedroom, and although I'd rehearsed a thousand conversations, I knew if I tried to talk to her, I'd mess it up and say something stupid.

The guide showed us pictures of the Sun King's frothed and dimpled courtesans as she discussed the artwork and the boudoir furniture. She explained that unlike most kings, Louis XIV looked after and educated his bastard children. She held up a picture of a woman in a nun's habit and said that when the king tired of her, Louise de La Vallière joined a convent and wore a spiked corset. This was how she atoned for her sins as a courtesan, and in return for her penance, the king acknowledged their offspring as his own.

Lisa pulled my sleeve, nodding towards a door to her left. We waited until the guide pointed out a detail in the cornices and then we slipped down the stairs to a basement cellar. A flight of stone steps led to a terrace overlooking a grassy moat.

Lisa fished in her bag. 'That guide's disgusting,' she said. Her face caught the afternoon sun, and green glitter sparkled on her eyelids.

She lit two cigarettes, passing one to me.

'I was enjoying it,' I said. 'That stuff about the illegitimate children.'

She took a drag and walked on ahead. 'That's because you're fucked up.'

I puffed on the cigarette. It felt stupid, like I was kissing it.

She called back, 'And that's why you're always alone. Last in the queue, at the back of the group. Always wandering off—' She stopped and turned to me. 'Why is that?'

It was a brutal thing to say, but I didn't let it show. 'Well, this time it's because I'm following you – someone who's even more fucked up than me.'

She laughed and we sat on a wooden bench, hidden by hedges and rows of potted trees. The distant, lazy drone of a lawnmower cut through the air.

She watched me, amused by my attempts to smoke.

'I don't fit in either,' she said suddenly, her eyes wide. Golden strands of hair drifted across her face.

I laughed. She was the most popular girl in the class.

And here she was touching me, pulling me in close. That time in my bedroom – she knew a lot, acted older. Now she was choosing to be with me again, and her eyes held the promise of – what exactly?

I brushed the hair from my forehead, hoping I didn't look too dumbstruck. Her leg was warm against mine, and a few leaves fell off the trees and fluttered to the ground. The lawnmower stopped, and everything became bright and still, sharpened by the slanting light and the smell of cut grass.

'It was fun, that afternoon at your place,' she said, swinging her leg over mine. She shuffled in closer, her breast against my arm. It was almost too much to bear.

She exhaled, regarding her cigarette with distaste. 'I wish we had something better to smoke.' Her cigarette was covered in red lipstick the same shade as her nails. Some of it had come off on her finger, which she licked and rubbed on her tights.

'Do you have any more of that weed?' she said sweetly, rolling the butt between her fingers.

So this was what she wanted.

She wriggled closer, letting her skirt bunch up around her thighs, and then tossed her hair. She fiddled with a loose thread at her knee, slowly pulling it into a ladder.

'Just there's a party this weekend and I wanted to ask you along,' she said. She'd dropped the wheedling tone and was speaking matter-of-factly now. 'The guy having the party is a friend of Tomas.'

She watched me carefully.

'Wow! What an invitation!'

'It's just an idea,' she said, her green lids sparkling in the light. Then she grinned. 'Get some more of that stuff and come with me.'

'Are you serious? Did Tomas tell you he'd kick my teeth in too? That'd be a fun party trick for you all.'

'It'll get him off your back. The stuff they smoke is shit, and it would change their minds about you.'

'A party with Tomas? No way! The guy's insane.'

'Seriously, their parties are fun. They'll respect you.'

'*Respect?* Who do you think they are? Some kind of *gang*?'

I stood, and she grabbed my sleeve. 'Alex, forget trying to fit in here. It won't happen unless you have the latest tech, clothes, haircut. You can't compete with them on that level.'

I pulled free. 'Do I look like I'm trying to fit in?'

'I'm not saying you have to be like them, just go along with it. Play their game.'

'What fucking *game*?'

She grabbed my shoulder and kissed me on the cheek – a little peck of encouragement for the quest ahead. 'Think about it.'

She touched my cheek and kissed me again – on the mouth this time. The warm smoky taste of her surged through me like fire.

Perhaps she had a point about getting him off my back, I thought as I watched her walk towards the chateau, her hair swinging in the light. I felt torn – on the one hand insulted, yet my senses buzzed with nicotine, excitement and an overwhelming need to be somewhere, anywhere, with her again.

I walked to the wall bordering the moat. The stonework was clean where the sun hit it during the day, the shadows damp with moss. I leaned against the wall, feeling the warmth in the stones. As I closed my eyes, I caught a fleeting scrap of something, a remnant of the past that flickered just out of reach. I imagined I'd been in this place before, in another time. Not as part of the king's court – a builder or a servant, but as some kind of creeping thing, illicit and ashamed, like the black moss that clung to the damp underside of the stones.

It was as if everything was spiralling outwards, hurtling away and dragging me with it. I felt the place where Lisa had kissed me, my fingers cool against my burning cheek, and I had the sense I was moving fast, racing towards all that golden light.

NOW

Thirteen

Aubervilliers

'YOUR APPOINTMENT WAS TWO HOURS ago,' my parole officer says, pushing the door wide against a stack of empty bottles.

Sunlight floods in behind her, panning across the room like a searchlight. She steps carefully over the stained tiles, taking in the mess all around. 'Looks like it was some party,' she says.

I tell her about the break-in and she nods dubiously, then hands me a plastic vial. 'Make it quick,' she says, her eyes cold. 'You've already wasted most of my morning.'

When I return from the bathroom, she's at the table writing her notes. I place the sample in front of her, its warm contents fogging the sides. Usually she bags it quickly, but this time she leaves it there between us as a mark of her contempt.

'There was a problem with your last sample. You tested positive for morphine.'

'*Morphine?*'

She sits back, pointing her pen at the jar. 'What will it be this time? Cocaine? Cannabis?'

I force a weak smile. 'What is this, some kind of joke?'

'Denial just makes things worse, Alex. Drugs are a parole violation, you know that,' she says.

'But you test me each week.'

'And you didn't show up today.'

'*I slept through.*'

She rolls her eyes.

'This is a mistake,' I say, but my voice is thin, unconvincing, and my mind races. Did someone spike my drink? The water? But no, that's not possible – no one's been anywhere near me.

'Mistakes on these tests rarely happen,' she says, ripping out a page and handing it to me. 'Get a full blood test by tomorrow, at the latest. There's a clinic opposite the metro. If you go there now they might do it this morning.'

She holds out her key to my flat. 'And why doesn't this work?'

'The locks were changed yesterday, after the break-in. I was going to get a spare one cut for you and bring it today.' The words come out in a rush, defensive, and she laughs at the blatant lie.

'You were going to bring a key you don't have to an appointment you missed? Come on, Alex, don't just make things up. This is serious.'

She drops the old key on the table, puts the sample in her satchel. 'So what did they take?'

'I just said. I haven't taken anything!'

'No, I mean your robbers,' she says, emphasizing *your* as if they were friends I'd invited in for the night. 'Computer? Phone?'

'They didn't take anything. Not even the TV.'

She surveys the room. 'So they just broke in and made a mess?'

'And dumped dead fish on the floor,' I say, pointing to the tiles where the grout channels are stained a dull pink.

She scans the floor then looks at me sceptically.

113

'It makes it worse when you're like this,' I say.

'Like what?'

'Always suspicious. Never believing me. It's like I'm on trial again.'

'I'm not suspicious,' she says, gathering up her things. 'I'm careful.'

Outside the sun clouds over, chilling the room, making everything feel disturbed and unfamiliar.

'I can't stay here after this,' I say quietly. 'Can't you move me someplace else?'

'This is a hostel, Alex. It's not Club Med. You can't just call reception and ask for a nicer suite' – she looks out of the window to the darkening towers – 'a sea view. Something a little further from the lifts.

'Last time we met you said you were going to speak to your mother. Perhaps she could help,' she adds cautiously.

'I haven't had a chance.'

That was a lie. My mother called the day I got out and sent me some money, which I spent on food and a phone. She promised a weekly amount, but it had been two weeks and no more had arrived. She had two other children now and I was just a messy reminder of a past she'd rather forget. I'd always been an embarrassment, even before I became a criminal, so I knew the money would fade from the agenda, like her promise to visit.

'Get a job and live wherever you like, which you'll have to do soon,' says my parole officer. 'You need to focus on the future. So far, all you've done is obsess about the past.' She points to the chaos all around, like it's my past hunkered in around me.

'Who's going to give me a job? They see my record, and it's over. I don't stand a chance.'

She comes closer, perches on an armchair. 'We've been through all this. There are apprenticeships, programmes, courses you can do.' The chair wobbles and she bends down, gathering papers about my trial from beneath a leg. She glances through and shakes them at me. 'Forget all this. Put it aside, you need to get on with your real life.'

'*Real life?* And what's that exactly? Being imprisoned here? Being harassed? Getting my place trashed?'

'Alex—'

'Is that the real life I need to be getting on with?' I say, yelling now. 'That stalking charge from Lisa, and now this fake drug test! I'm being watched all the time. Followed and chased.'

'You need to stop all this travelling into Paris—'

'How do you know where I've been?'

'Stop digging around in the past.'

'Have you been tracking me?'

She leans forward. 'I've been *listening* to you. Every time we meet there's a new crisis. There's always somebody following you, chasing you. There's always someone out to get you. It's time to move on.'

It was pointless to talk of moving on. It's like there's this force pulling me back. Each time I start to break free, it's there, tugging at me, and the more I struggle, the more it tightens.

'Look,' I say, pulling up my shirt to show the eczema on my back, then revealing my forearms. 'It hasn't been this bad since I was a kid. This place – all the stress, these new problems – have brought it back. Even in prison it wasn't like this.'

She sighs. 'I noticed that on your arms last week. But listen, burglaries happen around here all the time. It doesn't mean they were after you. Maybe someone heard you'd just moved in.' She stands and smiles, places her hand on my shoulder. 'Even after your years in prison you still look like a rich kid, perhaps they thought you'd have some valuables. There are other explanations, Alex. It's not always about the past.'

'What's it about, then, since you know everything?'

She looks around the flat. 'Well, the place has been torn apart.' She nods towards the kitchen. 'There's no need to trash cupboards like that. So what were they after?'

'No idea. Somebody did this to scare me.'

'But why? Why would someone want to scare you?'

'It's like they want me back inside.'

She walks to the window, then turns. 'It's hard being released after so long inside. I know you still hold a lot of guilt about the past. Maybe that's what you're feeling.'

There's a cold shifting in my stomach, a tightening in my throat.

'It's understandable, this anxiety. While you were in prison, you had a routine, you were focused on the future, on getting out. Now you're outside, you're forced to confront the things you left behind. Freedom can be hard to accept,' she says. Her voice is low and patronising as if she's explaining something to an imbecile.

'I feel *watched* and *followed*. Not guilty,' I say, but she's right. Guilt about my father, and about blaming Sami hollowed me out. It overwhelmed me. Freedom means nothing if your conscience is still locked up.

'So, who's watching you? Who's following you?'

I stare at her for several seconds. Sami's the only person who hates me that much – the only person who has a good reason, anyway. And the fish guts.

'Don't be so gutless,' I whisper. One of the last things Sami said to me.

'What did you say?' she says.

I just shake my head. I can't tell her any of that. Bringing him up will just make things worse – it would feel like another betrayal.

Later that morning, my aunt arrives for our trip to the storage depot to collect my old things. Everything I packed in a hurry before I went into prison. I figure if I haven't missed something in seven years, then I don't need it, but she insists, saying it's time to face up to it.

Face up to what? To the reality that the life those boxes hold is lost and gone forever? Well, I got used to that a long time ago, and sorting through that old crap won't help. I tell her it's a waste of time, but she says someone needs to collect it all and she won't do it alone.

I wait in the car park, hoping she's forgotten, but she arrives on time and on the way there she chats about her job and her recent holidays. Her calm voice relaxes me, and I tune out, knowing she won't ask questions to check I'm listening. My father would often laugh at her cheerfulness, saying she was *pathologically optimistic*, as though her positivity was a kind of illness. Like him, I used to find her chat annoying – just white noise filling the air, but now it's soothing. She deals with adversity by not dwelling on it, by not teasing out the threads and staring into its dark heart. That doesn't make her stupid – she just feels its throb and moves on. It would have made her a bad journalist, but luckily for her she became a teacher.

She's optimistic about me, too, never letting on she doubts me, even when I tell her blatant lies and stories about my father that I know she likes hearing. When we talk about him together, it's like we play a game where we reconstruct the past with only good memories – holidays at my grandfather's place, trips to the beach, and Christmases together when I was small. I play along, rearranging the facts until we build a fantasy of the family she lost and inhabit it together.

It's sad that the person convicted of killing her brother is the only family she has left, and I wonder if she sees the irony of that. I don't know, but despite everything that's happened, there's no trace of the fear I saw in Elena's eyes, or the weary suspicion of my parole officer. Béa believes in me because she wants to, and that kind of faith amazes me. I'm grateful for it, but sometimes all this pretence feels thin, it gets exhausting, and I wonder whether my father was right, and that optimism is a weakness after all.

To tell you the truth, her belief in me is unsettling. There's a weight to it that requires something of me, something I can't provide, and I often think it'd be easier if she just blamed me. At my trial, people like May, and Paul Chambière gave evidence about the difficult relationship between my father and me, citing arguments in the months leading up to his death. When it was Béa's turn to speak, she hardly acknowledged any of it. It's as if she has her own version of the past, bullet-proofed and shielded from attack. Testimony that chipped away at my father's reputation seemed to make her sadder than the fact I was on trial for his murder. At the end of the day, her rose-tinted memories are as much of a fantasy as the lies made up in court.

I look over, nodding at something she's just said, even though I didn't hear it. She glances back, and I get a shock because she looks a lot like my father. Now she's old, her features have sagged into his, and she wears her grey hair cropped short at the back, like he did. She has his fine, papery skin and the same purplish shadows under her eyes, like old bruises that refuse to heal.

To offset these looks, she wears a lot of make-up. Glancing at her now I see this strange, painted image of my father peering at me from beyond the grave. His sad eyes rimmed with black liner, and his gaunt, powdery face smeared with rouge.

'I know this isn't what you want to do,' she says softly as we pull off the Péri, mistaking my shudder for anxiety about the trip.

'Let's just get it over with. We can dump it in a skip or something,' I say, as we drive past the building sites, through a grey wasteland of corrugated warehouses and fulfilment centres.

She looks over at me, shocked.

'I just want to get rid of it all. I can't even remember packing it,' I say.

That's not true – I remember the cop who stood outside my door as I packed the things I was allowed to take to prison, and tipped the rest straight into those boxes. I recall the heat on that surreal June morning, the acrid smell of road tar from the works outside. Béa and my mother moved around each other cautiously, Béa going through my father's things while my mother, dressed in black, went tearfully between us, speaking in low tones on her phone. The situation was a nightmare in which she had a starring role, and my father's death was something that had happened to her, not to him.

The storage facility is beside an underground car park, and we walk along a narrow corridor flanked with padlocked doors, lit by buzzing strip lights, and smelling of damp, forgotten things.

The attendant leads us into a small storage room and points to a flatbed trolley we use to take everything to the car.

We fill the car with boxes until we can't see out of the back, then drive in silence against the flow of traffic. The cheerful mood from before has gone, and the ghost of my father crouches in among the crates, his presence looming over us, as dark and fathomless as one of his black moods.

My aunt still lives in the building next to our old apartment, and my stomach flips as we swing into the narrow street. We leave the boxes in the car and head upstairs, my aunt ushering me into her small dining room. It's the first time I've been here since my release and my father's old furniture is all around. It looks out of place, as though the room has twice the number of things it needs.

She sees me looking as she lays the table. 'All this furniture is yours whenever you want it, you know. I'm just keeping it here until it finds a home.'

'I was thinking about the rest of his stuff. Where it went.'

'Most of his clothes I gave to charity shops, other things to friends like Patrick and Elena. I kept his favourite books, and the more personal items, of course.'

'You know Patrick died recently?' I say, when she returns from the kitchen.

She eyes me carefully. 'Yes, I went to his funeral.'

There's a pause as if she's considering whether to continue. 'Actually, he came here quite a bit. He spent some time looking through Eddy's things,' she says. 'In the weeks before he died.'

'What things?'

'His old papers and notebooks.'

'You have his papers?'

My interest startles her. 'They're down in the cellar. I haven't been there for months, not since Patrick died, in fact.'

'Why was he looking at them?'

'I ran into him in the street and for some reason, we started talking about Eddy's papers. I said I couldn't bring myself to go through them, so he offered to do it. He even apologised for not offering sooner.'

She shrugs. 'He thought it would take a couple of days, but he was here for several weeks. I set him up with a desk, a radiator, gave him his own key. We often had lunch together.'

'For weeks? Why so long?'

'I don't know. I was just happy for the company, to be honest. At one point he told me it was a puzzle. "It's all a big puzzle, Béa. I'll tell you once I've worked it out myself."'

'Can I go down there? I want to see what he was looking at.'

'It's too late now,' she says, pushing her plate aside. 'The spare room's made up. Stay here tonight, and I'll take you down tomorrow.'

My heart pounds at the thought of looking through my father's stuff, and I'm not sure whether it's excitement or dread, seeing his notebooks and papers sorted and ordered by another dead man.

Fourteen
Saint-Germain

MY AUNT'S SPARE ROOM FACES out over the narrow street. The apartments opposite are in darkness, except for a woman's face in a laptop's blue glow, as still and perfect as a hologram. I can't sleep so I stand at the window until it starts to rain. Then I lie on the bed and watch the shadow play of light that moves across the walls.

Sometime in the night, I wake. Rain sheets sideways across the window, pursued by the wind, which moans around the building, rattling the chimney grate, sucking air from the room. Outside in the hall, the parquet squeaks as if someone's approaching. It's not quite footsteps, more a soft scuffling, like my father's loafers padding the hall. Then the rattle of bottles in the fridge and I'm back in my teenage bedroom, ears straining for the click of lights, shoes dropping to the floor, and other sounds that come through the walls.

Back at the window with the same tight throb in my stomach, hoping it's just the familiar surroundings conjuring his ghost, rather than the shame that pursues me constantly. I wasn't innocent, but I didn't kill him, so why does he come for me? Is this what my parole officer meant – the guilt from the past that now has air and room to spread? Like an ancient pathogen, activated by release. I've spent so much time believing my own story, but now I'm not so sure. I left him bleeding on the threshold, and yes, I lied about Sami. But who lied to me? The stories are all mixed up and the truth so hard to find, that I think my memory is the biggest liar now, making links and connections where there's just a void.

Soon, the rain eases, and dawn is not far off. Grey light washes the building opposite, its balconies framed by iron railings, like viewing galleries on a ship that ploughs a tarmac sea. Up high, mansard roofs and bull's-eye windows catch the first glow of a weak sun.

Light creeps slowly around the room, sliding across shelves, over my father's books – the worn, leather-bound *Pléiades*, gold spines glinting like Bibles. Below, the biographies of Napoleon and De Gaulle nudge up against sepia photos of Béa and Eddy as children standing stiffly with their parents. On the desk is a vase of flowers and a worn notebook. His computer is there too. I flip it open, my finger hovering over the keyboard before turning it on.

'I thought we could spend the day together,' my aunt says at breakfast. 'There's a film I'd like to see.'

She doesn't mention the cellar, and I'm about to remind her when I remember: the blood test.

'Ah, no, I forgot. I need to get back. A doctor's appointment.' It's a thin excuse and doubt crosses her face, making me feel terrible. For a moment she looked so happy.

'I'll come back tomorrow. We can go then and I'll visit the cellar too.'

She hesitates. 'I was thinking last night after we spoke. I shouldn't have mentioned all that, and Patrick being here. It might be too much ...'

'Too much what?' I say, sensing some kind of prohibition.

She looks away. 'All of his things down there. There's a lot there, a lot to take in.'

I let it drop and bring up the subject of his computer instead. Most of what's on it is corrupted, but I might be able to get it fixed. She looks surprised when I ask to take it, and for a second I think she's going to keep me from that, too, but then she agrees.

After breakfast, she drives me back to the hostel and waits by the car while I take the boxes inside. When I come down, she's talking to the maintenance guy who looks after my block.

'Hamid was telling me what happened, Alex. Why didn't you say something?' says my aunt. The circles under her eyes are dark, almost mauve, her brow furrowed. Hamid gives me an apologetic look.

'I didn't want to bother you. It was just some kids. And it's fine now. Hamid's changed the locks.'

I walk Béa to her car and say goodbye. At the entrance, I turn, and she's still watching me, a worried expression on her face. I make the thumbs-up sign, and she waves back.

Hamid helps me upstairs with the last of the boxes.

'The place looks better,' he says, lighting a cigarette on the walkway outside the flat. 'Your aunt's a nice lady, but I've got her worried about you now.'

'Do you really think it was someone who lived here before?' I ask.

He shrugs. 'There are plenty of break-ins here. And the flats are sometimes trashed, like yours. But I've never seen the fish guts before. You got special treatment there.'

He runs his hand over the new lock. 'Don't worry,' he says. 'These are tough, you won't have any more problems. If you do, just come and find me. I'm usually over at the allotments on the old fort.'

'Fort?'

He points over the motorway to a stretch of land where trees rise behind a high brick wall. 'The fort's abandoned now. All that's left is a few disused buildings and a salvage yard. The allotments are near the new developments on the far side of the fort, just beyond the cemetery. You can see them from here.'

On the way to the clinic, I pass the entrance to the fort – a wide driveway blocked by iron gates, security cameras and a wall made of exposed stones thrown together with thick, haphazard mortar which wraps around the entire site. There's a small group of protesters outside with banners. Further on, set back from the road behind a wire fence, are the allotments – a series of small vegetable plots and run-down huts, their roofs bent under the weight of gardening equipment. They look like something from another era, out of place against the steel gates, the fort and high rises all around.

Beyond the allotments are the construction zones Hamid mentioned, the ones I can see from my room, and all around there's the subterranean thump of excavation, the ground shuddering with dull blasts, but nothing rises above the sightline except a faint dust haze.

In my room that evening, I go through the boxes of my old belongings. Objects ordinary and familiar, now surreal:

schoolbooks full of perfect cursive written in faded ink. Toys, drawings, rocks and broken shells. Lost keys and coins. A blue parrot paperweight. My father's death and the years in prison had crashed through my life so completely I can barely remember the boy who had owned all these things. It's like looking at stuff belonging to a distant cousin, one I'd played with a few times but have since forgotten and it fills me with dread, as though this unknown child had been killed along with my father.

Some of my father's belongings are in there, too, and I dig through it all cautiously, trying to keep the memories away from the light. Coming across his personal stuff – cufflinks, bankcards, reading glasses – recalls his room, and our apartment. I see his unmade bed, his bedside table with these things on it and his books all around. I put them carefully aside before they overwhelm me, and dig further in, bringing out armfuls of documents, invoices and old paperwork. There are newspapers and magazines featuring articles he'd written with drafts attached. I don't look too closely at these, just put them near the door to sort through later.

At the bottom of one of the crates is a shoebox. Inside are several bundles, each of them bound with tape so perished it disintegrates when I pull on it, and old photos of my father and a woman fall out. They're sitting on café terraces, at the beach, laughing, with their arms around each other. In some, the woman poses for the camera, and in others, she's caught off-guard. She's very beautiful, with pale eyes and short dark hair clinging to the sides of her face.

In another bundle, there are pictures of my mother. It must have been when they'd just met, and she looks so young and happy – like I've never seen her. There are photos of me as a baby, and the three of us together. I put them aside quickly, not ready to go back this far yet.

Finally, right at the bottom of the shoebox, gathered in a long, slim envelope, are images of Céline Chambière. There are studio shots of her in swimsuits. Clipped to these are a bundle of letters and other pictures – close-ups of her naked body, and another, grainy shot where she's wearing heavy make-up, thick chains across her chest, and a tight corset. A man and a woman next to her are dressed in similar gear, and the shot is taken through a window, blurred, as if captured from a distance, the perspective shortened. Another photo shows my father in the same window, naked from the waist up and holding something in his hands. On the back of these photos are the words 'Matrix Club', and the names of those featured. I flick through the pictures of Céline, wondering why my father had such explicit pictures and what he did with them.

He was a dirty bastard, and it was just like him to keep pictures of women in a shoebox. He probably kept it under his bed with the newspapers and the cigarette butts. I spread Céline's letters on the table, trying to piece them together with my memories of that time. I've never read or written any kind of love letter, but they're not at all what I expect – more business-like, than the words of lovers, with talk of dinners with Céline, Paul and their friends. Although there are references to other, more secret *rendez-vous*, they seemed to be carrying out their affair in plain sight, oblivious to who knew.

The last letter, dated 21 December, is written on formal headed paper with just her name and mobile phone number in a fancy cursive swirl.

I'm sorry, Eddy, but I can't help you anymore. Paul is getting suspicious. I'm asking about work all the time. It's too much. I care about you and what happens between us, but I don't want to dwell on the past. You're always drawn back there.

Given the formal tone of the letters I go back and forth, wondering whose work she's referring to. I read through them all again and work is mentioned several times, but there are no details. Finally, on impulse, I call the phone number on the letterhead and after several rings, Céline answers abruptly. When I hear her speak I remember how she was that day on the porch at Épernay smoking through the drizzle.

It takes her a while to register who I am, and then her voice drops, tight as elastic. When I ask about her relationship with my father, she hangs up.

I wait a couple of minutes, then take a shot of one of the photos and text it to her. She phones me straight back.

'What do you want? Money? Is that what this is about?'

'No, not at all.'

'What is it, then?'

I pause, wondering how to frame it. 'Tell me about your relationship with my father?'

There's the click of a lighter, sucking of air.

'I'm offering your photos back,' I say.

'We had an affair, that's all. You know that.'

'How did it end?'

'The way these things always do. The differences between us were exciting at first, but they soon became annoying, and it fizzled out.'

128

She sighs theatrically and I see her on a balcony across town, blowing smoke into the night. 'It lasted about eight months, and before you ask, it ended well before he died.'

'There's a letter here written less a week before his death.'

'It was over long before then. That's what I'm saying. We remained friends, still wrote to each other.'

'Why? What about? I need to speak to you properly. Face to face,' I say.

There's a shift down the line. It could be relief, impatience, or even fear.

'I just want information, that's all.'

Finally, she agrees to meet at their apartment that Friday when her husband is out at lunch.

Later that evening, my parole officer calls to say my test is all clear.

'Now do you believe me?' I say.

'I believe you about the test.'

'Someone's messing with me.'

'Look, it's late, I don't want to go into it now, but I thought you'd want to know.'

'Someone's setting me up. Can't you see that?'

'It's probably just a mix-up at the lab.'

'Now you're going to tell me that happens sometimes.'

'It happens sometimes,' she says, hanging up.

THEN

Early November

Fifteen

Saint-Germain

OUTSIDE, A RUBBISH TRUCK SHUDDERED to a halt. Shouts, the rumble of bins, then a pause, before gallons of glass cascaded into the truck. Our narrow street was like a ravine that amplified street noise as it ricocheted up the buildings. I rolled over and reached for my phone: six thirty, Monday morning.

I thought of Tomas and a knot tightened in my stomach.

It had been several weeks since the beating and I'd managed to keep clear of him all that time, but last week I saw him getting into the back of his father's car. He turned as it pulled away, his ugly face framed in chrome, staring at me from the rear window like a demonic family pet. Then on Friday he shoved me out of the canteen queue, pushing in with two of his lackeys. Be my guest, I thought, moving away from the hot lights of the service bar where crusted couscous and bright pink sausages sweated in a pool of grease. Tomas elbowed me hard in the ribs, and then messed up my hair. Everyone was looking so I just laughed and moved back, which was a mistake, as one of his lackeys laughed too. Tomas was annoyed – he wanted more from me now he'd had a taste, and I could tell from the look in his eye that he was just dying to get his hands on me again.

For the rest of the day I was on guard, making sure he didn't catch me alone. It meant hanging around the main quad with the younger kids, and using the staff toilet near the classrooms, but I knew I couldn't do that forever and eventually he'd find me again. The relief when the bell rang that afternoon was physical, and I felt stress fall away as I ran towards the metro.

But it was Monday now and he'd had the whole weekend to plan his next move.

I lay in bed, considering options, and then crept into the study.

My father had been working late and his laptop was on the desk beneath a pile of notebooks and a glass tumbler stained with the filmy dregs of last night. I slid it out then tapped in the code. Although he had a perfect memory for facts, my father could never remember a password so he always used the same one. I emailed the school saying I was sick, but as I did so, I noticed his mailbox filling up with emails from different addresses, all of them spam. I scrolled down – hundreds of emails had arrived during the night and were continuing to pour in. Then suddenly, mid scroll, the screen went blank. I closed the lid and slipped the laptop back in its place.

In the kitchen I set coffee on the stove, and went out for bread, still thinking about what had just happened to the computer.

'You're up early,' my father said when I got back. His eyes were bleary and his hand shook a little spooning sugar into his cup.

'It's a bit early for you too,' I replied, hoping this early start meant he'd be out all day and I'd have the apartment to myself.

He breathed on his coffee. 'Got a meeting at *La Globe* this morning.'

'Are you working there now?' I asked.

'I'm doing a story about them. Something that happened years ago. It'll be strange seeing the old place after all this time.' He turned to the window. It was dark, and his reflection was bordered with the spikes he'd put on the ledge to stop pigeons nesting there. 'It'll be strange for them to see me too.'

He leaned against the stove so our reflections levelled up in the glass. I wondered what could be so strange about seeing old colleagues. Perhaps he was still drunk.

'What about you?' he said. 'I got a message about another detention.'

Fear shot through me like a pilot light.

He reached over and wiped the window with a cloth, as I counted – *one, two*—

'What's it for?' he said, rounding on me. He tried to soften his face to make it less threatening, but it just went slack and jowly.

'Give it a rest, Dad. The sun's not even up.'

'What's it for?' he growled.

The chair scraped loudly along the floor as I stood up and walked to the door. 'It's Mme. Joubert,' I said over my shoulder. 'The history teacher.'

'And?'

'I compared Napoleon to Hitler. You know, the stuff you always talk about – nationhood, expansion, all of that.'

The bleariness vanished from his eyes. 'You should tell me this kind of thing, Alex.'

'Why? So you don't just think I'm thick?'

'I know you're not *thick*. But I want to help. I know how this place works, this country. I'm not blaming you, but you can't go around saying things like that about Napoleon. He's a cultural icon, like Mohammed, or Jesus.'

'You're always blaming me.'

'No, I'm not. But you need to know how to frame it. How to get your point across without being too blunt.'

'Oh great, so now I'm blunt *and* thick?'

He reached for the coffee, but it had overheated and boiling liquid erupted from the spout, bubbling down his hand like lava.

'Jesus!' he yelled, thrusting his hand under the tap. 'Why did you leave the coffee on? It's red hot!'

'Blaming me again. *You* left it on.'

He plunged his hand into the sink, breathing heavily. 'I'm sure that's not the only reason she's on your back. Your marks last term were a disgrace.' His face was inflamed, as though the scalding had shot up there.

He dabbed a tea towel on his hand. 'Your school's one of the best in the country. If you don't get with the programme, you'll be straight out of the door!'

He stormed from the kitchen, the towel bound tight around his fist like a boxer's wrap.

I turned to the stove to clean up the mess. This was typical of him – escalating every conversation into a battle over grades as if he couldn't even *think* of anything else when it came to me. I hated this new school, and I couldn't understand why he was so desperate for me to do well there, why he rated it so highly when it went against everything he stood for. He always droned on about state-funded schools, not private education, and if you listened to the way he spoke about the teaching staff, you'd think they were all fascists. He knew the only reason the school was 'one of the best in the country' was because they threw out the slackers before the Bac so it didn't mess with their stats, and that's clearly what he thought would happen to me. I didn't get it. My father had resisted the elite all his life, but here I was at a school rammed with their kids. On one level he resented them, yet he also wanted their polish to rub off on me. Well, none of it was working – the experiment was a failure, because the only polish I was picking up was the kind that came off Tomas's boots.

I acted as if I was going to school, but my plan was to head back to Montparnasse and find the girl on the street. I'd been thinking about what Lisa said. I didn't think scoring drugs would get Tomas off my back – it wasn't that simple, but then again, it couldn't hurt. Mostly, though, I wanted to talk with her again. Or more precisely, I wanted to be with her again in my room. I was never going to be like Tomas or his mates, so I needed to find another way to stand out. My father's constant attacks were wearing me down, sucking the air from my lungs. If I wanted to be with someone like Lisa, I needed to kick away from him, away from the dragnet that pulled me back.

I waited until the study door closed, then rifled through his jacket. I took one of his credit cards and left the apartment.

By eight, the Jardin du Luxembourg was in full swing, teeming with joggers doing circuits of the outer tracks. Newly cropped plane trees lined the paths, and a mower cruised over a broad sweep of grass, its lazy drone underscoring the slap of tennis balls. Vapour trails streaked the sky, and the smell of manure wafted up from the flowerbeds.

I left the park by the southern gates, withdrawing fifty euros at an ATM near the restaurant we were at the other night. I always felt a tug of guilt stealing from my father, but he never noticed. I was careful to make these withdrawals near his favourite places, so if he saw it on his statement, he'd think he'd done it during one of his drinking sessions.

I walked around Montparnasse until I came across the makeshift tent in the street off the cemetery. The street was quiet, the bars and clubs all closed, and the tarpaulin sagged with rain. The empty little begging bowl sat guarding the entrance half filled with water. Another stab of guilt hit me, and I almost walked away, but then I saw them up ahead, arguing.

She was hitting him, her long plait whipping across her shoulders as she threw herself into the blows. He yelled back, his hands easily grabbing the balled fists she flung at him. When they saw me, the girl shouted and, alarmed by her aggression, I took off, running into the next street, but it was a dead end and Sami was right behind me.

He charged at me like a bull, grabbing me in a headlock. We struggled, but I could feel how strong he was – sinew and muscle all through to the bone with the tough edges of the street thrown in. After a few seconds, my feet gave way and I was on the ground, his knees pinning me to the concrete, straddling my chest. I was looking straight up his nostrils, inches from his cracked brown teeth and he stank even worse than before.

'I thought you stole my wallet,' I gasped, as he pushed his knees into my arms.

'I didn't steal your fucking wallet,' he said, reaching into my pocket. 'But I have it now.' He took the fifty euros and flicked through my cards.

I tried to snatch it back, but he had leaped up.

'This is the problem with you people. You take things that aren't yours. You steal,' he said. 'You have no conscience.'

'Hey, give it back!' I yelled, trailing after him and pleading until we reached the girl, now sitting with the baby.

He shook my wallet in my face, his eyes narrow. 'Not only are you a thief, but you're violent.' He pointed to the girl. 'She says you attacked her.'

The baby was crying, trying to strain free of its blankets. The girl laid it along her legs, so its head rested near her ankles. She rocked her feet sideways, back and forth.

I felt suddenly ashamed of the way I'd behaved and guilty, too, like I was somehow responsible for them being on the street. But I didn't know who they were, let alone where they came from. They weren't my problem. I'd taken a small foil of grass, but so what? Apart from that I had nothing to do with them.

I tried to smile.

Sami waved his arm in the direction of the baby, the girl, the whole miserable scene. 'You smile? This amuses you?'

The baby continued to cry, and the girl placed it in a cardboard box then scowled at me.

'I'm sorry!' I yelled, my hands in the air. I was sick of whatever game he was playing, and I would've walked away, but he had my father's card.

He came in close. 'Why have you come here?'

'I came back to apologise.'

He scoffed, his black hair shining almost blue in the sunlight. 'No one apologises unless they want something.'

Just then, the girl leaped to her feet and ran across the street to a small traffic island where a woman was stuffing a bag of clothes and junk into a recycling bin. The girl pushed the woman aside, grabbing the bag and the things hanging out of the bin. The woman shouted at the girl as she backed away, while the girl gathered everything up and dragged it back across the street where she spread it on the ground.

Sami went over to the haul and pushed a few items around with his foot.

'I know what you want. But it's good stuff, the real stuff, not the usual shit you buy round here,' he said, distracted by an old transistor radio. He turned it on and then tossed it back onto the pile. He looked at me as though I was just another piece of discarded junk. 'If you want more, then bring another fifty euros on Friday afternoon at five. I'll be waiting there,' he said, pointing to a bench.

I had no idea of the price, but I knew I should haggle, so I said it was too much.

He stared at me, his eyes dark and penetrating, then laughed. 'Fifty euros for a quarter, or a half, what the fuck would you know?'

He tossed me my wallet and turned to the clothes on the ground.

When my father came home that evening he went straight to his study. Later, he knocked on my door.

'Don't play your games while I'm talking to you. Look at me,' he said.

I sighed, pausing the game.

'Where were you today?'

I kept my eyes on the screen.

'I told them you had a doctor's appointment,' he said. 'But why did you skip school?'

My skin started burning, heat creeping up my chest. I didn't know what to say, so I thought the best thing to do was just ignore him while I bought some time. I replaced my headphones and brought my avatar into position.

My father reached for the console, ripped out the cables and pulled it off the shelf. 'I said, don't play those games while I'm talking to you.'

I lunged at the machine, tried to wrestle it back, but he pulled it from me and smashed it on the floor.

I couldn't believe it. I stood there, feeling the hum of shattered electronics deep in my guts. He picked it up and smashed it down again, glaring at me. A splintering echo went through the apartment, and the aftershock of fury coming off him sent me reeling back.

'I'm not slaving my guts to send you to the best school in the country just so you can sit at home playing these games!' he screamed.

I stared at the dusty gap on the shelf where my console had been, at the rows of games cartridges, all of them useless now. I couldn't believe what he'd just done. It was like he'd knocked my teeth out.

'I hate you!' I yelled after him, blubbering through the tears streaming down my face.

It wasn't until much later that I remembered to return his card. After I left Sami, I withdrew more money. I wasn't worried my father would notice the withdrawals, but I knew he'd miss the card. His wallet wasn't by the front door, but passing his bedroom, I saw it on the chest of drawers.

'What are you doing, Alex?' His voice boomed in stereo, from all corners of the room.

I slipped the card into his wallet and whipped around to face him, the evidence splayed on my hand as I fumbled for an excuse. 'We had a school trip, and I borrowed some money from Nathan. I need to pay him back.'

He swirled his glass of whisky and ice. 'So just ask. There's no need to go sneaking around my room.' He took his wallet and then handed me twenty euros, tamed now by whisky. 'I'm sorry about the console. I'll get it fixed.'

'Sure,' I said.

He started to walk away, then stopped. 'You haven't used my computer, have you?'

'No,' I squeaked.

'Just I turned it on this morning and there was nothing. It's completely dead.'

I shrugged. 'I know how you feel.'

'I had some important stuff on it,' he said, and then moved forward to ruffle my hair. 'I'm sorry, it's been a tough day. Don't skip school again. I won't cover for you next time.'

Sixteen

Montparnasse

O N FRIDAY, SAMI WAS WAITING for me on the bench. I sat down beside him and passed him the money tucked into a handshake, the way I'd seen it done in films.

'Not like that, you idiot,' he said, laughing as he pocketed the note. 'Always act like someone's watching.'

He pointed to the tall apartments all around, their dark windows gawping down at us.

'Go to the cubicle on the corner and put the bags somewhere against your skin, not in your pocket,' he said, placing a cigarette packet between us.

'Against my skin?'

'Yeah, in a sock or down your pants. The police will only check your pockets.'

Fear knuckled my throat at the mention of the police, but I swallowed it down. He scrawled a number on a scrap of paper, and then put his hand on my shoulder. His voice was calm and reassuring. 'Don't worry, nothing will happen here. If you have any trouble or want more, call this number. I won't answer, but I'll call you back.'

I took his number and the cigarette packet and walked towards the toilet, the silent audience of windows tracking my movements. I kept my head down, feeling the force of surveillance as a physical thing. Cold air crept around my collar, puckering the skin on my neck. Approaching the block, I had an urge to bin the packet and keep walking, to head back home and away from this crazy deal with its stupid exchange, but something else had taken over and my legs just kept moving.

I thought of Lisa's face. The twitch of her mouth, and her green eyes like slivers of glass. I remembered her look that afternoon in my bedroom when she'd focused on me as if she saw what I needed. I knew she didn't have all the answers, but I thought she'd be a good place to start.

I hesitated outside the toilet, engulfed in the stale reek of urine, and I decided in the split second I stood there that I'd do it just this once, to show her I wasn't a loser. She'd know the first time I scored wasn't a fluke, that it wasn't just luck, and I'd prove it to myself too. But even then, as I pushed away fear and took the next wild step towards her, I felt the edges of something darker wrap itself around me. I knew I wouldn't be able to stop what I'd started, and that once it had hold, the tighter it would bind.

The cigarette packet held two small bags – one with clumps of weed, the other six white pills. I stuffed a bag into either sock and later, I called Sami. He called me straight back on another number and I asked about the pills.

'I couldn't get as much weed, so I gave you those instead. If you don't want them your friends will. Take them clubbing.'

Finally, I had something Lisa wanted. My urge was to tell her straight away, but I decided to wait until she worked it out herself. She'd been ignoring me the past few weeks so I did the same to her when eventually she focused back on me. I deleted her texts, walked off when she approached, and avoided her eyes. I made sure she felt my absence.

Finally, she cornered me at school, putting her hand on the wall so I couldn't pass. When I told her I had pills, too, she was all over me, trailing me around school, sending texts and later, I sent her a picture of the pills in their little plastic bag. She was beside herself and called me immediately, making me promise to bring them when we went out that Friday. It was the first I'd heard of any date, but I wasn't going to argue. My plan had worked.

On Friday evening, I stood naked in front of the bathroom mirror. Surveying the extent of my eczema was something I rarely did, but as I stood there, I imagined I was her seeing it for the first time. Angry red blotches swept my torso like a chain of islands whose inflamed landmass shifted and moved with the seasons. An ugly, hand-shaped cluster flared across my chest, its fingers reaching for my neck, while a galaxy of spots grazed my arms and shoulders, giving the whole area the look of plucked chicken skin. The largest area, just above my groin had the texture of elephant hide and cracked to form painful fissures, which spread and deepened if I moved too quickly.

I layered cream over my body and stood there like a painted tribesman, waiting for it to soak in. Any girl would be repulsed, that's for sure – unless she was drunk or high. That was the idea, of course, but I couldn't even imagine someone touching it.

My father put his head around the door. 'Dinner's ready.'

His smile faded when he saw my body. 'I had no idea your eczema was this bad. Turn around,' he said, and I made a quarter turn, craning behind to catch my reflection in the mirror.

'It's getting worse. It looks painful. Do you want to see someone? A dermatologist? The one we saw at the hospital, perhaps?'

'It's fine,' I said. 'They just suggest more of these stupid creams, and they never work.'

'We could tell her that. Perhaps try something else.'

'I'd rather not.'

'I thought it had gone away . . .'

I leaned over the sink, washed my face. 'Well, it hasn't.'

'I can see that, but let me know if you change your mind.'

I got dressed, choosing a collarless shirt that I buttoned to the neck, a pair of jeans and a khaki jacket.

'You didn't have to dress for dinner,' he said, putting a steak in front of me. It was cooked the way I liked with a melting disc of garlic butter at the centre. 'I bought that DVD you were talking about. I thought we could watch it tonight.'

I cut into the steak. 'Sorry, Dad, I'm going out.'

He gave me a blank look.

'Just the Champ de Mars, then along the river, you know,' I added.

'Who with?'

'People.'

'Who?'

'Just people.'

Pierre's was a twenty-four-hour cocktail bar near Bastille, one of those touristy, American places with waiters who don't ask for ID as long as you can afford the drinks. A group of kids from school took up most of the outside tables. They sat in a row under the candy-striped awning wearing fur-hooded jackets, their faces glowing under the radiators as they twirled umbrellas and straws, poking at the fruit in their cocktails.

At the side of the bar was a nightclub, and Lisa and I shared a drink as we shuffled forward in the queue. Inside, the heat made my eczema go crazy and I almost left straight away, but Lisa grabbed my hand and led me downstairs to the bathroom. She found an empty cubicle and perched on the toilet seat like the queen of the club. As she fished in her bag, the fabric of her dress slid up, and I saw a mass of pink scratches grazing her kneecap. Perhaps it was eczema like mine, I thought, but looking closer, I saw a row of longer, wider scars further up her thigh.

I thought she must have been in an accident, then realised the scars were too precise, too fresh and too neat. They'd been etched deliberately, both knees symmetrical.

She showed me then, and I stared at the wounds on the insides of her legs and higher, where the patterns became more frenetic, a series of wild cuts that made increasingly terrible patterns the further they went, disappearing into the line of her knickers. Just below her hip was a fresh injury, the skin puckering, all red and tight. It looked like it had only just stopped bleeding.

I touched her knee, afraid of the wounds, which looked so raw and painful. The veins of my hand stood out against her scars, and I felt a throbbing under my skin.

She brushed my hand away. 'Get off!' she said, pulling her skirt down. 'Stop touching me, you're freaking me out.'

I gave her the pills and she went to work, placing a mirror on top of the toilet lid and telling me to stand with my back against the door.

Lisa bit one pill, swallowed half, and gave me the rest. Then she tapped out some powder from her bag on the mirror, crushing the lumps with the edge of a card, chopping it one way then the other. Her hands were shaking, and some of it fell to the floor. Sweeping her hair over her shoulder, she snorted a line through a tiny silver straw. When she came up, she shuddered, and then kissed me. Her tongue was dry and bitter.

I tried to copy what she did, snorting the powder through the silver tube, but I only managed to get halfway through before the powder seared my nostrils.

'You'll get used to it,' she said. 'Try doing it quicker.'

I managed to get the rest up my nose, but it formed a bitter lump at the back of my mouth and sat there, burning for a while before eventually sliding down my throat.

A minute or so later, the drugs detonated in my head, propelling me backwards. I pressed my sweaty palms against the door, which thrummed with the vibrations of the music outside, building with the rhythm, getting louder until I realised the pounding wasn't part of the music, but someone banging on the door.

We pushed through the queue and back up to the club, which was now in full swing. I couldn't speak, my ears like two drums, as if the music in the club was coming from inside my head. Lisa spun around, the coloured lights reflecting in her hair, which surged towards me like a neon river.

The floor was packed tight, everyone pressing against each other, and I felt simultaneously disconnected from the crowd, yet part of it. Lisa reached under my sweat-drenched shirt, and for once my body wasn't itching, my skin no longer tight and painful. The drugs, or her touch, had anaesthetised it somehow.

Then for a long time, we just danced, bathed in soft shifting light and the music that pulsed over us in shuddering waves. Lisa had her arms around me, her hair brushing my face as we held each other, moving to our own rhythm until I lost track of time, and my problems with school, my father, and my wretched skin all disappeared into an oblivion of drugs and music. Sounds and senses merged until all I saw were hazy shapes and colours, my heart pounding like a galloping horse.

Seventeen

Bastille

W E STEPPED OUT OF THE club hours later into a
blue-grey dawn, the sky the colour of ice.

'What do we do now?' I said, stunned by the
cold and the sharpening light.

Lisa pointed towards the canal and I carried her coat, its fur
hood prickling my arm. My eczema had revived, and my body
crawled with itches.

I offered it to her, but she waved it away. Her hair was drenched
with sweat. Make-up smudged her face, and one of her eyes was
red and veiny.

'I just need some air,' she said, lighting a cigarette, our footsteps
echoing on the rough paving stones at the edge of the canal.
Grey light stretched and rippled on the water, and drifts of leaves
swelled between the boats moored along the towpath.

We went up some iron stairs to a square where there was an
early fish market. Men in white overalls and black rubber boots
scattered ice over metal trays, crunching it down, while others
laid out the fish, pressing their stiff, silvery bodies into neat rows.
Juice dribbled out of the fishes' mouths, staining the ice pink.

Behind the stalls the men worked fast – their large, blubbery arms gutting and slicing, then tossing the bones high in the air towards the bins.

A fish skeleton landed in front of us and Lisa squealed, slipping on the pavement. One of the men laughed as I helped her up, her dress wet and smeared with scales. He sucked on his cigarette, his swollen lips leering like a cartoon as he watched us weave around the puddles and crates.

We sat on a wooden bench at the edge of the square, the street lamps casting yellow light over the morning. Lisa kicked off her shoes, draping her legs across my lap, her dress riding up past her knees. Her pupils were enormous, and she looked beautiful and strange with her ragged hair and filthy feet. I traced the line of her legs, drawn to the memory of what I'd seen on her thighs. Her skin was blue with cold, and the scars on her knees looked surreal in the acid light.

We talked for a while about the night laughing and teasing each other. After a while, she rummaged in her purse and brought out several bags coated in powdery residue. She waved them at me. 'Do you have any more?'

I shook my head. 'Where did you get those other bags?'

'Tomas,' she said, smiling.

I shifted on the bench, overcome by a sudden wave of despair. 'Is he really your boyfriend?'

She shrugged and then pouted, nodding slightly, as though none of it mattered. 'Why? Are you jealous?'

'Maybe,' I said. 'But why are you with him? You know he beat me up for no reason. The guy is a psychopath.'

'He is a bit,' she said and went digging in her bag. 'We're not really together anymore. His mother didn't like me coming round.'

149

'Céline?'

She looked up. 'You know her?'

'His parents are friends of my father's.'

'She said I was a bad influence.'

'You led her boy astray.'

She moved in closer. 'I bet your mother wouldn't be like that. She'd be one of those cool mums who hands out condoms, and changes the sheets afterwards.'

I felt the heat prickle across my chest as she took my hand.

'She'd go along with it just so she could tell her friends, *We let them sleep together, so they don't do it in parks*. I've heard them say that, can you believe it? They think we're dogs!'

'Tomas isn't far off,' I said.

She laughed. 'Tomas's mum is way too uptight. She complained to the school, said I was a "little tramp". Those were her words!'

'That's ironic.'

'Even if I was, what business is it of theirs what I do out of school?' Lisa scratched her leg then looked up. 'Why ironic?'

'Well Céline seems—' I said, immediately regretting it.

'Seems what?'

'Nothing.'

She jabbed me in the ribs. 'Come on, tell me.'

'I can't.'

She put her hand on my crotch. 'Tell me, or I'll have to force it out of you.'

She moved towards me. Her touch and the way she looked at me was completely overwhelming and I felt my self-restraint drain away.

'My father's sleeping with her,' I said.

Her eyes grew wide. 'Nooooo way. How do you know?'

'Promise not to tell?'

She smiled, chewing on a strand of hair. 'Of course I won't.'

'I've seen them together.'

She put her hand over her mouth. 'You saw them having sex?'

'I practically walked in on them at her place. The country place.'

'Oh, God, that's gross. They're so old,' she said, putting her arms around my neck.

Hours later, I woke fully clothed, lying sideways across my bed. My nostrils were raw and swollen, and I breathed through my mouth in short, dry breaths. I rolled over and a dull thud radiated from the back of my head to the blurred edges of vision. The room shuddered, and a jagged spear of light pierced the curtains. As the sun moved, the spear lengthened along the carpet and I watched it, imagining it was my future creeping towards me.

My phone was full of messages from Lisa suggesting we meet up. I thought of our walk home that morning along the river as the sun rose and turned the sky pink. I hadn't expected to hear from her so soon. Her texts reignited the excitement from the night before, and I felt high again, my brain full of scrambled images of the club, the lights and her. I got out of bed and threw the curtains wide.

By the time I got outside, the promise of the morning had wilted into a damp afternoon. The sun was a glazed disc struggling behind heavy cloud, and shoppers packed the streets. Men in brogues and pastel sweaters sipped espresso at the cafés, their eyes sliding from newspapers to the women in heels who walked past, laden with bags.

I scanned the terrace at the café and went inside. Lisa was in the back room on a studded leather banquette next to a fake gas fire. Large ceiling lights tinged the place green and vintage jazz piped through the speakers.

She sat alone, twirling the straw of her oversized drink, looking small and tragic, and the excitement I'd felt at seeing her again evaporated.

Her skin was blotchy and there were dark circles under her eyes, one of which was badly swollen. Her hair, now more ashy than blonde, was pulled back into a greasy bun, making her face look sharp and pointy.

We chatted for a while, and she blew her nose until it grew all red, standing out like a ball of chewed meat against her pale face.

Finally, she asked about the pills – where did I get them and could I get more?

So again, this was what she wanted, I thought, my mood properly crashing as though I'd been hurled from a speeding car. Perhaps this was all she ever wanted.

Her questions annoyed me, and she looked worse the more inquisitorial she became, until all I saw was her pointy chin wagging at me, firing questions as she rubbed her eye with a tissue. I'd always worried that one day, my eczema would spread to my face, and right now, with her eye a glistening sliver beneath swollen folds, she was the living embodiment of those fears.

I shuffled back in case she was contagious. 'I'm not your delivery boy, Lisa.'

'No wait, don't go,' she said, as a hand slapped me hard on the shoulder. It was Tomas, his white teeth dazzling in the gloom.

He sat beside me, his legs sprawling out. He looked frightening, grinning with a deranged leer, his face glowing like he'd just come from an ice hockey game.

'I heard you guys had a great night,' he said, in a deep voice, running his hand through his hair, his breath a blast of mint.

'Did you arrange this?' I said to Lisa.

She grabbed my arm, her face pleading. 'Alex said he can get more,' she said to Tomas.

'No, I fucking didn't.'

'Hey, hey. Stay cool,' said Tomas, moving in close. A bitter edge crept into his smile – a reminder of the psychopath in the toilet block.

I laughed weakly. 'Come on, guys, what is this? Some kind of joke?'

They exchanged a glance, and Tomas leaned in further. 'I'm having a party in a couple of weeks. It'd be great to have some of those pills you had last night.'

'What do you think I am – your dealer?'

'No, seriously. I can make it worth your while. I mean it.' He was so close I could see the pores on his nose, smell his sour, piney deodorant.

Lisa chewed her straw. 'Just introduce us to your guy.' She looked at Tomas and I sensed the strong ties between them, ties that excluded me.

'We'll come with you. That way you're not doing the deal. You can just introduce us,' she added, smiling indulgently as if I was a child.

Tomas held a fifty-euro note casually between his fingers like a tip. 'Just call the guy. Arrange for him to meet you somewhere with the stuff, and we'll come and get it.'

I stared at the money. 'You want me to call him and make an arrangement?'

'Yeah. Just call him, just this once, and make the arrangement. We'll do the rest,' said Tomas.

'And what exactly is the arrangement? You want fifty euros' worth of pills?'

Tomas laughed and waggled the note at me. 'No, my friend, that's for you. A little incentive to get you started. As for the pills, I'll have as many as you can get your hands on.' He stuffed the note into my shirt pocket, and then slapped his thigh like he was some kind of bank exec who'd just closed a deal.

When Tomas went to the bar, I stood up and threw the money onto the table. I needed to get away from him, his money and his sickening smile. I looked at Lisa, expecting to connect. But there was nothing, just a vacuous, hungry look.

'What's the matter?' Lisa said. 'I wanted you guys to meet out of school so you'd see he wasn't so bad after all.'

'Not so bad? You saw the way he behaved. He's a total prick. A fucking nutcase. And he's only speaking to me now because he wants something from me. Like you.'

She walked around next to me. 'What's so bad about that? It's the way of the world. You scratch my back, I scratch yours.' Her face was sharp and humourless as she stuffed the fifty euros back into my pocket.

'What if I don't want my back scratched?' I said, the eczema prickling across my shoulders.

It was actually the last thing I wanted.

'Everyone wants their back scratched,' she said, running her nails along my spine.

I walked to the river, furious at the way she'd spring-loaded a trap then led me straight to it. She must have thought I was an idiot, tempting me to the café and then ambushing me like that. What made her think she could push me around and do her bidding – score drugs for Tomas, help her with her habit? It was insulting.

Tomas was worse. The way he'd edged in so casually – *I can make it worth your while*, so confident he could buy me with the shitty cash between his fingers like I was a member of staff. *No, my friend, that's for you.* So we were friends now, were we? Just because I was part of a transaction he wanted to pull off.

Someone needed to teach him a lesson, I thought, trying to imagine how. I thought of his parents, so satisfied with themselves, their houses and all their money. People like Tomas were so insulated in their world of weaponised cash that it was impossible to get anywhere near them.

As I walked along the riverbank, I said the words aloud, *I can make it worth your while*, trying to imagine the kind of person who'd say that. I pretended I was Tomas, and felt his arrogance swirl around me. I repeated the words, lost in his world until I sensed the edge of something else – something desperate and naïve in his belief that everyone had a price, and a twinge of fear in case they didn't.

As I crossed the road and headed home, some of my annoyance subsided, and I grew aware that I now had access to something he wanted. The more I considered the opportunity that had just arisen, the more it became loaded with promise – not of cash, but power at the thought that now he needed something from me. Suddenly, the isolation I felt at school receded, and in its place a kind of hopefulness took shape and the threat of him felt contained, neutralised.

I had access to these drugs and he didn't. I'd get them, but I'd do it my way. I'd turn the tables on him, make him grovel and beg for them, and he'd realise just how little power he actually had.

I felt instantly taller, as if gravity had become weaker, the ground a bit further away. The world had sharpened up and come into focus, and I felt good like I was in control and about to start winning for a change.

NOW

Eighteen

Saint-Germain

ON THE WAY TO MEET Céline Chambière, I pass some kids on the platform at Saint-Denis. One of them reminds me of Sami, and he's in front of me later at the Gare du Nord, jumping the barricades for Line 4, just like we used to. I follow, leaping over the turnstiles just behind him.

A whistle cuts the air.

You! Stop!

Up against the wall!

I freeze against the drumroll of boots, hands to my ears like a boxer up against the ropes.

A cop pushes me aside and I stumble to the ground, bracing myself for a boot in the back. But the cops are ahead of me now, crowding around the boys, frisking them.

The one who looks like Sami is pinned to the floor, the side of his face flattened and he stares straight at me, his eyes reaching for mine, for some kind of help. A cop cuffs him from behind, and then stands, wiping the sweat from his brow as he adjusts his belt. Another cop empties the boy's backpack and fillets the sides with a silvery blade.

The kid is sprawled on the ground surrounded by his things – towel, goggles, swimming gear. The police turn their attention to his friends and I step forward to help him gather his stuff, but then I think of my parole officer's warning – *Just stay out of there.* If the police call up my details they'll bring me in, too, so I just stand there, knuckles stinging from the fall, and then I melt back into the crowd, feeling the weight of another betrayal. I should have been able to help him, but I'm more powerless now than ever. It's times like these that prison feels close – one false move and I'm straight back there.

Coming into Paris means taking a risk even if I switch off my phone. The patrols have stepped up in Zone One – you can't move without permission now, and police line the stations on the Péri like bouncers at a nightclub – stopping and searching, checking IDs. It's a signal to the suburbs:

Stay out.

We're watching you.

Most people accept it's the price to pay for safe streets. It's like the city itself commands it.

I continue my journey, still thinking of Sami and the boy I didn't help as I drop my father's computer near Bastille to see what can be salvaged, then catch a bus to Odéon. Here in the heart of Paris it's another city, almost another climate, and sunshine through plane trees casts soft, shimmery light over the terraces and the slow, lunchtime crowd. Men in cravats browse rows of paperbacks, and cakes in the patisseries glisten like gems. Passing a sweet shop, a group of squirrels and birds stare at me through the glass, each feather and whisker carefully moulded in dark glossy chocolate.

My footsteps echo along the narrow streets where tall apartments rise like mausoleums, their dark windows silent and still.

Water drips from balconies, splashing the pavements and chilling the air.

After several wrong turns, I find the Chambières' building, enter the code Céline sent me and press their name on the lobby intercom.

There's a noise from the receiver like whispering static and then Céline speaks, as if to a deliveryman. 'No, I'm afraid you have the wrong apartment.'

I press the buzzer again and finally, the door clicks open. I walk up two flights to where she waits on the landing, hand on the door behind her.

'Didn't you get my message?' she whispers.

I shake my head, barely recognising her stunned face for the amount of cosmetic surgery she's had. Her lips and eyes are the only things that move, and she gapes at me like something in an aquarium.

She tells me Paul is still there, and waves towards the stairs, as if flicking me away.

I say I'm not leaving without speaking to her, and as we stand there arguing, the door swings open and Paul steps out. He wears gold corduroys, a white, open-necked shirt, and brings with him the citrusy whiff of expensive aftershave.

He peers at me, eyes squinting in the gloom, and I suppress an urge to laugh. They both look ridiculous with their matching tans and silvery, swept-back hair – like those billboard advertisements for retirement plans you see on the metro where the elderly couple has morphed into a blended mutation of themselves. I wonder what their expensive looks are supposed to be saying, or what they're designed to hide.

'Who is it, Céline?' Paul says.

Céline gives me an icy look. 'It's Alex Giraud. I wanted to speak to him first before telling you.'

'Good god!' Paul says, his face tightening as he steps towards me. 'What's he doing here?'

She puts a hand on his shoulder and tells him she'd contacted me thinking I may have heard from Tomas.

What? I almost say, wondering what on earth she means. We hated each other. She must know that.

Paul looks from Céline to me, then back again. 'Heard from Tomas? This is all a huge surprise,' he says, and I can't help nodding in agreement.

She keeps her hand on him, her eyes on mine as if drawing me into her lie, into this little three-way conspiracy.

'Why didn't you tell me?' Paul says, holding the door open. 'You'd better bring him inside, then.'

'But Papa is there. I think it's best if Alex and I go downstairs.'

'Nonsense. If it's about Tomas I want to hear it too,' Paul says, standing back and ushering me in.

Light streams through tall windows and blazes along the wide, polished hallway of their massive apartment. Double doors open onto a large salon where a Filipina in a maid's uniform fusses over an old man in an armchair. The apartment is still, the windows closed, and there's something stale about the atmosphere like the old man might be dead. There's a yawning silence, too, as if even your thoughts would echo down the corridor.

Paul enters the salon, followed by Céline who looks at me urgently, mouthing something I don't catch.

The salon is decorated in the old style, with spindly antiques arranged formally at either end of a large Persian rug, and a vast

161

mirror extends from the fireplace to the ceiling. At the far end, folding doors open onto a dining room, and a large bowl of lilies fills the room with the heavy reek of cat's piss.

I take a seat, my mind racing. I have no idea what to say about Tomas, and glance at Céline for guidance, but she's looking at Paul.

'I really think it's best if I speak to Alex alone,' she says, her mouth a tight line.

Paul's ability to ignore his wife's wishes is impressive, and he turns to me, telling me they haven't seen Tomas for over seven years. His voice hardens as he tells me Tomas disappeared that January, just after I'd been arrested.

'When you left school Tomas took the blame for what happened. People twisted the story, said that Tomas put you up to it all. He never recovered from the association with your father's death. It was devastating.'

I nod slowly, unsure how to reply.

There's a noise behind us. It's the old man, banging on the floor with his cane.

Paul yells to him, telling him it's almost time for his nap, but the man ignores him and insists on knowing who I am.

'Bring him here,' he yells.

Paul turns to me in exasperation. 'Come over. You need to speak loudly, he's almost deaf.'

Paul introduces me as Tomas's schoolmate and the old man looks at me through hooded eyes. With his flaccid neck and gummy mouth, he resembles an ancient turtle, and his head sways slightly as if held by invisible threads. What remains of his silvery hair is raked over his scalp and his walking stick is laid across his lap like a rifle.

I extend my hand, my grazed knuckles still smeared with blood and there's an angry patch of eczema on my wrist. He regards me with disgust, his own hand remaining on his stick while mine hovers in mid-air.

'Alex what?' the old man shouts, and flecks of spittle fly from his mouth. He hooks the handle of his stick around my thigh and pulls me closer, gesturing to a chair beside him. His hand is marked with liver spots, and yellow nails curve over the pads of his fingers.

Paul calls for the maid and then tries to get his father to stand, telling him it's time for his pills, but the old man starts talking to me about the war, and then changes tack abruptly, quizzing me about my family and their connections. I tell him my mother is Croatian.

The eyes narrow, and I see Tomas's cold, ruthless glare.

'The Balkans. That was no war. That was a massacre!' His hand shakes as he wipes the moisture from under his eyes with a handkerchief. 'I was in Indo-China, and Algeria. They were proper wars, not like these days, with terrorists and bombs and beheadings in the street.'

The maid is beside him now with a tray of pills. She hands him a glass of water, and he fumbles for the pills, scraping them into his palm like pebbles.

'And the gypsies that come from there. The Balkans. Untold problems!' he says, his hand shaking as he looks at Paul. 'All that business with Tomas. Those people were responsible, remember.'

'It's time for your sleep now, Father,' Paul shouts, helping him out of his chair.

They fuss around the old man while I hover at a distance then step forward to say goodbye, but the old man swats me away.

Paul takes his father by the arm, and they shuffle out, the old man leaning on Paul for support.

Céline looks flustered as she scrapes the hair from her face, and then puts her hand on my back, almost pushing me towards the door and this time I'm glad to be leaving.

'We can't do this now. I'll tell Paul you had to leave suddenly.'

'What was all that about Tomas?' I say.

'I'm sorry, it was the first thing that came into my head.'

'No, what the old man said about him? What did he mean *gypsies?*'

Céline sighs impatiently. 'Tomas got caught up with some hippies, not gypsies. Paul's father gets confused. He reads too much news. He's unwell, as you saw.'

We reach the door, and she looks back down the hall. 'There's a café opposite the metro at Concorde. Meet me there tomorrow at eleven and bring the photos.'

Nineteen

Concorde

I T's DOG-WALKING HOUR IN THE Jardin des Tuileries. Men and women patrol the gravelly paths like an arthritic army, hands tangled in leads and walking canes. I watch from the park as Céline arrives at the café, lights a cigarette and checks her phone. Her hair is pulled back from her face except for a sweep of blonde fringe, and large gold earrings graze the collar of her white jacket. I wait until she finishes her cigarette then cross the road, and we take a table inside near the window.

She makes a show of looking at her watch. 'I don't have long. Tell me what you want.' She attempts a smile before her mouth takes on its usual downward slant.

I take her cue, dispensing with pleasantries, but reply cheerfully enough. 'You were helping my father before he died. How?'

I put her letter on the table and she glances down, uninterested at first. Then comprehension floods her face and she reaches over, her cheeks reddening. 'Where did you get that?'

I slide the letter onto my lap as the waiter arrives, sets down her tea things, my Coke.

I unfold the top page and read, '*I can't help you anymore,*' then pass it to her. 'What were you helping him with?'

She scans the letter, her face neutral. 'I've no idea. I can't remember writing that.'

I push the photo I sent across the table. 'Did Paul know?'

She covers it with her palm, and looks up, her eyes narrow. 'Paul knows everything. He knows we're meeting today, too, so don't think you can blackmail—'

'I said this isn't about money. What kind of help was it?'

She taps the table, pours her tea.

'Honestly, I can't remember. All I can think is I must have meant generic help, in the sense I couldn't *help* him. None of us could help Eddy towards the end.'

'Help him with *what*?'

'With his drinking. With himself, for God's sake. It was a break-up letter, Alex.'

It sounds so ridiculous that I laugh, wondering in what galaxy a break-up letter still existed. 'I thought you said you couldn't remember.'

'Look, our affair, if you can even call it that, was very brief – a few months at the most. It was little more than a two-night stand, really.'

This isn't quite what she said on the phone, and the flurry of letters between them comes across as more than just a fling. I think of the night I saw them together, my father's trousers around his calves as he strained against her in the utility room. That scene I couldn't get out of my head for weeks afterwards, and one I recall now aided by the perfume she still wears. The heavy floral scent that hung in our hallway for hours after she'd left, lingering on cushions and nooks around the apartment.

Her eyes soften, and she places her hand on mine, hot and clammy. 'His drinking was impossible. You know that.'

I remove my hand and she sits back.

'We were all to blame. We let it go on far too long. We talked about intervening, checking him into a clinic, but we didn't. Telling him the truth risked pushing him away.' She carefully sips her tea. 'For someone who was concerned with the truth, he never liked it applied to him.'

That was certainly true. I think back to that time: to the late nights and early mornings. I see him now, grim-faced, hands shaking in the cold morning light as he poured his coffee. The hands were always the giveaway – trembling proof that he'd lost his grip.

I read again from the letter. '*I can't help you anymore. Paul is getting suspicious. I'm asking about work all the time. It's too much.*'

I look up, but her face is a mask. 'Why did you say that? What kind of work were you asking about *all the time*?'

She affects a look of calm, but her hands are clasped together, knuckles white. 'Eddy spoke about work a lot – about what direction he wanted his career to take. He talked about PR, working at the UN, going into government. I thought we could help with contacts. But it was all talk. He was burnt out.'

She shifts in her chair. 'He wasn't really working at that stage, or even interested in work. He was too drunk most of the time to do any real work. It was awful. I still feel terrible about it.'

I follow her eyes to the street. Why is she going on so much about his drinking? They all drank back then. Does she want me to blame her for that? And what about blaming me? She doesn't seem to hold me responsible for his death at all. Perhaps that's because she knows I didn't kill him.

She looks at me sadly. 'I could have helped him. After you left home, he was in a terrible state, inconsolable, calling me constantly. By that stage, I'd called things off between us, but we stayed in touch. The drinking was out of control, dangerous. He thought it was his fault, the divorce, you moving around as a child, not fitting in at school. He thought he'd turned a blind eye to your problems, not paid enough attention to you.'

This was a huge surprise, and I stare at her in disbelief. I was never aware he felt remotely guilty about my upbringing. He referred to all of the moving around – my being dragged from school to school, as my 'international education', something I should have appreciated and been grateful for, and he never turned a blind eye. The things she says about him being too drunk to work don't make any sense either. He always worked whether he was drunk or sober, it didn't seem to make any difference. In fact, he often boasted he did his best work after a drink or two.

She's distant now as she fiddles with her tea things. Our eyes are locked, but hers are glazed as if she's looking right through me, and there's something detached in her voice. What she's saying doesn't ring true, and suddenly I don't believe a word of it.

I lean in, my face so close to hers that we almost touch. 'Why are you telling me all these lies?'

She reels back.

'Why are you exaggerating how much he drank, how guilty he felt, saying that you ended it months before he died?'

'It's the truth, Alex.'

'And Paul?'

Her face sours. 'What's Paul got to do with this?'

'Wasn't my father working with Paul?'

'None of this has anything to do with Paul. He knows even less than I do.'

It's hard to believe Paul knows less than she does, given that she professes to know nothing.

I return the letter to my bag and she looks at me down her nose the way she did when I was a child. Reaching for a cigarette, she remembers we're inside and looks around impatiently. The café is filling up with the lunchtime crowd and the waiter hovers nearby, keen for us to move on.

Outside, she lights a cigarette and I scan her face. There isn't a trace of the woman in the photos. With her bourgeois looks and manner, she isn't the sort of woman that usually attracted my father. Then again, I can't imagine he was her type either.

She registers my expression and looks at me with contempt as we cross the road and climb the steps to the park. We walk along a sandy path to a bench on the edge of a fountain. In a clearing beside us, a group of elderly people practice tai chi with sad, determined faces.

Taking a seat, she turns to me. 'You're a fool, Alex, opening this up. Eddy was trampling on a minefield, poking at things that were buried long ago. Things were bound to blow up.'

'What do you mean? What *things*?'

'Give me those photos.'

I reach into my bag and hand them all to her, together with the letters.

She starts flicking through. 'You have all my letters. And *these* photos too.'

'I'm giving them back. They're yours.'

She nods, relieved.

'Tell me what this is all about,' I say.

'Eddy was investigating an old story, something that happened a long time ago,' she says. 'It was a scandal involving his old colleagues from *La Globe*. Something that took place when they were all young.'

'When who were young?'

'Your father and several others whom you don't know.'

She lights another cigarette and the smile vanishes, her face now severe. 'Back then, in the seventies and eighties, some of the journalists at *La Globe* were agents.'

'*Agents?*'

'They called them agents of influence – more like infiltrators or moles. They took information and put a spin on it, or made things up. These days you'd probably just call them influencers.'

'And they influenced what?'

'They ran false stories – spread misinformation and propaganda, forged documents, started rumours and stirred up animosity. It all happened years ago.'

'So why was my father interested, then?'

She looks thoughtful. 'He was troubled about his role in it, I think.'

'His role?' I pull my coat against the sudden chill. 'What was his role?'

'I understand he was tricked into it.'

'How?'

'I'm not sure. I tried to get it out of him, but he wouldn't say. He was embarrassed, or perhaps he didn't trust me. He told me it was time to come clean, to get to the bottom of it and write some kind of memoir.'

At last what she's saying makes sense. My father always said he wanted to write a book. I remember him working at his computer late into the night, his old notebooks spread out on the desk.

'So how did you help him?'

'Eddy wanted to know which other journalists were involved, and he needed information and contacts. He'd drifted away from most people while he was living in the US, but Paul and I hadn't. He wanted access to our lives, the people we socialised with, and he needed me to help him.'

She drifts off as if remembering something then shrugs. 'I invited him to our dinner parties so he could meet them all again. At first, I thought he just wanted to reconnect with people. But actually, he wanted more than that.'

'What did he want?'

'He wanted to know who was behind it all, how far it went.'

'Did he find out?'

She doesn't answer, just looks at me intently for a moment then looks away.

'And what was in it for you?' I ask, eventually.

She laughs. 'If you're asking what I saw in him, I couldn't really say. There were many sides to Eddy. I never knew which to expect.'

'Were you in love with him?' I ask. Somehow the question seems important.

She smokes for a while then shakes her head as if disagreeing with her own thoughts. 'Your father was very attractive. He had a kind of brutal honesty, and if he liked you, it felt like you'd passed some kind of test.'

'*Honesty?* You've just suggested he was some kind of traitor, who was sleeping with his friend's wife for information.'

'He knew he didn't always get it right, but he believed in himself, and he knew what motivated him, which is more than you can say for most people. And he and Paul were never friends.'

She looks at me. 'You're still very harsh on him. You don't remember him like that, do you? It's odd, isn't it, for all the scrutiny we put our parents under, we never see them very clearly.'

I think back to the weekend at their house. I saw the two of them pretty clearly then.

'And these photos. There are others too – of my father and other people.'

I reach for the photo of Céline and point to the name on the back.

'It says The Matrix Club,' I say. 'Were these photos taken there?'

She takes it back and smiles. 'Yes.'

'I looked it up. It's a strip club.'

'Back then it was different. A different kind of club.'

'An *échangiste?*'

'Yes, a swingers club. A lot happened through relationships back then. It was a time of change.'

'And exchange.'

'Why not?' she says. 'But it's not the kind of thing people boast about these days. Those clubs have a seedy reputation now.'

'I thought they were more popular than ever.'

She laughs. 'That's just tourists. No one in their right mind would use them now, times have changed.'

'You and Paul are respectable now.'

'Yes,' she says with a sigh. 'We are.'

'And that weekend we visited your house? Was that part of the scene?'

'There was no scene by then. It was all over long ago. That weekend was the end of our relationship. Eddy wanted information from Paul about certain people, personal details. I realised then he wasn't interested in me at all. We argued.'

'So not quite the drunkard you made out, then?'

'No,' she says quietly.

'Why didn't you tell me this before?'

Despite the sun, the breeze is cold and she pulls her jacket in around her. 'I worry about it all.'

'About what?' I say.

'About Eddy. I think perhaps he was onto something.' She looks at me, alarmed, as if she's only just thought of it, and then shifts and squares her body up to mine. 'One evening at our place, it was just before Christmas, I overheard him arguing with Patrick. Paul was there. They were discussing some kind of delivery, a messenger.'

'A messenger?'

'I asked Eddy about it later, and he made light of it, but I remember how startled he was when he realised I'd overheard them. More than startled, he was genuinely frightened.'

'Frightened you'd heard?'

She nods, her voice low. 'He was always quite open with me but when I asked, he clammed up, said it was nothing.' She stubs her cigarette against the bench and stands, puts the bundle of photos and letters into her bag. 'But he was too worried for it to be nothing. I didn't get to ask him about it again.'

She looks at me carefully, properly this time with her whole face. 'You know, you remind me a lot of him. Some of your mannerisms and the way you speak, constantly asking questions, never satisfied unless you've nailed things down. Eddy was like

173

that. He never let anything drop, just like you.' She laughs, 'And like you, he didn't care what people thought of him. He made enemies for no reason, attracted them like flypaper, but he didn't care.'

Then she pauses. 'The thing was – men tolerated him, women loved him, but no one really *liked* him, and he didn't mind. He enjoyed being an outsider.'

I watch her as she picks her way along the path, her spiked heels leaving puncture marks in the sandy gravel like the tracks of a sea bird stalking at low tide.

THEN

Late November

Twenty

Saint-Germain

I CALLED SAMI THE NEXT AFTERNOON, but he didn't call back. The shelter at Montparnasse had gone – a greasy stain on the pavement the only trace left. There'd been another crackdown, and the tents around the city had vanished. The Seine, Gare du Nord – all swept clear. The newspapers were full of stories about the 'Immigrant Invasion', and images of shanty towns and dirty, half-starved children filled the pages as they bulldozed the camps.

In our own apartment building it went on too. The residents vowed to douse any shelters that sprouted up on the pavement below with buckets of water from their balconies, like castle defenders in a medieval siege.

As I wandered the streets of Montparnasse looking for Sami and the girl, I tried to imagine where they might have gone, and whether there were even places that would take them. The girl and the baby – surely there would be some place for them, and so perhaps they had gone together to a refuge of some kind. But then I thought about the way Sami spoke of the authorities and I knew there was no way he'd be anywhere official. Each time I passed the greasy mark on the pavement it seemed to expand, until it took on an air of ugly familiarity, like the outline of a body at a crime scene. I wanted to find Sami because I needed the drugs, but the longer I looked for him the more anxious I became and the gloomier I felt. I started noticing things on the streets I otherwise wouldn't – drunks, addicts and other homeless types that drifted through the streets like ghosts. They had always been there, but I had never really seen them.

I'd almost given up when I saw the girl outside the metro a week later. Instead of the baby, she was with a small boy about four or five years old.

She looked frightened when I ran up to her and shrank back, pulling the boy with her. When I asked after Sami, she demanded money first, while the boy stepped forward and tugged at my pockets. I tried to grab his hands, but they slipped from my grasp, and then he lunged at me, laughing through gapped teeth like it was a game. I gave him a coin and wrote a message for Sami.

I passed it to the girl and she beamed at me, obviously thinking it was money. When she saw what it was, her face fell and I felt ashamed of myself, and the shame made me angry.

It was terrible they were on the street like this, dependent on the whim of strangers, on individual pity. I opened my wallet and gave her the note Tomas had given me the previous week, which I hadn't had the stomach to spend. It eased the guilt a little, or perhaps just made me feel a bit less helpless than her.

As I walked away, an old man shook his finger at me. 'These people are pests. If you give them money, you just encourage them to live on the streets like rats.'

*

At about midnight that evening, I heard my father come in. He opened my door a crack, and I pretended to be asleep. Afterwards, as I lay there, I had an idea – the first of many that seemed good at the time.

I waited until all was quiet then went into his study. He had a new laptop and a different password was scribbled on a Post-it note next to the keyboard.

I logged into the bank account he used most often and saw the withdrawals I'd made the week before camouflaged among similar payments to restaurants and bars. Scrolling through the list of payees, I found my account and transferred two hundred euros. I was just about to log out when I got greedy and went into another, dormant account for a second transfer of the same amount.

My palms sweated as they moved across the keyboard and once I'd done it, I felt ill. It was a lot of money I'd just stolen from my father, to do what? Buy drugs for Tomas and Lisa? I knew it was stupid. It was madness. But I was also thinking: how hard could this be? I was fed up with them pushing me around, throwing money at me, telling me what to do with their hungry eyes and inflated egos.

Just call him, just this once, and make the arrangement. We'll do the rest.

No, you won't, I thought. I'll do this properly, myself, and on my terms. I'll turn it round, and get the drugs with my own money. I'll win at this game, and you'll realise you're the ones who need me.

Like Tomas said, it would be worth my while, but not in the sense he meant. I'd buy the drugs alone, and then afterwards, once it was all done, I'd figure out how to pay back my father.

I closed down his laptop and sat there for a few moments, my head spinning.

Sami called me the next day and the line was noisy, full of static. I was excited to hear from him again, almost euphoric, and asked to meet that afternoon, before he changed his mind and I lost him again. When I told him how many pills I needed, he didn't sound surprised but said we couldn't meet in the neighbourhood this time as there had been trouble with the cops. He gave me an address up near the Péri and told me to meet him on Saturday, the day of Tomas's party.

I arrived early at the edge of a large street market. Stretched out along the road was a patchwork of blankets strewn with sunglasses, watches and cheap leather goods. Further down, people haggled over clothes, shoes and other junk. Hawkers jostled between the stalls, selling fake perfume and cigarettes from bags slung over their shoulders.

As I waited, two police cars pulled up. Their arrival sent a convulsion through the crowd and the stallholders scooped up their blankets, everyone scattering like birds. Within seconds the market had cleared, and in the space up ahead was Sami.

'See what I mean,' he said, nodding towards the cops who were checking the papers of some vendors they'd caught. The cops roughed them up a bit, putting on a show for those who watched from the shadows, waiting to set up again.

Sami darted across the road, and I followed, walking fast to keep up.

'We're going up north this time,' he said. 'Zone One is crawling with cops. They've stopped me three times this week.'

179

'What do you mean, *up north?*'

I patted the cash in my pocket for the hundredth time. I wanted to get the deal over with, and didn't want to go to whatever suburb he had in mind.

'Don't worry. They'll never stop you in this,' he said, pulling my collar. 'You look rich, so you can do anything. If you're poor, you're treated that way.'

I caught a glimpse of us in a shop window. He was right. His clothes were someone else's, even his trainers were the wrong size, making him shuffle and drag his feet. Although he had his own unique brand of confidence and swagger, he stood out, but it wasn't just what he wore. His face had a desperate, hungry look that nothing could disguise.

'We're meeting my cousin up at the camp,' he said, as we passed a row of butchers. Slabs of flesh and offal filled the greasy cabinets that faced the street. Further up, a group of women sold dried fish threaded on strings and bottles of home-made ginger juice from crates at the side of the road.

We took a bus north, leaving the cobbled streets behind as we followed a road flanked with sex shops and moneychangers. The bus swung through the tunnels of the Péri, then onto a motorway that cut through a low-rise stretch of warehouses and factories. Finally, we reached the Stade de France – the massive silver football stadium that hovered like a spaceship over the grey suburban wasteland.

We climbed over a metal barrier at the edge of a slip road and followed an overgrown track towards the canal. Rubbish clung to dusty trees on the side of the path, and plastic bottles lay wedged in the branches like toxic fruit.

After a while, the path widened and the camp appeared like a hallucination – a chaotic shanty town of cardboard, plastic, and corrugated iron hunkered in between a stagnant section of the canal and a building site. A smoky haze hung over the shacks, and the air felt close, almost thick enough to chew. A chill rose from the damp ground, and there was an eerie stillness to the place despite the roar from the motorway.

I stopped. It was getting dark and a sickening fear rose in me. 'I'm not sure about this,' I said, my skin starting to crawl.

Sami grinned and took my arm. His touch was like a flame and I recoiled.

'What is it?' he said, as I rubbed my arm wildly. 'Why are you always scratching yourself?'

'It's just eczema,' I said, trying to resist the urge to scratch my arm again. 'It's always worse when I'm nervous.'

'Come on, it's fine. You're with me. I won't let anything happen to you.'

I was reassured a little by his fearlessness, but I stayed close as he led me along the edge of the canal, past discarded oil drums and a burnt-out car on blocks. There was a stained mattress in the back seat, buckets and washing equipment in the boot and piles of rubbish all around. In one of the shacks further in, men watching television eyed us silently as we passed.

'There's power here?' I asked.

Sami pointed to thick cables twisting overhead and I saw the whole camp was rigged up to the mains electricity from the base of one of the floodlights on the Péri.

We passed some ragged kids poking at debris in the canal with long sticks, and I wondered what it was like to live in a place like this – right in the middle of a thriving city, but totally severed from it all, having to beg and steal for everything, even electricity.

I sensed the desperation of the place and was on high alert, patting my pocket constantly. As we went further into the camp, everything closed in behind us and I knew if anything went wrong, I'd be trapped. Chills spidered up my neck, but it was too late to back out now – I had to see it through.

'Do the cops ever come here?' I asked weakly, trying to sound calm, but wanting to see some sign of them now.

Sami shook his head. 'Everyone ignores this place – the government, the police. They keep talking about developing the site, evicting everyone, but nothing ever happens. If there's a fire, you can't get a truck, and no ambulance will ever come. But a no-go zone for them means a safe place for us.' He took my arm once more, but I was pretty sure I wasn't part of what he meant by 'us'.

Up ahead was a tightly built area of corrugated shacks leaning in against each other, rusted and falling apart like wreckage. Sami called out and a man appeared from one of the huts. He was short, but the forearms that stuck out from his sweater were like muscled ropes, covered with faded prison tattoos.

Sami took my cash and introduced him as Nick. I stayed back, trying to give the impression I wasn't nervous, but my heart thudded so hard I thought I was going to faint, and the whole landscape swooned around me.

'Whatever you need, call him first and then come here to collect it. Bring all the money, no credit,' Nick said in English as he counted the money. He had a strong accent, and spoke with a kind of slur as if the words were difficult to get out of his mouth. I couldn't take my eyes off his nose, which was flattened across his face like someone had tried to punch it through his head.

Nick and Sami spoke together in French for a while about some other deal, and then Nick raised his voice and threw in some angry hand gestures. I felt light-headed with fear, but I also got the sense Nick was putting on an act for my benefit, to let me know that even though he was short, he was tough. I had no doubt he was dangerous, probably capable of anything, but he'd overdone the performance, and it took the edge off my fear a little.

Finally, Nick turned to me with a cold stare, fanning the cash. 'There's not enough money here for what you want,' he said.

I watched him wave the money at me with a similar crazy confidence to Tomas, and suddenly my fear crystallised into an urgent need to get out of there. Something kicked into gear and I fell into role.

I looked at Sami. 'You already told me the price. Don't let him piss us around.'

Sami said something to Nick, which I didn't catch, but I got the sense he was on my side.

Nick spat onto the ground, the oily gob of phlegm landing near my foot.

We stood there arguing and trading prices for a while. Nick's face was hard and gave nothing away and although I was thinking fast, I realised I was stuck. Nick was already holding my money, and I had no idea how to even get out of this place, or what other dangers it held. Where there were drugs, there were also guns and knives, and I saw myself being chased by armed men along the paths between the huts if I even tried to make a run for it.

I knew I just had to tough it out as we haggled and Nick drew in closer.

I kept eye contact as I nudged my price closer to his, my heart thudding like a drum, until finally my persistence, or lack of options, paid off. Nick responded with a sharp nod as if we'd reached an understanding.

'This four hundred now, the rest next week,' he said.

When he said the amount like that, I felt a sudden paralysis and wanted to stop, to call the whole thing off. I knew it was reckless buying so many drugs, but I was in too deep, too high on the danger and smell of the deal, and so close to getting it, that there was no going back.

'Yes?' he asked, raising his hand. I thought he was about to hit me and I threw my arm up as a shield, but he laughed, grasped my hand and shook it in mid-air, then did a high five.

Finally, it seemed, we had a deal. The panic subsided and I felt a surge of relief, and a sense of power. I'd done this myself.

Nick invited me into his hut. A single bulb hung from the roof and damp rose from the bare dirt floor, which was covered by rugs a bit further in. A corridor of blue plastic sheeting led off to the left, to another room and the sound of a television. Nick pulled a plastic bag from a wall of milk crates stacked up as shelves. He counted out the pills, bagged them, and then watched as I rubbed the powdery residue from the bag along my gums the way I'd seen Lisa doing. It tasted bitter and I thought I saw him smirk as he watched me.

I felt like a fool standing there pretending I knew what I was doing. I thought of Lisa and Tomas, safe and comfortable on the other side of town, probably laughing together about their little drugs mule. But fuck them – here I was, doing this alone and they never could.

As I said goodbye to Nick, my phone rang. I reached for it then hesitated. It was the most valuable thing I owned. I didn't want Nick to see it in case he wanted it as collateral for the rest of the money I owed him, but he smiled and gestured for me to look at it.

When he saw my old phone, he laughed and went over to one of the crates, reached into a box and handed me the latest fake iPhone saying it was a present.

He shook my hand as we said goodbye. 'Don't forget the rest of the money next week,' he said.

Sami and I took the bus back. It was raining, and I watched through the windows as the darkening streets and factories turned back into smart apartments and tree-lined boulevards once we'd crossed the Péri. People relaxed in cafés, eating, drinking and enjoying their evenings.

I could still taste the powder, bitter on my tongue, and Sami looked at me with a new kind of respect. I wasn't just a pile of banknotes to him now, and back there with Nick he'd been on my side, helped me, and I hadn't embarrassed him. I felt closer to him now than Tomas or Lisa, or any of my so-called friends.

'I think my cousin likes you,' he said, putting his arm over my shoulder.

I laughed. 'What about you? You don't seem to get on that well for family.'

He winked. 'He's not really my cousin.'

'So who is he, then?'

'Just some guy I know who uses that camp as a front. He runs bars and clubs in Paris. Near where you met me that day.'

I thought back to when I'd met him and my admiration grew. He didn't have an overbearing father dragging him down, he was free from that, at least, but he was alone. Nick wasn't even his family.

'And you work for him?'

He didn't answer, and when I looked back, he'd gone. He was up ahead, behind a man with a map and a guidebook. As the man craned towards the fogged-up window, Sami took something from his pocket. The man hadn't noticed, just kept looking from the wet streets, back to his map. Sami weaved slowly through the crowded bus towards the doors and when the bus stopped, he leaped out into the night.

The bus lurched forward and I searched for Sami in the murky shapes beyond the wet glass but he'd gone. A police car levelled up, its red and blue lights hazing around the bus, its siren wailing. I zipped up my jacket and pressed myself into the seat as it swept past.

Tomas's party was held on a barge moored on a desolate stretch of river just south of Auteuil. Light from the motorway stretched across the water as I walked quickly along the bank, a cold wind driving through my jacket. I was tense after the trip to the camp and in no mood to celebrate. I knew I'd been invited to the party for one reason only, and I wanted to get the job over with – to give the pills to Tomas, get the cash and leave.

I hesitated when I saw the barge – a dark, rusty hulk strung with coloured fairy lights. Bad rap music blared from an empty dance floor on the first level, and it looked like a ghost ship that had drifted away from a theme park. A woman with a clipboard stood at the entrance above a red-carpeted gangplank and eyed me suspiciously. I patted my pockets, checking the pills were still there and then moved up the ramp.

Inside, a group of women sat around a table sipping champagne from brightly coloured flutes. I wasn't on the guest list, and the woman with the clipboard spoke to them, gesturing towards me as though I was a stray dog. As they sized me up, I realised that dropping pills here was not just a bad idea, it was insane.

Just then, Céline Chambière appeared with two bottles of champagne. She did a double take when she saw me.

'Alex!' she exclaimed. 'Come in. I didn't know you and Tomas were friends.'

I felt like a patient being admitted to hospital for some kind of awful procedure as she pulled two green rubber bands over my wrist – tokens for the bar.

A woman with big hair swung a camera towards me just as Lisa and her friends arrived. Lisa was back in party girl mode and wore a silky gold dress, her bare shoulders dusted with a kind of glittery powder and draped in a white fur stole. She squealed and threw her arms around my neck.

'I'm so pleased to see you,' she whispered, her breath smelling of alcohol and, faintly, of vomit. A dark slick of liner rimmed her eyes, the lids covered in glitter.

The woman with the camera veered towards us, and the girls fell into position, pouting as the camera flashed. I can still see those pictures now – Lisa's arm draped round my neck, Jeanne's head on my shoulder, their pupils dark pools. Seven months later, the papers got hold of those images and used them after my trial – a warning to the world about the dangers of too much pocket money. In those pictures I look like a pumped-up moron with a conceited, dimpled smile, but all I remember was feeling anxious and way out of my depth.

I followed the girls to the top deck. The barge swayed on the river, the breeze off the water cold and sharp. Up ahead, the river widened around a small island and distant city lights stained the clouds a dull yellow.

Lisa took a joint from her bag, toasting it carefully above a lighter, her white teeth glinting in the flame.

'You need to be careful tonight,' she said, holding the smoke in her lungs, then smiling mischievously as she exhaled. 'They think someone's *dealing*.' She tapped the end of the joint with a glitter-encrusted nail. 'Tell him, Jeanne.'

Jeanne took the joint and leaned against the railing. 'My mum found your skunk in my desk.'

'It's not *my* skunk,' I said.

'And when I got hold of her phone, I saw a thread about someone bringing dope to the party.'

'That's why all the mums are here. To keep an eye on things,' said Lisa, taking another drag. 'Don't look so worried. All I'm saying is they're onto it.'

'Of course I'm fucking worried,' I said, wondering whether I should just throw the pills overboard, like a drug smuggler avoiding the coast patrol.

'Relax,' said Jeanne, taking out her phone. She put the joint in my mouth and took a selfie with both of us in the frame.

'Don't worry, they're just jealous. And besides, they're too busy getting drunk downstairs,' said Lisa, finishing the joint before throwing it over the side.

At the bar, we traded our wristbands for tiny glasses of champagne. Lisa threw hers back, refilling the glass with vodka from her bag. Coloured lights strobed the dance floor, and a few people danced in a fog of dry ice. There was a queue along the gang-plank now, and people from school who usually ignored me waved through the windows.

Lisa toasted my glass. 'Your new best friends.'

I smiled, but the talk of the snooping mothers had made me think that the more people arrived, the bigger the problem.

It wasn't long before that hand was on my shoulder again. This time Tomas was completely out of it – pupils dilated, swaying and giggling, looking nothing like his usual hockey jock, psycho self.

'Your party's crawling with parents,' I yelled above the noise.

He laughed hysterically and led me across the room to a small utility cabin, the crowd parting before us. He was sweating, but the maniac was gone and his grin was just creepy under the bright cabin lights.

'I'm sorry about what happened before, man,' he slurred, taking the bag of pills from me and waving them around. He held them up to the light, trying to focus. 'I thought you were some kind of a loser, you know.'

He fished into the bag and took out two pills. Yellow powder flaked off on his fingers, and then he dropped the bag on the floor, the pills rolling around his feet.

'Oops,' he said, dissolving in a fit of laughter as he crawled around scooping up the pills.

When he stood, he moved in close, stuffed a roll of notes in my pocket and put his arm around me. 'I want us to be friends,' he said. He was hot and clammy through his shirt, swaying and waving the bag around. He lost his balance, and we both lurched towards the wall.

I was getting the sense that being his friend, even his pretend friend, might be worse than being his enemy, and I pushed him away.

There was a banging on the door and loud yelling above the music.

'This is a bust!' Lisa said, forcing the door open. She laughed at our expressions and went from Tomas to me, looking for the pills. Her arms were around Tomas now, and she held him in a way that was familiar to them both.

It was my cue to leave. 'Have a great time you two,' I said, and I left them to it as I hurried from the party.

The steady rocking of the metro soothed me on the long trip back to Saint-Germain, and my breath returned as the train took me further away from Lisa and Tomas and their crazy world. I felt like I'd won this bout, got Tomas off my back and clawed back some status and power. Yes, I'd been reckless, but now that I'd done it, I felt exhilarated. I had them in my hand now, and they needed me. You don't get all that without taking risks.

Twenty-One

Saint-Germain

'**I**s that you, Alex?' my father said, stepping into the hall. 'We've been worried about you. I've been calling.'

'What's wrong?' I said, closing the door, fear crawling up my back. Patrick and Elena were at the dining table, food almost untouched on their plates. They glanced at me, returning their gaze to the TV, which flashed with the lights of emergency vehicles.

'There's been a car bomb near Issy,' said my father.

'And riots at Saint-Denis,' said Patrick, gesturing to an empty chair. 'Come. Sit down.'

The screen showed a line of police, then paramedics lifting a foil-blanketed body into an ambulance. Flashing lights strobed the bewildered faces of a gathering crowd. Some were agitated, hands in the air, while others watched through their phones, filming. Then a wide shot to a car parked against a rough stone wall, red flames engulfing the front, thick black smoke billowing from its charred and mangled rear.

'It's near one of our offices,' said Elena, her hand shaking as she pointed her cigarette at the screen. 'Our office is just there. That car's in the space where I sometimes park.'

191

'Who is it?' I asked my father.

He shook his head. 'No one's claimed it yet.'

Patrick read his phone. 'People say it's an Islamist attack of some kind. The numbers are all over the place. Some saying two dead, others six. Some say none – just injuries.'

The screen switched to a newsroom – a panel of talking heads and commentary. They debated the possible culprits – a separatist cell, the Corsicans, various Islamist groups.

Patrick went back to his food. 'But what's the target?'

'I was there this afternoon,' said Elena, her face pale.

'It's near one of the old fort sites,' my father said, scanning his phone, his face full of concern. 'Fort D'Issy. Someone mentioned this to me a few weeks ago.'

'Mentioned what?' said Elena.

'I lost the material when my laptop was hacked. There's a lot of activity down there – demonstrations about a big new development.'

'The headquarters of the Gendarmerie Nationale is at the Fort D'Issy,' said Patrick, scrolling through his phone.

'Perhaps they're the target. The police,' said my father.

'There's also a refugee centre there. It could be that?' said Elena, more as a question than a statement. Her face was crumpled, agitated.

Patrick forked the air. 'Why would a refugee centre be a target?'

My father filled the glasses. 'In-fighting.'

'Doesn't make sense,' Patrick said.

'Then it's a warning of some kind.'

I sat with them as they debated motives for the attack. After a while, the discussion shifted and Elena spoke about the work she was doing with youth groups and charities in that area.

'You have to put up with Jean-Marc,' said my father. 'That would take more charity than I have.'

'Oh, come on, Eddy. You had lunch with him just the other week. Why have lunch together if you loathe him?'

'It was work.'

Elena was quiet as she stacked the plates. 'He's not so bad. He wants to do something,' she said softly.

'Well, he has the money,' said my father. 'It's easy to be public-spirited if you're loaded.'

Elena walked to the kitchen with the plates. 'A lot of people are loaded, but very few share it.'

My father raised his glass. 'Careful, you sound like one of his disciples now.'

Elena turned. 'What do you mean by that?'

'Paul and those other sycophants.'

'Are you saying I'm a sycophant?'

'Just that he's surrounded by them these days.'

'That says more about Paul than Jean-Marc,' said Patrick.

'Jean-Marc's made a lot of money,' said Elena. 'People respect what he's done. Money talks, Eddy, stop being such a purist.'

'But what does it say? That's the question,' my father said.

'You're offending me now, you know exactly what he does and that I work with him,' Elena said from the kitchen.

He poured another glass and raised it to her. 'Indeed.'

My father always talked like this with his friends, his banter amiable but barbed, and the shape of the debate was always the same. He would begin with something minor, but his anger would increase as the night wore on, fuelled by his drinking and the knowledge he couldn't fix things. He used to believe his job would lead to change, but now I sensed he wasn't quite so sure.

Many of his friends, like Elena, had ditched journalism altogether, and this often provoked him. He said it was an abandonment of the cause, but sometimes I think it was just envy that they made more money. I knew his anger flared with the amount of alcohol he consumed, and the uncertainty that now clouded the convictions he once held.

As he refilled the glasses, his voice took on a pompous tone. 'We see this more and more – having to rely on the whim of philanthropists for essential public services the government won't implement. It's worrying.'

Elena walked in from the kitchen with a platter of cheese. 'Jean-Marc's hardly a philanthropist. But as I said, at least he's doing something—'

'—and not just writing about it,' he said.

She glared at him. 'You said it, not me.'

'Although you seem to be writing for him these days too. Stories that subtly promote his interests, his plans for the suburbs.'

'How dare you say that! He's never told me what to write.'

'Perhaps because he doesn't need to.'

She turned to the cheese, hacking off huge wedges. 'Where does this self-righteousness come from, Eddy? And this hypocrisy! You seem to be forgetting you were told what to write once. That you had a job like that, and that your eyes were on the money.'

I stayed with them as they got drunker, the conversation circling around the same old topics – schemes to change things they never could, dissecting the motivations of people they didn't know. They only half-acknowledged me, glancing over when their arguments needed support which I gave by nodding or smiling. As the evening wore on, I barely followed the conversation, but I wonder now whether traces of what was said stayed with me so that the sudden understanding that came to me much later had actually been building for some time.

I was up early the next morning searching for the money Tomas had given me at the party. I checked my pockets, but it wasn't there. I was just going through my chest of drawers and trying not to panic when Lisa sent a series of texts:

> What kind of shit were those pills?
> We were all off our heads
> They had to call an ambulance
>
>
>
> Tomas wants to kill you

I tried calling, but she didn't answer.

I was used to Lisa's habit of making a big deal after a heavy night, so I tried to put it out of my mind. But I kept getting flashbacks of the party – the greedy look on her face when she saw the pills, Tomas's hysterical laughter, the powder that came off on his fingers, his slurred declarations of friendship, the two of them together. The scenes flashed in my head like the whirling lights of the dance floor, and the urgent flares of the ambulances and police cars on TV.

The next day at school, Tomas and some others were off sick. There was a weird silence in lessons, and Lisa avoided me until I cornered her after class.

'What's wrong? What happened at the party?' I asked.

'Sebastian collapsed and had to be ambulanced out,' she hissed. 'You're in trouble.'

'What? Why is it my fault?'

'Those pills were poison.'

'They can't have been,' I said weakly, sickness rising in me. 'And anyway, I did this for you. You're in this too.'

She leaned forward, jabbing my chest, her face sharp and vicious. 'No. I am *not* in this. This is your mess. *You* clean it up.'

The tense atmosphere at school continued to build for the rest of that week and everyone avoided me. My father was out each night and so I was alone in the evenings, panicking, googling 'ecstasy side-effects', 'drug sickness', then at eleven o'clock on Friday I was called to the head teacher's office.

I arrived at her door at the same time as my father, who looked a wreck – unshaven and in last night's clothes. Mme. Vaux regarded us both with distaste as she listed the charges against me. She described me as a menace to the student body and each time she criticised me, she bounced a pencil on its rubber end like a miniature judge's mallet.

I tried denying it all, but she said 'sources' had me down as the supplier of the drugs, and they had pictures of me smoking dope at the party. Most damning of all, Lisa had photos I sent her of the pills we took at the club on her phone. I tried saying it was all their idea, but Mme. Vaux shook her head as though I was insane.

I sat there, frozen to the seat, unable to do anything but stare back at her. Time stretched out in all directions as she stacked up the evidence against me.

I thought of the kids at the party and hated them all. It was so typical to blame the source, rather than the buyers, and what about the parents who gave their kids all that money in the first place?

My father made no real attempt to defend me. He spoke in unfinished sentences, his voice distant, as if coming from another galaxy. He looked bewildered, struggling to take it in, and I almost felt sorry for him, as full of shame and self-pity as I was.

When the police were mentioned, my stomach hollowed out. I sensed I was no longer in control of myself, or what happened next. I felt detached, like all of this was happening to someone else.

Finally, Mme. Vaux placed her hands on the table as if she was about to launch herself across the desk like a missile. She said Tomas's father would press charges unless I was removed from the school with immediate effect.

My father pulled himself together at this point and leaned forward with his hands clasped, saying that technically, I hadn't taken drugs to school, it was a private party. He spoke very politely, grovelled a lot, and tried to argue that expulsion was excessive for one stupid mistake. He asked that I be granted one more chance. I looked over at him surprised and impressed, at first. It was a good try, but it didn't work. Vaux said the school had a policy of zero tolerance concerning drugs. This was all bullshit, of course. She knew damn well those kids had more drugs than a Colombian cartel, with or without me.

The more my father defended me, the sicker I felt. I knew how much he hated pleading with people like Vaux – he thought it was way beneath him. The more he grovelled, the more furious he became beneath his calm facade, and I began to fear the punishment that would come later.

Finally, with a face like the grave, Mme. Vaux said the school's decision had been made and that I was expelled with immediate effect.

Afterwards, I felt weak, but partly relieved. Finally, a decision had been made, and I could escape from everything that had been oppressing me. I walked from school with my father, pleased he'd eventually stood up for me, and enjoying the feeling of us being on the same side for a change. I didn't care about school; in fact, the thought of leaving wasn't a bad idea at all.

As we entered the metro, the relief I felt took on a kind of euphoria, and I almost didn't care what happened next. Matters were out of my hands. I felt weightless and almost laughed out loud, but my father's face was thunderous.

His hand shook getting out his pass, and he stood with his back to me on the metro, knuckles white around the handrail. He didn't speak to me on the train or on the short walk home, and just glanced over once in the lift as if wondering who I was.

The brief sense of relief evaporated as we entered the apartment and his wrath came crashing down upon me.

'Sit down!' he roared when we got to his study. 'Tell me what's been going on.'

'She's been dying to get rid of me ever since I started there, you know that.'

'I'm not talking about school. Since when did you become a *drug dealer?*'

He turned to the drinks cabinet, poured a large Scotch, threw it back like medicine, and then immediately poured another. The afternoon sun flooded the room, reflecting off the glassy floorboards. The harsh light brought out the lines on his face, and he looked completely exhausted, his mouth a grim, bloodless streak.

I told him everything that had happened with Lisa and Tomas, saying I'd bought the drugs from a random outside school. Afterwards, there was a long silence. Finally, he buried his head in his hands and I thought for an awful moment he was going to cry.

'Everyone at school takes drugs, Dad. Mme. Vaux knows that. This is just an excuse to throw me out.'

He lifted his head. 'I can't believe you did all this for Tomas. What were you thinking?'

'You've always wanted me to be friends with people like him. It's the reason you sent me to that school in the first place.'

'But Tomas *Chambière*?'

He said the name in a way that made me think his main concern wasn't me, but the impact this would have on whatever was going on between him and Céline.

'Look at the way you suck up to the Chambières. Going to their place for the weekend, drinking with Paul at every opportunity.'

I was going to say 'fucking his wife', but I stopped myself.

'You're worse than Mum,' I said instead.

'Don't compare me to your mother.'

'At least she admits it.'

'I'm in contact with the Chambières because of something I'm working on. That's why we're friends. I know them through *work*. I didn't intend for you to become their son's dealer,' he said pompously.

His lecherous double standards enraged me. 'So how else was I to become his friend? Do I walk up to him and ask him nicely? Or perhaps I should have just slept with his girlfriend. Is that the way these friendships work?'

His face hollowed out. 'What on earth do you mean by that?' he said, hoarsely.

He turned and poured himself another Scotch, his hand shaking. His drinking had always been furtive in the apartment, he'd never drunk so openly in front of me at home before.

I had the urge to knock the glass out of his hand.

'Look at you with that Scotch. You've been out every night this week, getting pissed. And you think I'm the one with the problem.'

'Drinking's not illegal, Alex. And I've been out for *work*, not *getting pissed*.'

'How can you stand there lying and lecturing me about drugs while throwing back Scotch? You're such a hypocrite.' I grabbed my bag and jacket.

'Where do you think you're going?'

'Out.'

'Not after today, you're not. You're grounded.'

'Fuck you!' I yelled as I walked down the hall, slamming the front door behind me.

It was late when I got home and I entered the apartment quietly. There was a heavy smell of perfume, and the air felt unsettled, as if people had just been in the hall. A door closed softly up ahead.

Two wine glasses were on the sideboard, their bowls stained red, and under my father's door there was a faint glow. I heard a woman's muffled voice, and then the light went out.

I lay in bed, staring at the ceiling. A knocking started up against the wall. It got louder and, knowing what was coming next, I put my hands over my ears and curled onto my side. I couldn't stand this. I flipped over, pulling a pillow over my head and pressed myself into the mattress.

Later in the night, I woke. There was no moon, and I walked down the corridor. Stepping into the bathroom, I caught a whiff of the same perfume and sensed someone there. I stood still, and in the dim light I made out a form on the toilet. At first, I thought I was hallucinating and strained my eyes against the darkness. Her body was braced forward, her blonde hair over her face as if she was hiding from my sight. She wore something black and tight, shiny, like latex or leather and kind of trashy. I took a step backwards, and she screamed.

My father appeared in the hall, a towel around his waist, his hair wild. 'What the hell's going on?' he said, switching on the light.

I squinted away from the glare of the lights. 'And you think I'm the one with the problem.'

He grabbed my shoulder, but I shook him off. 'I don't care what the fuck you do, but don't tell me this is *work*.'

I pushed past him to my room and locked the door.

NOW

Twenty-Two

Saint-Germain

I WATCH CÉLINE WALK AWAY, TRYING to unravel the threads she's thrown me. Even if my father had been writing about himself and his colleagues, why did she want to hide it? She passed it off as an old story, something everyone knew, but this was the first I'd heard of it.

Like most journalists, my father loved to talk. He often presented his ideas as news, putting forward his opinions as facts, so the story about him writing a memoir makes sense. But while he sometimes overestimated people's interest in what he had to say, it was difficult to accept he was just digging up old news. My father, even as drink sodden as Céline claimed he was, would never waste time on an old story, even if it did involve him.

When I arrive at my aunt's, she's on the phone. She nods towards lunch preparations on the side, and I turn on the stove, chop ham and chives then pour the omelette mixture into the pan.

'Did my father mention he was writing a memoir?' I say, when she gets off the phone. 'About something he was doing years ago at *La Globe*?'

Her smile drops, her eyes dark and thoughtful against her pale face. 'No. Why do you ask?'

'Céline Chambière mentioned it.'

She looks startled. 'You spoke to Céline?'

'I saw her.'

I tell her how I found Céline's letters and photos, and about our meeting. She listens as she cuts her food into small pieces. When I finish, there's a long silence.

'Was this what Patrick was looking at down in the cellar?' I ask.

She shakes her head. 'Patrick said it was your father's work files that interested him.'

'Work files? Why was Patrick looking at his work files?'

'I don't know what he was looking at,' she says helplessly. Her evasiveness is starting to grate.

'I can't believe Patrick was here going through Dad's *work files* without discussing it, even vaguely. You said you often had lunch together. You must have talked about what he was doing down there.'

She puts her cutlery down sharply. 'I haven't seen Eddy's papers, and I don't want to. That's why I accepted Patrick's offer to sort through them.'

She changes the topic, and we talk about other things. Once we've finished eating, I revisit the topic of the files, reminding her that she said I could go down to the cellar and see them myself. Given what was in the shoebox, and Patrick's keen interest, they could be worth a close look.

She makes excuses, but I insist, spurred on by her reluctance and after we've cleared up, she leads me down the back stairs to the storage rooms in the cellar.

We walk along the dark corridor, empty except for a few rat traps and old cleaning equipment. Finally, she stops at one of the doors and gropes for the keys, her face silhouetted against the damp cement walls. Inside, she fumbles with a switch.

'The lights have blown,' she says, her voice tinged with relief.

I hold out my phone, and a beam of white light pans the small room. On one side, about ten cardboard boxes are stacked haphazardly against the raw, breezeblock walls. In the middle of the room an old desk with a fringed lamp gives the place the air of a military bunker, and next to the desk, there are two grey filing cabinets. Béa switches on the lamp, blows dust off the desk and looks around the room as if taking it all in for the first time.

'There might be enough light by this lamp,' she says.

Or we could just change the main bulb, I think, wondering if this is another way to limit my access.

She points to the boxes against the wall. 'He was sorting through all the papers in there. Anything still relevant on a personal level, he brought up to me, the rest he'd either throw out or put into some kind of order in these filing cabinets.'

She switches on a small radiator then touches my shoulder. 'I'll leave you to it, but don't stay long. Being down here will bring back lots of memories, I'm sure.'

She disappears into the darkness of the corridor and her steps recede, then a door slams.

I move to the boxes, open the top one and peer inside, aided by the torch on my phone.

It takes a while to focus on what I'm seeing – rows of wire coils, and then I realise the box is packed with the spiral-bound reporters' notebooks my father used. I remember them spread over his desk as he worked into the night. He'd flick back over their pages, then to the screen, checking his notes against what he'd typed.

He was always strangely guarded about these notebooks, which he tied into bundles and stacked high on the bookshelves. He never locked them away, but I knew not to touch them, and I feel the same prohibition now. His presence is so intense I get a whiff of his aftershave and glance around quickly, expecting to see him at the door.

Just looking, Dad, I say, blinking the image away as I carry the box to the desk.

Sitting down, I select a notebook. It's from his time in Cairo in the eighties. The paper is thin, torn from the binding, and the ink is blurred, seeping through where the paper has caught the damp. Reading his messy handwriting – notes, diagrams and his own shorthand – I'm overcome with memories of the language he used: a mix of French and English, his quirky sayings and sharp insights. As I read, I see his movements and hear his words, laced with irony and sarcasm, interrupted with short bursts of laughter. It's like turning the pages on a manuscript in a museum, one I've seen many times and know through the glass, but have never been able to touch.

I take my time, immersed in the strangeness of these snatched moments jotted down in haste in the busy heat of Egypt, now read slowly by me, more than thirty years later, in this damp cellar.

I have to stop after a few pages, overcome with the claustrophobic sense of him. I walk to the door, brace myself on the frame and take several deep breaths. I pace the corridor then come back inside, empty the box and stack the notebooks on the desk.

At the bottom of the box is a layer of business cards of politicians, embassy officials and diplomats. Then my father's press passes in French and English, and other official authorisations. Some have his photo attached, taken in the days when he had a full head of hair and a thick handlebar moustache. I lay them out in date order and scan the blurred snapshots, the thick-rimmed glasses whose frames gradually recede along with his hair until, finally, they are rimless, his hair greyed and thin.

I move to the filing cabinets. Inside, old manila folders hang in suspension files, some several inches thick, with headings in my father's handwriting.

There's a damp smell coming off them and lifting one out, I see spots of mould. I take several files to the desk and start sorting through them. Each folder contains newspaper clippings and magazine articles, some sections marked with highlighter pen, or Post-it notes.

I spend a few hours going through the filing cabinets and see that each folder has a different news story that follows the same pattern – a chronology of articles from small papers in remote parts of India, Asia or Africa. Then, several months later, the story is picked up in other, Western countries. In France, the stories were written by Paul, Elena, my father and Jean-Marc, together with several other journalists at *La Globe* whose names I don't recognise.

Finally, at the back of the cabinet, there's a larger blue file with pages clipped together – lists and email printouts. It's labelled VESTNIK in handwriting other than my father's.

There's a typed page with the following words:

VESTNIK

LISSA

GOLUB

KRASNY

OREL

LISSA is circled, and next to the other words are initials in my father's handwriting, some crossed out and replaced by other initials or question marks.

The next note, again in my father's handwriting:

The New Year's payments make my involvement clear as Lissa.

From 1974–8, I received 50,000 francs a year in salary, 72,000 bonus and 58,000 expenses. From 1978–1980, I received 57,000 francs a year in salary, 88,000 bonus and 65,000 expenses.

Who was Vestnik? Paul? – he bought the hamlet near Épernay in the eighties . . . but no proof.

His *involvement* as Lissa . . .? I think back to what Céline said when I met her.

It was a scandal involving his old colleagues from La Globe.

These must be the names of the agents she spoke about – and the crossed-out initials and question marks mean what? That he knew their codenames but not who they were?

He didn't know *exactly* who they were, apart from him, but he had his suspicions.

After this note, the word 'Vestnik' is repeated, with another question mark. There's a hole in the paper at the top of the 'I', like my father has ground his pen through with the effort of concentration.

The bank accounts attached are my father's, dated 1974–1978, and show various payments struck through with yellow highlighter.

I sit back and scan the files on the desk – piles of folders, each section containing different articles on the same story or news piece.

They ran false stories – spread misinformation and propaganda.

At the very back of the filing cabinet are newer documents and maps of Paris with places in the suburbs marked in red. Amongst these pages are random addresses, numbers and dates. Then there's a sheet headed 'Gateway' with a series of shorthand notes. At the bottom a phone number and a name, Mari, scrawled in large letters and circled several times. I take down the details on my phone.

It's colder now, and my fingers are starting to cramp. As I replace the files and notebooks, I see a brown envelope clipped to the back of the filing cabinet. labelled ISSY – CAR BOMB. Inside is a single CD-ROM and three fuzzy polaroid pictures of my father's beaten-up face, others of his body, bound in thick black ropes.

In the images he's clearly unconscious, beaten badly. I take the photos and the CD-ROM upstairs.

It's dark in the apartment, and my aunt's on her laptop in the kitchen.

'How long did Patrick spend down there?' I ask, sitting opposite her at the table.

'A few days.'

'But you said he was here for weeks.'

'He was. At first he was in the apartment. Then, after the robberies he moved everything to the cellar.'

'Robberies?'

'There were a series of break-ins in the building and after that, Patrick worked downstairs.'

'Why?'

She shrugs. 'He said things were taking longer than he thought and it would be better if he worked in the cellar. I told you I gave him a key so he could come and go as he pleased. It suited him not to have to wait until I was home.'

'So what kept him busy for so long? You said Patrick told you it was a puzzle. What did he mean by that?'

She moves her laptop aside. 'He was here a lot, but I didn't ask what he was doing. I knew he'd tell me when he was ready.'

She returns to her laptop, and there's silence apart from the click of the keyboard.

'Do you believe he killed himself?' I say.

She raises her eyebrows, but her eyes stay on the screen. 'That was what everyone said.'

'Do you believe what everyone says?'

She stops typing. 'Of course not, you know I don't.' She stands and walks across the room. 'It's all very sad. At Patrick's funeral, people said he was depressed. Perhaps that's true, and this was a diversion. Perhaps he was hiding it by throwing himself into your father's files.'

'But not throwing himself into the river?' I say.

She lets out a deflated sigh. 'I don't know. He *seemed* fine. But how do you know? And sitting there all day going through Eddy's files would be enough to make anyone depressed.'

I'm used to her putting a spin on things, but this is something else. After a while impatience gets the better of me.

'Can you just tell me what was going on?'

'Nothing was going on, Alex. I don't know why you're obsessed with all of this.'

'With what? What are you saying?'

'With these conspiracy theories. That someone else killed Eddy. That Patrick didn't kill himself.'

'Patrick was a war correspondent. He'd seen worse things than my father's files. You don't really think he killed himself, do you?'

She looks at me, helplessly. 'I don't know.'

'Well, I'll tell you what I think. I think Patrick's death is linked to my father's. I think Patrick was killed because of something he'd found out about my father, probably down there in his files.'

'He was just helping me! I'd hate it if that had anything to do with his death.'

She stands and walks across the room.

Finally, she looks over. 'There was a woman at Patrick's funeral who knew Patrick had been looking at Eddy's files. It threw me because not even Elena knew Patrick had been working here.'

'What did she say?'

'Not a lot. There were many people at the funeral. She took my number, and said she'd be in touch.'

'Did you hear from her?'

'No, but the strange thing was she found me and connected with me on Facebook.'

'Show me,' I say, as she opens up Facebook.

'That's strange. She's not here,' she says, pushing the screen away.

I take the computer and scroll through her friends. 'Do you mind if I look for a while?'

'Of course not,' she says, leaving the room to make a call.

It's been years since I logged into my Facebook account because we weren't allowed access to social media in prison. I enter my details, and it's all still there, dormant. I scan the updates and messages from people whose names I barely remember, whose lives mean nothing to me now.

I'm about to log out when a message pops up:

> Hi, Alex,
> Strange seeing you here again!
> Welcome back!
> Tomorrow 6 p.m. then?
> Lisa xxx

Twenty-Three
Les Halles

I STARE AT LISA'S MESSAGE, UNABLE to understand why, just a week after accusing me of stalking her, she'd write to me on Facebook. It doesn't make sense, but perhaps she hasn't changed and still feels the need to stir things up.

I think about her all night, trying to resist the strong pull back, more outrage now than anything physical, but in the morning, I still can't let it go. My parole officer said I couldn't contact her, but as she initiated contact, I can't see the harm in replying – that's not stalking, after all. So I message her back agreeing to meet at a bar that evening, then take a screenshot to prove she wrote to me first.

I spend most of the day in my aunt's cellar going through my father's files and then later, I ring Elena. It takes me a while to circle around the topic I actually want to discuss.

'Of course, I don't have a list of people there. Funerals don't have guest lists, you know,' she says.

'Béa said she met someone. A woman. I need to know who she was.'

There's silence down the line.

'They were discussing what Patrick was working on,' I add.

'Why would *Béatrice* be discussing what Patrick was working on?'

I listen while she lights a cigarette and takes a drag, her voice softening with the exhalation.

'I don't remember much about that day, Alex. It passed in a blur – people pressing my hand, mumbling support. I remember things like what Patrick was wearing in the coffin, and what Nathan said to me, but not much else.'

'His death doesn't make sense,' I say quietly.

'Suicide doesn't make sense.'

There's a long silence, and I almost think she's hung up, but then she speaks. 'The thing is, everyone wants an explanation as to why Patrick killed himself, and they want it from me. Was he unhappy at work? Having an affair? Was he gay? Surely I'd have known. I've been asked all these questions and blamed in many different ways, but this kind of speculation goes nowhere. It's a fantasy, a reflection of people's own obsessions and fears.'

'I think someone killed Patrick. And I think whoever it was also killed my father.'

She inhales deeply. 'Like I said, Alex – this idea their deaths are linked, that's just your fantasy.'

'So what's the explanation?' I ask.

'There is no explanation. Patrick was in a dark place, incomprehensible to everyone, including himself. Just leave it alone,' she says, then hangs up.

Before I leave the apartment, I make another call to the number I found in my father's files – Mari. There's no answer

214

so I send a text, explaining who I am and asking whether we could speak.

It's just past seven when I exit the metro at Châtelet. I hesitate at the ticket barrier, with an overwhelming urge to turn back, but force myself through, and then walk slowly past the shops and cafés leading to the Forum des Halles. The warm day has turned cool, and groups of people gather under heaters drinking and laughing.

Nearing the bar, a sense of disorientation takes hold. The light sharpens, pulling everything into focus, and there's a shift in frequency. Conversations, music, the clink of plates, all increase in volume like I'm tuning into several radio stations at once. I feel a wave of exhilaration, a kind of nervous dizziness like I'm sixteen again, and heading out on a date with Lisa.

Then I pass my reflection in the mirrored window of a shop – bad haircut, old clothes, scuffed trainers – and the feeling evaporates. She might not even recognise me.

But I have no trouble recognising her. She's on the terrace wearing ripped jeans and a grey puffa jacket, taking photos of a small white dog sitting at her feet, her blonde hair shielding her face like a curtain. As I draw closer, she turns for the ashtray, and then freezes, nothing but a winding coil of smoke between us.

'You haven't changed at all,' she lies, throwing her arms around me and pulling me onto the seat beside her.

'Of course, I have,' I say, laughing. 'At least, I hope I have.'

We talk for a while, and she tells me she's working as a reporter for an online journal, and then she lapses into silence, not looking at me, her hands fidgeting – patting the dog, smoking.

I want to come straight out with it – ask her about the stalking allegation, and why she wants to see me now, but I decide to wait until she mentions it. She doesn't say a thing, and I wonder if she's just buying time.

'Sorry I never visited you,' she says, bending down to grind her cigarette on the floor. A trail of mousy roots pushes out along the parting of her hair. Her legs are crossed, foot tapping nervously. Her knee pokes out of her jeans, which gape in frayed designer slashes all the way up her thighs, reminding me of the cuts she used to have there.

'It's fine. The thing is when you're locked up, visitors are just another part of the punishment.'

I always hated receiving visitors. The way they'd look around, logging the details, and asking about life inside as if it was some kind of holiday camp: *What's the food like? Are you getting enough exercise?* It was exhausting dealing with these questions.

She reaches over, places her hand on my arm. 'I'm sorry.'

Suddenly, I sense she's playing with me again. 'How can you be *sorry* after what you said to the police?'

'What?'

'You complained I was *stalking* you.'

'*Stalking me?*'

'Come on, Lisa. My parole officer said you called the police. Apparently, you saw me in a café at the end of your street.'

She shakes her head. 'This is the first time I've seen you in over seven years.'

'So who made the complaint?' I'm trying not to yell, but my voice is getting louder.

She backs her chair away. 'I have no idea. Why were you stalking me?'

The dog barks and I look up. The people at the next table are staring.

'I wasn't! Come on, Lisa, what's going on? Why did you want to meet me today? Is this a trap? Have you called the cops? What do you want?'

The dog snarls at me, lips peeled back to reveal ugly little teeth, white eyebrows bristling over beady eyes.

She bends over to soothe it. 'I didn't complain about anything. I don't want any more to do with the cops than you do. I was just glad to get your email last week.'

My chest lurches. 'What email?'

She rolls her eyes. 'Your email. You can't remember?' She picks up her phone, starts scrolling. 'Here it is. *Hi, Lisa. How are you? Want to meet for a drink?*'

I snatch her phone. The email, sent from my account, suggested we meet at a café near her place.

I stare at her as she chews her lip. 'Yeah, I thought it was strange to meet there and I couldn't anyway, because I had work, so I emailed back and then you replied, suggesting we meet there today.'

'I replied?'

'From another email. You freaked me out a bit, actually, after all this time. She shakes her head, takes her phone and shows me the other message. 'I didn't reply to that one. Then I felt bad when I saw you were back on Facebook last night, so I sent you that message,' she says.

Checking my own phone, I see nothing to her in my sent box. I feel dazed, not sure if she's lying and I don't want to know the consequences if she isn't.

'What the hell is going on? I didn't send those emails,' I say. 'Someone's hacked my account.'

'But who?'

'They'd have to hate me a lot to set me up like this. If I were actually stalking you I could go straight back inside.'

I look at the photos on my phone, find the screenshot of her Facebook message. 'Why did you say *Welcome back* if we'd already been emailing?'

She looks at it. 'Welcome back to Facebook is what I meant.'

I study the email on her phone again, trying to work out who it could be.

'But seriously, Alex, who would do this?'

I head into the café, and then downstairs to the bathroom, needing to get away from her to get some quiet, to think alone.

Is she lying to me again? But why? Or could it be him? I stare in the mirror, my mind on Sami, of course. There's a heavy ache in my chest and it feels bad blaming him, and unoriginal – like reaching for the same excuse just because it worked last time.

I turn on the tap, splash water on my face and notice that my hands are shaking. Guilt about Sami is distorting things, keeping me from seeing things properly, but there's a pattern now – the guy chasing me the other night, the break-in, the positive drugs test and now this stalking set-up.

It was too easy to blame Sami, although at first it made sense – I was convinced he was consumed by the same obsession as me. But now the harassment has increased, I know it isn't him. It's hard enough in prison to get a shower, let alone fix something outside. And while he has good reason to hate me, this just isn't his style. If he wanted revenge he'd just take it, not mess around with me like this.

I know it's not Sami. I can't blame him. I can't even say his name.

Twenty-Four

Les Halles

WHEN I RETURN TO THE terrace, my thoughts are broken by a mob surging across the square like a crowd at a football stadium. They move quickly, some carrying drinks trying not to spill them, while others are panicked, pulling their friends along. There's a woman with a pram, running and talking on her phone. The waiter comes outside with the bill and he stands beside us, watching. Then the crowd slows down. The people with the drinks walk back the way they came, and everyone disperses. It's like a film shoot, as though someone has just yelled, 'Cut!'

'That was weird,' Lisa says, as we leave the café and walk across the square. It's getting dark, and a fog settles over the street, spreading like smoke in the glare of headlights.

There are screams and shouts behind us. The crowd masses again, more people running this time. Lisa grabs the dog, and we move to the edge of the street. Bodies skim past us, people shouting and darting into shops for refuge, a sense of fear in the air.

We hear the judder of a machine gun – two, three bursts. It sounds close.

There's real panic now. So many people pressed together, surging forward, pushing us against the wall.

'Quick, in here,' Lisa says, running into a sports shop. Others stream in behind us, and we just make it inside before a tall man in an acid green tracksuit tries to pull the glass doors shut.

'We're closed!' he yells as people heave forward, a few squeezing through the narrowing gap. Those left behind press their faces to the glass. They're outraged, unable to believe he's just locked the doors on them, that they're being excluded. A small boy cries. He's wedged between two adults and our eyes meet for a second before the tide rolls along the street, carrying him with it.

The guy in green tells everyone to stand back for the security grille, which descends on the outside of the glass. A woman squeezes in between the grille and the glass, her head trapped by the metal cage. She screams, and the mob outside pulls on the grille to free her. Its hinges buckle, stalling at the halfway point, no one able to get in or out. People yell and bang on the glass, crying and begging to be let in.

'You can't just leave them there,' I say to the guy, feeling their desperation.

I lunge for the button on the grille, but it won't move. The people outside have no way in, and we're now trapped inside. Lisa drags me to the back of the shop where we take cover behind a rack of neon tracksuits and platform trainers.

The shop assistant is frightened and moves away from the doors. He looks for his colleague but she's cowering behind the desk on her phone, shaking her head at him. The man turns to the people inside – about fifty of us altogether.

'We're not sure what's going on outside, but we've closed the store, put our security procedures in place.' His voice falters as he clears his throat, tries to sound calm. 'Everyone must wait in the shop now until we hear from the police.'

There's murmuring behind me, a lone female voice. 'Let them in. At least some of them. There's plenty of room.' The woman stares in horror at the crowd outside banging on the glass.

A chorus of '*No!*' '*Don't open the doors!*' picks up around me.

Some people are booing.

'We don't know what's out there. It could be dangerous,' one says, fanning the terror that's ignited in the store. 'Look, it's a stampede,' she says, pointing to a heavier surge of people running past, screaming.

'The doors are locked. No one else is coming in. Everyone towards the back,' the shop guy says, herding us into a huddle. 'Stay at the sides, keep to the walls.'

I imagine someone in a balaclava bursting in with a machine gun, shattering the doors, crawling under the grille and spraying us with bullets. We're an easy target – hemmed in here like sheep in a pen. I think of the best position to adopt. Which part of my body should take the bullets, where would cause the least damage? It's frightening, but surreal, like we're actors rehearsing for a play. I step backwards and knock over a mannequin. Its head breaks off as it crashes to the floor and a girl screams.

Lisa pulls me into the changing rooms.

'What's happening?' people murmur, scrolling through their phones.

No one says 'terror attack', but it's what we're all thinking as everyone flicks through their feeds – texting, calling, feverishly skimming Twitter. Someone says there's a security alert at the shopping mall. Shots have been fired, everyone evacuated.

A girl yabbers at her phone in Spanish. She's in tears, red-faced, arm around her friend who's hyperventilating. I give them my seat on the changing room bench.

Lisa checks her phone. Breaking news on one of the news services reports that gunmen have taken over and the area is in lockdown. Someone says it's a bomb, that the police are working to defuse it. Then a man announces a device has gone off on the metro. It's carnage and scores have been killed. The Préfecture de Police on Twitter say the Anti-terrorist Unit has arrived, a warning to stay indoors, keep away from the mall.

Outside, sirens and the thud of helicopters.

Lisa reads from her phone. 'The Mairie says leave the area.'

Another person contradicts her. 'The police say stay inside.'

The shop landline goes down, and suddenly no one has a signal. The lights flicker, and people scream. Lisa grabs my arm.

We cower inside, listening to the people on the street with growing fear. What if they have the right idea? What if they're escaping the danger, moving towards safety, instead of here like us, waiting to be attacked? I want to run. The Spanish girls think the same, and they're up now, heading towards the back exit, arguing with the shop assistant, demanding to be let out. The shop assistant senses mutiny and makes an announcement: anyone who wants to leave can do so now, but he'll only open the door once.

Lisa grabs a sports bag from the shelves and puts the dog inside. A few others leave with us, but most stay. The door slams behind us and we're left in a dark alley flanked with wheelie bins, reeking of refuse. Sirens fill the air, and riot police with dogs move towards us in stalker mode, knees bent, guns ready, scanning the bins with torches.

They glare at us. 'Get down! Get back inside!' one of them yells.

Lisa bangs on the door, but there's no answer. The dog whines from the bag, and she turns to the cops in a panic. 'Which way? Where should we head?' A police dog comes over, growls at the bag.

'Head north. Stay out of the metro!' the cops yell as they disappear around a corner.

We walk quickly along the rue Saint-Denis. Sex shops line the street, their windows full of neon signs, latex and rubber. The buildings have been evacuated, and two girls in spandex dresses and leopard skin boots chat to a group of drag queens. Roman centurions gather at the corner wearing tight shorts and knee-high sandals, their golden helmets sprouting bright red plumage. One of the men is Caesar in a toga and a gold leaf tiara. They stand around smoking and readjusting the straps on their clothes like they've seen it all before. A beautiful woman in a suit of iridescent feathers struts along the cobbles in gold stilettos and two people kiss in a doorway.

Turning into an alley, I glimpse a couple through the steamed-up windows of a ramen bar. They hold hands across the table, oblivious to the commotion outside.

Someone runs towards us, saying there's a gunman at Les Halles and as we round the corner, a crowd surges again. The throng builds, and we're borne along, heaving back towards the square. We stumble over abandoned shopping and an empty pram with a handbag attached. A helicopter hovers overhead, like a wasp about to strike, its blades chopping through the tense night air, spotlights sweeping the alleys. There's shouting up ahead, the air thick with panic. A yellow, smoky haze pricks the skin around my nostrils, followed by acrid needling.

'Gas!' yells Lisa, wrapping her scarf around her face. She tows me along, pushing through the crowd as tears pour down our cheeks. I stumble and fall back, choking and gasping for air.

It's impossible to know if we're heading away from the danger or right into it, but we can't go back against the flow – we're in a crush now, carried along by the surging pack. Someone pulls at the pockets of my jacket as Lisa stumbles to the ground.

'Quick! Take the dog,' she says, passing the bag with its trembling weight. I haul her up just before the crowd moves past and together we're swept on ahead.

Near L'église Saint-Eustache the crowd thins. There's less smoke, but a heavy sourness hangs in the air mingling with the sense of menace, everyone watching each other, uncertain. People gather around the fountain flushing their faces with water. Up ahead, a line of riot police forms a human shield, barricading a restaurant and two adjacent cafés. People cower inside, behind a wall of upturned tables and chairs, lobbing bottles at the cops from the terrace and upper floors shouting, 'Fuck the police! Fuck France!'

A flare goes up as a tear-gas canister bursts through a first-floor window above the restaurant, then another. Plumes of smoke belch from the windows as the rioters go wild, streaming out of the building towards the police and their Perspex shields, who attack them with batons. A fire has started on the second floor, flames leaping up. There are sirens all around, helicopter blades juddering through the darkness, their spotlights lunging into the crowd.

People throw stones and bottles at the police, anything they can get hold of, while others further back watch the scene, mesmerised, like an audience at a festival. Fear has morphed into something else now, and there's an apocalyptic thrill in the air, a sense of wild exhilaration coming off the crowd who yell and howl in rapt anticipation of real, raw violence.

We stand and watch for a while, completely absorbed, then Lisa grabs my sleeve, pulling me away. I don't even ask if she wants to come to my place – it's clear she doesn't want to be alone and neither do I.

If she's shocked by the shabbiness of where I live, she doesn't say. Once we're inside, I draw over the bolt and start flicking through the channels on TV. There's the scene we just left – helicopters and police trying to control a stampede that's turned into a riot. There's aerial footage of people running through the streets, the crack of tear-gas canisters as the crowd disperses, then the sudden deluge from a water cannon.

A reporter says it was a terrorist attack masterminded from a Moroccan restaurant. Two of the gunmen are dead, and one is on the run. Hundreds of people are injured and many more arrested.

I pass Lisa a beer, and she looks at me, her forehead creased. 'A terrorist attack? Is that really what was going on?'

On TV, a government spokesman condemns the attack and the extensive property damage. He speaks excitedly, arguing to extend the counter-terrorism laws, saying the recent terrorist attacks have sparked a spiral of violence and anarchy that's out of control. He wants a form of martial law. *We have barbarians at the gate!* he says. The TV cuts to another spokesman who says these attacks will only get worse unless the government adopts a policy of zero tolerance.

Lisa attends to the dog, who's nosing the stained grout lines in the kitchen, then lapping at a bowl of water.

I mute the TV and put on some music.

'*Hundreds* injured?' Lisa says, unzipping her boots, sitting cross-legged on the bed. I feel that familiar pull towards her, equal parts attraction and fear. Our legs touch as we sit there drinking beer, looking out at the night sky, the distant throb of a helicopter rising above the music.

'I mean, I was scared at one point,' she says, pointing to the scenes of chaos on TV. 'All those people running – I thought we were going to be crushed, and then all that tear gas and smoke. I've never seen that before.' She twists a handful of her hair and brings it to her face. 'You can still smell it,' she says, holding the strands in front of my nose.

'But it didn't feel like an attack,' she continues. 'It was a frightened stampede. And where was all the *property damage*?'

'You saw them in the restaurant,' I say.

'Yes, but that was all. I didn't see hundreds injured or even any arrests. Something feels strange. I'm not sure.'

'You're probably in shock,' I say, drawing closer. We sit on the bed for a while, talking about the night and what we'd seen. We'd never spoken like this before. At school, she was never interested in what I thought only what I could do for her. And I never knew who she was either – beyond the lip gloss and mirrors.

She turns to kiss me, pulling me back on the bed. Her hand moves slowly over my chest.

'Is this allowed?' she whispers.

The dog barks, just as I was thinking it was good she hadn't changed that much, and she goes to it, leaving me with the scent of tear-gassed hair, the taste of cigarettes.

Standing in front of me later, I see where she used to cut herself. There are deep scars at the tops of her thighs, and lighter pink marks scoring the flesh below like twin tracks crossing the skin. I reach out, remembering the first time I saw them in the club that night when they were still fresh. I didn't notice their mathematical symmetry then.

'I'm glad you don't do that anymore,' I say, tracing a scar above her knee. 'These remind me of what you were like back then. You've changed a lot.'

She tears a condom open with her teeth. 'Seven years of therapy, so I hope I have,' she says, then pauses to put her hand on her heart. 'Or maybe it's just that the cuts are all hidden now.'

I laugh, pulling her onto the bed. 'Still the drama queen,' I say.

Outside, a helicopter grates through the sky.

I wake several hours later, shivering in the cold night air. There's a weight next to me on the bed and I reach over to the dog's warm body. Lisa's silhouette is at the open window, a cigarette flaring at her lips. A wave of relief that she's still here takes me by surprise, then a strange kind of dread. It's seven years since I've been with anyone and I hadn't expected to fall for her so quickly.

'You smoke too much,' I say.

She sits on the bed and offers me a drag. 'It helps me think.'

I take a puff and then recoil. 'Is this a joint?'

'Of course not! Don't be paranoid.'

'I'm not.'

She laughs. 'Yes, you are. Yesterday you thought I'd set you up with that stalking. Now you think I'm trying to drug you!'

I tell her about the urine test and point to the new locks on the front door.

'And I was burgled,' I say. 'Someone ransacked the place. They tore electric sockets off the walls, dumped fish guts on the kitchen floor. They totally trashed the place.'

She sounds shocked. 'Fish guts?'

'Yeah, mafia gang shit. *Be careful what you fish for.* The caretaker said it was probably a previous tenant, someone who still had a key, but I'm not convinced.'

'Then who?'

She touches my arm and something about the contact and the darkness draws out the fear. 'At first I thought it was Sami. He's the only person who hates me that much.'

My skin starts to burn. 'I thought it was revenge for what I did to him.'

'But Alex, he's in jail.'

'There are other people. His friends. I saw them.'

'Where?'

'Following me. I used to see them all the time. But now I just don't know.'

'If Sami could get you here, he could have got you in prison,' she says. 'He had seven years to do that. And how could he contaminate a urine sample? It doesn't make sense.'

'I know. So Tomas then?' I say after a while. 'It's just like him to send dead fish.'

'Tomas is an idiot, but he wouldn't do that.'

I wait until she moves closer, remembering what Paul had said about their missing son. 'You're still in touch with him, aren't you?' I say, feeling a surge of the old jealousy, which annoys me after all this time.

'Not really. We were friends for a while after school, but then he lost it. That business between his mother and your dad, plus all the trouble at school. Last I heard he was living in a commune in the south.'

'A *commune*? Hippies?'

'Yeah, it's some kind of farm. One of his mates inherited it, and it's full of rich kids growing dope, living up trees, making pottery. That kind of thing.'

THEN

Early December

Twenty-Five

Saint-Germain

I LAY IN BED, THINKING ABOUT the woman I'd just seen in the bathroom. Was it Céline? If so, why hadn't she said something? My presence in the apartment was hardly unexpected, so why did she scream like that? It made me feel guilty and unwelcome, like an intruder.

I listened for my father's tread, for the soft knock at the door. It was like I was ten again, waiting for him to come into my room, sit on the edge of the bed and console me. Instead, I heard his muffled voice through the wall, his measured tones interrupted by hers – agitated, disjointed. They spoke for a long time and when they finished, I waited, and when he didn't come, expectation soured into frustration, and I hated myself for my neediness.

My feelings seesawed like that until I fell asleep, and I woke to a morning of leaden emptiness. I had no school to get up for, and instead of relief, I felt exhausted at the thought of what lay ahead. Ranged against me were my father, Tomas, Mme. Vaux and potentially the police. I couldn't face them all off, or even just sit it out. I needed to escape until things died down, so I packed a bag and left the apartment.

Outside, it was cold and grey, the street loud and jarring. The city's tension invaded my body, short-circuiting my nerves.

I turned on my phone to a barrage of texts from Tomas, demanding his money back, threatening to beat the shit out of me. He sent pictures of the door to my building, Lisa's house and other places I went, making it clear he knew where to find me. I must have lost the cash in my rush to leave the party, or somewhere on the metro. My father was convinced his computer had been hacked so he'd added extra security. I couldn't steal from him again even if I wanted to. It seemed the only solution was to try and get the money back from Nick – I'd explain that the pills were bad and perhaps he'd see sense. It seems hopelessly optimistic now, but I was desperate. I called Sami endlessly, but he didn't answer and neither did he call me back.

I knew he worked near the market at Clignancourt some mornings, and it didn't take long to find him on the edge of a damp underpass of the Péri. Fake watches gleamed along one arm, gold chains hanging from the other. He looked hopefully at passers-by, extending his arms towards them in a glittering embrace.

He shook his head when I started pleading, not taking his eyes off the passing crowd.

'There's no way I can get that kind of money back from him. And anyway, there was nothing wrong with the pills. Your friends drink too much,' he said, as he fell into step with a man who'd glanced at the watches. A little further down, they stopped to haggle.

There were two large holdalls near my feet. I nudged them open. One held watches and chains in small plastic bags, the other shrink-wrapped perfume.

'Are these fake?' I asked when he returned.

He laughed. 'What do you think?'

'I think they're fake, just like those drugs.'

He came in close, and the chains brushed against me. 'Those pills weren't *fake*.'

'Stop pissing around. It's serious. One of the kids had to be taken to hospital, and I'm getting the blame.'

He shook his head as if the idea of it was crazy, unheard of.

'The police are involved,' I added.

He scanned the road, agitated now. 'What have you told the police?' he said, jabbing my chest, the jewellery glinting in the sun. 'If the police ask, say nothing. You understand?'

'You need to help me. Speak to Nick. Help me get the money back.'

'Don't forget you owe him money too,' he said, pushing me aside to follow a woman. I sat beside the bags, my back against one of the huge concrete feet of the Péri, determined not to leave until he agreed to help fix things.

He ignored me at first then after a while, he threw me a box of perfume.

'If you're going to hang around, you can help sell this shit,' he said, pointing to the opposite corner. 'Stand over there and hold them out. Go for the guys – they come here looking for cheap presents for their girlfriends.'

I had no intention of helping him with his work, but I soon got bored watching. I thought he probably made a lot of money if the number of boxes was anything to go by.

So I stood at the corner, thrusting perfume at passers-by. Most people ignored me, swerving and sidestepping around me. Two American tourists screamed when I leaped out in front of them, batting me away with their guidebooks and maps.

Sami came over and told me I was doing it all wrong. Stepping in front of people never worked, he said, it's too threatening. You need to walk alongside them, show them the box like you're offering them a secret prize, and then retract it. Withholding things always made people want them more, he said.

'Show them the price tag,' he said, pointing to the duty-free sticker that said 125 euros. 'Start with thirty euros. Get whatever you can, but no less than ten. Keep an eye out for the cops, if you see them, run, and if you get caught, don't even look at me.'

He demonstrated by sidling up to a middle-aged woman. He spoke softly, telling her she was beautiful, which made her smile. He held out the perfume, holding her hand as he sprayed her wrist like a salesgirl in a department store. When she gave him twenty euros, he put his hand on his heart, pretended to look hurt and offered it to her for free, saying it was because she had such lovely eyes. That made her laugh, and she gave him another ten, accepting the box as if it were a precious gift instead of the poisonous shit it probably was.

I watched him sell bottle after bottle like that and saw the pattern – flattery, smiles, humour, a soft voice. You just had to engage people, to reassure and captivate each one in their own way, make them think you were doing them a favour. It was amazing how stupid people could be if you made them feel good.

I tried it myself – flattering, praising and congratulating people, but they still ignored me. One guy kicked me away like I was a dog. I started to think it wasn't what I said, but the will behind it. Despite his desperate look, Sami had a survivor's instinct and the kind of determination I didn't have because I'd never needed it.

I'd sold nothing and was about to give up when a man walked up to me wearing a tweedy beret and red cords. I told him he had a beautiful smile and offered to spray him. He held out his wrist in a girlish kind of way, sniffed it then took out twenty euros. When I reached for the note, he took hold of my hands so our three hands were clasped together. Then he took the perfume and kissed me, releasing the note.

Sami was at my side, laughing as I wiped the moist imprint off my cheek. 'You're getting better at this,' he said, taking the note. 'Don't worry about him. He tries it on me all the time.'

I stayed with Sami for the rest of the day, helping him and trading stock with other vendors who arrived later with similar things to sell. Finally, he zipped the holdalls and heaved them onto his shoulders. I followed after him, saying I wouldn't leave until I got the money back from Nick.

He resisted at first, but then took pity on me and promised to call Nick later. Then we headed east along a stretch of road lined with fast-food shops, cheap bazaars, and grocery stores with their produce stacked out on the street.

After a while, the highway divided into two slip roads that curved up to meet the Péri, leaving a triangular traffic island in the middle. The area was covered with large wooden fruit crates bearing the stickers of origin – Kenya, Cameroon, Spain. It looked like the debris you'd see after a market, only instead of oranges and mangoes spilling out of the crates there were people.

Wrapped in blankets against the cold, they lay among piles of clothes and bags, looking at their phones, playing cards, talking. An overpass seventy feet above provided some shelter and massive pillars some privacy to a line of tents that shuddered in the slip-stream of passing cars, their guy lines tugging on roadside barriers. The ground underneath the crates was slick with filth, and the sour stench of unwashed bodies drifted over the road to us.

The people sprawled on the concrete island looked obscene, like injured bodies thrown from vehicles after a multi-car pile-up. The cars flashing by seemed oblivious to the sight and I wondered, as I looked over, what the people on the island thought of those in their cars who sped by on the snarling roads towards futures they'd never know.

A few minutes later, Sami stopped at a shop selling children's wedding clothes – garish princess dresses and miniature tuxedos.

He opened a door and inside, spiral stairs ascended steeply, the steps so narrow and warped that it was difficult to keep balance while carrying the bags. As we gained height, we went backwards in time, past ancient pipes, the walls all cracked and peeling like blisters. The faded paintwork and wooden stairs had large, ugly marks where dark liquid had hit them with some velocity. On each landing there was a squat loo – two concrete blocks in a stained gutter tray, the doors gaping open or kicked off their hinges.

By the seventh floor, I was gasping for air as I followed Sami down the narrow corridor. Through paper-thin walls, I smelled frying onions, heard TVs and people yelling.

He led me into a tiny room. It had a rough wooden floor and warped rafters under a bowed ceiling that sloped towards a window in the eaves. We were just outside the Péri, right on the edge of Paris. Vehicles thundered past on the motorway below, and just beyond, the panorama of the city spread out under the grey light of an early winter sunset. I'd never seen Paris from this perspective.

It was the kind of view that hits you in the chest – a beautiful, haphazard landscape of stone buildings, zinc rooftops, spires and golden domes all pressed in against each other, with the glistening sliver of the Seine snaking through it all.

'Amazing view,' I said, poking at the solid foam spray that filled the gap between the window and the frame.

'Yeah, Nick just cut a hole in this wall with a sledgehammer. He built this view,' said Sami, staring out.

'This is Nick's place?'

He reached for a mattress propped against the wall then pulled down a sheet and a couple of ragged blankets from a shelf near the door. 'He owns the building and lets me stay here as long as I work hard and help him sell perfume and the other shit.'

'You give him all the money?'

'Yeah. Most of it.'

I asked him to call Nick then, but he said Nick worked nights at his clubs and so he'd do it the next day. We sat playing cards until it got dark then went out for a takeaway. After we'd eaten, he offered me a small white pill.

'Here, take this. It will help with the sleep.'

'Are you kidding? Not after those other pills.'

'Suit yourself,' he said, swallowing it. 'I told you there was nothing wrong with them. It must have been something else – other drugs, what your friends were drinking, what they ate.'

There were no curtains on the window, and we lay on the mattress watching light slide across the ceiling.

After a while, the pill must have kicked in because he started rambling, his words incomprehensible, and when he spoke, he traced outlines in front of him like a shadow dance with his hands.

I asked him about his family, and I felt him shrug.

He said he had no family.

I turned to him. The dim light emphasised the faint lines and blemishes on his cheeks, like a relief map. I felt my own smooth face, bland and featureless by comparison.

At first, he said his parents had died. He rolled over and was quiet for a while. I thought he'd drifted off to sleep, but then he turned back. 'I lived in an orphanage in Lyon run by Americans until I was nine. They taught me English. They told me that crap about my parents dying until I realised they'd never existed.'

He walked to the window and sat on the sill, smoking. His eyes looked wild.

'Nick says I'm like the Devil. I have no family.'

He laughed, slipping back a bit and my stomach lurched – it would be so easy for him to fall. He steadied himself on the window frame, took a long drag and then pulled himself back inside. 'It was a long time ago. It's like a dream now. When I was fourteen, I came to Paris, and now I have this.' He gestured out of the window. 'Paris. This is what my parents gave me.'

'What was it like?'

He grinned. 'What's it like? It's Paris. You know! It's always beautiful.'

He reached to a shelf and brought down a packet of biscuits and a jar of peanut butter, and started spooning huge lumps onto the biscuits, shoving them into his mouth. 'I can't actually remember anything about it. But the crazy thing is whenever I think of that place, I feel hungry. So that's my main memory, I guess. Hunger.'

'If Nick owns this place, why does he live at the camp?'

'He doesn't live at the camp. He lives here. He just uses the camp to store stuff because the police don't go there.'

'What stuff?'

'Drugs, phones, fake stuff. You saw it.'

I was about to ask another question when he turned around. 'You ask too many questions. Shut up now. Let's sleep.'

Sometime in the night, I woke to voices in the corridor, a dog's bark, the clink of a metal chain. A cold draught under the door brought the sweet, rich smell of pipe tobacco. Turning towards Sami, I pulled the blanket around us, and the warmth of his body released a heavy strain of his own acrid reek. My shoulder dug through the thin mattress to the floor and further down the hall, a door slammed.

I needed to use the toilet, so I walked down the corridor. A man's silhouette loomed at the doorway backlit by a hanging bulb. He whistled and an Alsatian dog exited the toilet, its claws scratching at the bare wood floor.

In the morning, Sami made coffee on a camping stove.

'Your neighbour. He lets his dog use the loo.'

'Oh, yeah. Don't go in there. I forgot to tell you. The guy's a pig. Use the one downstairs.'

'I threw up.'

Sami grinned. 'Yeah, so you see it wasn't the pills.'

'Can't you just call Nick?' I said, feeling tired and desperate. My shoulder ached where I'd slept on it.

I hassled him until finally he took out his phone and sat on the window ledge.

He spoke quickly in French. *Problem with that guy here. Says it was bad. Yeah, yeah, that's what I told him. Yeah, I know. I know.*

I told him that, too, but he – OK. OK, I'll say that. Yeah, I got this. No, no, I won't. OK, speak later.

Sami hung up. 'He said there was nothing wrong with them. Forget it.'

'What? Come on.'

'He says you still owe him.' He shrugged. 'That's what he said. And if I were you, I'd be more worried about Nick than your friends.'

'I'll come with you today, then. You can give me a cut of what I sell.' I thought if I helped Sami, he might try harder with Nick.

He looked at me curiously. 'If your parents give you money, why do you need to come with me?'

'They don't *give* me that kind of money,' I said.

He handed me a coffee. It was bitter, like the dregs of an ashtray.

'So the money for the drugs?'

'My friends,' I said. 'And I took some from my father,' I added, turning away towards the window, suddenly ashamed at how bad it sounded and how easily I was now boasting about it. It was like I was talking about someone else.

Sami brought his coffee over. 'If I was rich, I would give my son everything,' he said, pointing out of the window at Paris as if to indicate the extent of the gift he'd give his son.

He turned to me. 'Why do you come here? Why do you get involved with this shit when you have a nice home, and parents who have money?'

I didn't know what to say. 'I want to be free, like you. Free to do what I want.'

He gestured around the small room, the boxes stacked against the walls. 'What's free about this?'

241

He was right – it was a stupid thing to say, but I remembered the way I'd seen him outside – the way he always got what he wanted and knew his way around, his ease and confidence with people.

'You're not tied down. You can go anywhere,' I said. There was a pause as we looked at each other. 'You have nothing to lose,' I added, putting my finger on it. I wasn't sure whether it was that exactly, but there was something about his lack of ties to anything that appealed to me. I didn't understand the attraction, but his life felt weightless and free, but at the same time dangerous, like falling.

'Having nothing to lose doesn't mean I'm free. It just means I've got nothing.'

'You're not weighed down by things.'

He laughed bitterly. 'I'm weighed down by the stuff I don't have. Look at all this shit.' He kicked a box of Christmas toys over. He took out a plastic handcuff and put it on his wrist. Then he pointed a toy gun to his head. 'I'm weighed down by this, and by the lack of everything you have.'

He lit a cigarette and smoked for a while, deep in thought, and then he turned to me. 'You know, it's a waste of time, selling stuff on the streets. We need to get hold of money from your friends, these rich kids you know.' He was angry, unlike I'd heard him before.

'Are you kidding? They won't give me money after this.'

He looked at me as though I was an idiot. 'I just need a name and address. I can talk my way in.'

I took in his hungry face, matted hair and baggy clothes. His whole air of wild desperation.

'I'll just tell whoever answers the door – it's always some member of staff, the cleaner, babysitter, whatever, that I've come to fix the Wi-Fi. People always have problems with the Wi-Fi,' he said.

'You're a good pickpocket and a hustler, but I don't think you should consider burglary,' I said, nerves stirring. I could tell it was something he'd done already.

'Well look at you – dealing drugs to your friends. You even steal from your own father.'

I nodded, aware of just how easily I'd done these things.

'It won't be that simple,' I heard myself saying.

'Just get me the door code and name. I'll do the rest.'

He explained how he'd do it, and I listened to his words, uncomfortable about the idea but relieved there was no role for me, beyond providing the target details. His energy and enthusiasm were infectious and I was drawn in. He had a tough life, but instead of whinging about it, he was doing things – he had ideas and guts, made the most of what he had, and I liked that about him.

He understood me, too, and unlike Lisa and Tomas, he treated me as an equal. He'd helped me more than anyone else, especially up at the camp with Nick, and here I was staying with him when I had nowhere else to go.

At the same time, I wasn't entirely stupid; I didn't think he'd go too far out of his way for me unless there was something in it for him. I'd already stolen a lot of money from my father and I didn't see why we needed to rob more people to pay for Nick's dodgy drugs. But then again, I didn't want to go back home either. I thought as long as I made him think we had the same interests, he'd let me stay a bit longer.

'I'm worried about the police,' I said. 'They say I could be arrested because of the drugs.'

He came in close. 'Listen carefully. Never say anything to the police. They'll betray you. OK? We have to deal with our own shit, solve our own problems. Remember that. The police are not our brothers.'

I nodded, and then I said, 'Nick isn't your brother either. Or your cousin. He's not even your family.'

He put his face close to mine. 'He *is* my brother – what he does affects me, and what I do affects him. That's what I mean by brother.' He clasped my shoulders, pulling me to him. 'And if you and I do things together, then we're brothers. What I do affects you, what you do affects me. We're brothers, understand? If the police ask, say nothing. "No comment."'

We stood there staring at each other, and then he squeezed my hand. I was surprised at his strength.

'OK?' he asked.

'No comment, brother,' I said, and he laughed, squeezing harder until it hurt.

Twenty-Six

Metro

I SPENT THE NEXT WEEK AVOIDING calls and angry texts from my father asking where the hell I was then blathering on about the lycée he'd got me into in the New Year. I couldn't face any of that, so I tried calling my mother, thinking I could stay with her for a while, but her phone kept ringing out. It seemed being with Sami was my best option, at least in the short term, so I stayed in his room near Clignancourt, selling watches and perfume in the morning, pickpocketing on the metro in the afternoon.

At first, I didn't know what he was doing on the train when he made a dash for the doors, but I leaped off just in time and followed him up the platform. He moved quickly, shoulders hunched, hands in his pockets as he weaved through the tunnels.

He turned a corner, pulled some cash from a wallet, and then threw it in a bin.

'First rule – get rid of the wallet,' he said, heading off down a passage.

'Second rule – change trains,' he said, as we boarded one heading in the opposite direction.

He always chose a crowded carriage, standing just inside the doors for a quick exit, and he dressed in his best jeans and trainers. He pretended to be absorbed in his phone, but his eyes scanned the people around us. Sometimes he'd talk to me, exaggerating his American accent to pass us off as tourists, while his eyes flickered over my shoulder.

He didn't take long to home in on his targets, always choosing those absorbed in their phones, their senses tunnelled into the thin wafers of metal. Phones were made for pickpockets, he said, and it was true. People may as well just hand over their cash when they took out their phones.

On one of the first trips, I saw it up close. A girl stood between us, handbag under her arm like a warm brown chicken. She turned so it pressed against him and he sidled in, talking to me in a low voice as the carriage filled up, jostling and swaying against her with the rhythm of the train. She shrugged, angling off, bringing her phone to her face, her bag close to him. The zip was near his chest, and his eyes darted sideways, back and forth, checking no one saw him reach up slowly, peel the zip back, fingers spidering into the gap. He felt around, and there it was. The soft little purse. Always at the top, always within easy reach. The train took a bend and he used the movement to take it from her bag. When the doors opened, he was ready, shouldering through the crowd, riding out on the soft exhalation of brakes before she'd even read her text message.

'Third rule – don't make eye contact.'

We zigzagged the tunnels with tourists near the Louvre, went further afield at rush hour, then later, in the bountiful hours near midnight, we'd be up near the red light district where everyone was wasted and careless. Fear and adrenaline fuelled him, fine-tuning his luck as he moved in and out of the crowds, unseen, unnoticed.

Sometimes we saw others he knew. He never acknowledged them so you'd notice, just glanced over for a split second as they passed. He told me when they were young, it was a game. They'd tease each other and compete. But none of them were young anymore, their faces hollowed and stained with dirt. The shadows under their eyes were permanent, like tattoos.

One afternoon, we came up at Montparnasse to drop some cash at one of the bars Nick ran. It was better to get rid of the money so we weren't caught red-handed, Sami said. It was hard to arrest someone for pickpocketing if they had no wallets or cash on them. We followed the Boulevard Raspail to the narrow street – Passage D'Enfer – where I'd first seen Sami that cold morning over two months before. I half expected to see the girl there, too, with her baby in a box by the tent.

Sami walked up to a shiny black door next to a boarded-up shopfront. He pressed the buzzer and soon a man appeared, unshaven, his eyes puffy with booze and sleep. He grunted to me in a way that said, 'Wait here,' and ushered Sami in.

There was a faded sign on the building opposite: FEUX DE L'ENFER – fires of hell. Bars and nightclubs lined the street, and they had names along the same theme: SEVEN SINS, JÉZABEL, TENTATION. The washed-out sign above the black door beside me said, PLEASURES OF PARADISE, the words written on a scroll held by a snake. Its body was covered in green scales beneath the fat smiling face of a cherub.

'This is where I saw you the first time we met,' I said to Sami when he emerged. 'What is this place?'

'It's a nightclub.'

'And Nick owns it?'

'He runs it. He runs all the places along here for some rich guy.'

'Who?' I asked but he didn't answer, just crossed the road back towards Montparnasse.

Nearing the metro, we passed the cashpoint I used to withdraw money from my father's account. Sami and I hadn't spoken again about the plan to rob my so-called friends, but it occurred to me that if I could figure out how to access my father's account one more time, I could get the cash to pay back Tomas and survive for a few weeks until I got back on my feet. I knew I was taking a risk, but I had few other options.

I entered the apartment and immediately sensed his presence. He called my name, and I closed the door softly, trying to gauge his tone. I walked slowly down the creaking hall.

'Are you all right? You look terrible,' he said when I reached his study. His voice was stern but tinged with relief. 'You're filthy. I can even *smell* you from here. Where on earth have you been?'

I slid my bag off my shoulder. 'Staying with friends.'

'Staying with what *friends*? What the hell are you playing at, Alex?'

'Just a friend, I mean. You don't know him.'

Any sense he'd go easy on me disappeared and my body started itching like mad.

'*First*, you're expelled for dealing drugs, *then* you disappear for over a week. *Now* you have the gall to come back here like nothing's happened, slinking through the door like a filthy dog.'

I picked up my bag and turned to leave.

'Sit!' he yelled, pointing to the chair.

It didn't take long to get into a full-blown argument. He'd found out about the money I'd stolen and he stood there, pointing a pencil at my face as if he was about to drive it between my eyes. He also blamed me for hacking his computer because he'd worked out I'd used it to access his bank account. Thanks to me he'd lost a ton of work and valuable documents. *Irreplaceable*, he said as he loomed over me.

My guts hollowed as I sank further into the chair, and I felt his fury physically, unsure what he was going to do next.

I said I'd pay him back, but of course I had no means of doing that. When I said he could cut my allowance, he actually laughed.

'If you live under my roof, you need to live by the rules.'

'I do live by your rules.'

'Drug-running and stealing are not my rules.'

'So what are your rules, then? Drinking till you pass out? Sleeping with your friends' wives?'

He looked at me, stunned. 'It's none of your business what I do.'

He moved over to the drinks cabinet, his hand reaching for the Scotch but then he hesitated and poured himself a glass of water.

'You started this. I hate living here. It was your idea to move back to Paris,' I said. 'So don't blame me for what happens.'

'Don't blame you? Who else am I supposed to blame? No one's forcing you to sell drugs. No one's holding a gun to your head while you steal money from me. Or have I got this all wrong?'

'What about Mum? Why can't I live with her?'

'We've been through all this before.'

I leaped out of the chair. 'You always said it was because I was at school in the States and she was here. We're in the same country now, or near enough.'

I'd never asked so openly before. I knew my mother and Olivier had sold their apartment and were moving to Monaco in the New Year, but it was worth a try at least for a few weeks until he cooled off.

'Why can't I live with her?'

'Because you can't. And while we're at it, you're grounded.'

'But I'm going to stay with Mum this weekend.'

'No, you're not. You're staying here until things improve.'

'You're such an arsehole. No wonder she won't come near you.'

He walked to the window. 'Don't speak to me like that,' he said quietly.

I grabbed my bag and this time he didn't try to prevent me leaving. I went to my room. May had tidied it up, and of course, the hash pipe was no longer on the balcony, the grass no longer in my drawer. Even my computer was gone.

I paced the room. He wasn't going to stop me seeing my mother. I'd had enough of living by his rules. It was time to start doing things my way.

I rang her number. There was silence down the line. I tried again. The same emptiness, so I stripped off and had a shower, attending to my eczema, which had worsened, then repacked my bag with clean clothes and a few other things I needed.

'Where do you think you're going?' he said when I passed his study.

'I'm going to stay with Mum,' I said, pulling my backpack onto my shoulder. I intended to go straight to her apartment.

He followed me down the hall.

'Listen to me,' he said, his voice tight. 'I don't know if you've heard any of your messages, but I've called that lycée. They can take you in January when term starts again. Work hard, get through your Bac and then you can do what you like.'

I watched his head move as he went on about the Bac, until finally, something snapped inside me.

'I hate you, and I hate living with you. Why do you always stop me seeing Mum? You can't stop me seeing her.'

He turned. 'Grow up, Alex. You're not eight years old anymore. I'm not stopping you seeing her.'

I yelled at him. 'Yes, you are! You've stopped me this weekend. You just said I'm grounded.'

He slammed his glass down, and water flew into the air like a fountain. 'She rang to say she couldn't have you this weekend. I don't even know where the hell she is, but wherever it is, she doesn't want you there. Olivier doesn't want you there! For God's sake, Alex, isn't it clear after all these years?'

All of the fatigue and exhaustion of the previous weeks came crashing in around me, and as I ran down the corridor, the walls seemed to shake. I couldn't stay with my father any longer. He was suffocating me with his rules and restrictions, and now he was poisoning my head with lies about my mother. I stood at the door and put my head against the cool metal panel, my mind a reel of images of her smiling, shaking her head, making excuses as to why I couldn't stay with her that night, that weekend, that holiday.

I stared at him as he stood there, water dripping over his hand.

Why did he have to say it so plainly?

But he was right. She never really wanted me with her. And the times we spent together were always cut short, plans changed at the last minute. He always backed her up, *colluded*, even anticipated those excuses by saying I couldn't go, I was too busy, or I had too much homework.

And what if he was only putting up with me because she wouldn't? What if he was only doing it out of the same worn-out sense of duty she'd discarded? My head felt tight, and there was a metallic taste in my mouth, like blood.

I needed to be by myself, away from both of them.

'Alex, wait,' said my father. 'Let's talk about this. I'm sorry.'

I opened the door and tossed my keys at him. They clattered onto the floor and slid along the corridor to his feet. 'No, you're not.'

I ran down the stairs.

He called from the balcony, but I didn't stop.

I just kept running.

NOW

Twenty-Seven

Aubervilliers

POLICE SIRENS WAIL OUTSIDE as grey light edges in around the blinds. Lisa opens a window and the muffled blare of a tannoy fills the room, followed by a wave of angry chants. It's a protest of some kind in the street below, she says, another *manif*. She's wearing my T-shirt, and as she leans out to get a better view, I see the tension in her legs up to the crease at her buttocks. It's weird seeing her in my clothes like she's my girlfriend or something, and I wonder why she's wearing my shirt when hers is right here.

She moves back inside, scanning the wall above the desk where I've stuck old news reports about my case. I get ready for her questions, but she just reaches up to attach the corner of an article that's come loose. She reads it carefully and then glances at me, as if checking something.

While she's in the bathroom, I do a quick recce of the flat. Balling up clothes, stuffing them in the wardrobe, sorting dishes in the sink. I leave the empty bottles on the table so she doesn't think I'm trying too hard.

I pass her bag, hesitating for a second before tilting her phone for the previews. This isn't something I'd normally do, but she's right here nosing around my things, so I figure I should know a bit about her too.

There are two messages: one from 2.34 this morning, the other an hour ago. They're both from the same person; someone called Steph.

> So how did it go?
> Come on, what's the story?

Could be anyone, I think, staring at the screen until the question marks quiver. Could be about anything, too, but I'm sure it's about me. The shower stops and I replace her phone. I'm glad the old Lisa's gone, but I don't know this new person either.

On my own phone there's a message from my parole officer about our appointment today, and another from the computer shop. They say they've retrieved some of the files on my father's laptop and it's ready for collection.

Lisa walks towards her bag, but she doesn't look at her phone, just gives the dog a biscuit and some water. A little while later she checks it, but goes straight to the news. The police are treating last night's attack as a terror incident. They've blocked roads around the metros and put security checks along the Péri.

Outside, there's tension in the air, a smoky haze and the sharp smell of burning rubber. The main road swarms with people, their faces painted white or covered in balaclavas and masks – The Joker, Guy Fawkes, surgical masks. Some blow whistles giving the scene a carnival feel, but there's no music or dancing, and no one's carrying signs. They march in lockstep, arms interlinked. There's a man with a CCTV camera around his face, the lens protruding from the top like a beak. He aims it straight at me and hands me a flyer about police surveillance. A woman, agitated and unmasked, points in the direction of the new high-rise, and says they're protesting about evictions from the estate. Like the scene last night, the atmosphere's tense, full of anger, as if things could ignite any second.

Lisa carries the dog as we push towards the station. We can't make headway on the road, so we hug the edges, surging with the crowd as it slinks north. Police in full body armour block access to the side streets and up ahead, gendarmes flank the entrance to the metro, stopping people and checking IDs. They manhandle the crowd and downstairs, people shove and jostle, while screens above the platform show most of the lines are down.

Finally, a train arrives and we squeeze on. The train noses forward slowly, as if unsure of what's ahead. It stops in the tunnel between stations and there's an announcement that no trains are crossing the Péri. If we want to travel into Zone One, we need to walk.

We get out at the next stop and head south past a stretch of derelict warehouses and boarded-up shops. Nearing the Péri, the street dips and joins a knot of larger roads that wind onto the motorway, and we cross over to a path that follows the canal. Wind ripples the water, bringing the smell of stagnant drains. On the other side of the canal is a large building site where bulldozers clear the land, their tracks leaving red scars on the flattened earth. A few tents cling to the edge of the site and men loiter among the debris.

The wind is behind us now as we pass under the Péri towards another stretch of cleared land. Suddenly, the place looks familiar: it's the edge of the camp I visited with Sami. The pylons and cables are still there, wires all frayed and limp, but the huts have been demolished. Household objects protrude from charred mounds and fill the bulging skips all around.

I'm still thinking about the camp when someone jostles me on the stairs at Clignancourt. There's a tug at my pocket, a glimpse of a face in profile – squashed nose, then a stubby hand shields it from view. The flash of a street-muscled forearm, dark with old tattoos. I try to catch him, but he moves ahead, his body lurching as he's swallowed up by the crowd.

Back on the metro, we shunt slowly through dark, empty platforms, while others are packed, teeming with police. Lisa makes space for the dog as the crowd pushes in. There's an announcement on a loop – most lines suspended, no service at all beyond the Péri now.

At the computer shop, the man hands over my father's laptop and a hard drive. He says a lot was already deleted or corrupted, but he's downloaded what he's found.

'You can run it through my computer,' Lisa says when we're outside, but there's my parole officer and our meeting this afternoon. I shouldn't even be in Zone One.

Just stay out of there.

'I need to get back,' I say, heading towards the bus stop.

'The buses will be worse,' she says, scanning her phone. 'There are no trains running beyond the Péri and they've put up roadblocks. It'll be chaos up there now. And besides, I want to see what's on that hard drive.'

'Why?' I ask, turning to face her. 'Why are you so interested?'

Her curiosity alarms me, but she's smiling, her eyes all innocence. 'You've got me intrigued after what you said last night – these people pursuing you, the robbery, that drug test and now these files.'

'I can't. I have an appointment,' I say, but she persists, trailing me down the street.

'Come on,' she says when we see the queue for the bus. 'I'm going to work; you'll be alone. I'm doing you a favour, you idiot. Can't you see?'

I see there's no real choice, and we hardly speak as we travel to her apartment in the sixteenth arrondissement. Her attention is on the dog, which she carries in her bag. The trains are running normally in Zone One and everything's calm, unnervingly so. There's no sign of the disruption beyond the Péri but that glimpse of the old camp has brought back memories of Sami. I remember the day we went up there together. How he looked after me with Nick. And later, when he let me stay, even though he could barely survive himself.

I know the conditions he'll be suffering under now. With his murder conviction he'll be in maximum security, locked up with others in a tiny cell and only released for an hour a day. I didn't think of him too much when I was inside, but now I'm out, each day that passes feels like another one I've stolen from him. He had nothing then except his freedom, and I've taken that away too.

I'm still thinking of Sami as Lisa leads me through the lobby of her building which is vast and glamorous, a modern Versailles. Huge mirrors throw dazzling light over cactuses and palm trees, their leaves sharp and silvery in the glare, and a thick red carpet seems to hover over the polished marble floor.

'Don't look so worried,' she says, as the glass lift floats up past a double staircase then an arched mezzanine beneath a huge chandelier. 'Even if my parents are here, they'll be in their rooms. I could drag a dead body inside and they wouldn't notice.'

'Or bring a murderer home,' I say, as we enter the apartment, the wooden floor tanned and glowing beneath our feet. We drift down the wide hall, past silent rooms immaculately furnished with sculptures and modern art, then a series of shadowy bedrooms. I'd forgotten this kind of opulence. Among my school friends it was normal, but now the quiet emptiness is eerie, the difference in our circumstances so huge, that I feel small and insubstantial. I watch Lisa as she deposits the dog with a maid, then turns and smiles. She seems to have hardly registered the changes in me, said nothing when she saw my place and it makes me wary, this lack of judgement. We walk past more rooms before Lisa leads me out of the back door and up a narrow staircase. At the end of a curved hallway is her tiny studio flat. There's a bed jammed against the wall and shelves all around. A desk at the window faces out over chimney pots and dark grey roofs.

She switches on the computer and logs on for me.

I call my parole officer to let her know I can't make our appointment and for once, she doesn't complain or ask where I am. The police have cut all links to the suburbs, she says. They think last night's attackers are there, and they've set up a full security block around the Péri, closing all transport routes and roads to the north.

I stare out over the silent streets below. By now the traffic will have done the rest, making everything beyond the Péri completely gridlocked. It feels insulated from all that here, like a separate city.

There's silence down the line. 'I need to talk to you about Sami,' I say, and then ask her whether she could help me arrange a visit to see him.

She takes a deep breath and replies quickly, saying she wouldn't advise it, but I tell her I want to help him in some way. If I can prove my innocence then I can prove his too.

'Come on, Alex. Get real. How will you do that?'

'It's not prohibited, then?'

Silence. 'No, it's not. But it's not a good idea.'

'So how does it work?'

'I can apply for a visitation permit for you. But he'll have to agree ...'

'And if he doesn't want to meet me, then fine. I'll drop it.'

There's nothing I can do to bring my father back, but I can try to do something about Sami. I need to try and fix things, at least see him again.

Lisa returns from the next room dressed for work, and when she's gone, I scroll through the contents of the hard drive. Random documents, their names erased and replaced with obscure codes and date stamps. I file them in chronological order, opening a few as I go along.

Most files deal with my father's personal admin. There are draft news articles, notes and research. Many of the files are entirely corrupted, just a series of hieroglyphics. I stare at the pages for a while as if that might unlock their secrets, but the symbols stay mute.

I work through some older files, grouping them and glancing through the topics, but not reading anything in full. The sun has moved behind the apartment and the desk lamp fills the room with yellow light. Outside, the sky has dimmed, my reflection just a silhouette against the grey. Being up so high there's an unnatural quietness broken only by a plant scraping on the window ledge, and the occasional shudder from the fridge behind me.

I move quickly through the bigger files – scans of newspaper articles and old microfiche. There's no order or sequence within the articles themselves, most documents just single pages, scattered randomly. It's impossible to work out which pages belong where so I focus on those that have a headline and a date, all of them going back to the seventies and eighties.

I keep filing in date order, the topics wide-ranging and uncon-nected but the same authors recur. My father's handwriting criss-crosses the print, and is scribbled in the margins. I stop to read some of the articles, zooming in on his comments or highlighted sections. The newsprint is hazy and nothing stands out.

I come across a series of images from a ledger book of some kind – columns of numbers and dates in neat handwriting. They're scans of my father's bank accounts from the seventies, the same ones that were in the blue file in my aunt's basement. Several large amounts are circled with a thick black pen.

Finally, among a more recent group of corrupted files, there are maps of Paris, sites highlighted and marked with prices and dates, notes written in shorthand.

I move quickly through the last of the files – again, they make no sense until finally, a document looks familiar. It's the list of agents' names I saw in the blue file, but instead of question marks, each name is identified in the final column:

SALARIES (excluding bonus and expenses – francs)

VESTNIK	100,000	Paul
LISSA	50,000	Eddy
GOLUB	30,000 (one-off)	Frederic
KRASNY	40,000	Jean-Marc
OREL	40,000	Elena

Following this is another document, a scan of a loose, handwritten page, signed 'Vestnik':

Frankly speaking, the services are becoming more difficult to supply given my new role, and I have sudden financial commitments I need to reconcile.

You might worry about the larger payments, but you need not. I have a bank account in Switzerland, and you can send the fees there instead.

— Vestnik

I sit back, not sure what any of it means, or if it means anything at all. It's like I'm racing around slippery corners only to cover ground I've just been over, then running straight into a dead end. Numbers and dates swim before my eyes.

Your father died in the middle of a puzzle, Patrick says, as though he's in the room with me. I feel once more the strange urgency of his words when he visited me in prison. *Women were always your father's motivation. They were his weakness. It was never money.*

I stare out of the window. Which women? What money? What the hell did he mean? If I thought, like Patrick, my father's files held the answers we were both mistaken. All I had now was more questions.

Twenty-Eight
Passy

A DRAUGHT CREEPS UNDER THE DOOR, cramping my shoulders and neck. I stretch out on the bed and try to piece all this together. I think back to what Céline told me – about my father being tricked into becoming an agent of some kind, trying to draw a connection between that, the articles and the names in his files.

There are footsteps along the corridor, a soft knock at the door.

'I thought you were asleep,' Lisa says, bringing the freshness of outside into the close, dark room. She puts down a large dish of noodles and chicken, two plates and some cutlery, and we eat cross-legged on the bed, plates balanced on our knees.

She breaks off a beer from a six pack and hands it to me. 'So what have you found?'

'Not much,' I say.

I roll the cold metal on my forehead, trying to freeze out the ache behind my eyes, then I reach over to turn off the computer.

'Wait. Let me have a look.'

She sits at the desk and starts scrolling through the documents, opening several. I feel a swell of anxiety, reluctant to let her pry through it all.

'I should be going now,' I say, my hand on the hard drive.

She turns to me. 'What do you mean?'

'It's late.'

She shakes her head. 'Haven't you seen the news? You won't be able to get home now. The attack last night. There's some kind of siege going on up at Saint-Denis. They've shot five men.'

'A *siege?*'

'Everything's shut down – metro, buses, roads. I thought you must have seen it since you're still here. It's everywhere on the news, and look,' she says, taking a leaflet from her bag. 'These were all over the metro.'

The leaflet is written in an elaborate cursive script on paper the colour of parchment. It says that the 'Soldiers of the Caliphate' claim responsibility for the Les Halles attack. They say it was inspired by Allah and his Messenger, and is part of a plan to cleanse and punish the people of Paris for their perversion and debauchery.

'We were covering it at work. It's why I'm late. Apparently, the attack last night is the first in a series. They're going for strategic points around the city.'

'So if the attack was at Les Halles, why is the siege going on in the suburbs?'

'There were gunmen at Les Halles, but they fled beyond the Péri. At least that's the word on Twitter. Although others say it was a bomb and the attackers were all killed. No one at work knows what's going on, and each of the papers is running something different. At the moment it's just speculation, but the whole area beyond the Péri is in lockdown.'

She turns to the screen and suddenly everything – my father's old documents, Lisa's interest, her apartment perched right above her parents', now this attack and lockdown – feels claustrophobic, stifling, and I need to escape.

'What's the matter?' she says, as I start to pack my bag.

I point to the screen she's looking at. 'Why are you so interested in all this?'

'Come on. I was there, too, remember?' Her voice changes pitch, suddenly serious. 'And I still feel bad about my involvement back then. I want to help you.'

It's the first time she's admitted any 'involvement', but it makes me suspicious – like I should have been about her all those years ago.

She continues scrolling, engrossed in the screen. 'It's hard enough restoring your own meltdown, let alone someone else's. All this material – it's impossible to work this out alone. I can help you.'

Suddenly, I don't believe her at all and I push her wrist from the keyboard.

'Hey, back off,' she says.

'What about those texts this morning?'

'What?'

'On your phone. When you were at my place.'

'You went through my phone?'

'I should have done it a long time ago. Who's *Steph*?'

She moves away. 'She's a work colleague.'

'Do you tell your *work colleagues* what you do at night?'

'Why should I tell you?' she says.

'And why should I tell you any of this? Why should I let you look through these files?'

There's a pause as she taps her fingers on her phone. Finally, she nods. 'OK, then. I was excited when I heard from you. I thought there could be a story in it. I told one of my workmates I was meeting you. So what?'

She bites her lip, clearly embarrassed by the way it sounds.

'*A story*? Is that what this is? Something for the gossip section perhaps: *My Friend, the Patricidal Maniac.*'

She smiles. 'Actually, you know what? It is a story. But not like that.' She points to the screen. 'If there's something here that proves someone else killed your father, then why wouldn't you want it published in every paper in the country?'

I stare at her, still not trusting her, but wondering what I have to lose. Perhaps she can help me, and she's right about the publicity.

'I scour archives all day. Research. Fact checking. This is what I do,' she says. 'And yes, this is interesting.'

'It feels hopeless. None of it makes sense.'

'Tell me.'

'I know he was hacked a few times, but these files are a mess,' I say. 'He was researching something. But I have no idea what it was.'

'And you think it's linked to his death?'

'Yes,' I say quietly. 'Sami didn't kill him. I know that, but I'm not sure who did, or why. I've been looking into this since Patrick died earlier this year. I think it's connected to Patrick's death, too.'

I'm used to people rolling their eyes at this point, telling me I'm a conspiracy theorist, deranged, *paranoid*, but her expression stays the same. I tell her about my meeting with Céline, how she was helping my father reconnect with people from the past, about him and his colleagues being agents of some kind. Then I take her back through the things I've filed.

'Céline said he wanted to know who else was involved and who was behind it all. She was a bit all over the place and I don't know what to believe. But she said she thought my father was onto something because he was too worried for it to be nothing. Those were her words.'

'And these articles?'

'They're old articles by the same journalists – my father, Tomas's dad, Nathan's mother, other colleagues. There are hard copies at my aunt's place.'

'The same articles?'

'Same kind of thing.'

I scroll through the files on the computer, showing her what's there, taking her through it all.

'What's that?' she says after a while. 'Go back. Let me see that.'

It's a document with a map, then a list of place names and addresses.

'I recognise some of those places,' she says, her finger sliding down the screen. 'Charenton, Ivry, Issy. They're places in the suburbs around Paris. Old forts. And this one's near you,' she says, moving the mouse so the cursor circles the name: Fort d'Aubervilliers.

The next page shows a valuation, the ownership of the Aubervilliers site, a list of tenants and a map of the area. There's a short article by Elena from about eight years ago about contamination at the fort, saying the whole area needs a massive clean-up.

Attached to her article is a series of surveys and pollution reports outlining past decontamination operations.

'And look at this,' I say. 'There's a version of this at my aunt's place.'

I open the file of names and salaries.

'These are the agents Céline told me about. See here, my father has identified himself as Lissa, and Golub seems to be someone called Frederic. The top one, Vestnik, is Paul Chambière.

'The payments for Lissa stack up with ones my father received,' I say, flicking to his bank statements, where the annual payment of 50,000 francs is circled.

She taps the screen. 'If your father was seeing Céline to get information from Paul and their friends, then isn't Paul the one you need to speak to?'

I tell her I saw him when I visited Céline, and that it's clear he blames me for Tomas's disappearance.

'What happened to Tomas wasn't your fault,' she says after a while. 'You can't blame yourself for everything.'

'I don't,' I say. 'What do you mean, *what happened to Tomas wasn't your fault?*'

She sighs heavily. 'He took off after I told him your father and his mother were having an affair.'

I pull on the chair, so she swivels around to face me. 'You *what?*'

'Well, it wasn't quite like that. He already suspected. I just confirmed it,' she says, her eyes fixed on mine. 'He told me ages before that he'd seen her phone, heard his parents arguing about your father. That's why he hated you. That's why he harassed you at school and beat you up. At first, I tried to convince him it wasn't true, so he'd stop. But then one night much later I got

269

drunk, and I told him what you'd told me – that you'd actually seen them together.'

'When was this?'

'It was after your father died. Sometime that January. That was the last I saw of him. He left that week.'

I flick through the files slowly, taking in what she's just said, and remembering all her destructive, meddling ways. I never asked her to get involved, and I hadn't asked for her help now. What was she doing back in my life? The memory of the old Lisa, the way she and Tomas manipulated me, comes flooding back like she's tricked me once again.

'You promised to keep it a secret,' I say.

'Come on, Alex. Didn't he have the right to know? Wouldn't you want to know the truth about that, especially if you already suspected? Isn't that exactly what you're doing now with all of this – trying to find out what happened?'

'Why didn't you tell me back then that Tomas suspected what was going on between Céline and my father?'

'Yes, I should have. Instead, I thought getting you two together as friends would help.'

'As *friends*? You mean, becoming his dealer? Well, that was a stupid idea. Just think how that backfired.'

'Look,' she says. 'I really do feel terrible about everything that happened. I know a lot of it was my fault ...' Her voice trails off, and she shakes her head. 'That's why I want to help you with this.'

I take another beer. 'You said Tomas was living in some hippy commune. Is he still there?'

'Right now? I'm not sure. Le Chapot, they call it. I went there once. He's OK. A bit lost.' She waves at the screen. 'But think about it. You could go to Paul, tell him Tomas's disappearance wasn't your fault. He might listen. And he might help you decipher all this.'

'Yeah, and he might not.'

I look at Paul's name on the screen above my father's then pick up the leaflet she found on the metro and read it again:

Paris, the city of corruption, will tremble beneath the feet of the soldiers of Allah and his Messenger, and its streets will draw narrow and run with the blood of unbelievers.

'The Messenger,' I say, shaking it towards her. 'Allah and his Messenger.'

I tell her what Céline said. About my father and Patrick arguing about some kind of messenger.

'If Paul was there then you need to speak to him,' she says eventually. 'And if he's on this list, being paid all that money, then you need to find out what it's all about. You need to find out what he knows.'

THEN

Mid-December

Twenty-Nine

Saint-Germain

I KEPT RECEIVING TEXTS FROM TOMAS – pictures of dead birds and vermin, messages saying I'd be next. He knew where I lived, so I couldn't go home, and home was the last place I wanted to be. I got no response from Sami so I wandered the streets near his building that first night and slept a few hours in a doorway. My mother still wasn't answering her phone; I even went to their apartment, but there was no one there. I considered calling my aunt, but she lived right next to my father. Finally, in desperation, I called Patrick.

Later that evening, he embraced me at the door and told me my father was there too. I tried to leave, but he gripped my arm and led me inside.

My father was on the sofa with Elena. We greeted each other awkwardly, and then Patrick followed Elena to the kitchen, leaving us alone. There were scratches on his cheek and he had a black eye – a drinking injury, I guessed.

He touched his face as if reading my mind while we made small talk about the weather and football scores, both of us relaxing a bit as the smell of grilled meat wafted over from the kitchen.

At dinner, I ate quickly, clearing my plate and helping myself to more. The atmosphere was tense, everyone choosing words carefully. We kept to non-controversial topics – Christmas, which was fast approaching, and the holidays. Patrick did most of the talking while my father and I cast furtive looks at each other. I realised I didn't even know it was the school holidays, let alone Christmas. It had been quick the way my focus had narrowed, and I felt even more disconnected from them all than usual.

After a couple of glasses of wine, his attention shifted from me, and my father started needling Elena about her work again. The youth clubs she ran in the suburbs had received a lot of attention following the car bomb the week before.

'They say we need to work closely with the police to monitor what goes on,' said Elena.

'Like what?'

'Well, they want names and addresses of whoever uses the space, what they do there. That kind of thing.'

'That's ridiculous. They can't prove any links,' said my father.

'They say they can, but of course, they're not in a position to disclose without risking their sources,' said Elena.

'They always say that. It's bullshit. But, you know, the local elections.'

'Rumours say it's a new terrorist group, and that the bombers have links to the refugee centres and camps along the Péri. They've bulldozed them all.'

'Since last week?'

Elena nodded.

My father kept asking about the youth clubs, and how much she had to do with them. At first, it felt like he was trying to avoid speaking to me, but as he drank, his questions became more insistent, as they had with her a couple of weeks ago.

'He's a veritable oligarch now, with his media and property interests.'

'Eddy, the properties are hardly high-end. They're affordable housing in the suburbs.'

'Don't be so sure. Pretty soon he'll be running for President. I wouldn't put it past him.'

I couldn't work out whether he was genuinely interested in her work, or just wanted to wind her up. The atmosphere grew tense until, finally, Patrick changed the subject.

Towards the end of the meal the topic of the Christmas holidays came up again, and my father put his arm around my shoulders.

'I thought we'd go skiing for a few days over New Year,' he said.

I looked at him, surprised. This was the first time he'd ever suggested we go skiing – I could barely ski – but he said it like it was something we did every year. It felt like a show he was putting on for Patrick and Elena. They must have known it was a sham, and I felt awkward, complicit in his phoney act.

'You look horrified,' he said.

I shrugged, not wanting to make a big deal of it.

'Come on, Alex, it won't be that bad. Think of all the opportunities to push me off a ski-lift,' he said, turning to the others.

Everyone laughed except me. He'd had a lot to drink and was doing his usual thing of running gags at my expense, belittling me in front of everyone. It was hard to take offence because as usual, they were *jokes*, and they also had a grain of truth, especially the bit about me wanting to push him off the ski-lift. I knew he was still seething after our argument the day before, and this pretence that he'd moved on was unusual for him. It made me much more anxious than if he'd stayed angry, and I didn't know what to think of his performance.

At the end of the meal, I helped Patrick in the kitchen. He told me I was welcome to stay with them as long as I liked if I wasn't getting on with my father. It was as if Patrick was trying to make up for his behaviour.

Just then, he appeared at the kitchen door as if summoned by our discussion. 'Yes, where *are* you staying now?'

'Mum's,' I said.

'There you go, lying again,' he said, filling his glass from a bottle on the side.

Patrick raised his hand in warning. 'Eddy, we agreed—'

He ignored Patrick and drew closer, slouching against the kitchen cabinet as he swirled the wine in his glass. 'I've just learned your mother's moved to the Bahamas, so unless you've joined her in the jet-set with a high-speed commute, I very much doubt it.'

I was thrown by the news and just stared at him, dumbstruck. She'd said Monaco. And worse, she hadn't even called to say goodbye.

'That's new, you two speaking to each other,' I managed to say, though I felt like I was falling.

It was then he told me what had happened. My mother wasn't joking when she spoke about the 'tax nonsense', but it turned out to be much more serious. Apparently, Olivier was on the run from the French authorities for some kind of fraud. All their assets in France had been frozen, and they never went to Monaco at all.

'Let's not discuss this now,' Patrick said sharply, ushering us back to the table where my father, flushed with alcohol and the triumph of revealing my mother's sudden disgrace, took off his sweater and sat down.

'Eddy!' Elena gasped, reaching forward to touch his neck, gently pulling aside his shirt. His collarbone was swollen and long reddish bruises extended down his chest. 'Eddy, that looks terrible.'

'It's fine,' he said, shrugging her off. 'It's not broken, just bruised. I fell off my bike.'

'Look who's lying now,' I said.

They all stared at me.

'Why do you believe his bullshit?' I said.

There was a deathly silence around the table.

'All of his lies about women, his drinking, this so-called *fall*.' I looked from Elena to Patrick. 'Why do you put up with it? He comes here, drinks all your booze, insults Elena about her work. He's always picking a fight. Why doesn't anyone ever tell him to just shut the fuck up?'

My father reached towards me. 'Alex—'

'You don't even have a bike,' I said, grabbing my bag as I left the apartment.

Now there was nowhere I could stay. I couldn't find Sami, he still wasn't answering his phone, so I walked the streets near his building until I passed a metro station in a square flanked by cafés and shops. It was a cold night, and there was a large vent above the station with three drunks sleeping over the grate. I huddled near them in the warm air that rose from the tunnels below.

I stayed in the area for the rest of the week, checking his building and the markets daily but there was no sign of Sami. I couldn't hang around and wait for him for fear of running into Nick, to whom I still owed money – so I staked it out from across the road. Each time I went near their place, I passed the people on the traffic island. At first, I'd been an observer, but now I saw the street from their perspective. Like them, I'd been thrown from my life. They were the wreckage of wars and misery, and although their trajectory had been very different from mine, here we were at the same place. I watched the people flashing past on the motorway, warm and safe in their cars like I once was, and I wondered if they ever glanced over to those on the island. Did they ever realise, as they sped towards airports and homes, how close they were to such a fate themselves?

I tried to buy food but none of my cards were working and when I asked at the bank, they told me my accounts had been frozen. So I started begging outside the metro, trying to catch the sympathy of tourists as they headed up towards Montmartre. At first, it was embarrassing, and most people looked away, but it was nearly Christmas, and if I stayed there long enough, someone would toss me a few coins, and that spurred me on. One day, a woman saw me and clutched her heart. I thought she was having a seizure after walking up all those stairs, but I think she was just shocked to see someone so young begging. I smiled sadly and ran my hand through my hair. It worked, and her eyes welled up as she emptied the contents of her purse into my lap. The drunks saw what happened and tried to get in on the act, calling out to her as she hurried off.

That was a good day, but mostly it was a waste of time. No matter what I sat on – boxes, clothes, wooden crates, the cold made its way through my flesh and numbed me from arse to heart, so it was hard to tell where I ended and the pavement began.

I got to know the drunks who spent their days on the opposite side of the square. In the mornings, they sunned themselves on a bench near the café, guzzling steadily from large soft-drink containers. Occasionally, they'd laugh and slur obscenities at the tourists, baring what few teeth they had. By the afternoon, they could no longer sit upright, so they lay on flattened cardboard and old newspapers. Fluids oozed from them in long dark stains, like tongues licking the gutter.

One day, I watched them tempt a pigeon towards them with crumbs from a baguette. One of them threw a blanket over the pigeon, handed it to another who sawed off its head with his pocketknife while the others cheered him on. Afterwards, they thrust the bloodied corpse at passers-by like a bunch of tulips and laughed like crazy as people screamed and leaped back. Finally, a man belted the pigeon with an umbrella and its headless body barrelled through the air, its wings outspread in one last groggy flap before landing on the pavement near the café.

The owner tried to chase the drunks away. He doused the pavement with a steaming bucket of bleach, and then jabbed them with the mop and told them to move, saying they were bad for business.

'We'll move for a drink!' one of them said.

Later, after a few hours of silent stand-off, the owner came out with a bottle of wine, offered it up for inspection as though they were customers, and then opened it with an exaggerated flourish. He told them they could have it if they moved on, and so they collected their things, and the whole heaving, stinking, mass of them lumbered over and took position right next to me.

They told me they used to perform vaudeville in the tourist restaurants of Montmartre. One of them had played the accordion while the others danced and did routines. They gave a drunken rendition of a song from their past, and it was surprisingly good – they could still carry a tune. They kept up the singing, but it soon became clear having them next to me was bad for my business as well. It detracted from my appeal as a down-and-out waif, reminding people of the all-too-ugly reality, so they'd sooner kick me than give me their money.

I had to make up a story to get rid of them. I told them Monoprix was having a sale on drink, that they were almost giving it away. I watched them argue and peck over coins – their flat, dark fingers running over greasy palms until at last, one of them reeled off to buy the booze. He was gone for hours, and in his absence, the other two talked about him endlessly: *Where was he? When would he be back? What would he buy? Where did he go again? How much could he carry? Perhaps he's drunk it all himself, the bastard.* Finally, they tired of waiting, gathered up their rotting cardboard, blankets and plastic bags, into a supermarket trolley, and went off in search of him. It was good to have the patch to myself again, but the next day they were back, greeting me like an old friend, forgetting all about the false lead.

Each day passed like that, more or less the same, while I became hungrier, colder and dirtier. The drunks didn't often behead pigeons, and only once did a woman empty her purse into my lap, but the grey light and filth of the square remained the same, and the bone-cramping coldness never changed. At night, the drunks gathered in their blankets and lay on the steel grate of the metro. They slept there all rolled up together, heads percolating with methylated dreams, bodies buoyed on rats' breath and fumes from the dusty tunnels below.

The more I got used to this routine, the less my old life felt real. I focused each day on essentials like getting money, charging my phone and finding something to eat while all around me people made preparations for Christmas. As my world shrank, things became easier – there were no decisions to make, but it worried me how quickly this had happened. I knew my life had swerved down an unfamiliar path, but I'd convinced myself this was a temporary thing, an adventure even, and my life would soon get back on track. I had plenty of time, I thought, not able to see that this little diversion had now become my course.

At first, I told myself it was the outcome of bad luck. It was certainly not my choice. But as time wore on, I became angrier. I was in this mess because of decisions others had made, and one person in particular. It was obvious there was one person at fault, and one person to blame. One person, in fact, who stood between my life as it was, and my life as it should be.

'You should call your father, Alex. I know he'd like to hear from you,' my aunt said when I finally managed to charge my phone and ring her asking for money. She said my father's bank had told him they could only reinstate the money I'd stolen if he reported it to the police and so he had. They hadn't brought charges, but it was a possibility and this was why my accounts had been frozen. There was no way I was going to speak to him.

I was about to hang up.

'Your father's been trying to reach you. He wants to make sure you'll join us at my apartment on Christmas Day.'

The last thing I wanted was to see him again, but I needed cash, and there weren't many alternatives, so I agreed.

My aunt said my father had told my mother everything and finally, she called me. It was then she said she was in the Bahamas. It was late there, and I could tell she'd been drinking. She begged me to tell her I was OK and so I did. I asked her for money but she refused, and kept saying the same things she'd said to me outside the restaurant: that things were complicated, that Olivier was involved in something *difficult*, that she was powerless but that she would try and get here as soon as she could after Christmas.

I kept checking Sami's building and finally one morning, the front door was ajar. I climbed the seven flights and found him stripped to the waist, washing at the sink, surrounded by boxes. There were bruises on his shoulders, and his face was a mess.

'What happened to you?' I said, but he shook his head.

He reached into a small plastic bag full of a yellow buttery substance and gently daubed some of it on his face where the welts were.

He held the bag out to me. 'Here. Try this,' he said.

'What is it?'

'*Karité*. Shea butter. I got it for you from the African market. It will stop all that itching you do.'

'Thanks,' I said, looking away from his face. The butter had made his black eye shinier and more menacing. I wanted to ask him if it was Nick who had done that to him, but I already knew the answer.

'Are you supposed to sell all of this shit now?' I said, peering inside one of the boxes that were stacked up against the wall – it was full of plastic toys.

'It's Christmas. Everyone wants that shit.'

I walked to the window, pressing my forehead to the glass.

Sami spoke quietly. 'Nick wants the money you owe him, and the money for the stuff you ordered and didn't collect. He wants it this week.'

I spun around. 'But I didn't order anything. And he's the one who owes me money for those bad pills.'

'Shut up about that,' he said. 'He knows you've been hanging around here and he wants rent. This will get worse.' He sounded tough, but there was fear in his eyes.

I had no intention of paying Nick anything, but I needed money and somewhere to stay. I knew that if I stayed on the streets much longer, I'd end up like the drunks, or worse. I kicked the pile of boxes where Sami had placed his clothes, and they fell to the floor. 'I know you make a lot on the metro. I could help you with that.'

Sami took a towel from under the sink and wiped his face. 'It's a waste of time, these small scams. We need real money, think of something else. What about your friends? Did you get the codes?'

I thought about the kids at school, the well-secured apartments with concierges. 'Thanks to Nick and his poisonous pills, that's not going to happen. They don't want to know me.'

'It wasn't the pills. It was something else they'd taken.'

'Let *me* speak to Nick. You said he lives here, right?'

Sami laughed sourly and pointed to his face. 'Why? So you can have your pretty face messed up too?'

A coldness gripped me, and I wanted to run, but I couldn't move.

He lifted up his shirt, showed me the bruises on his body. 'This is what he does. It's how he controls people.'

'What does he want?'

'He wants the rest of the money, and he's angry that you've been here, stalking the place. He said it draws bad attention.'

I stared at Sami's body, at the beating he'd taken because of me. It was only a matter of time before I got that too.

'These friends of yours. Just give me names, addresses. You don't need to be there,' he said.

The most obvious apartment was Lisa's. I knew where she lived. I also knew her parents weren't around much. But they had serious staff and it was risky, we couldn't do that. I shook my head. There was only one other place I could think of.

'What about my father's apartment?'

As soon as I spoke, I knew I'd gone too far. I don't know what possessed me, but I was desperate, not thinking straight. I was furious with him after his behaviour at Elena and Patrick's, and for reporting me to the police.

'Your *father*?' Sami said in disbelief, pulling on his tracksuit trousers.

He was right. It was a ridiculous idea, but my father was out most nights, and anything of value was insured. 'We could break in at night when he's out.' I said, thinking quickly. I knew that Sami had done it before. He'd know what to do and it might work. At that point it felt like our best option.

'Break in when he's out?' he said. 'Don't you have a key?'

'I left it there,' I said. 'But we could easily break in.'

Hearing myself speak those words, and actually think through what it would require, made it suddenly feel like a terrible idea. What if something went wrong? The guardian, or one of the neighbours might see us.

'Then again he doesn't have much to steal,' I added, but I knew from the look on Sami's face that the idea had taken root and there was no going back now.

He laughed. 'That's what rich people think, but there's always something. He has a computer, watches, yes? And money, cards, all this kind of thing we can take.'

I shook my head, as the cold reality of robbing my father sunk in. 'No. It's a bad idea.'

He was standing opposite me now, and he leaned in closer. I could see his crooked teeth up close, smell his sour, nicotine-slaked breath. I felt that same coil of excitement and fear from the first time we met. It was terrifying, but powerful, almost exhilarating.

'So we try your friends, then?'

I thought back to Lisa's place, even Tomas's. They were grand apartments, much more security, and there would always be someone home. 'No, actually our apartment would be better.'

He rubbed his throat. He hadn't washed his face properly, and the water had left streaks of dirt on his neck, like long brown scratches.

Then his body relaxed, and he smiled. 'Or you just call your dad. Tell him you're in trouble, you need cash. He has a lot of money, Alex. He should share it.'

'I'm not calling him. He won't give me money over the phone like that.'

He lowered his voice. 'OK, back to the plan, then. I'll break in, you know, make a mess. I'll make it look like a proper robbery.'

He went to the sink and rustled around with his washing and clothes. I knew the plan was crazy, the whole idea threw me into turmoil, but everything was closing in and we needed a way out. Sami seemed confident he could do it, and at that moment, he was the only person I could rely on. He needed to escape from Nick and I needed to get away from my father. We were bound together now in a common purpose.

'Why should you live like this?' Sami pointed around the room. 'He's your father, your family. It's your money too.'

I nodded, he was right, it was partly my money. If it went well, Sami could be in and out quickly. I could tell him exactly where everything was.

Sami came over, put his hands on my shoulders and pulled me towards him, his face close to mine.

'You don't have to come with me. You can stay here,' he said softly.

I felt comforted by his words, his warm, heavy hands, and relief flowed through me. I knew he would make everything work out somehow.

His voice grew softer, and he looked over my shoulder, out of the window. 'I have cousins in Lyon, Marseille. Real cousins. We could go there afterwards. It will be safe. We can get away from this place.'

Over the next two days, I tried to put the whole thing out of my mind. Being with Sami again was a bit like coming home, and we fell back into the same routine. Sami didn't mention the robbery again, but I thought about it a lot. I had the building code and the apartment itself would be easy to break into. Sami knew how to pick locks, and the place was by no means high security. May had gone back to the Philippines for Christmas, so there was no chance of running into her, but there was the guardian to get past and two sets of neighbours on the fifth floor to consider. Someone like him would be arrested if he was lurking around an apartment in the sixth arrondissement. No, he couldn't just break in. So I thought of a better idea and soon a plan formed in my mind.

When I saw Sami next, he was a mess. Another dark welt traced his eye socket, his lip split like a ripe plum, deep scratches all over his hands. He didn't tell me what had happened, he didn't need to.

'I'll call my father, tell him I'm sending a friend round to collect something – one of my books or something like that. Once he opens the door, you can just ask him for money. Say I'm in trouble and need cash. There'll be no need for violence or a break-in.'

Sami liked this idea, and he started calling me his brother again.

'I'll call him tomorrow, Christmas Eve. It's good timing, all the neighbours will be away.'

The next afternoon, we went to Castorama for gloves and lock-picking equipment in case my father was out. As we cruised the aisles, Sami picked up a hammer with a yellow and black handle and a claw head. He held it towards me.

'What do you think?'

He swung the hammer towards my knee, like a golf club. 'In case there's any trouble.'

I laughed, thinking it was a joke, but he wasn't joking. It wasn't just his usual bravado.

'Any problems with the neighbours, we need protection,' he said, his face suddenly savage, all twisted and swollen.

'No. Put it down.'

'If I'm going to do this, I need it,' he said, jabbing me in the ribs with the handle, hooking my sweatshirt with the claw end.

'You said it would be easy. You didn't say anything about a *weapon*.'

'It's not a weapon, it's a *tool*, and I won't use it. Just as a threat in case there's any trouble. People are terrified of a hammer,' he said, putting it in the basket.

Outside the shop, I borrowed Sami's phone and called my father. His voice was hollow with relief and I almost stopped there, but Sami was staring directly at me. I told him I needed my headphones.

'Where are you, Alex? Whose phone are you using? I've been trying to—'

'A friend's. Mine's out of juice.'

It was cold, and I was shivering. There was silence down the line. I heard the ice in the glass as he took a long drink. Then his voice hardened.

'Alex, I can barely hear you. You're making no sense. I don't see you for days, you don't return my calls, and then you call me demanding – what do you want – *headphones*?'

'They're in my room. He can come right now.'

'Who can come?'

'My friend. Sami.'

'Sami?' he asked.

'You know, the guy I'm staying with.'

'I'm not at the apartment now. I'll bring them to Béa's tomorrow.' He hesitated, his voice hopeful. 'Béa said you'd be there . . .'

Sami came in closer, shaking his head and pointing at his watch.

'Béa's tomorrow? Yes. But I need them tonight. Why can't he come now?'

'No, not now. I can't talk. I need to get back. I'm expecting someone—'

'When are you expecting them? We could come before.'

There was a long pause, and he sighed. 'OK then, come before nine thirty.'

'We'll come at eight. Sami will be there at eight.'

I closed down the phone. Hearing my father say goodbye sent a chill through my bones. I thought of stalling the plan – maybe wait until after Christmas. But then I looked at Sami's swollen face – no, we couldn't wait that long. If we were going to do this, we had to do it now, that night, when everyone was away for Christmas. I gave Sami the go-ahead, and we agreed to meet at the main gates to the Montparnasse cemetery just before eight.

NOW

Thirty

Saint-Germain

THERE WERE A FEW PEOPLE after my trial who surprised me with their support, but Paul Chambière wasn't one of them. His profile online said he still worked at Sciences Po, running one of the big graduate programmes in Paris. I tried calling him first to arrange a meeting, but he made it clear on the phone I was someone he wanted to forget, so I know the only way he'll speak to me now is if he has no choice.

His office at the university is in a townhouse behind high sandstone walls tucked away in an exclusive shopping district in the seventh arrondissement. I wait outside at lunchtime as preppy students surge through the arched entrance.

He leaves the building just after one, and I trail him at a distance until he enters a café. Taking a seat on the terrace, I watch him through the glass. When he sees me he does a double-take, says something to the people he's with, then comes outside.

'I told you there's nothing to discuss,' he says. 'If you continue to harass us, I'll call the police.'

'My father was working on something and he wanted your help.'

He stands there for a moment, stiff as a board. Finally, he gestures to his lunch companions, fingers spread to say, 'Five minutes,' and then points towards a side street.

'Céline said he was working on some kind of memoir. What was it about?'

He stops and waits for me to level up. 'It was a memoir, Alex. What the fuck do you think it was about?'

I stare at him, shocked by his tone.

'Your father was writing about his favourite topic – himself,' he adds irritably.

'If he was writing about himself, why did he need your help?'

A door clicks open behind us, and an old lady appears from the building. The sound startles Paul, and he moves off further down the street.

'Céline said it was about his old colleagues from *La Globe*. So what was it about – himself or his colleagues?' I say.

'For God's sake, Alex, how do I know? I didn't read it.'

'But he told you about it.'

He laughs unpleasantly. 'He said it was a memoir. But it would've been very dull had it just been about him. Even he knew that.' He carries on, his voice reaching a higher pitch. 'It was about things that happened a long time ago. Things no one's interested in now.'

'I'm interested.'

He takes a deep breath, turns to face me, and I see the shadow of Tomas. The same tight jaw, the mean, grey eyes. '*Why?*' he says, making the word into a sigh. 'I don't understand this sudden interest in your father. You were never interested in him when he was alive. Frankly, you behaved as if you wanted him dead—'

'I didn't want him dead—'

'—and now he is dead, you can't leave him alone.' He steps back. 'Of course, you wanted him dead,' he says. 'You made it happen. You let that thug into the building. You admitted it yourself.'

'That's not how it was,' I say, the blood throbbing in my ears, fists tingling with the urge to punch him.

'Guilt comes in many forms, Alex. You of all people should know that.'

'I'm not guilty.'

'You're not *legally* guilty,' he says, his voice loaded with sarcasm. 'But you may as well have the word tattooed across your forehead. Why are you so interested in his work? Why do you pursue these foolish conspiracy theories? What's that if not some kind of guilt trip?'

'It's nothing to do with guilt.'

'You're not sixteen anymore, Alex. You can't stalk people and threaten them on the street. Especially with your record.'

'I'm not stalking you.'

'Eventually, you'll have to take responsibility. It was blindingly obvious you and your friend attacked him—'

'It was so *blinding* no one saw anything else. I'm trying to find out what happened after I left him – *still alive.*' I'm shouting now, heat prickling my chest, cheeks burning. But my words sound desperate, weak with overuse. It's like I'm yelling into the wind, repeating the same thing over and over, *I'm not guilty. I didn't kill him*, hoping if I keep saying it, people will believe me.

There's a long pause, the air ringing.

'What's this really about?' he says finally. 'What do you need to know beyond what Céline's told you?'

'Since I spoke to Céline I've been going through his files.'

'Files?'

'He'd collected old newspaper stories – some in hard copy, others scanned into his laptop, many of which were written by you.'

I'm getting a reaction, so I exaggerate a bit. 'Hundreds of articles, together with drafts, research, notes.'

'What kind of articles?' he says, his voice low, face pinched with intensity.

'Ones from thirty, forty years ago. Why did my father keep so many of your old stories?'

His body flexes. Then he lets out a sigh like surrender. 'Let's not discuss this here.'

He makes a call to his colleagues, excusing himself from lunch, and we walk back to the university building.

We take a wide flight of stairs to the first floor, our footsteps muffled by thick carpet. He ushers me into a book-lined room, sunlight streaming through windows flanked by potted palms. His desk is at an angle, facing out across the room. A large abstract painting looms behind the desk like a theatre backdrop, and classical music emanates from a discreet sound system in the corner.

I stand at the window. Students returning from lunch fill the courtyard, their cheeks even rosier than before. It's a beautiful day – the budding leaves on the plane trees are an unreal shade of lime green, fresh and new in the crystal afternoon light. For a second, I see myself walking with the students outside, joking and laughing. I'm dressed like them in chinos, loafers, expensive coat, and I'm a few inches taller, full of confidence because I know whatever I say, however implausible, will be heard.

Unlike now.

Paul stands next to me, looking outside. 'Your father wanted you to come here,' he says, as if reading my mind. Then he laughs. 'Could you even imagine yourself at a place like this?'

'I had no intention of coming here, or anywhere like it,' I say, stunned by the bitterness in his voice. The question feels like an attack on my father's delusions, rather than mine.

'This place is a life-changer. Kids come here knowing nothing of life. And after three years they're opinion-formers.'

Rammed full of your opinions, I think, turning from the view.

'At least you realised you didn't have what it takes,' he says, walking back to his desk. 'I always thought it was strange. Eddy was clear-sighted about most people, but when it came to you, he really had no idea. He would boast about you and talk about your achievements, such as they were. Right up until the end, he had hopes for you. He never saw your true nature. It was pathetic, really.'

'Like you with Tomas, perhaps?'

A shadow crosses his face, dimming its spiteful glare. My comment has caught him off-guard. He's so wrapped up in my father's delusions that he's forgotten his own.

'You never anticipate the intensity of the disappointment your children can inspire in you,' he says, more to himself than me.

'Perhaps that's right, but without parents like you and Céline, Tomas may have stood a chance.'

He points towards the windows. 'Tomas would be out in that courtyard, or somewhere similar if wasn't for you.'

'Tomas didn't leave because of anything I did. He left because of Céline's affair with my father.'

He turns away. 'I know it upset him when it came out,' he says quietly, leaning on the desk for support.

'No, before it came out. He knew about them from the beginning, and he hated me for it. I only sourced drugs for him

295

to get him off my back. When it became so public, he couldn't take it.'

Paul goes quiet. Then he looks at me like he's forgotten who I am. 'You have no idea,' he says numbly. He sounds detached, like he's put up a wall between himself and the memory.

Anger surges through me. He knows Tomas hated me, but it's easier for him to just blame me for Tomas leaving rather than blaming Céline, or even himself.

What other easy lies does he believe? What other truths does he hide?

He walks to the cabinet and pours a drink. He stands with his back to me. I can only see part of his face, the side of his cheek and the muscles in his jaw, which slowly contract.

'Céline said you hadn't heard from Tomas,' he says finally. I can barely hear him. 'Do you know where he is?'

He turns to me, his eyes cloudy. The contempt is still there, but the hand with the glass shakes very slightly, and in that moment, a trace of understanding passes between us.

'No, I don't know where he is. But I could find out.'

He nods and the relief defuses him somehow.

'If you help me,' I say. 'My father wanted something from you. That weekend we drove to your house he told me he needed your help with work.'

Paul looks at his glass as if weighing up the possibilities. 'He wanted information. He wanted something to prove his own conspiracy theories.'

'About you?'

He laughs, spite returning to his face. 'He would have loved to pin something on me, but he never could and neither can you. Whatever you think you're onto, Alex, you're wrong.'

I reach into my bag and show him the sheet of paper with the words – Vestnik, Lissa and the others, and the names of those my father had identified on the right.

'Your name's here. Is this what he was trying to pin on you?'

He walks to his desk, sits down, and turns the paper over as if looking for clues.

'Who are those people?' I say.

'The words on the left are agents' names. The names on the right are, well, it's me, your father and colleagues of ours. He knew he was Lissa, of course, but he wasn't sure about the others. They were just guesses.'

'And you were Vestnik?'

'He thought I was, but I wasn't.'

'So what was it about?'

He pushes the paper away. 'They called it *active measures*, a scheme of recruiting journalists to influence public opinion through misinformation and propaganda.'

'Was this what he was writing about in his memoir?'

'I believe so.'

'Then this is what got him killed.'

He shakes his head and his jowls quiver. 'All of this happened a long time ago. Most of the people are retired now, or dead. The rest don't care.'

'Then why did my father care so much? Why did he sleep with your wife to get at you, or what you knew?'

'Céline thought he was sleeping with her to get at me, but perhaps he wasn't. Perhaps he loved her,' he says, letting out that condescending laugh again. 'Who knows what his motivation was?'

I point to the paper. 'And his motivation for this? Why did he do it?'

'Your father always said he'd been trapped. He said he'd been blackmailed into running their stories and propaganda, and that's why he left *La Globe*. Years later he returned to Paris full of remorse and an urge to come clean. That might have been fine, but he wanted to drag everyone else down with him, expose them all. That's where the problems began.'

'Problems for who? You?'

'Not me. I wasn't an agent. I wrote things I believed in, but others didn't. They did it for money.'

'So they were told what to write?'

'More or less. The Soviets or whoever would launch a story in a local paper – India, or Africa. It could be just a letter. Many conspiracies started life as an anonymous letter in an Indian newspaper – *The Patriot*, it was called. The paper was set up by the KGB for the sole purpose of publishing disinformation.'

'And they'd report on that?'

'Exactly. A journalist here would then pick up the story and get it published in the Western media as a secondary report. All your Cold War conspiracy theories – they needed someone to spread them, and they used people like Eddy.'

'Did anyone suspect?'

'Yes, but by the time they did, it was too late. A lot of the material started with a grain of truth. To manipulate the truth, you have to have a truth in the first place. And people want to *believe*. They want simple stories. The simpler, the better. And rumour does the rest. Like a pebble dropped into a pond, the ripples spread out and it becomes self-sustaining.'

The courtyard outside is silent, and there's a shift in the air, an emptiness in the room.

'Céline said Patrick and my father argued about some kind of messenger.'

He looks startled for a second, then recovers himself. 'I don't remember that.'

'Who was the messenger? Was it a reference to Mohammed?'

He looks out of the window, making a pretence of recollection, his eyes still. 'No, nothing like that.'

'And there were maps of Paris in my father's papers. Plans and drawings. What are they about?'

'I have no idea what he was doing apart from what I've just told you.'

'So why did my father think you were involved?'

'He dug up things I wrote and said they proved I had communist sympathies. I did back then, but I wasn't a spy.'

It's my turn to laugh now. I'd never seen a communist and didn't know what one looked like, but I knew it was nothing like him with his plush office, the artwork and the antiques.

'Yes, hard to believe now, isn't it? That's why Eddy never really believed it,' he says.

'I don't believe it either.'

'No. You wouldn't understand, but back then it was fashionable. Whereas today clothes, money, appearances are considered cool, back then it was what you thought. Now if anyone accuses you of being a communist, it's a joke, an insult. The focus now is on lining your pockets instead.'

He stands up and comes closer. 'Eddy wasn't a bad man, but you won't find absolution by looking into the circumstances of his death. Your father never achieved much in his life, so why would his death be extraordinary?'

'I'm not looking for *absolution*. I'm looking for answers, and I don't think the answers lie in ideals. My father was interested in reality.'

'No, he wasn't. He was side-tracked into a fantasy, and so are you.'

'It wasn't like him to dwell on the past, to chase down a dead story,' I say.

'The problem was it was his own dead story. His own central role made him biased. He believed it was still relevant because he thought *he* was still relevant. And he wasn't.'

Thirty-One

Vincennes

PAUL ESCORTS ME FROM HIS office across the wide, cobbled courtyard. He nods to the security guard as we pass through the gates then stops abruptly, extending his hand.

'I hope that's answered your questions,' he says, as though we'd just been discussing economics. He shakes my hand as if pushing me away.

When I reach the corner, I glance back. He's there on his phone, watching me.

Entering the metro, my phone beeps with a message:

> I know what he was working on. Meet me at the café opposite Vincennes this afternoon 14.30.

The text is from the number I found in my father's files with the name, Mari. I hadn't had a response since sending the message three days ago, but the timing is bizarre, as if the sender has just seen me say goodbye to Paul.

> Who is this?

I text back, but the message fails. I try to call, but there's no answer.

People swirl around me on the platform. Most are on their phones, and I search their faces, wondering if it's someone close by.

It's already 2 o'clock, and the limited service on the metro means I can't change trains in case I'm followed, so I just swap carriages a few times. My phone's on, and I know I can be tracked, but I don't care now.

The café is on the edge of a park, opposite a fairground, and there's a relaxed, out-of-town feel with music and carnival rides rising above the fence. The terrace is crowded with people finishing their lunch and enjoying the afternoon sun. I scan the tables. Only one person sits alone, absorbed in his phone. He looks familiar, and I linger nearby. Mari could be a man, Marion. But he ignores me, so I move into the café, taking a seat near the window with a view across the road.

A dark-haired woman follows me inside. Careful make-up so I can't tell her age, but I guess around fifty, and she's dressed neatly in a skirt and a black sweater.

'Hello, Alex,' she says quietly, glancing behind her. 'Do you mind if we sit further back?' she adds, and I follow her into the shadows.

She arranges her seat so it's facing the door and sits with her handbag on her lap. 'We met very briefly a long time ago. You won't remember.'

I shake my head. 'Were you a friend of my father's?'

'Not exactly a friend, but I knew him well.'

We place our orders with the waiter then she reaches into her bag and pushes a USB stick across the table. 'This contains all of the information I gave your father, and to Patrick.'

A chill slides in beside the stick, and I stare at her small, pale hand cupped over it like a croupier's over dice. She fixes me with a stern look, her mouth downcast. 'I sent it to them separately. To your father about a month before he died, then to Patrick earlier this year.'

I sit back, considering the implications of this.

'You need to be careful, Alex,' she says, as the waiter appears with our drinks. When he's gone, she speaks quickly, glancing past me towards the door as she stirs her coffee. There are white animal hairs on the sleeve of her sweater, a contrast to her otherwise controlled appearance.

'What's it about?' I ask.

'It's all on the stick. Some of it is explicit, I have to warn you. Hidden cameras, you'll see.'

'Cameras?'

'They had a camera across the road from the club in Montparnasse. There's old footage of your father. He was looking into that old material and that's what led him to me. At first, I gave him some photos I'd found of him and others, taken at the club – he didn't know. The newer material is more financial – plans for the development of the properties they're buying up in Aubervilliers, Bobigny, Montreuil and La Courneuve. Details of the offshore ownership, the directors and the prospectus for the Issy site. The background's all there.'

'Wait, wait,' I say, confused by the sudden rush of information. 'What is this?'

'I work for Ligne Rouge. It's a massive development in the suburbs,' she says, pointing at the stick that lies between us. She stops abruptly and checks her phone, and then scans the restaurant again as if she's not sure which holds the greatest threat. Her constant agitation fuels my paranoia, and the hairs stand up on my neck as though someone's right behind me.

'So what's the connection between all this and my father?'

'Eddy was investigating the activities of the company I work for. I'd been worried about it for years, but did nothing. It was only after Eddy got involved that I realised the full extent of it.'

A couple enters the restaurant, taking a seat nearby. She finishes her espresso and gets up to leave.

'No, wait,' I say, grabbing her wrist. 'Please. You're the first person I've met who can tell me what's going on.'

'It's all there,' she says, pushing the stick towards me. 'The hidden structure and ownership. I set the companies up through a network of trusts and offshore shell companies. In the beginning, I thought everything was above board, nothing out of the ordinary. Please – I need to leave.'

I look at the stick and then at her. 'Someone connected to all this killed my father?' I ask.

She pulls on her jacket, anxious now. 'I believe so.'

'And prompted Patrick to do what? Kill himself?'

She shakes her head impatiently, and then looks at me sadly. 'Of course he didn't kill himself.'

Everything fades as the certainty in her voice sinks in.

'What are you saying? How do you know?' I say, suddenly angry at her evasiveness and these half-explanations. 'Why did you give all this is to Eddy and Patrick? Why endanger their lives? And why are you giving it to *me*?'

'Someone needs to do something.'

'Why not go to the police? Since when did journalists become stand-in cops, on-call to investigate and mete out justice when other avenues had failed?'

'The authorities aren't interested, and besides, it could get me into much more trouble. Passing on this information is a breach of my duties, possibly even theft. I'm not supposed to do this.'

'But if it's illegal—'

'I didn't say it was illegal.'

I stare into her dark eyes. Her nervousness and the animal hairs on her sleeve make me queasy, and I feel like I'm sliding downhill fast. What if she's some madwoman – obsessed with a conspiracy theory, or some disgruntled employee who convinced my father to settle her scores?

I sit back, the possibilities swirling through my head, leaving a confused fog in their wake.

'And you, why are you still there? At this company?'

She laughs. 'I know too much. I can't leave.'

'Why not? Do they keep you chained to the desk?' I scan her clothes, discreet jewellery and expensive handbag. 'Or do they pay you too much?'

She looks at me, offended. 'As long as I'm there, I'm useful. If I leave, I'm a liability. You'll understand once you see it all. I can't explain here.'

She pays the bill and takes her bag as I reach forward and put the stick in my pocket.

She draws her coat around her. 'There's an old saying. If you wait by the river long enough, the bodies of your enemies will come floating by. Well, I've been waiting a long time, and the river just keeps getting wider, with no sign of them. No one believed me, except your father and Patrick. None of us can wait any longer.'

*

She leaves the café, and I follow her to the metro where she heads north. Using the skills I'd learned from Sami, I drop back, keeping distance between us. She stops several times to check her phone and look around, but she doesn't see me. Her nervousness is infectious, and as people crowd onto the carriage, I get the feeling someone's now following me. I keep my hand over the stick in my pocket, desperate to get home and see what's on it.

The trains are still disrupted and I lose her in the crowds changing lines at the Gare du Nord. There's still no transport beyond the Péri, so I get off at La Villette and walk north along the slow-moving canal, scanning the tow path up ahead. Flat, grey water laps the muddy banks where rubbish is scattered in amongst pale weeds. My eyes are drawn to an area of swirling bubbles that signal the decomposition of something beneath the water.

I head into the wind as it strengthens and skims a chill from the canal. There's a bend up ahead where the path enters a tunnel beneath the Péri, and the roar of traffic drowns out the seagulls squawking overhead. Exiting the tunnel, I pass a row of storage depots, then a large, boarded-up supermarket. Behind a high fence, the wind clatters loose metal in a scrapyard. Finally, a path signed AUBERVILLIERS leads away from the canal through a maze of suburban streets and bungalows.

I'm not far from my block when I sense it coming like a change of atmosphere – the gust of wind that arrives before rain, or the blue light of a snowstorm, everything sharpening and coming into focus. The noise is behind me yet the blow comes from in front as a car door opens, slamming my knees. There's a scuffle of foot-steps as someone grabs me from behind, arms tight around my shoulders. The first punch hits me like a sledgehammer – whiplash and shockwaves of light. I catch a glimpse of a face to the side – short, dark hair. There's blood in my nose, flowing over my lips, dripping down the car door, stark against the white paintwork. A dazed sluggishness overcomes me as the pain balloons, and I'm thinking, *Is this an accident? Have I walked into someone's door?* but then he peppers my kidneys with sharp, knuckly jabs. He hauls me upright, slings a rough cloth over my head. There are prickles of light, a cord around my neck.

Someone else punches me below the ribs and burning pain sends me staggering backwards. He puts his whole body behind the fist, breath hissing through his teeth. I'm doubled over, can't breathe. There are voices behind me, then the fighter pulls me up, frogmarches me forward as I suck in shallow breaths. His knees in the backs of mine, arms round me like bars. I lose my balance, tripping sideways onto the car. Grunts and that sick, close smell of sweat and fear.

I'm lifted, and then I fall, tumbling into the boot. There's pain down my side and everything moves slowly, like a machine shutting down. My head hits something sharp, exploding with agony as the door slams.

Now it's dark, and I'm shaking, knees drawn in. Blood fills my mouth and panic bubbles up from deep inside as warm piss soaks my jeans.

We drive fast for a while then the car slows, stalling over speed bumps, bouncing, my hands fumbling for something to hold. Muffled sounds come through the partition. I can't make out the words, just the hum of raised voices, and the quick rat-a-tat of an argument. Finally, the car stops and two doors slam. Then the boot opens. I feel a rush of cold air, specks of light through the sack. Traffic noise nearby and I'm pulled out of the boot and in through a doorway where something sharp hits my side. There's a strong smell of sweat, sour and animal, like wet leather, mixed with the chemical reek of bleach.

'This way,' a man says, taking the bag from my head.

I keep my eyes down. *Don't make eye contact. Don't let them see you seeing them.*

We're in a warehouse. There's a boxing ring on a raised platform in the corner, the floor padded with dark blue mats. About ten punch bags hang from wooden beams on chains and twisted ropes. Shafts of dusty light hit the mats, and birds flutter against the skylights above.

The one holding me ties a blindfold over my eyes.

'Take your clothes off,' another says, kicking the backs of my knees.

My legs buckle and I fall down, sprawling on all fours. I take off my sweatshirt, exposing my burning skin, the eczema alive with itches as I peel off my trainers and socks. I edge my pissy jeans down one leg, then the other, trying to think. My keys and belt jangle as someone goes through my clothes.

'Just take the wallet, the cards. The pin—' I say.

'Shut up,' one of them says, kicking my ribs.

He rifles through my pockets, and then presses something into my cheek. It's the USB stick.

'Look what I've found,' he says, twisting the stick hard into my cheek.

They speak among themselves, arguing about what to do. Someone drags me across a concrete floor. A door opens, and there's the smell of stale beer, cigarettes and bleach.

Downstairs the air is cooler, the floor gritty beneath my feet. Sounds echo all around and I stumble, falling onto a soft plastic mat. It's sticky and has an overpowering smell – sour again, like a wet dog.

There are others here now – two, maybe three more. One squeezes my neck, thumbs in my windpipe until my head throbs. Darkness then circling lights. The man releases me, and I fall back, gasping.

'Not like that, you idiot. We're not supposed to kill him,' one of them says, his voice slurred. 'Here, take this.'

'No, you do it. I don't know how.'

'Like this. Just take it. Hold it.' This new voice is angry now.

Then sick laughter. 'We could just say it was a mistake.'

The one in charge throws me face down and kneels on my back. There's a sharp sting inside my elbow and something warm moves up my arm – heavy and numb, like lead.

He flips me round. 'Stop sticking your nose where it's not wanted,' he slurs, before punching me in the face.

There's a rush of blood and my brain contracts, shrinking away from the sides of my skull, curling in around the edges like an oyster rippling away from its shell when doused in lemon juice.

Then I fall, down deeply, into the black.

Thirty-Two

Pasteur

I WAKE INTO A SWIRLING TUNNEL of white, edges furred with darkness. Slowly, the light twists and unfolds, bringing the room into focus. A thick bandage covers my face, my nose is blocked, and on the ceiling there's a grid of mirrored lights, one of which flickers in time with my heartbeat. My body's under a sheet, stretched out in front like a frozen landscape. Beyond the bed rail there are white walls all around. Everything is quiet and still apart from my breathing, the buzz of the light and my pulse, which sloshes in my ears like the sea.

There's a tingling in my head, like the dead waking up. I move an inch and pain blasts down my side. My arm's attached to an IV drip by a thin grey tube, and a pendulum of yellow liquid hangs from a stand on a little plastic noose. I move my arm, slowly this time, and the bag swings back and forth.

Are they poisoning me?

I try to pull away, but pain shoots to my shoulder and my arm drops back, throbbing. My body is on fire. I lift the sheet and see red marks across my chest like some kind of burning.

Next to the bed is a table with medical instruments on a starched cloth: the cold empty eyes of a pair of scissors above its sharp beak, a mound of soft bandages, swabs, a shiny metal bowl. I stare at a large, glass-barrelled syringe, imagining it engorged with my blood as sweat pools on my chest.

I lie back, panting, as images flash back, stunted at first – the rough hood, a kick in the back, a punch in the face. I try to move my hand to those soft places, stinging now and covered in bandages. The smell of sweat, the taste of blood and beyond that, darker recollections of a damp and cavernous room, noise like a packed stadium, people cheering. Ropes.

And then I'm falling again, drifting from the room towards the terror of the dark.

When I open my eyes, my father is there, mouthing my name, his voice a hoarse whisper.

Is Alex there?

Alex, are you there?

Static down the line.

Yes, I'm here, down here.

I feel his arm on my shoulder. *Alex, Alex, wake up.*

His eyes are murky green pools, heavy with questions, shifting and swirling behind fogged glasses. I blink, and they vanish, leaving veiny sockets. The skin on his face is yellow, tight across his cheekbones. His nose is decayed, his shrunken lips stretching into an obscene leer. A corpse seven years in the ground, skin like parchment. He reaches in, his grasp strong, binding me tight in the sheets, keeping me captive.

Speak, he says, eye sockets gaping. I strain against the weight of him, turning from his foul breath. Sweat prickles on my lip, rolls down my neck. My skin is on fire, the ceiling lights bearing down on me like a furnace. He whispers, goading me, drawing me in, and I roll my head, trying to pull free.

The sheets saw across my chest, and a wave of pain sets off starbursts of light. Then darkness.

Light builds again, and I turn towards it, gasping, with a throat full of ash. A hand cradles my head. A soothing voice, glass cool on my lips. Water down my throat, running over my chin. A blurred image in front of me.

My father again?

My father, but not my father. The heavy, rank scent of lilies. It's my aunt, hair short against her scalp like his. Deep-rimmed eye sockets holding his eyes – watery-green, concerned, anxious.

'Alex,' she says, her voice cutting through the fog, bringing me into the room, into reality.

'Can you hear me?' Her face over mine, eyes tracing mine, her mouth opening then closing, wanting to speak. I see into her nostrils, lit from above, red and transparent like rabbits' ears as they flare and pulse with worry. I try to answer, but my nose is swollen like a balloon. I close my eyes and let my head fall back onto the pillow, giving in again to oblivion.

Later, she's still there, her hand on mine. My throat contracts, a strange rasping sound. My head is hot and light.

She leans in, and I try to speak, but my words are just a low-pitched drone. She brings a glass to my lips.

'Shhh, just rest, Alex. There's no need to speak.'

I'm awake now, looking around and she takes my hand, anticipating questions. 'They found you on the Péri, near Saint-Denis. You were unconscious, your clothes in a pile beside you.'

I see a vision of myself at the side of the road like a heap of rubbish.

'A truck driver saw you and pulled over. He thought you'd had an overdose and called an ambulance.'

I touch the bandages on my body, the ache in my shoulders. Through the fog come images of the woman I met.

'The stick,' I say.

'What?'

'There was a woman. She gave me a memory stick.'

'What woman? A woman did this?'

'The USB stick. I put it in my pocket. Where are my jeans?'

'Shh, don't speak. Rest now.'

'Where are my clothes?' I say, trying to sit up. My aunt presses a button, puts her hand on my forehead and then a nurse arrives. She scans my file, takes my pulse and changes the gauze across my nose.

My aunt pulls on her coat. 'It's time for me to leave, but I'll be back tomorrow.'

'How long have I been here?' I ask the nurse when she's gone.

'Three days so far. You were badly beaten and lost some blood. There are scratches and friction burns on your body. Do you remember anything?'

'A little, but not much.'

'That's probably a good thing,' she says, checking my blood pressure, writing in my notes. 'The memories might start coming back slowly, so be prepared for that. You've had a shock, it might take a while.'

The nurse gives me something to sleep, and when I wake, the room is dark. The drip's gone so I can move my arm and switch on the light. There's an ache in my ribs as I sit up. My head feels better – more alert, and I'm hungry. In the far corner of the room is a basket of fruit in cellophane – grapes, bananas, pineapple, their flesh giving off a sweet ripeness that fills the room, making my mouth water.

I pull back the sheets and it's a shock to see my body criss-crossed with dark red welts and bruises, some like burns, others long scratches that carve deeply into my already damaged skin, and my ankles and wrists are still bandaged. I slide carefully off the bed and walk towards the table, the floor cool beneath my feet. The plastic crackles as I reach in and take a banana. I sit on the bed and work my way through the fruit – pears, grapes, dates. On a shelf beneath the fruit, there's a large hospital file with my name on it, and I start flicking through. There are notes about me as a baby, height and weight charts, immunisation records, details of the time I broke my collarbone. Towards the back of the file, there are details of my eczema – photos of various outbreaks, notes of appoint-ments and treatments.

Right at the back there's an envelope marked CONFIDENTIAL – DO NOT OPEN. It's in a plastic wallet stapled to the back of the file.

I prise off the staples and take out the envelope, placing it on the bed. I hesitate for a few seconds, and then tear it open.

Inside is a handwritten note:

Patient presented with skin condition, apparent since birth. Initial diagnosis of eczema made, but patient did not respond to usual treatment. Diagnosis of Ichthyosis was discounted at the time because the condition is hereditary, and neither parent had the condition. Diagnosis of Ichthyosis later confirmed after father disclosed that he was not the patient's biological father.

Confusion like vertigo as I reread the note.

Not the patient's biological father.

Is that me? Am I the patient?

'No,' I say, quietly at first. Then my voice gets louder, and I see myself as a child with flaming red, angry skin. Images crowd in, but nothing makes sense. I see my father's face. He's shaking his head.

The ground pulses beneath me, my blood drains to the floor, and I'm floating helplessly, light and flimsy, like an insect in the wind. I read the note until my head throbs, and I thrash out, pull the sheets from the bed, rip the pages from the file. There's a roar, then the ground falls away.

THEN

Christmas Eve

Thirty-Three
Montparnasse Cemetery

A MONGREL AND A ROLLED-UP NEWSPAPER.

Get him to hand over his wallet. He always keeps a lot of cash. Cards and cash.

My voice catches in the cold night air.

Sami grins, and my stomach turns to sand.

In the lobby, there are mirrored panels all around. I go from one to the other, rattling handles, pushing doors, but there's no way out.

Sami's on the other side of the glass. He rakes a hand through his hair, travelling up in the lift cage. The dim light hollows his eyes and cheeks, his face a death mask.

It's hot, and my clothes tighten like knots.

When my father speaks, it comes from above and all around.

Is Alex there? Alex, are you there? he booms, words crackling with static and disbelief.

Yes, I'm here, down here! I scream to the ceiling. My face shudders in the mirrored corners, flushed red with fear and rain.

He's still speaking.

317

I wait, counting heartbeats. Christmas lights pulse in the dusty glass, and my reflection dissolves, spins around.

Finally, Sami bursts through the door, my father's wallet open on his palm, brown and bloody, throbbing like a moth.

His eyes are full of fear and red like mine, flashing in the crazed Christmas lights.

He lunges at me, pulls my arm. The twisted bag with the hammer swinging at his side.

Come on. Don't be so gutless. We need to get out of here. Let's go.

He thrusts my father's wallet at me. *Remember our deal – you and me, we're brothers now.* Then he turns, fumbling with the latch before disappearing outside.

I look at the blood-stained wallet, splayed open in my hand. I want to run, escape from the scene and the horror upstairs, but something keeps me rooted in the doorway. I hear voices in the street outside – people are approaching.

Then I run in the direction of my father.

NOW

Thirty-Four

Pasteur

I TRY TO STRAIN FORWARDS, BUT pain shoots down my back, the muscles in my neck like iron bars. A chair scrapes along the floor then Lisa comes into view. She looks tired, make-up smudging the skin around her eyes.

My voice is slow and muffled, as if coming from deep underwater.

She puts her hand on my forehead, says I had a fit in the night and they had to restrain me.

Memories return like a kick in the guts, and I look past her to the medical file, but it's not there. The room tilts, begins to spin, and blackness hovers at the edge of vision.

I see him now. We're swimming out to the surf break near my grandfather's place where the sea is choppy, cold and murky, sand hissing under the water. My father holds me, his eyes hidden behind the fog of scuba goggles, his lips distorted and swollen around the snorkel. There are tiny bubbles in the strands of reddish hair drifting over his forehead. He releases me then swims away, arms low and strong against the current, waves frothing on his back.

He stops and turns, 'Follow me,' he calls. '*Suis-moi.*'

I try to reach him, but the current pulls me back as he swims further out. I thrash in the surf, calling 'Dad! Dad!' into the swell, and the wind drowns my cries.

I watch him at the break line, surf churning over his shoulders as he ploughs on through the water. Waves surge around me, dragging me down into a cathedral of foam and watery light, and then the sea thrusts me up like a cork. I rage and kick against the surf, fighting for both our lives, lashing out against the waves that are pulling me back. I call to him, but I can't make a sound. There's pressure on my chest, and a cold, rubbery hand grips my forearm. A sharp sting, then leaden warmth flows into my veins.

Later on, when it's dark, I wake again, dazed, exhausted, and then back to the sea, all murky and green. I float on the surface, staring into its depths and my father's face on the sand beneath me. His head is wedged between two rocks, the current wafting hair across his eyes, first closed and peaceful, now glazed and staring. Then his features change into Patrick's and the water turns thin and brackish, reeking of mud. His lips are blue with cold, eye sockets clogged with river silt. Patrick pulls a knotted rope to his chest, one hand over the other and it tugs at my belly. The rope is attached to me like an umbilical cord, a blood-clotted cable anchoring me to two dead men. The three of us are bound together, drifting slowly through the sand.

If you wait long enough, the bodies of your enemies will come floating by.

I twist and turn, trying to break free of the ropes dragging me down.

'What are you saying, Alex?' Lisa says, pulling me back onto the bed. The images fade as she unwinds the sheets from my wrists.

My lips are dry and cracked. My throat hurts.

'You need to rest. Stop thinking about it now,' she says.

My head falls onto the pillow, and beside me the tray of surgical equipment edges closer. The horror of the gleaming syringe, silver bowls and the wadding to soak up blood, scalpel to carve through flesh, dead-eyed scissors to snip it off. I point to the tray, the first aid symbol – a Swiss cross.

Red Cross. *Croix Rouge.* Was that something? Red Cross for Christians, Red Crescent for Muslims. Red, the colour of danger and emergency. The colour of blood. A red cross twisted into a crescent, into a sliver of moon at night. A bandaged moon, twisted and dripping with blood. Blood Moon. My father's head, his full-moon face, bloodied and groaning and staring up at me.

He was reaching out to me, but I left him there, bleeding.

His face like the moon stretched across the water that night, following me. Up in the sky, underwater. He beams at me from photos and reflections still. From newspapers and shredded memories. *Croix-Rouge. Croissant-Rouge.* Blood-soaked croissants on a tray. Half baked. Bloody crosses and crescents, blood-red bread. A hand grasping out of the sand to pull a cord, or draw a line. A line in the sand. A red line. Ligne Rouge.

'Ligne Rouge?' I mumble.

'What? Who?' Lisa says, holding my hand. 'Shhh.'

'The woman with the stick. Ligne Rouge. That's what they took.'

'What? Who's Lynne?'

Fragments of conversation. The memory stick. The boxing gym with the birds fluttering above. Blindfolded. My wet clothes in a pile. Then the blurred darkness, tied with ropes for the cheering crowd stretched out before me.

'Lynne who?' she says. 'Alex, you're scaring me. Shall I call the nurse?'

I shake my head; she doesn't understand. 'Not Lynne, Ligne. Ligne.' The effort of speaking, to be understood, exhausts me. Sweat gathers under my arms. It pools on my chest and soaks the sheets, smells vile, like a stagnant drain. Lisa mops my face with a cloth.

It takes all the energy I have to speak, and it comes out in a gasp. 'The woman I met. She said *Ligne* Rouge as in Red Line.'

'Ligne Rouge,' she says. 'Red Line.'

'Yes. A company. Ligne Rouge.'

Then I fall back into the sea, drifting on through the dark.

I stay in hospital another night until my bandages come off, and then I'm discharged. In reception, my aunt helps me fill out more forms reporting the assault to the police. She gathers my prescriptions and collects the medication. I was badly beaten, they say, bound tight and drugged with a sedative, but there's no lasting damage other than a swollen nose, bruised ribs and the network of rope burns crossing my body.

There's a fish tank next to me, one fish at the back, lodged between the glass and the air vent. It looks alive – fins and tail rippling on the flux of air and water, its swollen body hovering on the current. I look for movement in its gills or a swivel of its eye, but there's nothing. Like the dreams of bodies drifting, animated by tides. Bubbles under the water. Dead things beneath the surface.

Stop sticking your nose where it's not wanted.

We drive through Paris to my aunt's place, squinting in the sun's glare, the car trembling over the cobbled roads.

'Can I get you anything?' she asks quietly when we enter her apartment. 'Something to eat? The doctor said you need to eat.'

I stand in her kitchen, the ground beneath me shaky as if it might collapse or slip away like a magician's tablecloth. I say no to the food, but she prepares something anyway and I sit at the little laminated table as she moves around the kitchen, pale and drawn under the fluorescent lights.

'This is hard for you, I know,' she says, putting the food in front of me.

That's a fucking understatement, I think, and the absurdity of her words draws me back into the room. I almost laugh as I push the food around my plate.

'He always thought of himself as your father, Alex,' she says softly, putting her hand on my shoulder.

'What?' I say, stabbing a lump of meat so the fork skids across the plate.

She clears her throat and repeats the words, louder this time as if saying them again will make them true. It's a line she's heard in a film, just something she thinks she should say, and I wonder who she's trying to convince. Perhaps it's something she's rehearsed for years, preparing for just this moment and

I stare at her, chewing with my mouth open. I know it's rude, but I can't bear her feeling so sorry for me.

How the hell does she know what he thought? Did she discuss this with him all along? The idea of the two of them sharing this obscene secret, whispering behind my back, makes my throat tighten, the heat rising up my neck.

'He wasn't my father.'

'Alex,' she says, her voice strained.

'He was a fucking liar.'

'Don't speak about him like that.'

'Oh, yeah, sorry. I forgot. You're *related* to him.'

Feeling her hand on me releases a torrent of rage, and I slam my fork on the plate as she shrinks back.

'You're his *sister*. Or then again, perhaps you aren't. Have you ever bothered to check? After all these years, you might find that the old man of mystery wasn't your brother either.'

She goes to the sink, her back to me. I take a mouthful of food. It's disgusting – the watery rice, thick gravy, meat all stringy and overcooked. The taste of stale blood, abattoirs, dead things. I spit the meat onto the plate.

'Don't speak like that,' she says quietly after a while.

'Why are you whispering? We don't need to keep it a secret anymore, do we?'

She turns to face me, her face pinched. 'It wasn't like that. I didn't know either.'

Her words reverberate around the room, then the air is sucked from it, leaving a deathly silence in its wake.

'He either didn't know himself or . . .' She pauses, shakes her head. 'But that's not possible. He told me everything,' she says, before breaking down.

I should go to her now, but emptiness overwhelms me and I need distance from her – time to reassess this person as well. She's not my aunt now, after all, so I leave her at the sink and walk to the spare room.

Passing the mirror, I catch my reflection. *Who am I?* I ask, as I scan my face, scared and gaunt and unlike myself with a swollen nose and bruised, raccoon eyes. I think of the times I looked for Eddy in the blue flecks of my eyes, or the line of my jaw. All the times I dreaded finding him there, too. Even though I never saw any resemblance, I always felt something of him, some shared quality, in what lay beneath the skin. Now all the things I searched for then – that essence, those remnants, have disappeared, like islands off an old map. I stare in the mirror, wondering what I'm looking for, wondering what I'm looking *at*. Those are my mother's eyes, her nose, but what's lying in the shadows – who else is there?

Was my real father some one-night stand? A drunken hook-up on a business trip? Am I cobbled together from bits and pieces – wasted memories, shameful secrets, like a collage of rubbish from a skip? I tug at my thick, woolly hair, no longer French, but Italian perhaps, or Spanish. My eyebrows are dark and bushy, feathering together in the middle. Whose are those? And is my jaw on loan too from some fly-by-night prick at a bar? My soft, pouchy lips, framed by a pair of dimples, now look like a courtesan's arse in an eighteenth-century painting. One of the Sun King's bastards.

Later that evening, I'm on the bed in the spare room stumbling through a maze of images and half-memories, now dead ends and dim, shifting alleys, when Béa comes in to tell me she's been unable to contact my mother. It doesn't surprise me. They're always on the move, changing numbers, changing homes. These days it's impossible to hide, but the rich have bought the shadows, too.

She draws closer, scans my body. 'How are you feeling?'

'OK,' I say.

'I'm worried about you,' she says.

'I'm all right. I was walking along the canal. It was getting dark,' I lie. 'I'll be more careful.'

'That's not what I meant,' she says, then sits beside me. 'Let me tell you something, a story from a long time ago.'

I look at her, wondering if she's lost her mind. Now's not the time for any more stories.

'I should have told you this earlier.'

There's a creeping sensation around my ears, a dryness in my throat. 'Told me what?'

'It's about your father and a woman. It might help you under-stand things,' she adds. I've heard enough bad news lately, and from the look on her face, I'm about to hear some more. I have the urge to run, to get a long way from her and anything to do with my so-called father, but she takes my hand and brings it to her lap.

I'm only half listening as she tells me he met this woman, Lara, when he was in his early twenties. They fell madly in love, started talking about marriage.

I sit there listening numbly, wondering why she's telling me this.

'I was stunned. They hardly knew each other! At first, I thought it was a joke and laughed it off, thinking it was a cultural thing – Lara was from a small village, and perhaps all her friends were married, or she had family pressure.'

There's a fine band of perspiration across her forehead and her clammy hand tightens around mine.

'I warned Eddy it was too soon, that he should take care, but he told me to mind my own business. It caused a rift between us, and we didn't see each other for months.'

She stops to breathe. Talking about her brother's love life seems to stress her, and I imagine her back then – protective and frightened she'd lose him.

'When Lara got pregnant, it was a shock, but no real surprise. She'd been following a script she'd already written, and Eddy fell for the oldest trick in the book.'

'Maybe it was a trick, but maybe they were in love,' I say, not sure why she's telling me this now, and wondering where it's going.

'She hooked him like a fish on a line,' she says, her voice full of contempt. 'Then once she had him she played him for all she was worth. Lara told him she was already married, and couldn't go through with the pregnancy. Eddy begged her to leave her husband, have the child, marry him. She said it was impossible, and that her husband would find and hurt her, and if he couldn't find her, he'd get at her family back in Bulgaria. It went on for weeks, the tears – you've never seen anything like it. It was like an opera. Eddy was a wreck.'

'So what happened?'

'In the end, Eddy arranged for her to have a termination.'

'And that was the end of it?' I ask.

She laughs grimly. 'Not at all. It was just the beginning! After the termination, Lara went back home where she got sick, seriously ill, and then her husband appeared. He knew all about the affair. He came here first, threatened me. Then he found Eddy.' She reaches for a tissue. 'Eddy was blackmailed for money, and the husband threatened to prosecute him.'

'For what? Having an affair?'

'Back then, abortions were illegal in France. And not only that, he said the termination had damaged Lara, that she was ill and could never have children. He showed Eddy a medical certificate.'

'Eddy tried to find her but he couldn't track her down. So he paid the husband off, but it destroyed him. He had a breakdown and that's when he moved to North Africa. He wouldn't speak to anyone outside work, and I could only reach him through his colleagues.'

'Which colleagues?'

'Paul Chambière.'

'So Paul knows about this?'

She nods.

'And what happened afterwards? Did he see this woman again?'

'He never heard from Lara again, as far as I know, but Eddy would never discuss it. After that, the women came and went, always young, always glamorous, and I thought he'd fall into the same trap, but nothing lasted. He never let himself be drawn in again. Work came first. Until your mother.'

She shakes her head. 'With your mother, it was different. She also got pregnant very early in their relationship, but this time it was as if he saw the trap and threw himself in.'

'What do you mean?'

'I knew Eddy was never sure about her, but he wanted you. He wasn't going to let the same thing happen again – he didn't want to lose another child, so they got married.'

'Did you ever suspect I wasn't his?'

'It never crossed my mind.' She shakes her head. 'I've been thinking back, of course, looking for hints and signs about what he knew and when, but there's nothing. Honestly, it never occurred to me that he wasn't your father.'

I think back to the times he spoke about my mother, understanding now the depths of the resentment he must have felt about being so completely duped.

'And my mother?'

'They were never right for each other, and motherhood never suited her. She has had only one priority – herself,' she says bitterly, which surprises me after all this time.

An hour later Béa passes me her phone.

'Alex, I've been trying to call, Béatrice told me about your accident,' my mother says, her voice breathless, thin and distant. 'And she said you'd found—'

'Who was he?'

'Alex—'

'Is it Olivier?' I say, fighting down a swell of dread.

There's a long pause. 'No,' she says, finally.

'Then who?'

She doesn't answer and bile rises in me. 'When did Dad know?'

'I made him promise. Alex, listen. When Eddy and I got together, I was so young. I was alone and already pregnant. He

330

found out the truth when you were five, when I left him.'

There's an echo down the line, her voice shaky.

'Why didn't he tell me?'

'When I left I wanted to take you with me, but Eddy wouldn't have it. I told him the truth then, thinking it would change his mind, but it didn't make any difference, he wanted you to stay with him. And finally, I agreed,' she says. 'At first, I wanted to tell you. We argued about it constantly, but in the end it was me who made him keep it secret.'

'You're lying,' I say. 'I can tell by your voice. I can't believe he'd go along with this.'

'I convinced him it was dangerous.'

'*Dangerous?*'

'I can't say any more,' she says, her voice hardening. 'I'm sorry, Alex, I know it's inexcusable, but there are things at stake. Things I can't discuss.'

'This isn't some kind of negotiation, or some kind of deal you can strike to bury the past. This concerns the identity of my *father*, and so how dare you tell me things are at *stake*. What could be more at stake here than what's at stake for me?'

'It concerns others,' she says quietly. 'The children, Olivier.'

'But I'm also your child!' I say, my heart burning with hatred for her. 'This is not your secret to keep anymore. I have a right to know the truth.'

'Sometimes the truth is overrated,' she says.

'What the hell are you saying?'

'Alex, please, I'm frightened,' she whispers.

She starts to sob and fear ignites in me. 'Did you scare Dad off with these threats, these tears? Did you tell him that it was *dangerous*, that things were at *stake?*'

'No,' she says, too quickly. 'Look, I'll send you whatever you need, but please, don't pursue this.'

'*Pursue* this? Was it your money, your bribes, that kept him quiet?'

'Of course not!'

'What, then?

A pause as she gathers herself.

'In the end, he understood. And despite the lie I forced on him, I doubt he would have told you. Leaving you with Eddy was the best decision I made.'

When I hang up I feel numb, sick to my heart. How like her to give herself the final word, to twist self-interest into a virtue – the one where mother always knows best.

'I know very little about your mother, Alex,' my aunt says later. 'After they split up, Eddy hardly spoke about her. It was strange, and whenever he did mention her, I got the sense that he was talking about Lara.'

She gets up to close the curtains, and I sit back. There was always something weird about my father's relationships with women. I never understood the combination of coldness and desperation he had for them. In my eyes, his affairs made him pathetic, like a lecherous screw-up. And I never understood what they saw in him. But I can see now how his elusiveness might have been attractive – there was always a part of him that was inaccessible. Perhaps they saw something they couldn't get no matter how hard they tried, and often there's nothing you want more than something you can't have.

I think back to what Patrick said: *Women were always your father's motivation. They were his weakness. It was never money.*

Women may have been his motivation, but it was the disaster with Lara that meant he needed money.

I needed to find out more about this woman *and* the money.

Thirty-Five
Saint-Germain

G IVEN HOW COMFORTABLE PAUL LOOKED in the restaurant near his office, I guess it's his usual lunch spot. When he sees me waiting on the terrace again, it's as if he's expecting me and he comes outside immediately.

'You're still making enemies, then,' he says, his eyes tracing the bruises on my face.

'You didn't tell me about Lara,' I say.

'Lara?'

He continues to feign ignorance and so I tell him about the commune Lisa mentioned in the south, the place Tomas had been living last summer.

'So where is it? Do you have the address?' he asks impatiently.

'Tell me about Lara and my father.'

He sighs in frustration. 'For God's sake, Alex, that was years ago.'

He gestures for us to move away from the restaurant, and he walks close to me, speaking quietly into his scarf. 'I didn't know what was going on until much later.'

'You didn't know she was pregnant?' I say.

334

He turns to me, expressionless. 'She wasn't pregnant. The whole thing was a scam – the pregnancy, her marriage. It was a trick.

'She made it all up,' he says, walking on ahead. 'After the fake termination, the "husband" threatened to go to the police and have Eddy charged with procuring an illegal abortion.'

He smirks, unable to hide his pleasure at my confusion, and I imagine this is how he is with his students – patronising and superior. 'I told you he was blackmailed. Blackmailed into running their stories and propaganda.'

'He wasn't blackmailed for money?'

'It was a honey trap, but in the end, they paid him.'

'Who?' I say, completely lost.

He shifts uncomfortably. 'I only know what Eddy told me much later. After they hooked him in, they put him on the payroll.'

'And this was what he was writing about?'

'I tried to talk him out of it, but that just spurred him on.'

He looks down the street, pretending to think. He even scratches his chin to complete the charade. 'It wasn't long before he died. I reminded him one night when it came time to pay the bill that I'd lent him money all those years ago for the termination, and he'd never paid me back. It was meant as a joke about the bill, but he was drunk and got very offended and then it all came out. How he blamed me. How he thought I'd had a role in the whole thing.'

'A role?'

'He accused me of setting him up with Lara in the first place. He thought my opposition to his sordid little memoir was proof I was part of it.'

'And were you?'

'Of course not! He met her at a club we all went to back then.'

'The Matrix Club?'

He stops abruptly. 'You know about that?'

'He met her there?'

'He was introduced to her there.'

I stand at a distance, trying to imagine this world they inhabited then – the deception and the many layers of lies. No wonder my father didn't know who to trust. I want to ask Paul whether he knew Eddy wasn't my father, but I can't give him that pleasure and who knows – if they all swapped partners, it may even be Paul himself. The thought sickens me, but why not? I may as well prepare myself for the worst, and the idea that Tomas is somehow my brother is just about as bad as it gets. As I watch Paul with disgust, it occurs to me that this is how secrets prevail, and why no one tells the truth – because no one really knows.

'Eddy was set up?' I ask.

'Yes, but not by me.' He lets out one of his condescending laughs. 'It was typical of the way Eddy's paranoid mind worked, especially when he was drunk. He thought I was out to get him. I wish I'd never lent him any money either. Never do anyone a favour, Alex. They'll hate you for it.'

'So why did he hate you?'

'I've no idea. Your father was played by Lara and then trapped by her so-called husband. He was the victim of an operation, and then a smear campaign, but rather than blame himself or the perpetrators, he blamed me.'

'Is that why he was with Céline? To get back at you for something that happened in the past?'

He stops. 'Who knows? He resented my success for sure, but he could have had that. When he was younger, he was brilliant.'

'You said he never amounted to much.'

'He didn't,' Paul said, not meeting my eyes. 'He could have, but after Lara, he lost it. It wasn't his fault – he was deceived brutally, but once you cross that line, it's very hard to come back. He hated himself for being so easily fooled and for what he did after. It destroyed him.'

'But he carried on working. He moved to Egypt.'

'That was my idea,' he says, pointing at me. 'Jean-Marc wanted to get rid of him. Eddy was drinking and making mistakes. Making a clown of himself in the office. Eventually, I persuaded Jean-Marc to send him to Cairo. Sitting it out somewhere else was the only way for him to survive.'

'And Jean-Marc?' I ask.

'What about him?'

'Where is he now?' I say, thinking I need to see him too.

Paul taps his chest, ahead of me now. 'Last I heard he was in hospital. He's been unwell. Lung infection.'

I walk quickly to catch up. 'So why did Eddy want to write about all this?'

'That was the incredible thing. After years of hiding and deliberately losing contact with everyone, he suddenly wanted to get to the bottom of it all. He had an appetite for revenge, I guess.'

'Why didn't you tell me this before? Why did Céline try to hide it from me?'

'Céline wanted to protect me,' he says irritably.

'The swingers' club?'

'Yes.' He gestures back in the direction of the restaurant, his office. 'She was worried it would compromise my position here if that was all dragged into the light.'

I think of the photos in my father's shoebox. 'The sleaze, the exploitation. It's not that fashionable anymore.'

He raises an eyebrow, but doesn't take the bait. 'It was clear what Eddy wanted from Céline, and she didn't want to expose me like that.'

'And Patrick?'

'What's Patrick got to do with it?'

'He visited me in prison. He asked if I could remember what Eddy was working on before he died, and then two weeks later he's dead too. It's more than a coincidence.'

Paul shakes his head. 'That's just another conspiracy. Patrick killed himself. There was an autopsy, an inquiry. The reports he filed before his death – he was depressed. He hated it back here, hated being tied to the desk after years as a correspondent. He and Elena weren't getting on. His death has nothing to do with this.'

He loosens his collar and affects a casual look.

'And those codenames – Vestnik, and the rest?' I say.

He shifts impatiently. 'Vestnik means *messenger* in Russian. As in journalist, newspapers. Eddy thought Vestnik was the ringleader, the mastermind. He thought that person was still active.'

'Still *active?*' I say, imagining some kind of volcano, smouldering away in a backroom filing cabinet.

'Still involved in things. He thought Vestnik hadn't just gone away, that he'd just moved on to different things.'

'What kind of things?'

'For God's sake, Alex, I don't know. Eddy wanted to track him down, find out what he was doing now. His view was that these kind of people didn't just disappear, they went on to other projects.'

I hand him a piece of paper with the location of the commune. 'Why did he think it was you?'

He takes the paper and gives me a sour look. 'You know what? Eddy always distrusted me, but I was only ever helpful to him so forgive me if I don't remember your father kindly,' he says, before he walks off.

Paul occupies my thoughts as I walk back to my aunt's. The way he always has an answer, yet never tells me the full story. All this talk about helping Eddy, then how much he disliked him, but drinking with him all those times. If my father really hated Paul, then surely they wouldn't have spent all that time together.

As for the past, Paul said he wasn't involved, but that's just his word and he's hardly been totally straight with me so far. If Eddy was on the payroll, then why wasn't Paul? He's an academic now, and before that, he was a journalist. Neither of those are the kind of jobs that buy their kind of apartment, let alone a country place and a fleet of vintage cars. I think of Paul and Céline standing at the door the other day, a fragrant blur of matching pastels. That carefully cultivated look they think is so subtle, the discreet uniform of the rich.

Back at my aunt's cellar again, I sift through the files to the note from Vestnik, this so-called messenger, referring to *a new role* and *sudden financial commitments* with the direction of money to a bank account in Switzerland. Had Paul received that kind of cash? And if so, what was he doing in return?

I delve further back through the files, thinking about how Paul might fit into the puzzle when I receive an email from Lisa:

In the hospital, you mentioned Ligne Rouge. I found a
few companies with that name. There's one registered

> in the Seychelles. It looks like they own properties in the
> suburbs here in Paris. The strange thing is they're all
> clustered around the forts – those places you showed
> me on your father's computer.

I ring her and she picks up straight away.

'What do you mean *forts*?' I say, opening the attachment she's sent. It's a list of public spaces – parks and gardens, sports facilities and gymnasiums.

'The old forts around Paris,' she says. 'There are sixteen of them, all built around two hundred years ago as defence against the Prussians. The government now uses them for high-level security purposes: police training, emergency services, security, surveillance. There's one dead opposite you – the Fort d'Aubervilliers.'

'And Ligne Rouge?'

'Ligne Rouge is a holding company for businesses that seem to run migrant centres, clubs and gyms all over Paris but mainly near these forts. Its shareholders and directors are Seychelles companies, so it's impossible to see who actually owns it all.'

'Gyms?'

'Yes, it's odd they'd go to so much trouble to hide the owner-ship of gyms.'

'There was a gym. When I was attacked last week, I was taken to a place that had a gym,' I say.

I think of the bulldozed camp we passed, the face in the metro, his fighters' muscles, the boxing gym. That same slurred voice and the persistent sense of being followed. Nick and Sami weren't related, but they were 'brothers', and although Nick really didn't care about Sami, he was a useful asset, a hard worker. If someone's taking revenge for Sami, then perhaps it's Nick.

Whoever attacked me wanted whatever Mari had given me on the stick and it was probably the same people who broke into my room. But why would Nick want that?

I really need to visit Sami now. I need to find out more about Nick.

Later that afternoon I head back to my flat for the first time since the attack. When we spoke, Lisa insisted I stay with her until I've properly recovered, but I need to collect some things first. I keep to the main roads and nearing the hostel, I pass the fort site. There are protesters outside the gates as usual, large makeshift posters and people with clipboards gathering signatures.

In the lobby of the apartment I see Hamid, who's carrying a box of vegetables from his allotment and we catch the lift together. I mention the protesters I saw near the fort.

'It's valuable land, though, isn't it?' I say as we step out of the lift onto the walkway between the buildings

He passes me the box and then cups his hands around a match to light a cigarette. 'Not really. They say the land's contaminated, so no one wants to build on it. Some think the whole site's radioactive.'

I look over the motorway and beyond to the two construction sites. Next to the site are the allotments – a thin strip of land producing a few beans and cabbages.

'The army did nuclear experiments in the bunkers of the old fort,' he says. 'Madame Curie had labs in there before that. The place is full of contaminated waste.'

'They tested bombs here?' I say, and he laughs, making me think it's all some kind of joke.

His laugh turns bitter. 'No, not here,' he says, flicking ash from his roll-up. 'They tested the bombs at a safe distance – in Algeria, three thousand kilometres away. They kept it all a big secret, but everyone knows. The temperatures were so high it turned the desert sand to glass.'

'And they say the fort's still contaminated?' I ask.

'They say the levels are high, but no one knows. It's the usual thing. The protesters say one thing, the government says another.'

'If it's contaminated why would you grow stuff there?'

He exhales casually. 'Yeah, that's right. It could be made up.'

I look at the produce in the box, which now seems deformed. The beans are too large and woody, the tomatoes bulbous and mottled. I know that's the way home-grown ones usually are, but suddenly they all look toxic, and there's a heavy smell on the late afternoon air.

He sees me eyeing the vegetables. 'Occasionally they take samples for testing but they never tell us what the results are, so we assume everything's OK. I probably get more trouble with these,' he says, grinding his cigarette on the railing. 'Or the fumes from the motorway.'

'But they'd tell you if there was a problem?' I ask.

He looks up, and there's an edge to his smile. 'Maybe not. It's mainly Algerians living out here, too, so maybe it's like the desert tests. Why else would they let us farm it?'

'You'd prefer not to know?'

There's a pause and he shrugs.

'I didn't say that. But if they do proper tests and find it's contaminated, we'll have to leave. If it's not, the developers and bulldozers will come. We lose both ways.'

'You think they'd throw you off?'

He nods. 'Of course. There's already talk about development,' he says. 'That's what all the protests are about.'

'Development of the whole site?'

He nods. 'There are always rumours about what's going on here. The latest is that the attack at Les Halles the other week was caused by someone from the travellers' camp on the edge of the cemetery. There are rumours the old labs are being used as a bomb-making factory, that terrorists are making sarin gas in the tunnels. Someone even reported that the Imams have converted the gypsies to Islam and they're manufacturing nuclear bombs in the bunkers again. The whole thing's out of hand. It's crazy.'

'Who says all this?'

'The papers never let it go. They call the area a no-go zone. The police have ramped up security and that's just made it worse.'

'Why?'

'Because now there's so much more focus on the area and it gives the place a bad reputation. Apparently, they're going to bulldoze everything like they have at the Fort D'Issy. The story is they want to decommission the old labs, clean up the site and build luxury apartments.'

We say goodbye and I'm still thinking of the contamination next door when I see an email from my parole officer. She tells me my application for a visitation permit with Sami has been denied. There's no way he'll see me, and who can blame him? I need to come up with a better plan.

Later that night, I'm starting to write a letter to Sami when a message flashes up on my phone. It's from an unknown number with a video file that takes a while to download. Even before I see it I know it's me. My body naked on a blue plastic mat, and bound with black ropes. The image lasts for two seconds, and then it's gone.

That night I dream of Sami and I wake up sweating, tracing the marks and bruises across my body.

THEN

Christmas Day

Thirty-Six
Saint-Germain

I WAS SHAKING WHEN I ARRIVED at my aunt's on Christmas morning. I didn't know what had happened to my father after I fled the apartment the night before, but I knew he'd been hurt and was bleeding. I was expecting my aunt to say he'd had an accident, or that he'd be late, but she was listening to a broadcast from the church – all choirs and organ music, as she went around opening shutters, singing and humming to herself.

I stank, my clothes filthy and damp, but she pretended not to notice. I stayed in the kitchen, helping out as best I could – peeling vegetables, frying the stuffing. Listening out for the sudden crack of change.

When she handed me the table settings, I almost gave her one plate back. Arranging a place for my father among the candles and decorations marked the beginning of a chain of deceit I was powerless to stop. I'll go to hell for this alone, I thought, my legs half buckling beneath me as I lay his dish at the head of the table with the cutlery he'd never use on either side. I pressed them hard into the lace tablecloth in case like pitchforks and daggers they leaped to my throat.

When the call came, she took it in the sitting room. I watched from the doorway as she sank to the sofa, phone pressed to her ear, the other hand cradling her jaw like someone had just hit her.

Her eyes reached for mine as fear tore up her face.

'No, no. Please, no,' she said in a soft whimper, the kind that knew it was already beaten.

When she said 'the body', I knew that my father was dead.

Somehow I made it to the sofa. She clung to me and told me through sobs that a neighbour had found him that morning.

The room swam, and I saw him lying in the doorway, heard his groans, felt his hand reaching for me. I wanted to run to our apartment, kneel by him, revive him, but of course, it was too late for that. Last night I heard someone on the stairs. I thought they would help him. What on earth had I let happen?

About an hour later, the police arrived. The female officer was young, and her close-set eyes – dark, unblinking – were like a double-barrelled shotgun aimed straight at me. The man sat behind her wearing a knowing kind of frown as if he'd seen what I'd done and was just waiting for me to break. I knew I had to be careful, not say I'd been anywhere near my father, but beyond that, I didn't know how to behave. Did my fear come across as grief, or was it the other way round? When they offered their condolences, I just looked at my aunt and the shadows that crept along the wall.

The woman did most of the talking. She told us they'd been called to the *scene* by a neighbour that morning. His throat was cut, he'd been almost decapitated, she said, and he'd bled out on the threshold.

No, that's not what happened, I wanted to scream, but my lungs had no air. I shook my head. *No, no, no. I saw him. His throat wasn't cut. When I left, he was alive.* But of course, I couldn't say that.

The woman said the time of death was between ten and midnight on Christmas Eve, and since there were no signs of forced entry, my father probably knew his attacker. Her voice rose into a question, and my aunt looked at me with a sudden wildness, which the two of them registered.

At that moment, I had three sets of eyes tearing into me, so I said I hadn't seen him since that night at Patrick and Elena's, but that people like postmen and firemen often visited the apartments at Christmas for donations, so perhaps it was one of them. It felt like a brainwave at the time, the kind of brilliance that only comes under pressure, but looking back it was the stupidest thing I ever said. There was a long pause, as if my words hung in the air so everyone could examine them. The man made a note, and said ten o'clock was a bit late for the utilities. I shrugged and wanted to say I'm just trying to help, but my mouth went dry.

For the rest of their visit, I focused on controlling my face while they asked all kinds of questions.

Did my father have any enemies?

Any debts we knew of?

Was he expecting any visitors last night?

I kept my answers short, eyes steady and fixed on the wall or, when the woman spoke to me directly, on the bridge of her nose. It must have made me cross-eyed, but I didn't care. It's always better to look stupid than guilty.

As I listened to their questions, my mind raced back over the events of the previous day. I'd called my father on Sami's phone.

There'd be a record of that, for sure, but that's probably all. When they said they had an image of a dark-haired man on CCTV icy fear twisted in my gut, but I seized on the word 'man' – *singular, just Sami and not the two of us*, and hope swelled in me like a life raft.

After they left, I sat on the sofa with my aunt. Even though I was cold, sweat pooled under my arms. I've learned a lot about fear since then and how close it is to grief. I felt a terrible mixture of the two, but mostly I remember the cold, stomach-shrinking dread, a sense of the coming darkness, and walls closing in. When my aunt put her arms around me I wished I could have comforted her, but I shrank from her touch.

All that effort controlling myself backfired. Their suspicions were aroused and the police returned to question me further. Finally, a couple from the second floor identified Sami as someone they'd seen leaving the building on Christmas Eve. He already had a criminal record, was known in the area, and the CCTV footage was of him outside the metro. Even though they'd arrested him, the police kept at me, asking where I'd been that night. I said I'd slept on the banks of the Seine, but there were no witnesses. In the end, they told me to get legal advice.

I had a few days to get my story straight before I met my lawyer, M. Dintrans. He wasn't at all what I was expecting – fat, like a marshmallow stuffed in a suit, all soft and bulging in places where his clothes failed to hold him. Every so often he'd swivel his trousers around on his hips then hoist them up. He had so much blubber around his face that it erased all expression, so it wasn't clear what he was thinking, and it didn't inspire confidence. How would he handle my case, I thought, if he couldn't even manage himself?

He was suspicious of me from the get-go, and that really threw me. He didn't believe I'd slept by the river, and the more he questioned me, the more confused I became.

My aunt stayed with me for the first hour or so. When Dintrans left the room to take a call, I asked why he was defending me when he didn't seem to be on my side at all. She was silent for a while, and then explained these were the kind of questions I'd get in court, so I needed to get used to them. She said he specialised in difficult children's cases and I was lucky to have him. Some of my father's old colleagues had gathered around, and Jean-Marc had helped find him. It was only when he got involved that Dintrans agreed to take me on. Some lawyers only worked for rich clients and Dintrans was one of them.

When he returned, he asked my aunt to leave.

I stuck to the story I'd told the police, and he made me repeat it again and again until everything I said felt tired and worn out and I wasn't sure if even the truth was real. It was hard to keep track of it, and I contradicted myself many times. In the end, I was more focused on trying to remember what I'd said to Dintrans than recalling what actually happened. His queries about the small details stumped me the most – like how my father seemed when I last saw him, what he was wearing and what we'd talked about.

I said that he seemed the way he always had. Stressed. Confrontational. Drunk. Patrick and Elena were there that last time, so I had to remember it correctly, but nothing I said went down well.

Dintrans had a habit of taking off his glasses and pointing the chewed arms at me. If I hesitated, he'd jab them at me with this nasty look that said, *If you can't remember something small like that, how can I believe you about the big stuff?*

In truth, I was more scared of him than the police. He dragged his seat to the window where the streaming light made my eyes sting. Whenever I looked away, he raised his voice and told me it came across as *evasive*, so I forced myself to stare at his large silhouette, but the glare of the sun made it hard to see his eyes.

At one point, he leaped up out of his seat, which squeaked and sprung up like something released from captivity. He turned on me, criticising my *demeanour*. My father was dead, practically *beheaded* on his own threshold, so I'd better sit up straight and start looking as though I gave a shit. I needed to start dressing properly, too – none of this *streetwear*.

I sat up, tucked my shirt into my jeans, and tried to look more respectful even if I didn't feel it. It wasn't true that I couldn't give a shit – I was shit scared. Fear is like fire; it engulfs everything. If he couldn't see that, then there was something wrong with him.

After that, he got down to business and made me admit my relationship with my father had been difficult, but he twisted my words so it sounded like I'd bullied him, even beaten him up. *Where did he get all those scratches and bruises? You say he didn't even have a bike.*

I said it wasn't like that and if anything, my father had been the most violent, but mainly to objects like my games console.

Dintrans managed to turn that around too. *No,* I said, *it never got physical between us, and he never sexually abused me either if that's what you mean.* After that, he told me not to try and second-guess him. This line of questioning made me light-headed and queasy, my eczema itching like crazy all along my arms and up my back where I couldn't reach it.

It wasn't until later in the day that he played his trump card. He must have had the plan all along and was just waiting until he'd worn me down. He put his hands together, nodded and turned his back. I thought he was going to say we'd reached the end of the session, but instead, he reached for an envelope among the mess of papers on his desk. He opened it slowly and then thrust an A4 photo at me.

'Who's this? Think fast.'

It was a bad photo of Sami. A shaven-head mugshot from three or four years ago. His eyes were dark, gloomy pools that threatened to consume me.

The sudden injection of new fear just when I thought we were done made my mind go blank. All I could think of were the last things Sami said to me.

Don't be so gutless.

Remember our deal – you and me, we're brothers now.

I should have confessed to at least knowing Sami then, but I was frozen. Unsure of where to turn, I built a wall of lies.

'I don't know,' I must have finally spluttered as I stared at the mugshot, unable to take my eyes off Sami's face.

Dintrans continued to fire questions, and my short, terrified denials chipped further at my credibility.

Where had I met him? *I hadn't.*

Who introduced us? *No one.*

Why did he call my father? *No idea.*

Was he the one who slit my father's throat?

He said my father had written 'Sammy' on a piece of paper on his desk, and Dintrans sat back triumphantly. My eyes itched, sweat prickling under my arms. *He's the guy the police need to question, then, not me,* I said.

I knew I needed to keep one step ahead, but I was losing traction and the room was swimming. Blinding sunlight bent across the sprawl of papers on his desk and everything splintered. My mind was running in all directions, and it was only when Dintrans stood over me and told me that if I was going to keep up the lies, then I needed to learn how to control my nervous tics, that I realised I was moaning and squeezing both knees to keep them still.

After that, he said nothing, just stood there, staring out of the window. Then he walked back to the desk, selected another photo and held it up. It was a crime scene shot of my father on the entrance mat, a tape measure and pointers in the frame. I wasn't prepared for it, there was dark blood everywhere and I nearly threw up. I looked away, but he shook the photo and asked me again why my father had the name 'Sammy' on his desk.

Then he held the two photos together – my father's and Sami's.

'There's a missing link here,' he said, moving the photos apart, so there was space between them. He leaned forward, placed a photo on either side of my head. 'It's an ugly portrait to be sure, but the truth is rarely pretty.'

He passed another photo – a close-up of my father's dead face, all bruised and swollen like a drowned man.

'This one isn't very pretty either,' he said, looking from the photo to me, and back again. 'You're lucky you don't look much like him. Not yet, anyway.' He waited for a long, painful moment as the image moved closer to me and then he said, 'Do you worry your friend might do this to you if you tell the truth?'

'He's not my friend.'

He nodded, affecting a look of concern. 'Why was his blood at the scene?'

I saw Sami in the lobby, covered in my father's blood and the genuine confusion wiped my brain of focus.

'His blood?' I said.

He smiled, registering the fear in my face now.

'Yes, Sami's blood was at the scene. Come on, stay with it. You're acting like someone who's guilty, Alex. You're not guilty, are you?'

I shook my head. I wasn't guilty of killing him, but robbing him was my idea. I didn't know how it worked, but I thought a judge would see that as just as bad. And a son running away from his father when he was injured, well, that was probably the worst thing ever.

'Do you know how I can tell you're lying, apart from your twitching knee and the way you glare at me?'

I shrugged.

'When you tell the truth, you sit up straight the way you did when we talked about the bruises on your father's neck. But when you lie, you sulk like a brooding dog.'

He shook a bunch of papers at me. 'It gets worse the more you read. You were even *stealing* from his bank account.'

He spread his arms wide. 'Alex, you're the only real suspect here, the only one with any possible motive—'

'I didn't kill him.'

'Why did your father write down Sami's name?'

He held the photo of my father's bloodied face, a dark pool of blood extending over his chest like a bib.

'Perhaps he was expecting Sami. Perhaps Sami called him.'

He kept at me like that, nodding his head like one of those dashboard bulldogs, up and down, side to side.

'Well, is that right? Did Sami call him?'

Finally, I shrugged. 'I guess so.'

'You *guess so*? Well, guess what? If I've guessed it and you've guessed it, then others will guess it too. And I don't want this case to be about guesswork. I need this case to be about facts. My facts.'

He pulled his chair in close so our knees were touching. I could feel the heat coming off him, his damp breath smelling of garlic and the sour reek of lunchtime wine. He held out his hand, and the weird thing was I took it, even though I resented the old bastard then more than anything. He spoke softly and told me not to worry. He said he knew I was scared, and wanted to help me. He said it didn't matter what I'd done, he would get me acquitted. He put his other clammy hand on mine, and said the thing that worried him was he didn't think he could get me acquitted with this *narrative*.

'I need the real story,' he said, and for the first time, he sounded sincere.

He stood side-on at his desk shuffling papers, arranging them in piles. 'I'm on your side. I'm *paid* to be on your side.'

He turned to face me. 'It's my job to take care of you. I know it doesn't feel like it, but that's because you're not telling me what I need to hear.'

He sighed and returned to the glare of the window so I couldn't see his face. 'What we have is a case where the spotlight is shining on you. We need to move it, so it shines somewhere else.'

He held up Sami's picture again. 'He may not look like it, but this guy is a godsend. No one will believe him – a thug from the suburbs who already has *form*. We need to twist the spotlight around so it shines on him.'

He let the photo sag in his hand. 'You've heard of telephone records, Alex? Caller data?'

I nodded, my stomach flipping like a fish.

Dintrans said my father received a call at nineteen minutes to four on the day he died. He explained that once someone had been arrested, or was even under suspicion for a crime, the anti-terrorist legislation gave the police the right to look at all the data on their phone. Dintrans had seen the geo-locators for my phone which put me in exactly the same area, possibly metres apart from the phone that called my father on each of the three days before the attack.

I went cold. 'Maybe we both visit the same places.'

'Alex, yours and Sami's phones spent whole evenings nuzzled up together. Your location parallels are at a level that makes it impossible to say you didn't know each other. We'd be laughed out of court.'

I tried to speak, but my breath stuck in my throat.

'If you deny knowing Sami, and it comes out that you did know him – and believe me it will – the jury won't separate the two of you. You'll both go down as joint killers bound and thrown in the river like a couple of pups in a sack.'

He dropped the file on his desk like he'd just closed the case. His skin was shiny with perspiration, and he mopped his neck with a handkerchief.

He went to the bookshelf and drew out a red, leather-bound volume with gold lettering on the spine. 'Do you know how different cultures view cases of patricide?'

He opened the book and propped it on one of the shelves. 'In China, the convicted criminal is beaten and then sewn into a sack with a dog, a cock, a viper and an ape,' he said, scanning the page then looking over at me. 'I'm told this still happens in some rural areas. Can you believe it? God knows where they get the ape. The sack with the animals and the criminal is thrown into the sea, or a river; and if there's no water, it's thrown into a hole.'

He replaced the book and walked slowly towards me.

'In France, it's dealt with less imaginatively, but the punishment is severe. In the old days, the patricidal son was taken to the place of execution barefoot wearing nothing but his shirt, his head covered with a black veil. He was then exposed on the scaffold, his right hand cut off and immediately put to death. The punishment is not that bad now, but it's still one of the toughest in Europe.' He leaned in towards me. 'It's thirty years.'

He put his hand on my shoulder. 'Alex, I just can't think of a way to keep you out of this, and you're not going to be able to keep up your lies throughout the trial.'

I sat there feeling the last dregs of hope drain away and so I did what any good loser does – I gave the dice one more throw. I didn't like Dintrans, and I was sure he hated me.

I shook my head. 'I've never met that guy.'

He walked around the desk, head bent as though he was thinking.

Then I don't know what came over me. Perhaps my confusion was greater than my fear. Sami didn't have a knife. My father's throat wasn't cut. The story was way beyond my control now. I felt my mouth open and words came out.

'The thing is, I don't think Sami killed him,' I said.

Dintrans turned to me with a look of satisfaction and said softly, 'Why don't you just tell me what happened?'

In the end, I took Dintrans' advice and said in my statement that it had all been Sami's idea. I knew that wasn't true, of course, and that robbing my father was my plan, but Dintrans said that was just a detail. I think it was this lie that made me feel the worst. Sami had been in custody all that time, and he hadn't mentioned me.

It was a relief to speak freely, to confess after holding it inside for so long, and afterwards, I could think clearly again. It was like the problem was no longer mine, it was Dintrans' now, and I almost wanted to kiss him for taking it on.

I said we'd rehearsed it: that Sami was just supposed to ask my father for money, that the hammer was just in case things got out of hand. I told Dintrans I didn't really think about what that meant, and yes, of course, the whole idea was *out of hand* from the beginning, but I had no idea he was carrying a knife.

All this time, Dintrans sat perched on the edge of his desk, taking notes.

'Describe what you saw when you ran upstairs after Sami fled?' he asked for the hundredth time.

I told him I saw my father sprawled on the entry mat. The place was a mess, the contents of the sideboard lying on the floor around him. He was still conscious, but there was blood on the floor. He was writhing and groaning, and his slippers had fallen off. I said I noticed his socks were red like the bloody fingerprints on the door frame.

'And what did you do once you'd stepped inside?'

'I spoke to him. He grasped my arm, and I told him to hang on, that I was there. Then I ran to the kitchen to get some water and a cloth for his wound, but once I got there, I just stood at the sink unable to breathe, panicking at the sight of the blood on the floor. Then I heard noises.'

'What kind of noises?'

'A kind of thudding sound. At first, I thought it was the radiators inside the apartment, but as the sounds got louder, I realised it was someone coming up the stairs.'

'Which stairs?'

'The main stairs. I assumed it was a neighbour. Then I remembered my father said he was expecting someone.'

'Expecting who?'

'He didn't say, but I guessed it was a friend. A woman, most likely.'

'When did he say this?'

'When I spoke to him on the phone that afternoon. He told us to come before nine thirty, when this person was due.'

Dintrans asked me what happened next and I told him I thought Sami had just given him a light injury – you know how scalp wounds can bleed. I didn't know what to do, but was convinced whoever was on the stairs would help him. I couldn't stay there – I'd be blamed for what had happened – so I made a split-second decision and ran down the back stairs that led straight from the kitchen to the rear of the building.

And that's the way it was, my legs flying down the service stairs and straight out of the back door, past the bins and into the back courtyard, the blood fizzing in my head. If I'd been a dog, my ears would have been flat along my skull, eyes white, swivelling around in fear, and I felt charged up as I burst onto the street.

Being Christmas Eve, the restaurants and bars were packed and lots of people were outside. The world looked surreal and garish after the rain, like there was a lacquer spread over everything.

I ran to the river. When I got there I felt a strong pull back to my father, but an even more powerful fear, hot and feverish, propelled me onwards and I crossed the bridge to the Île de la Cité.

The stairs leading down to the water glistened yellow from the streetlights, and my steps echoed on the stone like I was entering a dungeon. The black river lapped high on the cobbled banks, flowing fast and surging in currents. Further out, lights from the opposite side shimmered and dissolved across the water like flames. All of the bridges were hung with lights that cast shadows on the cavernous arches and made the river look as if it had been strung with massive Christmas decorations.

I stood on the bank, which seemed to sway beneath me. In the apartments opposite, dark silhouettes moved in the buttery light making Christmas preparations. Bells rang out across the city, loud and insistent against the wail of sirens and the background hum of traffic.

I found some old blankets on a low wooden trolley a homeless person had left behind, and I dragged them to the pointed tip of the island under a large willow tree whose branches drooped into the water. I lay there all night, and for a while, it felt like a refuge. It was as if I was on the prow of a ship, steaming away from the city, everything bad receding behind me with the flow of the river.

At some point I drifted off, and when I woke, the sky was clear. The wind bit through the blankets, and a full moon stared down at me.

Where are you, Alex? Why did you leave me?

I tossed and turned but I couldn't escape my father's words which carried on the wind like the flames of light that rippled and stretched across the water.

'OK,' Dintrans said when I'd finished, placing his pen on top of his notebook as though everything was settled.

He put his hand on my shoulder. 'I'm glad we understand each other now.'

It was just as well my evidence was pre-recorded because the whole trial passed in a blur and I had no idea what anyone was saying. It was as if they were speaking a language I knew once but had since forgotten.

In the end, the jury believed Sami was the mastermind and that he killed my father in a scuffle on the threshold. Dintrans told me not to mention going upstairs or hearing someone arrive, and to say that Sami had a knife.

'Even if it's not him, at least there's one less on the street,' he said on the final day of the trial.

Sami was convicted of murder and got a twenty-five-year sentence. I ended up with fifteen years as his accomplice, reduced to seven because I was a minor at the time.

So in the end, Dintrans didn't get me off completely, but he was right, and the jury went for the 'stupid plan gone wrong' story. It was the easiest option, and it worked. It appealed to their fears and their darkest beliefs. The jury didn't have to think too hard, they just needed to believe the simple story Dintrans told them.

And for a while, he even made me feel it wasn't so far from the truth.

NOW

Thirty-Seven

Passy

THAT MORNING BEFORE I LEAVE my flat I finish the letter to Sami. All prison correspondence is read, so I'm careful how I express myself. I can't say straight out that I'd lied in court, so instead, I tell him there were things about my evidence I hadn't meant to say, things about that night I'd left out and most of all that I'm sorry for what I'd done. I make it clear that I want to help him get released, and I write the same to his lawyer, too, so he knows I'm serious.

If he wants to get his case reopened he'll need my help. No one listens to you inside, and it's impossible to get hold of your records. Even if you do, you can't keep any documents in your cell, and as for being allowed the time to go through them someplace else – forget it.

I finish the letters, seal the envelopes and leave the flat. I don't want to stay with Lisa, but after the warning and the photos on my phone, I realise there's not much choice. I'm careful on the way to hers and I'm still thinking of Sami as I turn on the back stairs to her flat, like his in many ways – each floor the same as the last – the bare wooden steps and peeling paint, the identical toilet on each landing. Suddenly, everything seems so long ago, now just fractured recollections. The past still holds me in its grip, but the clues to the puzzle I'm trying to solve are out of reach, like a dream, and I'm not sure how anything fits together, or if it's meant to at all.

'The door's open,' Lisa says.

She shuffles her chair to make room for me. On the screen is an advertisement for an apartment project. It's the kind of thing you see on housing development billboards on the edge of the city – tall apartment blocks silhouetted against blue sky, bright sunlight skimming the glass and balconies overflowing with plants in full bloom. At ground level a cyclist waves at a radiant couple with dog and pram. It's an architectural vision of the perfect life, but the colours are too real, too bright, the whole thing chilling in its flawlessness.

'What's that?' I say, wondering why she's looking at ads for suburban apartment buildings.

'This is Ligne Rouge,' she says, then reads from the screen:

> Urban environments are under ever-increasing stress.
>
> Disruption caused by mass immigration, over-population, civil unrest and environmental crisis is expected to exceed the resources of future governments.
>
> Ligne Rouge helps cities transform to face these challenges.
>
> The initial project, **Gateway to Paris**, is a unique opportunity to invest in the City of Light. The project will future-proof Paris against the external shocks that threaten to attack and destroy it.
>
> The **Gateway to Paris** heralds an exciting future and a revolutionary new way to live!

'What the hell is it?'

'It's a fortress city,' she says, flicking to a page showing an aerial 3D view of Paris with a ring of new apartment blocks tracing a line just beyond the Péri.

She flicks to another page and reads:

> Once complete, the **Gateway to Paris** apartment complexes, together with the natural defences of the river Seine, will fully encircle the city. The development will ensure the security and financial prosperity of the central Paris zone. It will safeguard and preserve the city's beauty, protecting its heritage, statues and monuments from external attack.

I stare at the screen. 'What do you mean *fortress city*?'

'I mean, literally. They want to build luxury apartment communities on the old fort sites around Paris. The plan is to link them up with a rail network, creating a ring around the city.'

She flicks through to a map showing the forts all joined together, encircling the city.

I scroll through the pages. 'Where did you find this?'

'On an investment site brokers use to exchange information. I did a search for Ligne Rouge. At first, I couldn't get access because it was limited to approved fund managers. But I found a phone number and spoke to one of the secretaries. I gave her the name of a broker I met on another forum who spoke about the site, said I was his assistant, and she let me in.'

I point to the line on the map linking the sixteen forts. 'Ligne Rouge owns all these forts?'

'The prospectus says they have ninety-year leases on five of them so far.'

'And the others?'

'They're owned by the Ministry of Defence and currently used for high-level security purposes – police headquarters, army barracks, training centres, that kind of thing. Some of them have surveillance and radar activities, others house divisions of the secret police, intelligence services, riot squads, the French Foreign Legion. A few of them are prisons and detention centres.'

'So what's going on? Ligne Rouge is developing these sites?'

'From the looks of things, yes.'

She moves the cursor around the map, circles several of the forts. 'They've started on three already – Issy, Vanves and Aubervilliers.'

'The building sites at Aubervilliers – I can see them from my window.'

She scrolls through photos on the screen. At the end of the architectural presentation, there's a series of bleak images showing the consequences of a failure to invest in the project – pictures of tent cities across Paris, run-down settlements in the suburbs, graphic shots of the aftermaths of terrorist attacks and scenes of environmental havoc.

On the next page is a panorama of burning cars, street violence, riots, angry strikers in yellow vests and finally, queues of dishevelled immigrants making their way through a devastated landscape towards the city.

Built on land once occupied by military fortresses, the **Gateway to Paris** development will fully encircle the central Paris zone, providing the first line of defence against the kind of urban stress Paris has experienced in recent years.

To maintain order, a municipal passport system will be introduced so that only residents and authorised visitors can enter and move between the apartment developments and the central Paris zone. Public demonstrations and gatherings of more than 1,000 people will not be permitted inside Zone One, which will house and protect the key infrastructure of government.

'Is this for real?'

'It's a luxury buffer zone all around Paris. A fortified ring of concrete and steel,' Lisa says, flicking ahead several screens. 'It's justified on the grounds of public health.' She reads from a page labelled CONTAINMENT:

Health pandemics exacerbated by high-density living and globalisation present a serious problem for future gener-ations. The circular, fortress structure of the **Gateway to Paris** means that the Périphérique can be closed and the city put into lockdown within twenty-four hours. In addi-tion, the defensive layout and placement of security checkpoints along the periphery means that the army can be quickly mobilised to guard the main exits and keep the peace. Controlled access to the central Paris zone and key governmental hubs will allow for ease of screening, quarantine and containment.

Further pages expand on logistics, stating that the complexes will have their own emergency services and police network, plus a highly developed security system, alarms, CCTV and other surveillance.

A series of pictures show the internal features of the compounds, each of them surrounded by what looks like a large moat.

> Despite the emphasis on security, a sense of open, pastoral calm is assured through ingenious landscape design. A network of ponds and water features will be incorporated into each complex, and low garden walls, hedges and terraced elevations will create natural, unobtrusive barriers and privacy.
>
> The perimeters of each complex will be reinforced with a defensive border zone fifty metres wide. This zone will protect each hub from penetration by truck bombs, terrorist blasts and unauthorised entrants.
>
> Each 'smart city' complex will combine world-class architecture and high-specification luxury interiors. In addition, each hub is designed to be entirely self-sustaining with state-of-the-art technology, high-speed internet, Wi-Fi-enabled green spaces and office blocks, on-site electricity generators, waste management and water filtration.

'The initial investment raised three billion euros, and there's a second round. People are still investing,' Lisa says.

'Go back to that page with the pictures of the tent cities,' I say.

Lisa scrolls through photos of protesters filling the Champs Élysées, Republique, the Bastille. Scenes of suburban riots and public disorder, societal collapse. Vandalised statues and monuments. Scores of pictures intended to instil fear and panic.

'There,' I say, as she flicks past strikers in front of billowing clouds of smoke, others drenched with a water cannon. 'Go back.'

She flicks back to a picture of a burnt-out car in front of a rough stone wall. Thick black smoke engulfs the front end of the vehicle, and there are bodies strewn across the tarmac as if thrown from the blast.

'Do you remember that?' I ask.

She shakes her head.

'It was at Issy years ago. The night after Tomas's party – the one where everyone got sick. I came home, Patrick and Elena were there with my father, and it was on the news. They never found out who the attackers were. Didn't you say one of the sites they've already built is at Issy?'

'Fort D'Issy,' she says, flicking to the screen showing the new apartment development.

Line 12 cuts a diagonal path across Paris from Aubervilliers in the north to Issy in the south. We emerge from the station into a bleak, windswept square at the edge of a building site. The drill of jackhammers competes with the drone of the motorway, and cranes reach up into the pale sky, their jibs pointing towards darker clouds closing in from the east.

A narrow road winds uphill, past low suburban bungalows to the old Fort D'Issy. As we gain height, the distant skyscrapers of La Defence rise out of the flat land as though they've erupted from the earth, their jagged silhouettes dominating the skyline and pulsing in the shifting light like living things.

Lisa navigates on her phone along the narrow streets, until we reach the fortress walls – five metres high, and built from the same rough stone that wraps around the Fort d'Aubervilliers. Up ahead, a boom gate and two empty sentry boxes guard the opening to an arched tunnel with the words FORT D'ISSY carved into a sandstone lintel. Lisa points her camera up at a tattered French flag that whips around a rusted flagpole. Despite all the building activity we passed, the area is deserted – as though an enemy army had just stormed through.

We pass beneath the arch and inside, a wall of plastic fencing blocks the way. Through a gap in the barrier, we see an abandoned construction site – muddy, cleared ground and the deep trenches of excavated foundations, now full of water.

A narrow path hugs the perimeter of the development. Eventually, the path widens to an open space erratically planted with frail saplings, their trunks still wrapped in plastic sleeves. Collapsed road barriers block the way so we pick our way over bollards and striped traffic tape flapping in the wind. Further along, a wall of hurricane fencing surrounds a large grassed area where metallic boulders, spikes and jagged ironwork erupt from the grass like the creations of a sadistic sculptor. At the edge of the development, anti-tank obstacles lie across a wide bitumen road.

Up ahead, a man in high-vis gear steps out of a makeshift site office.

'This is a private land,' he says, walking towards us.

'We're just looking for the way out,' Lisa says.

He stares at her camera. 'You can't take photos in here. It's private property.'

His hand reaches to his belt, as if he has a gun, but it's a walkie-talkie. He barks into it, reporting our unauthorised entry.

'You need to leave,' he says, pointing the antenna back the way we came.

'What is this place?' I say as Lisa pulls me away.

'It's dangerous walking around here. Leave now and don't come back,' he calls after us.

We retrace our steps, skirting the edge of the site back towards the exit. Or what we think is the exit, but we've taken a wrong turn. There's no gate, just the same haphazard stone wall on one side, plastic fence on the other.

Lisa pokes her camera through a gap in the sheeting and part of it gives way. We push through to a demolition site, the ground torn up by bulldozers and scattered with corrugated iron, bricks and blasted cement. The earth is pockmarked with excavation holes, and massive dumpsters overflow with mattresses, rugs and smashed furniture. Further on, a couple of ragged tents cling to the side of a half-demolished wall.

I walk ahead, but she pulls me back. 'He said it's dangerous.'

'It's not dangerous. It's just a construction site,' I say, as we pass mounds of rubbish and household debris. Lisa is taking photos of a pile of broken children's toys when the first figure appears. He's little more than a kid himself, but stocky, and walks towards us as if he wants something – a light or a cigarette. He draws closer, then there's someone else behind him, and one look at his beaten-up face tells me we're in trouble.

'Run!' I yell to Lisa as others appear.

It's what I should have done last week, I think, the ground a blur of dirt and gravel beneath me.

It's not dangerous. It's just a construction site.

Of course, it's dangerous, poking around in someone else's business. Getting carried away. But not getting carried away fast enough, not when it matters, because the first guy has me now, his arm around my neck.

And the ground rises up and hits me in the chin.

The one with the smacked-in face has Lisa. There are muffled screams as she struggles, and I flex against the kid on my back. He's probably only about sixteen, and I could probably shake him off, but the other one is bigger, and Lisa doesn't look like she's going anywhere.

They frogmarch us along a raw track back towards the tents. The earth is covered with oily stains and the ashy residue of fires.

They lead us into a concrete bunker; some kind of half-built block, the inside covered in graffiti.

I try to think. *Keep your head. They're just kids.*

But there are more of them now, some of them older, and they force us to sit back-to-back, our hands tied together around a cement column.

One of the older ones, a man, steps forward and grabs Lisa's camera as she struggles against me. 'I've told people I'm here. People know where we are. If you do anything to us—' she says.

'Did the company send you?' he asks, kneeling beside her. He begins going through the photos, deleting them. 'Who are these for?'

He takes her bag and fishes inside, going through her wallet, her cards. He holds out her press card to the others. 'The company sends in journalists now.'

'*What* company?' asks Lisa.

'The construction company,' he says, dropping her wallet into her bag. 'They come here all the time. Roughing us up, taking photos to get us evicted.'

A group has gathered around us now – ten, maybe twelve men and a few teenagers.

'We're just trying to find out what this place is,' she says. 'I'm taking photos of the site, not of you.'

The older guy finishes deleting the photos, then gestures to the others to untie us.

'You shouldn't be here,' he says, handing Lisa the camera. 'You need to leave now.'

'That's what the guy said outside. Who are you?' she says.

'Some of us used to live here. Our families had flats near the old barracks, but we were evicted a few years ago.'

'So, what's going on?' I ask. He looks at me for a while as if considering the meaning of the question.

'They want to clear the area for construction. After the first eviction notices a lot of people left. Then they cut the electricity and the water. Finally, they sent in the riot police, gave us an hour to pack our things and took us away on buses. They said there were faults with the buildings, that they was unsafe, and we would be rehoused elsewhere. But no one was. Then when we came back, the place was all boarded up. Now it's being demolished.'

He points to the tents. 'A few of us stayed. But they say we cause disturbances, trouble. They say we're a security risk and sometimes people come here, start fights and take photos to keep up the bad press. That's who we thought you were.'

We follow his gaze through one of the empty windows and I imagine a horde of people cresting the hills of debris outside, wielding baseball bats and Molotov cocktails.

'You need a permit to enter the site at all. Proof of residence.'

'But no one lives here,' I say.

He shrugs. 'Exactly. They mean future residents. You saw the spikes and boulders around the fort, the guards at the gates. They're increasing security more and more. That's why they have all that stuff there. Makes it impossible to come back, but we do. This is where we've always lived. We're not leaving. They need to know we're not giving in.'

'Go, now,' he says, pointing to the exit. 'One of the guys will show you the way out. There's further development down near the station if you're interested. A lot of billboards have gone up. More places have been requisitioned. You'll see,' he says, turning back to the others.

The wind picks up as we walk back to the metro, past a cluster of boarded-up houses. Trees scrape against billboards depicting glossy apartments and perfect lives played out under sunny blue skies.

Along the bottom of the poster is the slogan:

THE GATEWAY TO A NEW LIFE!

The pictures are the same as the ones Lisa showed me on the website.

Beneath the slogan:

The Fort d'Issy digital sustainable neighbourhood is supported by Digibank Immobilier and Gateway Développement

Thirty-Eight

Montparnasse

I<small>T'S ALMOST DARK WHEN WE</small> reach the station. Now there's a curfew against travel at night, and the platform is deserted save for a few solo travellers and a drunk weaving dangerously close to the platform edge.

Lisa shivers, pulling her jacket around her. 'Next time, we leave when I say.'

'You were the one taking photos, stirring things up.'

'You knew that place was trouble,' she says sourly, drawing half a step ahead, and silence settles between us with the growing darkness.

Finally, a train arrives, and a few stops later, there's a message on my phone.

It's the same scene as last night and it's clearly me – naked and blindfolded, tightly bound in thick black ropes. There's a knife on the mat beside me, a few inches from my throat.

I rear back, almost dropping the phone.

'What was that?' Lisa says, craning in as the picture vanishes from the screen.

'Did you see it?'

'Not fully. What was it?'

'It was me. When I was attacked.'

Then a text message:

You've been warned.

And another:

Stop sticking your nose where it's not wanted.

'Who is it?' Lisa says, twisting my phone towards her.

The echo of the slurred voice, the chewed words.

Through the window, the station's name we're pulling into, Montparnasse, swims past on a blue banner as the train slows along the platform, and images rush towards me.

Nick's voice.

Stop sticking your nose where it's not wanted.

Sami and the girl in the street near Montparnasse.

The bulldozed camp at Issy, and the one I visited with Sami.

'Alex, wait!' Lisa calls, but I'm already halfway down the platform.

The bars in the Passage D'Enfer are closed, and the sign PLEASURES OF PARADISE dissolves into darkness behind a low streetlight. Beneath the sign is a plain glass window, the interior draped in green satin and dimly lit with thin white candles. As I approach, a taxi stops and a couple emerge. The woman wears black heels and a coat, the man a suit. The lacquered door to the left of the window opens and they enter straight away.

I press the buzzer and finally the door opens an inch, the gap widening to reveal a woman dressed like a flight attendant in a dark blue jacket with heavy shoulder pads.

'No single men tonight,' she says, her elaborate blonde hairdo stark against the void behind her.

'No trainers either,' she adds, slamming the door.

I press the buzzer again.

'No single men,' she says, viciously through the intercom. 'No jeans. And no *trainers!*'

When Lisa and I return an hour later, I'm wearing her father's clothes – chinos, a white business shirt and a new pair of loafers. By now a queue has formed, each couple presenting themselves to a bull-necked bouncer installed at the entrance.

Inside, the woman gives Lisa a sugary smile as she takes the door fee, then ushers us towards a staircase that leads down two flights to a cavernous basement.

The walls are bare stone, covered in a lurid varnish that makes them glow with a deep golden sheen. Low banquettes hug the walls, and velvet chairs are tucked around small tables scattered with candles giving off a deep woody scent. A group of people mill around a bar at the far end of the room, laughing and talking loudly, and there's an air of expectation as each new arrival is scanned and appraised. When we reach the bar, a woman detaches herself from the group.

'Want a dance?' she says, taking my hand.

I can't see a dance floor anywhere, but she smiles and nods towards a doorway. Her crooked teeth glow in the light like the gleaming walls but the top half of her face is hidden beneath a lacy mask.

'Drink, then,' she says beckoning the barman. She leans forward and something about the way she moves and her nervous smile makes me think she's young.

The girl slides two glasses our way. 'You've been here before?'

Lisa rolls her eyes. 'I'll be back soon,' she says then heads off through the crowd.

I chat to the girl and tell her I'm looking for someone called Nick. 'Short, flat-faced, tattoos on his hands. You know him?'

'No, but that description doesn't narrow it down much,' she says, lighting a cigarette and turning away.

I take my drink and move away from the bar, through a door and down a long, crowded corridor in search of Lisa. There's a mirror along one side, which reflects the activities going on in a series of arched vaults. In the first one, a man stands naked, facing a black leather-padded wall. His wrists are manacled to heavy chains and a rusty anchor is suspended from a cage above his head. There's the grinding of metal on large pulleys and people watch as he's hoisted up until finally, he hangs by his wrists in mid-air. In the next alcove others watch a similar spectacle, this time a woman on all fours being led around by a man in a latex balaclava. In a bigger, recessed bay further down, naked bodies writhe on a large mattress. There are grunts, sighs, everyone going at it with serious faces, like they're rehearsing for a film but have dropped their lines for the run-through. A few smaller alcoves have private dances taking place and cool air blows along the corridor from vast air-conditioning units overhead.

At the end of the passage, there's a large cloakroom, toilets and a fire escape. I retrace my steps and find Lisa in the viewing gallery of the first chamber, taking surreptitious pictures on her phone.

As we pass the bar, the girl points to a table. 'Take a seat,' she says. 'The show is starting soon.'

Lisa hesitates, but I lead her towards the table and soon the room starts filling up with people coming in from the corridor, red-faced and glowing in the flickering candlelight, adjusting their clothes as they look around, smiling at the novelty of seeing each other dressed. There's a hum of anticipation and some take seats while others swell towards a pair of long satin curtains, which shudder then rise to reveal a small spot-lit stage.

Two women emerge dressed in red latex corsets and the same kind of masks as the girl at the bar. The crowd pulses with excitement and several men shoulder their way to the front, towards the women who make them stand in line. One of the women runs a riding crop along the men's faces, slapping them lightly back and forth until finally, she chooses one, pulling him forward while the other woman wheels a padded bench onto the stage. It's covered in black vinyl with brass buttons sunk deep into the padding.

The man strips, unable to control his excitement as he lies on the bench. His nakedness whips the audience into a frenzy of howls and catcalls. Slowly, the women circle him, tying his body to the bench with thick ropes. Their focus is intense, muscles flexing as they turn and bind him in elaborate knots until his body is a mass of twisted cables, white flesh bulging between the rigging. Another pair of women wheel a wooden church altar onto the stage and then, with candelabra and priestly torches, they drip red wax onto his belly. The man is moaning now, blindfolded, his feet clamped into a set of stirrups. The women beat him with paddles and slap him with knives, running them over the length of his bound and waxed body.

'What the hell is this?' says Lisa, totally transfixed by the spectacle on the stage.

The throng surges forward, pressing around us so I don't notice someone crouching next to me.

'Quick, put this on,' the girl from the bar whispers, passing her mask. 'He's just arrived. You need to leave.'

She nods towards a figure at the side of the stage. At first, he's just a vague silhouette, an outline that seems to suck the light into itself, as if he's his own shadow. Then he turns to watch the crowd, which is yelling and whooping now. Nick – his lank hair slicked over his head, in a dark suit and a wide lapelled shirt. He carries a white-topped cane like a circus showman surveying his audience.

His gaze returns to the stage, and then very faintly, he raises the cane, nods to the women on stage, and then dissolves into the curtains' dark folds.

Rabid howls of excitement come from the crowd as Lisa looks at me in horror. 'I'm not watching this,' she says, moving away from the table.

The man on the slab is screaming but I can't see him because everyone has surged forward in a crush. Suddenly, the crowd stills and through the silence comes a soft whimpering from the bench, then hollow, muffled sobbing. There are horrified gasps from the crowd, a soft squelching sound, then the crack of a whip and shrieks of agony, before everything goes quiet.

The girl follows me. 'That way,' she whispers, pointing towards Lisa who heads down the corridor, the alcoves on either side empty now.

Behind us a fury of clapping from the crowd, then cheers. Up ahead, a man pulls Lisa into the bathroom.

'Leave her, André,' says the girl as we enter behind them.

'She was taking photos,' he says. 'That's forbidden.'

'This place should be shut down,' says Lisa, reaching to grab her phone from André, but he steps back and then, with a sweeping underhand, throws it into a toilet bowl.

I follow her into the cubicle while the others argue, then André leaves.

'This place is insane. What is all this?' Lisa says, retrieving her dripping phone.

The walls of the bathroom are covered with old cabaret posters – images of leering performers doing various circus tricks, and others engaged in murkier spectacles, like the ones in the alcoves. The top left-hand corner of each poster is embossed with name of the club, and the symbol of the reptilian creature on the sign outside. A series of older posters with a different name catches my eye and I rip one of them from the wall as Lisa pulls me from the bathroom.

Outside, the girl leads us through a set of double doors into a back service area, then up a flight of stairs to a large room, open to the rafters. The floor is padded with blue mats, there's a boxing ring in the corner, and that unmistakeable, wet dog smell of cramped muscles, pain and sweat.

She sees my expression. 'It took me a while to recognise you, but yes, you've been here before. This is where they brought you. They drugged you and put you on stage.'

'On *stage?*'

She grabs my arm, traces the marks, now faint bruises. 'These are rope burns. You were part of the performance. I don't know what sick game they're playing.'

'You saw it?'

'It was like tonight, but you were out of it, drugged, a different performance. You were tied with those ropes.'

I stare at her, appalled by what she's saying.

'What's going on? What is this place?'

She opens the door onto a small back street.

'Just stay away from here,' she says, stepping back inside.

Thirty-Nine

Clairvaux

S AMI'S LAWYER CALLED AS SOON as he received the letter and asked me to come in and write a statement, saying all the things I didn't say in court – how I went upstairs after Sami left and found my father injured, but alive. I wrote that Sami didn't have a knife, and that when I heard someone coming, I took fright and ran down the back stairs.

Things moved quickly after that and now I'm in a visitors' queue outside a maximum-security prison east of Paris.

I'm panicked about the letter and regret the statement badly, knowing at the very least it's an admission of perjury. My fear grows as the queue moves forward, my heart thudding louder with each step. Nearing the checkpoint, I want to run back to the train station, knowing once I pass through the gates, there's no guarantee they won't just throw me into a cell, but it's only when the guards run checks on my ID do they even give me a second glance.

The visiting hall is crowded and when I see Sami, he's staring straight at me. Up close he has that prison look – dull flaky skin, eyes wired and bloodshot, and his expression is full of contempt. He's thickened up a bit around the neck and chest with a shape that comes from working out in confinement, from doing the same exercises over again, like a lion pacing its cage.

I take one of the flimsy plastic seats and look at the guard, willing him to move away, but he stays close. I keep back, thinking Sami might even lunge forward and attack me, but he just stares at me with a blank scornful look.

I'd prepared a speech, explaining how I thought I could help him and how sorry I was. I had a couple of carefully framed questions about Nick, too, but all of that goes out of my head.

I start to ramble. 'My lawyer tricked me into confessing, into blaming you, into saying you had a knife. He made it seem like the only way out.'

I say all this quietly, ashamed at how pathetic it sounds. I remember the way I felt back then – desperate and afraid, but concerned above all to save myself. I was such a coward.

'It was *your* only way out,' he says.

'I'm sorry for what I did,' I say, trying to make the words sound meaningful, but they're embarrassing, just further insults.

'*Sorry?*' he says in disbelief.

'I was scared. I had no idea what I was doing.'

'And you have a better idea now?'

'I know you didn't kill him.'

'Ah, well that's a start,' he says, the sarcasm in his voice rising. 'They believed your story then but now you want to change it – why?'

'I know my father was killed by someone else. Not you, and not me. I couldn't prove it then, but I will now.'

His expression changes and he almost laughs. He straightens up and I see something of his old confidence, but then his face hardens again. 'No one will believe you. If you say any of this you'll just prove you're a liar. You can't win. It's impossible.'

'You can win, though. You can get the case reopened by saying I lied. You have my statement.'

He nods. 'That's the only reason I'm here now. But why are *you* here?'

'Tell me what happened that night,' I say quietly. 'What happened up there with my father?'

He takes a while to answer, looking to the guard and then to me.

'I said what we agreed – that you were in trouble, needed money. He was angry, kept asking where you were. Finally he took some cash from his wallet. But he was drunk and when I reached for it, he threw himself at me. He attacked me, nearly knocked me out. I told you that.'

'And then you hit him with the hammer?'

'I didn't hit him with the hammer,' he says.

'But there was blood on the hammer, I saw it downstairs.'

'I didn't use the fucking hammer.'

'You were covered in his blood. His wallet was stained with blood.'

'We were covered in *my* blood,' Sami says. 'My head hit the edge of the cabinet as I went down. I was bleeding all over the floor, all over him.'

I sit back, remembering what my lawyer said about Sami's blood being at the scene. At the time I thought it was just another trick to make me confess.

'But he was hurt. You hit him,' I say.

'I punched him, that's all. He got my hands, twisted them around my back and straddled me. He started shouting, said he'd called the police. Then the entryphone started buzzing and

I panicked. I wrestled him off, punched him hard a couple of times, and it was enough to wind him. Then I ran.'

'You never said this. You never mentioned this in court.'

He leans forward, agitated now. 'Yeah, and you didn't tell the truth in court either. You grassed me up to get yourself off. But what good did it do you?'

We stare at each other for a while and there's a fear in Sami's eyes I've seen before. I think of his belief in keeping quiet, that brotherly code of silence. But this time it's more than that – he knows I didn't do it.

Then it occurs to me – he saw someone.

He saw them in the street and it was someone he knew. That's why he said nothing in court.

A bell rings and Sami glances up at the guard who's behind me, so I just mouth the words, *Was it Nick?*

Sami shakes his head and looks away.

'Time's up,' the guard says, and Sami stands. He looks desperate, as if part of him is straining.

'Almost,' he says softly.

It wasn't Nick, but it was someone Sami knew. Someone connected with Nick.

I watch as the guard escorts Sami away. At the door he looks back and nods, and with that gesture he throws me a chance to save us both, and I can't let him down this time.

When I get back that evening, Lisa's at the computer.

She holds up a jar of rice and in it, her dead phone.

'It wasn't a dream,' she says, pointing to the screen. 'And look what I've found. These are the Ligne Rouge companies.'

She takes me through what she's discovered about the companies we'd seen on the billboards near Issy. Digibank Immobilier is some kind of finance company registered in Cyprus, and Gateway Développement looks just like any other commercial property developer, its website full of glittering office blocks, glass atriums in the sky, and invitations to *Step into a World of Luxury*.

Lisa brings up a list of directors of Gateway Développement and scrolls down the page. There are thumbnail photos and names of the directors.

'Hang on,' I say. 'Go back.'

Lisa flicks back to the photo of one of the directors: a woman, Marianne Balard.

I crane in closer. The woman on the screen is blonde, younger than the person I met out at the Parc de Vincennes, but she has the same anxious eyes, the same stern mouth. 'That's her!' I say. 'The woman I met last week.'

'I can't get any more details about the company from here, but my father has access to this kind of information. I'll go down and use his computer,' she says.

When she's gone I go through my backpack for the CD-ROM I found in my aunt's cellar with the sticker in my father's handwriting:

Car bomb Fort D'Issy, 28 November (source: M Balard).

I insert the disk and click on the video link.

A jerky, handheld camera pans silently across an empty car park. The screen blurs then refocuses on a chaotic scene: seven figures on the ground near a wildly burning car. Three of the bodies appear to be children. The vehicle, a white Renault, is parked against a rough stone wall. The bodies are bloodied and face down apart from one man who crawls slowly across the ground on his elbows.

The screen goes black for a second and then pans jerkily across a crowd of anxious faces nearby, watching the scene.

The people stand back in a huddle, agitated. Some have their fists in the air, others have their mouths open, shouting. An ambulance pulls up, emergency workers run into view and attend to the wounded bodies on the ground. The whole thing lasts about thirty seconds.

Next on the disk are a series of screenshots of tweets mentioning the car bomb at the Fort D'Issy.

Then there's a report from one of the news agencies:

CAR BOMB WOUNDS SEVEN AT FORT D'ISSY

PARIS – A car bomb wounded at least seven people at the Fort D'Issy in Paris on Saturday, police and medical staff said.

The car detonated in the southern district of Issy on the site of the old fort which is now used as a centre for refugees and immigrants.

Interior Ministry spokesman, Bruno Drianel, said seven people were wounded, including one policeman.

It was not immediately clear if the bomber had driven the vehicle to the target or if it was a parked car bomb, police sources said.

There's a second video on the CD-ROM. Grainy surveillance footage of the same car park. There's a date stamp on the top right corner that flicks on and off: 28 November. The camera's vantage is higher, looking down over the scene.

It shows a man in a blue shirt and black trousers standing on the passenger side of a white Renault speaking to someone inside the car. It's in exactly the same place as in the previous video, but the car is intact, the surrounding area empty. The man steps back and the other man gets out of the car, and the two men walk to a white Toyota truck and drive away.

A few seconds later, the car explodes in a burst of white light. No one is near it.

The car burns for a while, and when the flames have died down, four men and three small boys run into view, their clothes heavily stained. They drop to the ground and play dead. The scene is the same as in the first video now with the car belching black smoke.

Moments later, an ambulance pulls up. Emergency workers leap out and attend to the people on the ground.

Next on the CD-ROM are screenshots from a Facebook page dedicated to 'The Fort D'Issy Bombing'. The photos show the aftermath of the same location and were uploaded the next day. The car is now a burnt-out shell against the familiar stone wall.

Finally, there is a series of news clippings about the incident.

I go back through the videos and photos, and when Lisa returns, I show her.

'Can you see it's fake? The CCTV footage shows this bomb was faked up.'

She turns the screen towards her. 'They're saying at work that the attack last week was fake too. I tried verifying some of the quotes but the police the reporters spoke to had just evaporated.'

'Show me that page you had yesterday. The pictures of the tent cities,' I say.

Lisa opens the Gateway to Paris site and scrolls to the images of tents, vandalism, protesters on the streets of Paris.

'That's it,' I say as the screen comes to rest on the burnt-out car, the stone wall, bodies strewn across the tarmac.

'It's the same picture,' she says, going from one to the other.

'Exactly. Look, it's the same stone wall around all of the fort sites. These are the so-called disturbances on the site. The trouble.'

'All fake,' Lisa says.

I show her the reference to M Balard on the tape.

'It could be a coincidence. It's a common name.'

'Not that common.'

She hands me a printout of company details. 'Gateway Développement's registered office is a firm of accountants in Guernsey. I called the number. They say they're not authorised to release any information, but look at this.'

I scan the list of directors. Dates of appointments and resignations.

'Marianne Balard became a director in January seven years ago.'

'That's a month after my father died.'

'That's not all. Look at who she replaced.'

'Elena Landis.'

I see Elena in her sitting room that day, the look on her face as she turned to me. *I stopped working for them years ago.* And the articles she wrote about contamination on the Aubervilliers site, even though she was no longer a journalist.

'Elena worked for immigrant charities and refugee centres in the suburbs.'

'The list of the fort sites in your father's papers. The link to this Mari woman. This is what your father was working on. It wasn't about the past at all. It was about the future,' Lisa says, tapping the screen of the Gateway to Paris development with a pen.

'Your father was investigating this kind of future.'

Forty

Champ de Mars

USING LISA'S SPARE PHONE, I text Elena, signing off as 'Mari'. She replies straight away, inviting me to her apartment the next morning.

All of the commuter train lines are down and the metro is disrupted, too, so I leave plenty of time, reaching her neighbourhood early. Cool air rises from the rain-slicked pavement as I take a seat at a café and order a drink.

Digging in my pockets for change, something grabs my attention across the road – the shape and look of someone familiar standing just outside the supermarket. His jeans sag on his hips, and dark, matted hair gathers in the hood of his grey sweatshirt. He looks like Elena's son, Nathan, but his face is blank and washed out, his cheeks hollow. He reaches out to passers-by who shake their heads and weave around him. It's only when a woman opens her purse that I realise he's begging.

He lights a cigarette and sits at the foot of a tree beside a dog curled around some blankets. Part of me wants to go over to him, but I shrink back. He looks as desperate as I feel, and whilst shame draws some together, for others it's divisive – there's nothing about it you want to share. It's like a filthy habit you hate even more when you see it in someone else.

He stubs out his cigarette and gathers his bags. I finish my coffee and move quickly away, keeping under the shadow of the terrace.

When I get to Elena's, she buzzes me in as though she's been waiting at the door. I walk up slowly, past the stained-glass windows that cast drab light on the dusty stairwell.

Her door is ajar and a crisp voice calls from inside, 'Come in.'

When she sees me, her expression collapses and she moves past me to the landing, peers down the stairs.

'Why are you here?' she says coldly. Finally, the penny drops. '*You* sent that text?'

She steps back inside and I follow her to the salon.

'Why did you pretend to be Mari? After all this time?' she says.

It's my turn to be puzzled as I glance around the familiar room, at the dark wood bookshelves with their leather-bound volumes and careful assembly of photographs that show an ordered life, or at least ordered memories. 'What do you mean "after all this time"?'

I watch her at the window, a shaft of light falling across her shoulder, and I recall the last time I was here when she stood in that same pose, smoking and watching me as I probed the dark, unsure of what to say, and clutching at small talk. An oppressive déjà vu overwhelms me now, and I feel I've done all this running around just to end up at the very place I started.

'You knew about her, surely?' she says, watching me closely.

'Knew what about her?'

'You knew she was seeing Eddy.' Then a pause and something like pity clouds her face, 'Didn't you?'

I hear her voice and the intensity of her words, but a gulf has opened up between us, and she recedes into the bluish cigarette haze around her.

'Seeing Eddy ...' I start, as an image rises from the depths: the woman in the bathroom that night, her blonde hair falling over her face. Then Mari, her dark hair but with the same pale complexion. The two memories swirl and disappear, then stack up slowly, like cards thrown onto a table at the end of a game.

'I thought that was Céline,' I say, more to myself than Elena. 'I saw Mari last week.'

Elena turns abruptly. 'You saw her last week?'

'She told me about Ligne Rouge. That you were a director there too,' I add, groping forward with the few facts I have.

Elena points her cigarette at me. Her nails are very red. 'What on earth are you saying, Alex? You're making no sense.'

'She told me what Eddy discovered before he died.'

Elena shakes her head as she stumbles over the words. 'Eddy was determined to make something of it, but all he did was annoy people by probing into their pasts, and Mari just encouraged him.'

'But it wasn't just about the past, was it?' I ask.

I walk to the bookshelf, to a photo of Nathan and Patrick. 'Did Mari encourage Patrick too?'

'Don't drag him into this,' she says, lowering herself onto a chair.

'They always seemed so close, Patrick and Nathan. It must have been hard for Nathan when Patrick died – such a horrible shock,' I say, taking the photo, digging deeper. 'But worse than that, Nathan must have thought he wasn't worth sticking around for. That he wasn't nearly as exciting as the frontline. Is that what Nathan thinks? That his dad committed suicide?' I watch her carefully as she wraps her arms around her chest and braces forward.

'Suicide isn't a revenge fantasy,' Elena says coldly, her face washed with fear.

'No, but in relation to Patrick it's just a fantasy, isn't it?' I say. 'I didn't mention it before, but Patrick visited me in prison just before he died. He was his usual self when he came to see me, not depressed at all. I'm sure Nathan would want to know that.'

'Leave Nathan out of this, Alex,' she says hoarsely, her voice low, almost a growl, and I sense her fear – raw and close to the surface. I can tell from the way her eyes dart around the room, seeking answers from the dead flowers and the dusty shelves, that she's lying, or at least hiding something.

'What is it you want from me, Alex?' she says eventually. 'Why have you come here again?'

'Tell me what you were doing at Ligne Rouge.'

'Promise me you'll keep Nathan out of this.'

'There's no reason for me to bring him in,' I say, and her face relaxes a little. 'But if you don't tell me what's going on, I will. I know where to find him.'

She takes a deep breath as if working up the strength to talk. 'I thought getting involved with Ligne Rouge would make a difference. I was sick of sitting on the sidelines, doing nothing. I was tired of all the hypocrisy,' she says.

'But you were a journalist. You weren't doing nothing.'

She waves the air, as if batting my words away. 'No one reads the news anymore. These days it's just entertainment and scandal. People flicking through news sites like porn, gorging on death, tragedy and hatred. They get their adrenaline fix and then move on.'

'Sometimes they react. Natural disasters, for example, people donate.'

'But no one wants to do anything. Reality makes people uncomfortable.'

I want to disagree, but I sense her shifting away, so I nod slowly. 'So you decided to do something.'

'I thought I could change things. And when Jean-Marc asked me ...' she says bitterly, her lips pursed. 'It was just after he'd bought *La Globe*. I was disillusioned, needed something different. He wanted to create a legacy and I thought I could help.'

'You wanted to help Jean-Marc with his *legacy*?' I ask. She'd spent her life scrutinising people's motives, and suddenly she was interested in a rich man's legacy?

She glares at me, her dark irises like pinheads against the white. I don't believe she worked with Jean-Marc because she wanted to help him with his legacy, but if I challenge her now, she'll just clam up.

'A lot of wealthy individuals want to create a legacy, to give something back,' I say, making my voice fluid and gentle, like a river she might allow her thoughts to drift into.

'I knew the charities were a vanity project, but at least he was doing something. They were helping refugees and the homeless, tackling problems in the suburbs. It felt like such a positive thing, and it was a change from journalism, from the endless cycles of gloom.'

She carries on, not only trying to convince me of the good she was doing, but herself too. She looks calm, but her hands give her away, clasped in front of her, the knuckles white.

I keep her talking, nodding and agreeing with her, until suddenly, she stops.

'Look at you, sitting in judgement on me. What would you know? You never had to fight for anything.' She steps forward so she's standing in front of me, her body shaking, the fabric of her dress quivering, and I see how thin she is beneath it. 'The private school, the expensive holidays, your allowance? Did you ever wonder where the money came from? Did you even care?'

I look at her blankly, wondering what on earth she's talking about. I want to ask questions, to challenge her, but people tell you a lot when they're angry.

'I never thought about it,' I say.

She points at me, a crazed gleam in her eye. 'Jean-Marc paid for your education like he paid for Nathan's. Jean-Marc betrayed Eddy, stabbed him in the back, and then bought his silence, as he did mine.'

I lower my voice, so the question's barely there. '"Bought his silence"?'

She moves across the room, her face shadowed. 'Jean-Marc paid Eddy from the start. All those years through Paul. Jean-Marc kept him on the payroll, kept him at *La Globe* to keep him quiet, keep him close.'

She mutters quickly, saying things I can't hear or don't understand. I want to ask her to slow down, but something's switched inside her, and she's in a trance, enjoying the transformation of thoughts into words, the way they fill the room. I stay quiet, having felt this myself – the need to self-justify again and again, irresistibly, to the point of confession. The act of speaking is a release, and so I just let her talk.

'Paid him through Paul?' I say eventually. 'Lara?'

'Lara was a set-up all along. The whole thing! She fooled Eddy into thinking she'd had a termination, that she was ill, and then they threatened to report him to the police.' She exhales with the burden of remembering it all. 'Eddy was out of his mind with grief. He was worried sick about her and did as he was told.'

'Who were these people?' I think about my father, twice fooled into thinking he'd fathered a baby. *Women were always your father's motivation. They were his weakness. It was never money.* No fucking kidding.

She raises her hands. 'I don't know exactly who they were – agents of some kind, mafia, who knows? They stayed in the shadows and had people like Jean-Marc carry out their business. Jean-Marc's always had those kinds of connections. He was on their payroll too.'

'Jean-Marc was Vestnik, their messenger,' I say.

Elena lowers herself onto the sofa opposite me, her body taut like a shield she's drawn in and wrapped around herself. 'As an editor at *La Globe*, Jean-Marc could influence things. He didn't recruit journalists personally or even tell them what to write, people further up the chain did that, people like Lara and her so-called husband. But Jean-Marc controlled them, and he edited and placed the stories they wrote.'

I hold her gaze despite the glare of the windows behind her.

'They used *La Globe* to push their agenda. Some of it was political, but mostly it advanced their criminal activities. They hated that idea of European unification, for example, so they encouraged anything that was critical of the plan.'

'I can't believe my father did this.'

'Lara's fake husband was from somewhere in eastern Russia, so Eddy thought his orders came from there, but that's as far as he traced it. Eddy never knew exactly who was behind it, or how far it went. Eddy was controlled for five, maybe six years.'

'Who knows about this? How has it remained secret?' I ask.

'We were a little clique. We swapped partners, went on holidays together. It's no real secret anymore, but no one discusses it either. It's too embarrassing now.'

'The place in Montparnasse. Passage D'Enfer.'

I take out a crumpled piece of paper from my pocket. It's one of the old cabaret posters I tore off the bathroom wall in Nick's club. On the corner the name and address: *Matrix Club, 16 Passage D'Enfer.*

'Where did you get this?' she says and I tell her about the visit to Nick's club and about the photos in my father's shoebox.

'The club was Jean-Marc's idea. A way to draw people in, get dirt on them while they relaxed, then compromise them later with scandal, with clandestine footage. He kept all those tapes and photos in a filing cabinet in his office. If you have those kind of secrets, you keep control of people.'

'No one wants them exposed. Everyone's respectable now,' I say.

'The thing about it all, the tragedy of what they did to Eddy . . .' her voice trails off. 'The stories Eddy wrote under their influence were used to smear his work, to destroy his reputation so that anything he did later was contaminated. Jean-Marc implied he was bent all the way through. It was a way of diverting the focus from what was really going on. He got him in the back, and the knife stayed. Eddy could never move beyond it.'

'And everyone just thought he was a drunk, a letch, a fool,' I say.

'Exactly. And so he set about to write this memoir as a way to purge himself of it all. He knew other journalists were involved, and that most of the stories could be linked to Jean-Marc – either written or edited by him, and he worked out that Jean-Marc was behind it all.'

'So this was why you worked for Jean-Marc? He had you too?'

'We all end up doing things we don't like,' she says with a shrug as if this was just a minor thing, like taking the bins out. 'We all end up compromised, doing the wrong thing, turning a blind eye. We're all just puppets.'

The room is quiet, the air stilled, almost bending towards us. 'So how did Jean-Marc pull your strings?' I ask.

She turns to me and then laughs hollowly. 'Look at you sitting there as if you've never done anything wrong. You of all people.'

She walks to the bookshelf, to the photo of Patrick and Nathan. 'I was so stupid,' she says clasping her face, and she looks so distraught that for a second it feels cruel to continue.

Then she sits, placing the photo flat on her knees.

'One day, not long after I'd started working for him, I accompanied Jean-Marc to a meeting,' she says, looking down at the photo, then at me, as if addressing an audience of me, Patrick and Nathan. 'I thought it was to discuss the charity's tax status, but once we arrived, the man told us that the company's accounts were under investigation. He stuck barcodes on all our documents and took them for evidence. Afterwards, Jean-Marc spoke to him, offered him a bribe to drop the case, and he accepted.'

She sighs deeply. The light has changed in the room, and her silhouette is small and drab against the opulence of the silk cushions like she's collapsed in on herself. Her eyeliner is smudged, making her eyes dark hollows against her pale face.

'Initially, I was horrified at the bribe, but then relieved when the man accepted it. The threat of an investigation scared me, even though I'd done nothing wrong.'

'It was a shock,' I say.

'Yes,' she says, looking at me gratefully. 'The moment was so surreal I just sat there, frozen. Afterwards, I felt tainted, guilty. I didn't stop him. I couldn't stop him.'

'But that didn't mean you had to go along with it,' I say, not really believing it myself. I knew how easy it was to be led along.

She shakes her head. 'I was frightened, confused. And fear does strange things – it takes you out of yourself, way out of your depth and you just do the easiest thing. Later, when we got back to the office, Jean-Marc twisted the story. He said the bribe was my idea, and congratulated me. He reassured me that it was a one-off thing, but it wasn't. There were more payments and he told me to keep signed records of all money sent and to keep it quiet, to keep it between us.'

She looks around as if we might be overheard. 'Not long after that, I received a salary increase and a huge bonus. He told me I was one of them now and that this would all be very much worth my while. It was like an initiation ritual, but it wasn't even real.'

'What wasn't real?'

'The man wasn't from the authorities. He was one of Jean-Marc's cronies. I only found this out later. It was a set-up to hook me in.'

'Hook you in to what?'

'The charities were being used to launder money, and they weren't charities at all. I found out later they were a front for other criminal activities.'

'And he told you all this?'

'I didn't find out until months later when it was too late. When I discovered the extent of it all, I told Jean-Marc I didn't want to be involved. He acted all innocent, asked me to explain what I'd discovered. Once I'd finished, he reminded me of the bribe, the paper trail of documents I'd signed, money transfers I'd authorised. He reminded me that I was a director of the companies that had made the payments, and that I was personally liable. Then he laughed and said, *If you look at the evidence, Elena, you'll see that you're the mastermind behind this.'*

'He'd set you up.'

She nodded. There was no evidence anywhere of his involvement in anything. The further up the chain you went, the ink dried up. Vanished. He made me believe that I'd done something illegal and that if I squealed, it would be me who carried the can.'

'So what did you do?'

'I did the only thing I could do.

'What was that?'

'Nothing.'

Forty-One

Champ de Mars

OUTSIDE, THE SUN IS DIRECTLY overhead and intrudes into the room like a spotlight. It fills the space where Elena stands with an intense light, showing the dust in the air, the streaks on the windows. She reaches up to the blind revealing dark patches beneath her arms.

'Did Patrick know any of this?' I ask.

Her grip falters on the cord and the blinds shudder.

'And the money Jean-Marc paid you?' I add quietly.

'The money allowed me to buy this apartment, a new car, Nathan's school fees. I told Patrick the money came from an inheritance,' she says eventually.

I need to keep her talking, so I keep reassuring her. 'You took on the burden of the lies and the fraud. You deserved to be paid for that.'

Flattery and reassurance. The best ways to get people's confidence and draw them in. Skills I learned from Sami on the streets all those years ago.

She looks at me like I've just thrown her a lifeline. 'By then, I was well and truly trapped, up to my neck in the illegality, complicit in the lies. I'd been checkmated and had no choice but to keep going, and from that point, I did other things – washing dirty money through his nightclubs and gambling ventures. Jean-Marc had me where he wanted and there was no turning back.'

She pulls at her hair as if trying to drag it off her scalp.

'Couldn't you go to the police?'

She shakes her head. 'Mari wanted to do that, at first. He'd hooked her in too. She confronted Jean-Marc, but he just laughed in her face. He said that if we brought any kind of action against him, he'd make us look like two disgruntled employees looking for a payout. He made it clear that worse would happen if we went to the police.'

'And you believed him?'

'Of course. He may seem harmless, stupid even, but that's just an act. He's dangerous, and he means what he says.'

I move to the bookshelf, drawn to a black and white picture of my parents and reach in, wiping the dusty glass with my sleeve. It's a holiday shot, the two of them in the front seats of a convertible car. Elena and Patrick are in the back, and standing by the car on my father's side are Paul and Céline Chambière. They're all wearing casual summer clothes and behind them is an old stone house in a pale field, the photo blurred and bleached with age and the light of that sunny day.

'Is this Jean-Marc?' I ask, pointing to a man standing on my mother's side of the car. Although I'd met him years ago, I didn't recognise the slim man with a full head of dark, shining hair.

'Yes,' she says. 'That was twenty years ago, maybe longer. We all used to go on holidays together to Jean-Marc's villa near Épernay. Your father usually found a way to get out of it, but he must have come that year.'

'Jean-Marc looks so different.'

'Corruption has made him ugly. Eventually, people get the faces they deserve. The poison surfaces at some point, like a boil.'

She talks for a while on this theme, telling me that Jean-Marc's bile has worked its way through his body to his lungs, and that he's ill in a hospital in Neuilly. I only half listen to her, looking at my father in the picture. His face is partly obscured by the glare of the car's windshield, and although he's handsome, his smile is anxious, hands gripping the wheel like he wants to escape.

I trace my jaw automatically, feeling for remnants of him out of habit. It's a reflex I can't shake even when I know there's no likeness and the impulse annoys me.

'He was good-looking once, like you,' Elena says, reading my thoughts.

'I don't resemble my father at all. I never have,' I say, wondering if she knows, but she looks away.

'And Céline and Paul. What did they know? How far were they involved?' I ask.

'Paul was always Jean-Marc's sidekick. He helped set Eddy up with Lara at the Matrix Club. Paul more or less ran the place, but he's managed to distance himself from it all. The place is just a seedy strip club now.' She raises her eyebrows and I can't tell whether she's embarrassed or disappointed.

'With S&M nights,' I add.

'I've had nothing to do with any of it for years,' she says. 'I know Jean-Marc still owns several places, but the clubs are run by others now.'

'And Paul?' I ask.

'He's the face of respectability these days, but he was never involved in Ligne Rouge.'

'So my father just used Paul and Céline for access to Jean-Marc?' I ask.

'Yes. Eddy was always suspicious of Jean-Marc, surprised at how powerful he'd become. He worked out that Jean-Marc was the ringleader all those years ago and from then on, Eddy was on a mission to bring him down. He started looking into Jean-Marc's current activities. The ownership of *La Globe* that gave Jean-Marc clout and the ear of politicians and business leaders, and the murky political loans which have smoothed the way for his real estate deals.'

'The Gateway to Paris.'

'Mari told you about that?' she asks, fear crossing her face. 'That was very foolish of her.'

'She gave me the information the same way she'd given it to Eddy – on a stick. But I was attacked and it was stolen.'

'Attacked?'

'I ended up in hospital. I lost the material, but I found the investment site online.'

She moves towards me, puts her hand on my shoulder. 'You must be careful, Alex. Mari has her own agenda. She was Eddy's last, most dangerous relationship. I don't know the status of the Gateway project, but I know Mari still works with Jean-Marc's investors.'

'Why did she tell Dad? Why endanger him like that?'

'She can't go to the police as she's in too deep, but she has a score to settle with Jean-Marc. He used her and she wants to punish him for that, and for dragging her into it too. When the legal system doesn't work, you use investigative journalists.'

'I tried to contact her again. I was worried after I'd been attacked. I thought they might have got her too.'

'Don't worry about her. She knows how to look after herself, that's why I was surprised by your text yesterday. After what happened to Eddy, she just disappeared. She felt responsible for his death but it didn't stop her continuing to take Jean-Marc's money. I haven't heard from her in years.'

Elena drifts off into her own thoughts. 'At first, I didn't know Eddy knew Mari, or what she had told him. I just thought it was odd that Eddy was seeing Jean-Marc socially. Eddy had always loathed him, but there they were having lunch, drinking together in the lead-up to Christmas, laughing and joking like old friends.'

Elena turns to me as if she's just remembered something. The light catches her off-guard, and her cheeks look sunken, dark lines etched into her face. 'The last time I saw them together was just before Christmas, in fact. Eddy and Jean-Marc came back to the office after lunch and I could see them from my desk. You know these stupid glass cubicles that they put in offices these days that are supposed to signal transparency and openness? You can't hear what's going on, but you can see it. They were shouting and then Eddy left abruptly.'

'He confronted Jean-Marc.'

'Yes. Eddy called me later that night, accusing me of being involved, of using the Ligne Rouge charities to stir up tension. Eddy said that Jean-Marc had set up gyms and sports centres in areas he wanted to develop. His thugs used them to create trouble in those areas, drive down prices, get the government onside to make it easier for him to buy up the land cheaply.'

She looks at me, her whole body transformed, like she's unfolded and the words are just coming out now.

'Eddy was right. It was a crude plan, but it worked. Jean-Marc sowed animosity between the police and local groups. *La Globe* ran stories on the lack of effective policing, accusing the authorities of losing control, terrifying everyone about the suburbs and no-go zones. Jean-Marc sent in his own security to maintain order, but that just made things worse because they provoked things further. What he was doing suited many people's agenda. Making the suburbs out to be dangerous meant they could increase policing, gain votes. He didn't have to do much apart from light the fuse. There were riots and demonstrations, and things just got worse.'

'And your stories about contamination at Aubervilliers.'

'At least they were true,' she says, looking at me defiantly, 'but yes, of course, the stories exaggerated the problem to reduce the value.' She shrugs, as if it was all an obvious, reasonable thing to do.

'And the car bomb we saw that time that you and Patrick were at our place. That was all fake?'

She looks away. 'Yes.'

'What about the Les Halles attack?'

She raises her hands in a protective gesture. 'I have no idea about that. After Eddy died, I resigned from the charities and distanced myself from Jean-Marc. Everything went quiet on the scheme for several years and I hoped it had all just gone away.'

'But all the news reports say the gunmen were from the site at Aubervilliers.'

She nods. 'I don't know if Les Halles was a real attack or not. Whatever it was, Jean-Marc will have used it to advance his agenda. I know he wants that site cleared.'

'So that's the plan, is it – to get control of the forts around Paris and develop the land?' I ask.

'Eventually. At the moment, the sites at Issy and Aubervilliers just look like normal developments. The first stage is to acquire the forts, enhance security, and then build high-tech apartment complexes on each site. The final stage is to link them together into a security ring that will surround the city.'

'Ligne Rouge. A red line around Paris. A luxurious borderland separating rich from poor. The whole thing is madness,' I say.

'Jean-Marc really believes in it. He thinks it's high time to protect the super-rich, insulate them from the rest of us, and by God, he wants to be one of them.'

'It's not as if they're on the same planet as us now, anyway.'

'No, they're not, but they're keen to make their mark on this one, and to tell the rest of us how to live.'

'So how is he keeping all this quiet?' I ask.

'Jean-Marc is litigious; he'll sue anyone who criticises him.'

'So people know?'

'A few people – journalists – have tried to find out what's going on, but they've been threatened with legal action and worse. The Ministry of Defence owns the forts and their dealings are classified, so the sales and leases to Ligne Rouge and its affiliates are secret for now. And the Ligne Rouge companies are held in a complicated network of offshore companies and trusts, so Jean-Marc's stake is doubly hidden.'

'And the money?'

'The investors are the same people Jean-Marc worked with all those years ago. Oligarchs, criminals, money men keen to invest and hide their dirty money. Your mother's husband is involved too.'

'Olivier?'

'Yes, that's the reason they left Paris. Olivier had a falling-out with Jean-Marc and the other investors. He became a threat to their project and these are powerful people. They have so much cash that they've run out of places to keep it, and they've invested billions into the project. There are similar schemes planned for other major cities – Sydney, Shanghai, Delhi. There's a rumour there's even one to be built from scratch in the American desert.'

She paces the room, muttering again, like she's reprimanding herself, twisting her hands. Then she turns to me. 'I didn't know the full extent of the plan, but the future cities sounded like Utopia. They'd have gardens, zoos, and the canals of the Seine would be diverted into waterfalls and lakes. There'd be beaches and swimming pools in the summer. The developments would have sustainable energy production and organic food grown on-site.'

'If Jean-Marc had gone to such lengths to hide everything then it was dangerous Eddy being so open with him,' I say.

'Of course. Eddy should have kept it to himself until he was ready to blow the lid and publish the story. But he hated Jean-Marc and couldn't resist letting him know he had the power to destroy him, his grand project, and to drag his past out into the light. If the scheme had become public, investors would have panicked, the money would have vapourised. If it all came out about Vestnik, then the project would have collapsed, along with Jean-Marc's reputation. I think it was the damage to his reputation that concerned Jean-Marc the most.'

She's agitated now and keeps getting up only to sit down again. There's a bottle of water on the side, and I pour her a glass.

'I warned Eddy to keep it quiet, but he ignored me,' she says.

'When did you warn him?'

She takes the glass, her eyes unreadable. 'The week before Christmas. At dinner. You were there too.'

'So you knew they were going to harm him?'

She grabs my arm. Her hand is hot and clammy. 'Of course I didn't! I warned him they were dangerous, that he shouldn't be so open about what he'd discovered. But you and Patrick were there, and then you had that argument and Eddy was drunk.' She looks pained and her voice catches. 'I was in an impossible situation. I didn't know the lengths they'd go to keep it secret. Jean-Marc was working with dangerous people who had millions invested and a lot to lose, but I had never met them. To me, they were just company names on documents.' She stops herself and then says as almost an afterthought. 'Though I should have known. Eddy had been attacked.'

'Attacked?'

'He tried to pass it off as a bicycle accident that night, you remember. I just froze. I couldn't say anything with you and Patrick there.'

'And on Christmas Eve? When Sami and I were there? The person that came later was sent by Jean-Marc?'

'Eddy told me he'd arranged to meet a whistleblower. He said it was someone from the Ministry of Defence. God knows why Eddy agreed to see them on Christmas Eve, let alone invited them into his home.'

'You must have known he was in danger. You knew what the stakes were. You knew that Eddy had already been attacked!'

'I didn't know this person was sent by Jean-Marc. Oh, God.' She puts her head in her hands and collapses on the sofa.

'And then Sami and I set the scene up so well, leaving Eddy helpless and sprawled in the doorway so that all his killer had to do was finish him off,' I say, pacing the room. 'And that's why Jean-Marc was so helpful in finding me a lawyer. Dintrans was working for Jean-Marc, too, making sure I implicated Sami, that we both went down and left no loose ends.'

She looks up at me, nodding through her tears, and I'm overcome with rage. 'Why didn't you say something when we were charged? I spent seven years in jail being treated like an animal for something I didn't do! How can you live with yourself?'

'Please, Alex, understand – I didn't know all this back then. I really thought you and Sami *had* killed Eddy. You always hated him so much. I only found all this out later, much later.'

'When?'

'These last years. As I said, I had distanced myself from it all, but last year development started on the Aubervilliers site, and then earlier this year, Patrick started looking into Eddy's death. He became obsessed with it and found out about the Gateway to Paris project and tried to publish something about it.'

'Didn't you warn him? You knew how dangerous it was.'

'He had been threatened but he said he wouldn't be intimidated. I told him enough so he'd see I was implicated, and that if it all came out, I'd be found guilty. I told him to keep it quiet and to be careful. I didn't tell him everything because I knew I'd lose him ...'

Her voice trails off, and I realise she knew she'd lost him then already. The reason Patrick hadn't told Elena he was looking through my father's files or that he'd visited me in jail was because he suspected her.

'There were so many lies between us,' she says, crying softly. 'Then, one weekend, Patrick pretended to go away. He said he was going to eastern Europe on a job, but I knew he was lying. I thought he was having an affair.' She wipes her cheeks and laughs bitterly. 'In fact, I hoped he was. I can't bear the thought that he died thinking I was involved in Eddy's death.'

She seems so pathetic that it's hard to maintain my anger. She's consumed by remorse and has been for years. The frailty of her body shows that. Jean-Marc had tricked her, and no matter what she did, she'd never be able to fix it. She was trapped forever with her own brand of guilt. She'd lost herself within it and I know how that feels.

'And they're after me too,' I say. 'These people have been following me, harassing me ever since I got out of prison.'

'They know you're following Eddy's trail, that you have something on Jean-Marc, the Vestnik material. I tried to warn you that day you visited.'

It occurs to me that I need to leave town and go somewhere no one knows me for a while. A plan is forming in my mind, and it's dangerous to stay. They've attacked me once, and they'll come for me again.

'I promise I won't contact Nathan. But I need you to do one last thing,' I say.

She shakes her head. 'I don't want any more involvement in this.'

'You can't be any more involved than you already are, and you can't escape this anymore. I'm going public with all this, I'm going to show Jean-Marc who the real messenger is, so prepare yourself.'

I tell her I need her help to get Sami released, and that she needs to speak to his lawyer, to give a witness statement.

Afterwards she looks spent, wrung out, but there's a lightness to her now that wasn't there before.

Before I leave, I go back over to the photo of my parents and Jean-Marc. I bend in and take a picture of it with my phone, and then suddenly it hits me and I have to lean against the

413

bookshelf as shock crashes over me, and I stand there stunned by what I've learned, and by what's staring straight at me.

A few minutes later the intercom buzzes and Elena looks at her watch, flustered.

'It's Nathan,' she says. 'I need to leave.

'It's Father's Day,' she adds awkwardly. 'We're going to Patrick's favourite restaurant.'

I follow her from the apartment to the landing, numbed by what I've discovered about my father and Jean-Marc, confused by the sudden appearance of Nathan.

She opens the heavy iron door, steps into the lift and stands facing me.

'Wait here a few minutes, he mustn't see us together. Not yet,' she says. Then, just before the lift doors close, she reaches out and touches my arm. 'It's true, you don't resemble him, but you're more like him than you know.'

Left alone on the landing as the lift descends, the sympathy I felt for her amid all the confusion and the echo of her parting words sours into an overwhelming sense of rage. I want to destroy her life like she's destroyed mine. How dare she tell me I'm like Eddy on *Father's Day* of all days, and then just go downstairs to meet her own son and carry on with her life, unburdened now by her confession.

Anger surges in me like a fever, and I race downstairs. The lift's empty, and there's no one in the lobby, but they can't be far. I push the door to the street and see them a little way ahead, crossing the road. They're talking, Nathan looking at her with the sunlight on his face. He's well built, his hair short.

He's not the beggar I saw this morning at all, and I shrink back, confused.

I watch Elena's small frame as they pass onto the pavement, into the shade. Is the rage I feel now because I see in her something of myself? My deals with Tomas, hers for Jean-Marc, both of us checkmated by the same fear, the same cowardice. And then me, blaming Sami for my father's murder. We both made one false step and then just carried on, putting one foot in front of the other because it was so much easier to do than anything else. We were absorbed in something larger, something we couldn't stop, our guilt like grit, rubbing uncomfortably for a while, but eventually becoming such a part of us that we didn't notice it anymore.

I look at them one last time – Nathan with his arm over her shoulder, and Elena looking up at him, smiling at something he's said. I release my hand from the door. What would be the point of destroying her now? What would that do? And besides, I have an urgent visit to make, an overdue score to settle. I let the door close behind me and walk in the opposite direction towards that hospital in Neuilly.

Forty-Two

Aubervilliers, 18 June

MY ROOM HOLDS THE AFTERNOON heat, and outside it's all sky – vast and blue with threads of pink cloud where the sun burns fat and gold on the horizon. Pollution swells at ground level like the city's last exhalation. The haze softens and blurs in a grey mirage that shifts and glimmers in the light.

Twelve storeys below on the Péri, an ambulance shrieks above the roar of diesel engines as they grind through the gears. To the south, at the edge of the fort, the Ligne Rouge building sites sit a mile apart, each one surrounded by a scar of cleared ground. The half-finished hulls of apartment blocks lie open and exposed, like the ribcage of some giant beast. Scores of cranes crowd in, their jibs like beaks, pecking and guarding the carcase.

The sun drops, bulging on the skyline, drenching everything in orange light, and it's like the city is on fire around me. The wind picks up, and the windows shudder as I turn from the view.

*

A backpack's best when you're on the run, something that won't slow you down. I've kept it light for the trip south to a place I can wait until the story's published without fear of what they'll do. A change of clothes, a sleeping bag and waterproofs with money sewn into the lining.

I've stacked my father's stuff against the wall for my aunt to collect once I'm gone. She'll keep it safe until things die down, when I'll return to make sure Sami's released.

I've been back to his lawyer, expanded my statement and handed over my father's wallet, too. I had it with me on Christmas Day at my aunt's all those years ago, and I hid it at the back of a cupboard. It was still there after all this time, underneath a floorboard, wrapped tight in a plastic bag. If Sami's right then it's stained with his blood, not my father's, and so now it's evidence that will help him.

There are pictures of my father taped along the wall. Photos at work, with friends, with me, with my aunt. I peel them off one by one and stack them on the desk. The paper's crisp and warped, colours faded by the sun.

I look at his face in the photos, remembering the times I scanned it for my likeness, and the relief I felt at seeing none. But even then, beneath the relief, there was always something murky and unexplained: why didn't I resemble him?

It was a question I never asked, perhaps because I always knew. Maybe I guessed long ago, tapping into some intuition at a deeper level, like those frequencies of sound only dogs can hear. Or perhaps I just want to believe I wasn't as easily fooled as him.

And what about him – how far *was* he fooled? He knew I wasn't his son, but did he know whose son I was? Did he look at my face the way I did his, repulsed by my bushy brows and dimpled cheeks, and repulsed for a reason? Or was that the kind of thing that only came to him in nightmares?

I think of our fights, of the times I said I hated him. He must have wanted to tell me then. What a punchline it would have been – so how did he resist? But he never let on. Not once in any of his booze-fuelled rants did he succumb to the urge to hurt me like that. I was a complicated puzzle he hadn't chosen and I feel the shame of it now. How unworthy I was of his restraint.

I look at that photo of us together – his hand on my shoulder, my pixelated face leaning into his on that sunny afternoon a lifetime ago. We look like friends sharing a joke, the way it should be. It was the newspapers' favourite because we seemed so ordinary, so out of place beside the twisted story of the son who killed his father. *If it happened to him, it could happen to you,* the picture said.

I wonder if they'll use it now to sell the papers once again.

I replace the picture and step back from the window. They say photos are memories and it's true – they keep hold of a lot, but they hide secrets too. And some photos aren't memories at all. They're just evidence of lies you've been told.

The photo I saw at Elena's this morning revealed a lie, too. She'd arranged her life across the ledges of her sitting room, the colours gradually bleeding into recent photos, so you could almost date them by the intensity of the light. Sepia pictures of her and Patrick on their wedding day, baby shots of Nathan and bright family portraits.

Lurking in amongst it all was that photograph of my parents. A once-sunny morning, now a grainy image in a dusty frame, hidden in the shadows of her shelves. I kept getting drawn back to it until finally something shifted and fell into place.

My parents are in a convertible car with the roof and windows down. The car is stationary, but my father's at the wheel, staring straight ahead. My mother is young, while the others are quite a bit older. She's in the passenger seat, smiling and leaning against the door, her arm resting on the ledge. Her hair is loose, flowing over her face like she's just turned to the man standing at her side who's bent over the car, whispering in her ear. He has his hand on hers, out of sight of my father, and something passes between them that only lovers share.

I was studying the photo at Elena's this morning as she spoke about my father and Jean-Marc. In the picture, my father looks concerned, like he's scanning the road for danger. Paul and Céline are standing next to the car, and Elena and Patrick are in the back. Elena can see the lovers holding hands and is close enough to catch what they're saying.

When I saw them together like that – my mother and Jean-Marc sharing a moment caught forever, a scene once private now exposed, I knew he was the final piece of the puzzle I'd been trying to solve.

He was good-looking once, like you, Elena had said.

I looked at my father gripping the wheel, his brow furrowed, almost scowling.

'I don't resemble my father at all. I never have,' I said, too quickly. I glanced over, but she'd already looked away.

When I spoke, I meant Eddy, of course, and it didn't occur to me until later, when I went back to the photo as I was leaving,

419

that she'd meant Jean-Marc. The realisation crept in slowly, but once inside, it grew, cascading around me like fear.

A crawling sensation filled my head as I leaned in and looked closer. When I met Jean-Marc at the Chambières', I didn't notice our resemblance, but in the photo, he still has the features that age buries or strips away – all those traces I'd looked for in Eddy but never found. Jean-Marc's thick, bushy hair that had ebbed to nothing but a monobrow and a moustache by the time we met, sixteen years later. The dimples, too, that would recede into the fat around his face. Seeing him standing there smiling, his hand on my mother's, was like scraping back sand to reveal my own face. Excavating the past to find the future. Those eyes, that arrogant nose. I stared at the picture for a long time – at my mother and Jean-Marc, wondering if I'd been conceived at that point, or whether that was all to come. I leaned against the bookshelf, stunned by the irony that the only person who understood their secret look was me – the very person they'd kept it from all these years.

But perhaps I wasn't the only one.

'You knew it was him, didn't you?' I said, eventually.

She sighed. 'I was never sure.'

'Not sure, or just didn't ask?'

'Of course, I didn't ask.'

'And Eddy?'

The ceiling creaked overhead like an eavesdropper shifting position and she reached for the photo. 'Eddy knew about them, of course. As for whether he knew you were Jean-Marc's son, I'm not sure. The timing would have been a dead giveaway, but he never let on.' She glanced out of the window. 'I think Eddy knew the truth but chose to ignore it.'

I think back to that night at the Chambières'. I wasn't supposed to be there that weekend. We'd sat next to each other at dinner, and Jean-Marc had asked me about school and girlfriends, like the parody of a real father. How dare he play that role if he knew I was his son.

Eddy, on the other hand, was anxious. At the time, I thought he was worried I'd embarrass him, but now I see it was something much darker.

'If the timing was right, then Jean-Marc must have known too.'

She raised her eyebrows. 'Jean-Marc's able to deny the undeniable. If he doesn't like something, he'll bulldoze through it, especially when he's riding high like he was back then. It's why he's been so successful. He can ignore the truth even if it's staring him in the face.'

'Like I was that night.'

'I watched him then. He knew who you were.'

'But how could he have ignored it all these years? If you know, others must,' I said.

'It's possible. As for Jean-Marc, he's his own reality. His needs and desires are all that matters. The rest is fiction, something that happens as a backdrop to the main event, which is himself.'

I looked again at the photograph, at Eddy's worried face as he grips the wheel, skidding along the edge of an uncertain future in which his son would grow to look less like him and more like his boss, his enemy, his murderer.

I reached the bus stop at Neuilly late this afternoon, and ran across the bridge, worried that visiting hours had ended. It was warm, and the drone from the Péri merged with the buzz of insects that hung over the water like mist. I paused outside the hospital to straighten my shirt before passing through the entrance security.

The waiting room was more like a gentlemen's club than a hospital, with its soft light, panelled walls and newspapers on long wooden hangers. I signed the register as 'Alex Garnier', surprised at the steadiness of my lying hand, while the receptionist watched over me, and then gave me a pass and directions to his ward. When I saw the date on the pass it didn't register at first but my legs felt weak as I walked down the corridor on this day that now held the weight of two dates – my birthday, as well as Father's Day. I walked slowly, wondering whether this was a blessing or a double warning. I tried to compose my face for the CCTV, but my soles squeaked on the vinyl floor like the opening yelps of a siren.

The nurse on his ward looked confused when I said my name. 'I've not seen you here before,' she said, leafing through his notes.

I told her I lived out of Paris and had made a special trip for Father's Day, then I asked whether his lung infection had improved. Finally, she smiled and closed his folder. 'His temperature's eased with the antibiotics, but he's having trouble breathing.'

'His asthma. The ichthyosis.'

'It makes things difficult.'

'I inherited that from him,' I said, showing her the scaly patches on my forearms.

At the door to his room, she put her hand on my shoulder. 'It's getting late. You shouldn't stay long.'

'Don't worry. I'll be quick.'

She went in first, checked the monitors and gadgets at his bedside, and then left me there alone. For a while, I stood at the door, taking stock of the sterile room, the background hum of machines and the bedclothes tight as bandages around his body. I closed the door and stepped forward softly.

They'd shaved his moustache and taped an oxygen tube under his nose. Grey stubble shone in the perspiration above his lip, and his face and neck, though thick and fleshy, were damp and very pale. It was as though a thin, whitish film covered his skin, and it glowed with a sickly tinge under the bright fluorescent lights. His body was still, the only movement coming from his mouth and chest, and he didn't so much breathe as fight for it. Each inhalation was slow and grasping, like he was extracting something from the air, his chest trembling on the rise, and then collapsing with a shudder.

I stood there for a while, making out the landscape that was my real father.

When his eyes opened, they were watery blue like mine but glazed and unfocused, and they strained with the effort to see me. Dried spittle had collected in the side of his mouth, and although he opened his mouth to speak, his voice was just a whisper.

His right arm moved under the sheet, and when his hand appeared, I saw the skin on his palm was cracked and scaly like mine. I had an absurd thought that maybe he was reaching for my hand, but in fact, he was fumbling for his glasses, so I took them from the nightstand and placed them on his face, folding them carefully over his ears.

When he recognised me, he tried to slide his body up and away from me. He looked so helpless that I almost felt sorry for him, but seeing his fear spurred me on, as if it were an endorsement of my plan.

His hand reached for the emergency cord, but I got there first. The tendons in his neck strained as he tried to raise his head from the pillow, but I pushed him down. His forehead was hot, and the terror that caught in his throat made him cough so hard I thought he'd do the job himself.

I leaned over with a cup of water from his bedside. His mouth gaped for the drink, and once he'd taken a few gobbling sips, he strained against me.

'What do you want?' he said hoarsely.

'You killed Eddy,' I said, my voice deep and hollow, unlike my own.

His words were in short supply, but I didn't need to hear his response. I could see the answer in his eyes, which rolled like those of a captured animal.

'You destroyed him, and then had him killed when he found you out. And you let me take the blame.'

'You did that yourself,' he rasped.

'And had your thugs harass me. Nick and the others.'

'Nick's making sure you don't make Eddy's mistakes. You should be grateful. They were never meant to harm you,' he said, his eyes closing against the weight of the lids. He breathed deeply, his body straining with the effort. 'Don't be stupid, Alex. None of this concerns you.'

'Of course it concerns me! I spent seven years inside for something I didn't do. And Eddy. He was an old friend and you stabbed him in the back,' I said, our faces almost touching.

He stared up at me, and I felt a strange contraction in his body, as though he knew the game was up. His lips twitched as he struggled with his breath.

'I never stabbed him in the back,' he said, as his eyes blazed. 'I always got him in the front.'

When I pressed the pillow over his face, his body stiffened. His legs kicked out, so I climbed onto the bed and straddled him, my knees pinning his arms to the mattress, the tight bedclothes doing the rest. It's not an easy thing to smother someone, but adrenaline lends a fierce kind of power. I was overcome with an unstoppable drive as he thrashed against me, vigorous for an old man. *There's some strength in the old bastard yet*, I thought with a flicker of satisfaction at the idea that perhaps I'd inherit that too.

As he struggled, I felt my power pitted against his, mine growing as his waned, each of his convulsions weaker than the last. I was inflamed with rage, stronger than anything I'd felt before, more powerful at that moment than my own urge to live. As I pressed down, I sensed that the fight was almost over, and it was in that moment of racing to meet death head-on, of feeling his life in my hands, on my terms, that suddenly, my anger faded and something else, something stronger, surged through me, creeping up my back like fire.

It wasn't vindication or the sweet purity of revenge.

It was the edge of a huge emptiness. As if I was flying low over a vast and barren landscape wracked by misery and despair. I removed the pillow from his face, and stood at the end of his bed, stunned by what I'd nearly done, still seething with the adrenaline that almost propelled me to commit the crime for which I'd been falsely convicted. I backed away. How easy it would have been to keep going.

I stood there, my heart thudding and slowly, I felt the desolation and disgust recede, and in its place crept a deep sadness and longing for Eddy.

Jean-Marc meant nothing to me and Eddy meant everything, and I felt the loss of him then as if a blade had just severed him from me, a loss as real and aching as the shame that went with it.

I could never get Eddy or those wasted years back, but killing Jean-Marc wouldn't get them back either. It would just be assuming the legacy of devastation Jean-Marc intended. There'd be nothing gained from destroying him. It was no more than he'd done himself.

Jean-Marc's mouth was flaccid, and his tubes hung loose like a dismantled toy. He'd fainted, but he was still breathing, calmer than before, but the breath was there.

Peering into the old man's collapsed face, I saw the things he'd taken from me – my father, my youth, my sense of myself. And in his face, I saw traces of the things he'd taken from others too – their money, their freedom and the reputations of people like Elena whom he'd drawn into his dark world.

Elena couldn't stop him, and neither could Eddy or Patrick. You can't stop people like Jean-Marc, but you can't be swept along with them either, I told myself as I replaced his tubes, readjusted his head on the pillow and smoothed away the signs of struggle.

I took the TV remote and switched it to his own news channel. His demise would be the first thing he saw when he woke up.

'You didn't win this time,' I said. 'The story's out. It'll be on the news tonight.'

My shoes squeaked as I walked back down the long corridor. Although I hadn't killed him, the will had been there, and I thought something around me would acknowledge that. The hairs on my neck stood up as if waiting for a shriek from behind me: *That's him! Stop!*

But the nurses just smiled as I passed, then went back to their papers.

I walked through the hospital reception, thinking an alarm would finally sound, that the wind would hammer at the glass, shatter the doors and pin me to the ground until the police came.

But everything was the way it had been and outside, a slight breeze rippled through the trees, making their branches sway and nod in silent approval, if anything.

I slip the photo of Eddy and me into the lining of my backpack as orange light slides across the windows of the tower block opposite. The wind rattles the glass against the frame, gently now, a farewell.

And down on the Péri everything's calm, the traffic quiet as I close the door to my flat behind me.

All this time I've been trying to piece the lies together, matching edges to borders, but time moves on, making lies into memories, then fixing the glass and tightening the frame until the picture looks real. Jean-Marc may have been Vestnik, the messenger of lies, but I would deliver the truth of what he had done.

I step out of the lift and the warm night air surrounds me as I walk from the place that's held my freedom hostage all these months. The past still stalks me, but I can see a way ahead. I know who I am, and I'll try to start again. The choices I make are mine now.

I can finally say after all these years that I didn't kill my father. It feels good, and this time, I might just get away with it.

BREAKING NEWS

Aux Barricades!

La Globe owner charged with murders of two journalists in massive property development scandal

LISA DALLET

Jean-Marc Garnier, owner of *La Globe*, was arrested today in connection with the deaths of two journalists, police have confirmed.

Edouard Giraud, a former journalist at *La Globe*, was stabbed to death in his apartment on Christmas Eve, seven and a half years ago. His son, Alex Giraud, and Sami Lantou were convicted of his murder. The body of Patrick Landis, another former *La Globe* journalist, was found in Ivry canal on 25 March this year. Police have launched an investigation into the deaths of the two men.

MediaNOW! has discovered that at the time of their deaths, both Giraud and Landis had been investigating a property development deal linked to companies associated with Garnier, who is currently in hospital under police guard.

The scheme involved the development of a ring of sixteen high-luxury apartment complexes around Paris which, when completed, would fully encircle the city.

Papers exclusively revealed to *MediaNOW!* show that Garnier is a director of the scheme's developers, Ligne Rouge, a company incorporated in the Seychelles. Ligne Rouge, owned by a trust registered in Nevis, has links to the $12 billion 'Future City' development in Dubai. A fund administered out of Guernsey is believed to have raised $3 billion in investment for the project.

Today the suburbs of Paris are home to diverse, often first- or second-generation immigrant communities. Garnier has long depicted the suburbs as dangerous breeding grounds for extremism, claiming in headline editorials that 'We Are On The Verge of Civil War', and that there are 'Barbarians At The Gate'. It is alleged that Garnier has used his position as owner of *La Globe* to build support for the project.

Applications have been filed for the immediate release of Lantou, and to overturn the convictions of Giraud and Lantou.

Neither Garnier nor his representatives were available for comment.

Further updates to follow . . .

Author's Note

In the US alone there are on average 242 parricides a year. That's about five instances a week of a child killing a father or mother.[1] This seems a lot, and once I became aware of these numbers, I started noticing parricides in the news and elsewhere. A couple of acquaintances had stories about a friend of a friend who had killed a parent, and there was a case at my sons' school where a boy killed his father in a dispute over his allowance. In the majority of cases, the perpetrators are white middle-class males without a history of violence. Often a parricide happens because the youth fears for their life or is desperate to end a cycle of abuse, but there are also cases where a child kills in cold blood.

It was these latter type of cases that interested me and I started thinking about the child-parent relationship in general – how volatile it can be, and how often a child goes through adolescence

---

[1] This statistic comes from a 2007 analysis of US parricide cases over the period 1976-1999. Heide, Kathleen M. and Petee, Thomas A., *Parricide An Empirical Analysis of 24 Years of U.S. Data*. Journal of Interpersonal Violence, December 2007. In countries where access to firearms is more difficult there are many less cases.

at the same time that one or both of their parents are experiencing a mid-life crisis. Often it is the child's unreasonable behaviour that is highlighted while the parents' conduct goes unremarked. It was this collision of tensions I wanted to explore in setting Alex up as the falsely accused murderer of Eddy.

I also wanted to explore the tension that comes with living in a city, particularly one like Paris which often feels like it's about to erupt into a clash between the older, vested interests of the central zone, and the newer immigrant communities in the suburbs. I started writing this novel just after the Paris terrorist attacks of 2015. Five days after the attacks, police fired nearly 5,000 rounds during an hour-long siege in the suburbs at Saint-Denis where some of the perpetrators were hiding. I was living in Paris at the time and overnight, the city was transformed into a battleground with riot police on every corner and many places suddenly inaccessible without ID and security checks. The boulevard Périphérique was already a gridlocked motorway that separated central Paris from the suburbs, but after the attacks it was like a barricade.

This state of tension is familiar to Paris as it is a city built on defences. From the city wall that once enclosed the central island of the Île de Cité in Roman times, to the Thiers wall and the ring of forts that were built around Paris in the nineteenth century.

After the Paris attacks, I imagined how those forts might be used once again, not necessarily for defence, but for containment – to enclose and safeguard the vested interests and heritage of the central zone. The rich already live separate lives to the rest of us metaphorically speaking, and they increasingly live physically separated as well. The pandemic has exacerbated this, and it's not hard to imagine a scenario where permanent physical separation of the super-rich within their own city-states develops not just on the basis of tax and affordability (as is the case, for example, in Monaco), but also for reasons of public health and 'security'. Schemes are already underway to 'future-proof' cities and Paris has always had a special appeal for the rich.

Part of the inspiration for Eddy and the other journalists in *The Messenger* comes from Cold War stories of espionage. The Mitrokhin Archive, a cache of top-level KGB documents smuggled out of Russia in 1992 by Vasili Mitrokhin,[2] provides details of the Soviet Union's secret intelligence operations around the world, including post-World War II infiltration of the West, and French *active measures* during the Cold War. According to the Mitrokhin Archive, a number of French journalists were Russian 'agents of influence', and several publications were set up in France to disseminate pro-Russian propaganda and misinformation.

Material in the Mitrokhin Archive suggests that the French newspaper *Le Monde* was codenamed Vestnik (which means 'Messenger' in Russian) by the KGB[3] and that during the 1970s and early 1980s, the KGB claimed to have influenced *Le Monde* articles and used it to disseminate misinformation and advance

---

[2] The official historian of MI5, Christopher Andrew, together with Vasili Mitrokhin, a KGB archivist, compiled two volumes based on material in the Mitrokhin Archive: *The Sword and The Shield: The Mitrokhin Archive and the Secret History of the KGB* (New York: Basic Books 1999) and *The World Was Going Our Way: The KGB and the Battle for the Third World* (New York: Basic Books 2005).

[3] Andrew, C. and Mitrokhin, V. *The Sword and The Shield: The Mitrokhin Archive and the Secret History of the KGB*, p.469

smear campaigns. Mitrokhin's notes also identify six agents and two confidential contacts within France's main news agency, *Agence France-Presse.*[4]

The romance between Eddy and Lara in *The Messenger* is inspired by a series of successful honey trap operations staged by KGB agents against various Italian diplomats working in the Italian embassy in Moscow during the 1950s-70s.[5]

The swingers' scene of the fictional Matrix Club in *The Messenger* is inspired by the story of Karl and Hana Koecher, Czech agents who worked for the KGB and also for the Czech intelligence agency. The Koechers were active in the US in the 1970s and early 1980s, and Karl Koecher is thought to be the only foreign agent to have infiltrated the CIA. The Koechers were said to be active in the sex club scene in New York and Washington in the 1970s where they liaised with personnel from the CIA, Pentagon and other parts of the US government.[6]

---

[4] Andrew, C. and Mitrokhin, V. Ibid, p.470

[5] Andrew, C. and Mitrokhin, V. Ibid, p.477-9

[6] Andrew, C. and Mitrokhin, V. Ibid, p.199-202, and also Kessler, Ronald, *Spy vs. Spy* (New York: Scribner's, 1988)

Acknowledgements

Thank you to Peter Straus and Lena Mistry at Rogers Coleridge and White.

To my brilliant editor, Kelly Smith at Bonnier Books UK.

To my writing group friends, Emily Ford, Elizabeth Macneal, Sophie Kirkwood, Campaspe Lloyd-Jacob, Tom Watson, Richard O'Halloran, Naomi Ishiguro and Gemma Reeves.

To my first readers, James Scudamore, Karen Norman, Kelleigh Greenberg-Jephcott and Sarah Newell.

To Patrick Markey for early inspiration.

To James Brabazon, Elliot F. Sweeney and Preeti Jha for reading the whole thing.

To Giles Foden, Philip Langeskov and Andrew Cowan at UEA.

To the lovely people at the Bridport Prize and the Lucy Cavendish College Fiction Prize and the judges Kamila Shamsie and Sophie Hannah.

To Anna South and Victoria Millar for editing advice.

To my friends Danielle Rowe, Anna Funder, Kate McGeever, Joan Moynihan, Nick Campailla, Douglas French and Margot Nightingale.

To Sally Murray.

To my parents who are not in this at all.

To Louis and Dylan who helped enormously.

And last and most to Tom for love and support at each of the many turns along the way.

Keep reading for an exclusive early preview of
Megan Davis's next thriller

BAY OF THIEVES

One

THE MONEY, WHEN IT COMES, arrives in the night, slipping in quietly like a welcome guest. It's a guest who needs no greeting, no towel or change of sheets. For it's been here before, this guest of yours; it owns the key to your door. You remember its smile, its sparkling wit, how it leaves the desire for more.

Vanessa's phone rang just as she was closing down her computer for the evening. It was her boss, Rob, calling from London.

'There's a big tranche coming in tonight,' Rob said. 'I need you to make sure it's dealt with.'

Vanessa took her phone from her ear to check the time. She'd been at her desk since seven that morning and was already late for drinks with her friend, Kate.

'It's Friday evening, Rob. I was about to leave. Why are you only telling me now?' Vanessa said. Kate was a lawyer too so she'd understand, but still.

'Napier's been here with me all day, following me around like a bloody shadow,' Rob hissed. 'I've barely had a moment free.'

Tension gripped the back of Vanessa's neck. Napier was the firm's managing partner.

'What was that about?' she asked.

'Year-end billings.'

'Are you sure?'

'Pretty sure.'

Vanessa edged back in her chair and looked out of the window over the marina in the direction of the bars that flanked the port of Monaco. 'How much is it?'

'Seventeen million. But there's been a mix-up with the money and Amir used their Cyprus account.'

'Why Cyprus?'

'Some of it came through the casinos.'

'OK,' Vanessa said, tapping the keyboard on her laptop to open the spreadsheet for their client, Amir. 'Which company is he using?'

'Kasan Tech. But the thing is – the funds need to be here in London for completion on Monday,' Rob said.

'Monday? Who on earth completes on a Monday?'

Rob's voice dipped several degrees and he spoke through gritted teeth. 'It's a property deal. And it's only available if we complete on Monday.'

'He can't send that amount to you from Cyprus by then. He'll have to do it in several tranches at least.'

'That's right, he can't do it direct. So you'll have to run it through the firm's Monaco account tonight. Amir's already cleared it with his bank. It's on its way.'

Vanessa stared at her phone as if it were malfunctioning. 'The trust account? You know I can't do that.'

'It'll be in the firm's account tonight and then you can send it to me.'

'Not with with Napier breathing down your neck. No, Rob, we can't do that.'

'We did it last month.'

'We were desperate. We had no choice—'

'We're desperate now—'

'It's way above the reporting amount—'

'You can override it.'

'We shouldn't even be having this call. You know the protocol.'

Vanessa glanced around the room, her eyes coming to rest on the almost-empty bottle. It was 7 p.m. and she'd only had one drink so far, or at least that's what she told herself. Normally one gin wouldn't have made any difference. It would have slipped down easily, hardly touching the sides and would have made her sharper if anything. But tonight there was something off. The light in the room seemed hazy somehow, and the shadows cast by the evening sun seemed to tilt unnaturally towards her.

Rob sighed impatiently. 'It's the only way. Get the transfer cleared tonight.'

Despite her unease, Vanessa was thinking fast. It was only her voice that gave her away. It was a little shaky, as if it were having trouble keeping up with her thoughts. 'Stephen's on night duty. He'll check everything before he finishes. You know what he's like.'

'It won't go through till late. You can pre-authorise it now before he starts.'

'Come on, Rob, I can't—'

'And another thing. You need to instruct James out in Road Town to transfer Amir's share in Kasan Tech to Elanka's mother.'

'Elanka's *mother*?'

'For fuck's sake, Vanessa!' Rob barked down the line. 'Do I have to spoon-feed you every step of the way. Just get it done!'

The gin fizzed in her head as Vanessa texted Kate to say she'd be late. Then she reached for the bottle and poured herself another. Vanessa drank to calm her nerves and to relieve the guilt. Sometimes she couldn't tell them apart, but tonight it was definitely her nerves that needed soothing.

Vanessa brought the glass to her lips, glancing out over the bay. Yachts flanked the port, three or four stories high, their carefully oiled teak decks taking up so much space in the harbour that there seemed barely enough room for the water. Each interior was equipped with the kind of luxury that was now required for life at sea – jacuzzis, wrap-around bars and wide lounging furniture that jutted out towards the marina in a sun-drenched, open-air display of inaccessible wealth. Vanessa moved her laptop closer, logged into Amir's account and waited for access. Rob was an arse. He'd always shown the potential to be one even back in law school when he strode into the lecture hall in a chalk-striped suit and a cloud of expensive aftershave and sat next to her on that first day. She thought he was being ironic and gave him the benefit of the doubt, but little did she know then how perfectly he would fulfil that early promise.

He told her he wanted to be a partner before he was twenty-five, as though that was the pinnacle of human achievement. He managed it by twenty-four with the kind of ruthlessness that made it look easy. It was hard not to admire his drive, the way he worked late and every weekend while their contemporaries were out getting drunk and having fun. Like most psychopaths, he started young and perfected his skills through monotonous repetition and now, twenty years later, he was head of the firm's London office.

Vanessa had been much more cautious, but her prudence had paid off and she now ran the firm's compliance department. Her job was to vet clients, monitor money coming into the firm and to be on the lookout for suspicious transactions. It was the perfect place to work if, in fact, you were going to get involved in some suspicious transactions yourself.

She scanned the figures on the screen once access to Kasan Tech's Cyprus account had been authorised. She saw the seventeen million had come in from various sources. The bulk of it was from the British Virgin Islands where Kasan was registered, and there were several cash deposits made in Cyprus – most likely the gambling money Rob mentioned. Finally, there was a tranche that had come in from Dubai. Vanessa saw that instructions had been given to send it all to the firm's trust account. She moved back to her workstation and filled in the necessary forms authorising the transfer of the money and assigning the codes that would make sure it passed under Stephen's overworked radar.

This part of the transaction was simple and one that she'd done countless times before, but the prospect of what she had to do the next morning made her feel nauseous. Once the money arrived into the trust account it had to be transferred immediately to London. If she got up early enough, she could wait until it came in and then make the transfer before anyone picked it up. She set her alarm for 5 a.m. now to make sure she didn't forget.

Vanessa wiped her hands and poured another gin as she looked back out over the yachts of Port Hercules and above to where the sun was a burning disc behind the Prince's Palace. It was a hot evening and people would be out in force along the bright wooden tables at the Brasserie de Monaco and then filling the terrace restaurants of La Condamine. Whatever doubts she had now she knew she would feel fine when she was outside, among others who, like her, serviced the rich and hid their money. There was comfort in numbers, in knowing that those around her shared a common goal. She would feel better tomorrow when the transfer to London was done, and her adrenaline could release. Better still on Monday when the property deal would complete.

She knew it was wrong – there was even a time she used to say each one would be the last. These days though she didn't say that or even bother to think she should, and she smiled at the irony: deception had taught her to stop lying to herself. That was something at least, she thought as she changed her shoes and fixed her make-up. It was easier not to think about it too much. It was easier to just get it done. Vanessa swigged the rest of her gin, gathered up her phone, laptop and bag, and went downstairs.